Gods of Mist and Mayhem

Chani Lynn Feener

ALSO BY CHANI LYNN FEENER

The Underworld Saga

Unhinged
Unleashed
Unbound
Unabated

The Xenith Trilogy

Amid Stars and Darkness
Between Frost and Fury
Within Ash and Stardust

The Roses Red Trilogy

Tithe
Revelry
Accord

Seven Deadlies

Bad Things Play Here

The Goblin Path

Two Worlds Duology

Across From You

Ulalume

A Bright Celestial Sea

Gods of Mist and Mayhem

Chani Lynn Feener

To Brie who helped keep this project alive when I would have given up on it 😊

I.

Cornered

Chapter 1:

"Run faster!" Jade slowed and stepped behind Amelia, planting both palms against her back and giving a good shove.

The push helped propel her best friend forward by a few feet.

It wasn't going to be enough.

Behind them, the shouts were getting louder, closer. If they didn't pick up the pace, they weren't going to make it.

"How did they find us so fast?!" Amelia cried over her shoulder, the words whipped away by the howling winds starting up around them.

Jade glanced up at the quickly forming clouds and cursed under her breath before snapping back, "Think about that later! Run now!"

Even though they weren't going to make it.

The screeching sounds of rubber on the road ahead came only a split second before the large SUV burst into view and came to a halt at the end of the street they were on. It blocked off the only exit, men dressed in black already pouring out and forming a line to bar their way.

"That mother fucker." Jade grabbed onto Amelia's arm and pulled her to a stop, putting herself in front of her as the men swarmed from both ends of the wide alley. Trapped.

In the midafternoon sunlight, the metal of the guns raised at them winked. The group, around thirteen total, had their weapons raised but also kept a wide berth, a show of respect that almost had Jade laughing.

Almost.

Their respect was a gimmick, a parlor trick. Their loyalty was to her grandfather, not to her. Wouldn't be until the old man died, and maybe not even then, not if she didn't submit beforehand and agree to become his official successor.

A thing she would most certainly never do.

Worn brick walls rose up on either side of them, the buildings flanking the wide alley path stretching high enough they would have blocked out most of the sun if the clouds weren't doing that already. The city, usually alive and bustling this time of day, seemed empty as Jade stood there, silently praying for someone to come along and notice two girls being cornered by thugs.

Well-dressed thugs, but thugs nonetheless.

Jade had chosen this city for the abundance of people, the seemingly never ending sound of tires on pavement and laughter in the streets. There was a safety in numbers that couldn't be found when one was alone, not only as a means to provide coverage, but also as witnesses. The Emeralds hadn't made it this far by being reckless enough to get caught on camera and plastered all over social media. Of course though, they'd found her today of all days, when a storm was rolling in and everyone had already abandoned the streets to stay dry.

"Miss Blakely, please we don't—"

This time she did laugh, the bark sharp and insulting to the point even she thought maybe she'd laid it on too thick. With no chance to go back however, she was forced to continue, to bury the fear she was feeling deep in her gut and pretend like everything was peachy.

"You don't want to get hurt *by* me?" she finished for Jason, her grandfather's right hand man.

The two of them were only five or so years apart in age, and even though he was older, she was at a higher skill level. If it came down to a fair fight between them, she would win every time.

She knew it.

He did too.

Jason's mouth thinned into a line, but he didn't argue her statement. Without the guns, thirteen people—even those trained under a kingpin as powerful as Owen Blakely—wouldn't be too big of a challenge for Jade.

Still, she felt foolish for how quickly they'd been found. She'd thought leaving the country would have been enough to get him off her trail, but no. There was no escaping the Emeralds, especially if you were the heir to the proverbial throne.

If you had power.

Jade's hand twitched at her side, fingers curling in on themselves slightly. The move was practically imperceptible, but the men were ready, watching.

Jason lifted the gun a fraction higher, aiming directly at her forehead.

She snorted. "What? Going to shoot me? Seriously? I'm not worth much to him dead."

"You're not worth much to him as a defector, either," he pointed out, and there was enough edge to his words that she actually found herself pausing.

She heard the sound of Amelia's shoes scrapping against the asphalt as she retreated a step. Jade moved back with her, not because she wanted distance—there wasn't enough space in this alley for them to safely move far enough from a gun—but to ensure she remained a protective shield in front of her friend.

Her grandfather killing her was questionable.

There was no doubt in Jade's mind, however, he'd let Amelia die without batting an eyelash.

Amelia Smith had been her best friend since high school, almost six years now, and yet she'd never once come in direct contact with the Emeralds' or Jade's grandfather. Somehow, Jade had managed to keep those two parts of her life separate. It'd become easier when she'd gone away to college, far enough out of Owen Blakely's reach that she'd been able to form her own life. Figure out who she wanted to be.

And who she didn't.

The next kingpin to the Emerald's? Yeah. Not on her potential career list, not if she had any say in the matter anyway. Sadly, according to her grandfather, she didn't.

And it wasn't because she was his only surviving blood relative, or her impressive fighting skills. It was because she'd been touched by the gods, gifted, marked.

In this day and age, so very few believed in gods or magic. Jade thought it was stupid for them to hold onto old traditions the way her grandfather insisted. Who cared about her power? In the long run, there wasn't really much she could use it for, at least not when it came to the Emeralds. Unlike Owen, who could turn anything that was steel into gold, Jade's gift was...Well.

Not that monetarily inclined.

Thinking on that fact, Jade felt a lump form in her throat.

Maybe her grandfather had given a kill order after all. The same way he'd had her father murdered all those years ago, a fact she'd only recently discovered, and part of the reason she'd fled.

"Last chance," Jason said, as if sensing her hesitation, her doubt. "Come with us, Miss Blakely, and no harm has to come to your other friends."

She may have simply followed that order, already so unsure about her current situation and likelihood of leaving it alive, except for that one word that stood out to her like a flashing neon sign.

An angry, violent red one.

Her eyes narrowed. "Other?"

"Did you think we didn't know about them?" Jason asked, clearly not noting the sudden fire in her eyes or the way she'd tensed all over. "About the one with the power to—"

Jade snapped. There was one thing she couldn't stand for, and that was anyone threatening her friends. Especially the ones who were like her, just trying to survive with the shitty hand that life had dealt them. The curse that others tried to call gifts only because it could bring *them* something favorable.

She rushed him, sending the rest of the men scattering backward to avoid her, guns still trained on her despite the fact no one pulled their triggers.

Well. That answered that question.

Probably.

They weren't here to kill her despite Jason's attempts at making her believe otherwise.

The lie only made her angrier.

She grabbed the barrel of his gun in one hand and twisted, shifting him off balance enough that she could take advantage. She kicked out, swiveling her hips and lifting her left leg to deliver a blow to his side.

He grunted, and artificial cherry scented breath gusted into her face. He was always chewing that damn gum.

One day, she was going to make him choke on it.

She dropped to the ground before he could recover, rolling on her hands and heels, to get a better position before hooking her foot around the backs of his ankles and tugging with all the strength she could muster.

Jason went down, and she got up, intent on delivering another blow while he was vulnerable.

The sudden gun shot was loud enough to send her scrambling back, back to Amelia who was shaking in the same spot she'd been in this whole time. Jade put herself in front of her and held out her arms, glaring at the short man who'd let off the round.

His arm was still held aloft, the point of the gun aimed at the gray sky above.

Jason cursed and sprung up, shoving at the man, asking him if he was crazy.

The shot could have alerted the police. Someone. It most definitely would have drawn attention to them that they didn't want or need.

Jade reached back and grabbed Amelia by the hand, shifted them a step to the right with the intention of fleeing while the men were all distracted.

Jason shoved the older man again, harder this time, sending him tumbling.

In the man's haste to right himself, his arm flailed, gun still gripped tightly in his hold. Too tightly. Because a second later the sound of yet another bullet ripping through the air cut across the alley.

Everyone froze.

And then slowly, all eyes turned toward Jade.

Her arm burned, hot and awful, unfortunately not an unfamiliar feeling. On the bright side, the bullet had merely grazed her. There was blood, but it was nothing. A minor flesh wound.

"Jade..." Amelia's voice shook.

She turned, the reassurance that she was all right already on her lips when she saw what had actually captured everyone else's attention.

Sure, they were probably scared over the fact they'd shot the heir, even if the injury was minor, but that's not what really had them all frozen in place.

The bullet had grazed Jade's arm...

...and gone straight into Amelia's.

She pressed against the wound, covering it from Jade's view, but it was obvious from all the blood that was pouring through the cracks in her fingers. Amelia had turned white as a ghost, shock the only thing keeping her on her feet or from screaming and crying.

"It's okay," Jade rushed to tell her, eyeing the location of the shot. It'd gone straight through the other girl's bicep. As long as they took care of it, stopped the bleeding, removed the bullet if it was still in there, she'd be fine. She wouldn't die. "It's okay."

Her best friend had just been shot by an Emerald member sent by her grandfather to kidnap them. Nothing about this was okay. But Jade couldn't think about that, had to push those truths away or risk the guilt eating at her to the point of distraction. She couldn't be distracted.

Amelia retreated a step—stumbled, more like— her feet splashing into a shallow puddle left over from the rain storm they'd been watching from the safety of the coffee shop window only an hour ago. Her sneakers instantly began soaking up the water, and when she stumbled a second time, Jade caught her around the wrist to keep her from falling over completely.

The move had Jade stepping into the puddle as well, and she grit her teeth against the wet and the cold. A single drop of blood rolled from the graze wound and plopped into the puddle, just between the toes of their shoes.

This wasn't going to work, they were out of options. Both of them needed medical attention and they wouldn't get it standing here in this filthy alley. There was also little chance of them escaping the men, now that they were even more amped up than before. Their anxiety practically snapped and crackled on the air.

They needed a way out. Any way.

They needed a damn miracle.

Jade grit her teeth and gave in to the inevitable. "We need to go with—"

Amelia dropped, and at first Jade thought she'd merely lost control of her body and had fallen, but no such luck.

The actual floor within the puddle just vanished, and suddenly Amelia was falling as if through a hole in the ground.

Jade tried to stop her decent, tightened her grip on her wrist and made to step away from the puddle itself but she was too late. The weight of Amelia and the sudden lack of asphalt under the foot she still had in the water was too much.

With a scream she was not at all proud of, Jade was sucked down into the darkness as well.

* * *

She was drowning.

Water filled her throat unforgivingly, pouring down her throat before she even realized what was happening. She struggled to see through the murk and darkness that surrounded her, eyes stinging as she flailed and desperately searched for the surface of...whatever nightmare body of water she'd ended up in.

Because she wasn't inside of a puddle, that was for sure.

A glimmer of light finally caught her attention and she forced her burning lungs to wait a bit longer as she shot upwards. The second her head breeched the surface she gasped, sucking in air as water ran rivulets down her forehead and into her eyes. She blinked, twisting around until she spotted Amelia almost ten feet away.

They'd somehow ended up in what appeared to be a medium sized hot spring of sorts. Now that she wasn't sucking down water, she was able to realize how warm everything was, and she noted the steam that skated around them.

Jade was somewhere near the center of the pool, but Amelia had surfaced closer to shore, right at the side of the end of a wooden dock. She was sputtering, blinking in the same harried way as Jade.

The two of them registered they weren't alone at the same time.

Perched on the edge of the dock was a man. From this angle, Jade could only make out the curve of his back and a set of strong hunched shoulders. The man was staring down at Amelia with wide eyes, clearly taken aback by her random appearance.

It might have also had something to do with the fact she was perfectly positioned between his spread legs, her head dangerously close to—

Amelia screamed and shot backwards. For a second she went under, but surfaced again quickly. She turned toward shore and swam, desperately putting space between herself and the man.

The very naked man.

Jade took a moment to be grateful she hadn't come up in a similar position before movement at the shore caught her attention.

Amelia, who was still struggling to make it the bank, didn't seem to have noticed yet, but she was swimming straight for a group of armored men.

The guards—because it was clear that's what they were—came out of nowhere, and she counted five before she was moving herself, dropping beneath the surface to swim underwater. She wouldn't make it before Amelia, obviously, but she might be able to just beat the approaching guards.

She came up for air once, head tilted in the direction of the man on the pier. She almost gasped when their eyes locked and a fizzle shot down her spine.

She was pretty sure his eyes weren't normal.

But then again, *none* of this was.

As he continued to stare, she forced herself to focus, dropping back down and making it the rest of the way without having to come up again.

Her feet slipped against smooth wet stone, but she pushed herself out only a minute or so behind Amelia who was hacking on all fours on the ground.

Her friend still hadn't noticed the guards, despite their proximity.

Jade grabbed onto Amelia's shoulder, careful not to touch the gunshot wound still bleeding a few inches below her hold. Like she had with her grandfather's men, she put herself in front, hunkering down slightly in an unmistakable fighting stance.

The armor on the guards was odd too, weird swirls and symbols embossed in the shiny metal. They each held a short sword, which admittedly made Jade wary, and considering their tight expressions, they didn't really seem like the types to negotiate.

They stopped a few feet away, leaving just wide enough of a berth for her to feel slightly less threatened but with nowhere to go. Unless, of course, she wanted to head back into the hot spring, which wasn't looking like too bad an option really. Better than getting cleaved in half by a sword in the middle of some unknown location.

Whoever they were guarding, whoever they worked for, had to be close, otherwise they wouldn't have stopped at all.

It gave her a moment to check their surroundings, confusion only solidifying the more she took in. They'd been in the city before, but gone were the brick buildings, shopfronts, and the parking lots. There was nothing but dense foliage on her left and surrounding the other side of the hot spring, and rocky paths ahead that twisted and turned toward buildings constructed of wood and grayish white stone. It looked as though they'd fallen into some expensive nature retreat, except the presence and dress of the guards made it obvious there wasn't going to be hot yoga offered in the evening.

"Well that was...eventful," a brisk voice said to her right.

Her head shot in its direction, gaze landing on a tall man with dark hair, wet and slicked back. He was dressed in only a pair of thin pants, which showed far more than Jade would have liked, and was leaning against a wooden building. The building was large, with a wide entrance leading inside and a long balcony that attached to the dock.

Another man dressed similarly stood a few feet away from the one who'd spoken, looking as if he'd just stepped out from within the seating area. His hair was a shade lighter and tied up in a loose bun at the back of his head. He had a prominent scar on his face, starting at the outer curve of his right eyebrow and ending at his chin.

There was an air of arrogance around them, clear in the set of their shoulders and the intense yet almost lazy way they both watched her.

Having been around powerful men all her life it didn't take Jade long to decide that, while clearly they held high stations, they were not the one in charge here. Just as she thought it the soft sound of bare feet padding against wood reached her ears.

She couldn't risk turning all the way, needed to keep her body toward the guards, but she tilted her head as much as she was able and waited for him to step into her field of vision.

The air caught in her lungs as soon as he did, because now that she wasn't practically drowning and she'd wiped the lingering droplets from her eyes she could see him clearly.

The man who'd been at the end of the dock made his way down it. He'd thrown on a thin white robe and tied it at the waist. It covered his lower half, but left the bare flesh of his chest practically on full display.

If she hadn't been so confused and freaked out she may have gulped at the view, but as it were, instinct was telling her caution and not attraction was imperative here.

He stopped next to the one who'd spoken, at the top of a short set of stairs that led down to the area where she and the guards had congregated. His eyes hadn't left hers since she'd spotted him, and now he cocked his head, looking down his nose in a way that screamed authority and danger.

Of course it was him. Because why would any of this be easy?

Vaguely, she wondered if he'd accept a simple apology from Amelia over having seen…well. All of him. Jade hadn't been at a good angle, so she hadn't really seen anything other than corded muscle here and there but she'd probably have to apologize as well, just for good measure.

"How did you get in here?" the man asked, voice low and deep and husky, the kind of sound that blanketed over you in the dead of winter and breathed a little heat against your chilled skin.

It was momentarily distracting, but eventually his words reached her and she paused.

She hadn't yet thought of a good explanation for how they'd ended up there, so she just went with the truth.

"No idea." Some of the guards shifted on their feet but she forced herself to maintain eye contact with the guy in the robe. He was in charge here. Only what he said mattered. "Would you believe we fell through a puddle?"

His eyes—pink, she realized now, that's what was so off about them, they were pink—narrowed slightly. "A...puddle?"

She couldn't really blame him for not buying it but...She didn't like the way his voice dropped even lower. She wasn't an idiot; their situation wasn't looking good. Not only did she have to figure out where the hell they were—because it most certainly wasn't Bangkok—and how to get back home, she also had to come up with a way to diffuse the guards with the sharp objects currently pointed their way.

Her grandfather always told her she could talk her way out of a paper bag. She'd never doubted him before, but now, staring at the guy with pink eyes, she was starting to.

Magic wasn't very prominent in the world anymore, most people believing it to be a myth. Jade, who'd grown up watching Owen Blakely encase disloyal subordinates in gold, was even shocked by the series of events that had just befallen her. Hell, she knew for a fact magic was real, and she'd question someone if they told her they'd suddenly fallen through a puddle.

And yet…

"It's crazy sounding, trust me, I know. But it's what happened. I don't really understand the how or why of it, but that's the gist." She risked a quick glance over her shoulder toward the hot spring. "If you'll let me, I'll go back in and check, see if I can find an entrance or a hole in the ground or…something. Anything so that we can go back home and out of your way."

Amelia's breaths were still harried, and beneath Jade's hand, her body shook.

They needed to get her injury tended to asap, which meant there was little time left that could be wasted on standing around talking.

"It doesn't seem like she's aware of where she is," the first man who'd spoken hummed.

"Or she's a good liar," the one with the scar grunted. His gaze was steely when he placed it on her, but still nothing compared to the darkness that was swirling behind those pink eyes the one in charge owned.

Jade was starting to feel a sick sense of dread climb up her back, pushing some of the adrenaline that had been helping her through this to the side so that she almost lost her resolve and dropped her eyes away from the men on the deck.

Instead, she steeled her shoulders. She knew what it meant to appear weak in front of those with power.

Humiliation.

Pain.

Death.

Neither she or Amelia were going to die here today, especially not when there were so many unanswered questions now swirling in her mind.

"The Grazer will find out," the pink eyed man said after a moment of silence, and just like that the discussion was over. He took a step back, as if about to walk away now that it'd been decided.

Jade felt a pinprick of annoyance, but didn't have time to think much on it for in the next instant the guards picked up their advance.

Amelia said her name, the sound so filled with fear that she found herself reacting without bothering to question whether or not it was a good idea to do so. Playing all her cards wasn't typically a smart move, but she was soaking wet, exhausted from the swim, and Amelia was hurt.

There was no telling if she'd be able to take on five guards in full armor wielding swords under normal circumstances, let alone these ones.

So, she did what she had to do to tip the odds in her favor.

"Sorry about this," she said to the nearest guard, not because she meant it, but because she wanted to confuse him long enough to stall for another second or two.

It worked. He paused and canted his head, dark brows furrowing deeply.

Jade twisted her free hand around so that it was palm up, then she brought her fingers together and snapped them.

The rain fall was instant, sheets of it pouring down from the sky like a river just let loose. There were cries of panic as they were all doused, as the water made it difficult to see.

Power thrummed through her veins, bringing with it a confidence and calm that allowed Jade to refocus. Though the rain was too heavy to see through, she could sense every single one of them.

"Stay low," she ordered Amelia.

Then she attacked.

Chapter 2:

There were few things that Jade could thank her grandfather for and actually mean—this was one of them. As bad as it sounded, and despite how badly she wanted nothing to do with the family business, Jade loved fighting.

She loved the rush of it, the excitement of having to predict her opponent's moves, of taking a hit and delivering a blow of her own. It was wild and intense and fierce. Freeing. More often than not, her combat training was the only time she'd felt like she could be herself at all, fully, one hundred percent, just herself.

She'd climbed the ranks within the Emeralds swiftly, even at a young age—her grandfather had started her lessons less than a day after her parents bodies had been put in the ground. Her tiny seven year old self still clad in her black mourning clothes.

Jade didn't like to think about that.

So she didn't, turning her attentions toward what mattered. The present.

One of the guards lashed out with their swords, slicing frantically through the sheets of rain, clearly uncaring if he ended up injuring one of his own.

Jade dropped to her knees and rolled, gripping onto his left ankle with both hands and tugging, allowing the already muddied ground beneath them to aid her.

He slipped, hands pin wheeling back, sword all but forgotten, and then slammed to the earth.

She didn't wait to watch that part, snatching up his weapon and twisting toward the next opponent. It was temping to attack with the sharp blade, but even amidst all the chaos she was smarter than that. They had no clue where they were, how they'd gotten there, or who these men worked for—aside from the guy with the intense pink gaze, which, really, told her nothing.

Jade had been trained in killing, though she'd only ever actually done the deed once, and it'd been more an accident than anything. Still, she didn't cringe at the idea of taking a life, not if it was necessary.

Now might not be the time yet. It might make things worse, and with Amelia injured, *worse* wasn't an option. She needed to protect her friend, get her out of here and somewhere where her wound could be looked at and bandaged. She didn't have time for this squabble, as much as she was enjoying the rush of adrenaline and the way her muscles burned.

Jade shifted the handle in her hand and brought the flat edge of the sword down on the back of the nearest guard, hard enough he stumbled. They were still struggling to see in the storm, unlike her, which made it easy enough for her to dart between them, delivering attacks here and there, just enough to send each and every one sprawling to the mud like the first.

Once they were down she didn't hesitate, returning to Amelia's side and snatching her wrist in a firm grip that may or may not have hurt. When her friend cried out, Jade grit her teeth and reassured her, practically dragging her between the guards who were already regaining their footing.

There was a path she'd noticed behind them that broke off and went in two directions. The one to the left appeared to head deeper into whatever grounds they were currently on, while the one to the right disappeared around the back of the large bathhouse building attached to the hot springs they'd come from.

Jade paused for a split second to debate, nibbling on her bottom lip, but she couldn't afford to linger long. The sound of clinking metal came all too soon and she silently cursed her earlier caution. If she'd killed them, they wouldn't be after them still. But doing so risked pissing off their boss.

"Stop them!" a voice demanded, dark and deep, causing a shiver to skate up her spine.

The guy with the pink eyes.

"This way," she said to Amelia, dragging them to the right before she could second guess herself. All of her instincts were screaming at her to put as much distance between them and that guy as possible, that though he hadn't held a weapon and was barely dressed, he was a thousand times more dangerous than any of the guards she'd just dropped.

Around them, the rain was starting to slow to a trickle, and soon the only cover they had would be gone. Jade needed to get them out of sight before that happened.

Her power didn't last long, just bursts here and there. No matter how much training her grandfather had forced her through, she was never able to hold it, never able to keep the rain coming indefinitely.

She turned onto the white pebble path, sneakers crunching and sliding against the small stones as she urged them to move faster. Her eyes scanned ahead, seeking out an exit, or at least a place they could successfully hide until the people chasing them passed.

Wherever they were, it was nothing like the city they'd just come from. There was a slight chill to the air that seeped through their thin, wet clothes. The grounds were green and well kept, the buildings all wood with paper screens over windows and sliding doors wide enough to fit three men shoulder to shoulder. The paths twisted and ambled in every which direction, and there was a tall stone fence surrounding the property, at least where Jade could see it.

"This way." She pulled Amelia over toward a stack of what might have been firewood that'd been set up against the side of a portion of the stone wall. Dropping her friends arm, she retreated a couple of steps to try and get a look over the wall, but all she saw was blue sky and the roofs of a few surrounding buildings.

They were going to have to take the chance that there was a town on the opposite side and not just an extension of this place.

Behind them, calls from the guards reached their ears.

"Hurry," she shoved Amelia toward the wood pile. "You have to climb."

"What?" Amelia shook her head, but Jade wasn't having it, forcing her to lift her leg and begin the shaky assent. The wood creaked beneath her weight, but surprisingly none of the logs rolled. "This is—"

"Talk later," Jade cut her off, listening intently to the guards drawing ever near. "Get to the top. Now."

She almost slipped once or twice but Amelia made it, pulling herself over the edge of the stone wall even with her injured arm. She glanced back at Jade with her legs dangling off the edge, face pale, blonde wet hairs clinging to her puffed cheeks.

"What do you see?" Jade asked.

"It looks like—"

She heard the guards turn the corner and shout, knew without having to look they'd been spotted.

"Doesn't matter," she started scrambling up after Amelia. "As long as it doesn't look dangerous below, jump."

"I mean—"

"Damn it! Jump, Amelia!"

Jade took the spot her friend vacated a second later, leaning over quickly to watch as her friend hit the dirt road below. Amelia groaned once, but other than that seemed okay, and with a sigh of relief, Jade jumped up onto the edge, ready to follow.

"Stop." The order was delivered coldly, quietly, almost impossibly so, but it had the same effect as if it'd been screamed directly into her ear.

Jade stiffened, crouched on the edge of stone which was only three or so inches wide, and told herself not to look. Her head didn't seem to want to listen to that, however, and she found herself twisting slightly on the tips of her toes, turning so that she was staring back the way they'd come at the speaker who'd somehow momentarily taken control of her.

The man with the pink eyes stood amongst the guards. Even though they'd chased after her, he didn't look out of sorts at all, wasn't even breathing heavily like the other men around him. Instead, he appeared calm, with just a hint of dark interest sparking in his gaze.

It was the looked that snapped her out of it. Something whispered in her mind that having this man's interest was the same as courting death, and she had no intentions of dying today. There was a darkness surrounding him, an intensity that she either hadn't noticed before or he'd had under wraps. Either way, she was noticing it now.

And she hated to admit it, even to herself, but she was afraid.

The man took a single step toward her. "Come down."

With a flash of horror, Jade realized her legs were in motion, turning her more in his direction as if she were about to follow his command.

What the actual hell was happening?

Gripping the rough edge of the wall, Jade felt the stone scrape against her skin, welcoming the sharp pain it brought. She stopped herself from moving any further.

The man's eyes narrowed in to dangerous slits.

Below, Amelia called out her name.

That was all it took to completely break the man's spell.

She didn't bother turning herself safely back around. Merely leaned back, tipping over the edge and off the wall without giving him a chance to do or say anything else that might magically sway her body.

She would have to seriously think on that later, once they were safe, but not now. Now was the time for running.

Another thing Jade was excellent at.

She'd estimated the drop to be about eight feet, so doable. Of course, it made a big difference when one fell backwards, and she hit the dirt with a grimace, pain ricocheting throughout her entire back and down her arms.

Amelia was instantly there, helping her up. "Are you all right?!"

"Fine," she said, and it was clear by her tone she was lying. On her feet, Jade took a quick glance around.

They must be in the middle of some kind of city, with the market place straight head where rows of street vendors could be seen unpacking the wares they'd just protected from the sudden rain. Fortunately, most of them seemed too busy with that to have noticed the two girls climbing over the wall.

The road they were on stretched the length of the wall itself, branching off to the market place and two other ways at either side. Wanting to get them off the main path and out of sight, Jade snatched Amelia's hand once more and raced across to the right, onto the street that seemed less busy from where they'd been standing.

The space between buildings here was much narrower, and they had to be careful not to knock over any of the boxes or stacks of discarded trash as they ran down it. About halfway, Jade noticed another opening, and she turned them down there, twisting to the left when there was yet another, this one snug between white and sandstone walls. The two of them had to turn and practically shuffle down it.

Amelia kept quiet the whole way, trusting Jade to lead them. She didn't know much about Jade's life outside of the college where they two had met four years ago, but she'd been told a thing or two.

The magic that pulsed through Jade's veins for instance was no secret between them, and neither was her grandfather being the kingpin of the Emeralds. All the times she'd had to escape from something or other though—a rival group, a scorned member, hell, a pissed off recruit she'd beat in the ring—those stories she'd kept mostly to herself. She hadn't wanted to scare her best friend unnecessarily.

Then Jason and those goons had found them halfway across the world and…

Well.

Now they were running through a strange city with an even stranger man and his guards hot on their trail.

Jade didn't stop them until fifteen or so minutes later, when they poured out of yet another tight alleyway. There were a string of clothes on a line before them, and after taking a quick look around for anyone and noting they were alone, she snatched the nearest garment from it and tossed it back at Amelia.

"What's this for?" her friend asked with a frown, holding up the brown dress.

"Didn't you notice what everyone else was wearing?" Jade had. The people in the market hadn't been dressed like someone from back home. "Your blue jeans will stick out like a sore thumb."

After only another second of hesitation, Amelia tugged the thick material over her head, settling it around her waist. She only winced twice, made a soft sound of pain as it rubbed against her wounded arm. As soon as it was on, she removed her jeans, bundling the wet material up and holding it out to Jade.

She'd dressed in her usual black skinny jeans and matching leather jacket earlier that day. There'd been enough people wearing pants she thought she could probably get away with keeping hers, but the jacket might cause a problem. Unfortunately, there didn't seem to be much else on the line aside from under garments which wouldn't be helpful in this particular instance.

With no other options, she ended up removing her jacket and folding it over her arm, hopeful that her charcoal t-shirt would blend in enough by being unimpressive. The cold air instantly nipped at her flesh and she clenched her jaw, as she discarded Amelia's jeans in a pile of trash, making sure they were fully covered by bits of rotting paper and broken glass.

"Is this going to be enough?" Amelia tugged at the hem of the brown dress. It only reached a bit beneath her knees, but the long sleeves covered her injury and as long as they moved quickly, Jade was hopeful it would be enough not to have anyone who did spot them giving them a second glance.

She tipped her head back and took in the darkening sky. "It'll be night soon," she said. "It'll be easier for us to move around unseen, but we need to find shelter." There was no telling what types of things happened on these streets once the sun set, and she honestly wasn't in the mood to find out.

"How?" Amelia rubbed her hands together and held up the cell phone she'd removed from her jeans pocket. There was a small attachment to the back where she kept her credit cards and a bit of cash. "I doubt they take dollar bills."

"Caught on to that too, did you?"

"Where the hell are we?" Amelia nervously wrung her hands, clinging to the phone. "We were in the alley and then…"

"I don't know," she told her truthfully. "But we can't figure that out here."

"Clothing is one thing," her friend said, "how are we going to steal a hotel room?"

A thought struck her and Jade reached beneath the high collar of her shirt and pulled out the string of tiny green gem stones she always wore around her neck.

There were tiny golden beads between each of the green ones.

"No." Amelia shook her head. "You can't."

"I'm not really seeing any other choice." She sighed. "Doesn't this place look like something from an Asian drama?"

Jade was half Chinese and spent most of her time watching Asian television over American shows. She and Amelia had actually bonded over a few when they'd been freshmen and newly introduced as roommates.

"It's not exactly like it," she went on, motioning towards the space around them. "There are some things that appear modern and some that don't."

"Stop changing the subject," Amelia snapped.

"I'm not."

"What this place looks like right now doesn't matter. You can't pawn your mother's necklace, Jade. You just can't."

It was the only thing left she had of her parents, even the photographs had been taken and locked away by her grandfather. He'd wanted her to form bonds with her new family and her new way of life, not weep and grieve for the one that had left her the night her mom and dad had died in that accident.

She'd always sort of hated him for that alone. For the fact he'd allowed her one tiny, wrinkled photo of the three of them taken at the park only weeks prior to their deaths. Even that, she'd hidden away, always fearful that he'd change his mind and take it too.

That hatred had grown however, when she'd discovered his secret. It'd been an accident, she'd recently graduated and had gone home to his estate under orders. She'd only been looking for her passport, which he'd always kept under lock and key, so that she and Amelia could spend the summer back packing in Europe before they returned and her friend had to start her adult job at the law firm she'd gotten hired at.

Jade had found her passport. But she'd also learned the awful truth. Her parents accident hadn't been an accident at all.

"How do you even know that'll pass as currency here?" Amelia tried again.

"I saw some people buying things when we passed the market. They used gems."

She blinked at her. "We were standing in front of that place for like, a minute."

"And?"

She opened her mouth, closed it. Then sighed. "Why are you so perceptive?"

"I was trained to be," she said. "That training is going to help us get off the streets."

"Don't you think it's weird though?" Amelia asked a moment later once they'd started moving again. They stuck close to the sides of buildings, trying to remain in the shadows even as the sky darkened above them. "We end up in a place where your necklace happens to pass as money?"

She shrugged. "Not really? It's jade and gold. That's got worth in our world too."

Amelia missed a step, and Jade worried it was the blood loss and all the running, but when she looked into her eyes it was clear it had little to do with exhaustion.

"I think I need to sit down," the words were barely a whisper and Amelia didn't wait for her Jade to reply, dropping to the ground right where she stood. She pressed her good arm against the wall and squeezed her eyes shut.

"Are you okay?" It was a stupid question, but there wasn't really anything else Jade could think to say.

"I get that this isn't as earth shattering for you as it is for me," Amelia told her, still in that quiet, shaky voice, "what with you having known about magic your entire life. But this is really freaking me out. You just said we're in another *world*, Jade."

"It's only a guess," she replied dumbly.

Amelia thought so too, for her eyes snapped open and she glared.

Jade held up her hands, palms out. "Okay, sorry. For the record though, I only know about things like other worlds and magic as a whole because of the stories my dad used to tell me as a kid. Bed time stories. My grandfather told me some too, but his were even less believable. I didn't think they were real."

"Didn't think that until we fell through a puddle, you mean?" Amelia scoffed.

Jade was typically the one of the two who utilized dry humor and sarcasm. The fact that Amelia was falling back on it now could either be a sign she was struggling to come to terms with their situation, or she was coming to terms and accepting it for what it was.

Bat shit crazy and impossible.

But also their new reality.

"In these stories, what's the other world like?" Amelia tucked her knees under her chin.

They shouldn't be doing this, wasting time out in the open. Any moment, one of the guards could stumble upon them. Jade's rain trick would only get them so far. She lacked the power her grandfather controlled, as well as most of the perks that came along with it.

Amelia wasn't ready to get up, though, that was obvious, and Jade nibbled on her bottom lip debating the best course of action before finally giving in.

She motioned at her with a finger, telling her to turn and rest her back against the wall. That exposed Amelia's shoulder to her. As she got to work rolling up the sleeve of the dress, Jade spoke, mind struggling for a second to recall the stories she hadn't heard in over a decade.

"It was a story about our family," she said softly, inspecting the bullet wound. It was a relief to see that it'd gone clean through. At least she didn't have to worry about digging metal out of her arm in the middle of these filthy streets. "And the other families like us, the Legacies that have powers."

The Legacies were families spread throughout the globe, all with magic coursing through their veins. Sometimes it skipped a generation, sometimes more than one. Jade had only ever met four people she wasn't related to that also had an ability like hers, two of which were other Legacy children she was introduced to.

Ones her grandfather hoped she'd pick a partner from.

Part of her wondered if that was the reason he'd sent Jason after her now. She was turning twenty-two in a month. Old enough to start at least considering marriage, or an engagement, at least as far as he was concerned.

Security for the family, as he'd put it.

"Our ancestors are supposedly from another world. They carved through the veil between them and entered our realm, where they remained. The start of my lineage was injured during travel and only survived long enough to meet a woman and start a family with her before he passed."

"Sounds kind of convenient," Amelia drawled.

"That the only person who could actually prove this crazy story is real also happens to be dead?" Jade snorted. "Yeah, agreed." She'd said as much to her grandfather once.

He'd beat her as a lesson.

She had gotten something out of it, she supposed.

Jade had learned how to take a beating.

"Sucks that now it's looking like the story might be right, huh." Amelia cracked a tired smile, head lolling slightly to the side as she grimaced when her wound was prodded at.

"We need to get this stitched up," Jade told her. "Honestly, I can't believe you're still conscious."

"Probably wouldn't have been," she admitted, "if not for the whole falling into a hot spring bit." She sobered some and then added in a lower tone, "That guy...the one with the eyes. You don't think...He's not going to still be chasing us, right? It can't be that big of a deal that we saw him—"

"*You* saw him," Jade corrected, unfolding her jacket to grab a small sewing kit from the hidden inner pocket. The needles had all been sterilized and the thread had been changed to sutures a long time ago. There were also a couple disinfectant wipes and a few bandages.

"Fine," Amelia rolled her eyes, wincing again when Jade tore open one of the wipes and began cleaning the wound, "I saw his dick, not you. Happy?"

"Depends," she shrugged, "was it worth it?"

"That's not funny." Despite her words, Amelia's mouth twitched upwards. "Can I ask you something? Have you done this before? Stitched someone up on the streets while on the run?"

Jade pretended to think it over as she threaded the needle. It was getting more difficult to see in the dark, but after a few tries she managed to get it. "Not while on the run, but otherwise, yeah, once or twice. Some of the guys I worked with would get injured on a side job or whatever."

"What about from a rival gang?"

She clucked her tongue. "We aren't a gang, Amelia. We're a syndicate. There's a bit more to it than running into a group of gangsters at the same ice cream parlor and having a fist fight in the streets."

"Sure, Miss Blakely," she rolled her eyes a second time, this time with more gumption, "my apologies."

"This stuff will help with the pain," Jade squeezed a bit of the advanced numbing cream she'd gotten from a doctor friend years ago onto the surrounding area and gently rubbed it in, "but it won't mask it entirely. This will still probably hurt like a bitch, just...less of one."

"Great." Amelia clenched her other hand into a tight fist and inhaled slowly before giving a single nod as Jade lifted the needle. "Okay. I'm ready."

She wasn't ready.

Jade tried to work as quickly as possible. Her friend bit at her fist and even buried her head against her arm to try and stifle the sounds, yet that was only so affective. They needed to hurry just in case those guards really were still following them.

On the one hand, Jade thought that Amelia made a valid point. Surely the pink eyed man had better things to do with his time than hunt down two random girls because they'd peeped on him in the bath. However...

She'd seen the look on his face, recognized it for what it was.

Whatever his role in this world might be, he was used to getting his way. Inexplicably. People like that were dangerous.

She lost track of time as she worked, squinting in the shadows, hoping she didn't make a mistake. Once it was done, they were both covered in a sheen of sweat, muscles achy and shaking slightly from the strain of everything they'd been through. As she packed her things away, she realized it was far too late for them to even attempt trying to find an inn. They needed somewhere nearby they could just hole up in for the remainder of the night.

She glanced back at Amelia whose eyes were closed, breathing labored. Moving at night was smarter, but there was no way her friend was going to be able to do so. It'd have to be some place they wouldn't have to worry about being caught in for at least most of the day tomorrow as well—they couldn't afford to move around in daylight, not until they were certain that those guards were no longer after them.

Plus, they needed time to come up with a game plan, figure out possible ways to get home.

Because they had to get home. They sure as hell couldn't stay here, wherever the fuck here was. They didn't have any money and didn't know anyone, which would make things a lot harder considering the only solution Jade could currently come up with was getting out the same way they'd come in.

Through the hot springs.

She'd made sure to keep track of all of their twists and turns through the city, was confident she could follow her mental map back to the place they'd escaped from.

The real hurdle was finding a way in undetected.

"Come on." She tapped lightly at Amelia's knee and rose to her feet.

The shadows had thickened around them where they hovered against the side of a tall three story building, shielding them from view for the most part of any passersby at either end of the alley. So far, it didn't seem as though anyone had noticed them, and she'd only counted four people walking by. With any luck, that meant most of the city were in the process of heading home for the night.

They started moving once more, Amelia sticking close while Jade peered into every window they passed in the hopes they'd happen by a storage unit or something of the like. At first there was nothing, just shops or private homes—she couldn't really tell, just knew they were occupied and well kept—then after at least an hour or so of searching they finally came upon something doable.

"There." Jade pointed across the dirt road.

Amelia followed her finger and then groaned. "Damn it."

Chapter 3:

The sound of voices woke Jade first and for a moment she remained still as a statue on the itchy bed of straw she and Amelia had used as a mattress. The building she'd found was a stable with the horses kept at the front. There were three rooms attached, a main one where most of their things were stored—bridles, saddles, brushes—and another that appeared to be a sitting room for workers to rest in during the day. The other was a half barn filled with barrels of hay. That's where the two of them had hidden last night, in the left corner farthest from the two wide doors that'd been closed and still where.

For now. The voices were coming from directly outside of them, and Jade held her breath, silently praying that whoever was out there didn't intend to come in.

"What—" Amelia gasped when Jade's hand slapped over her mouth, but quieted as soon as her still half asleep brain caught up and realized what was going on.

Jade listened intently, able to make out sentences here and there since the men were standing directly outside the doors and not moving.

"—can't believe it. Who do you think would be so stupid?" one of the voices said incredulously. From the sounds of it, he was an older gentleman, maybe not as old as her grandfather, but probably around there.

"I have no idea," another man, younger, answered. "The punishment for sneaking into the palace is death already. But the punishment for peeking in on the royal bath…"

Her eyes went wide with realization.

They were talking about her and Amelia.

Amelia had obviously figured that out as well, for fear entered her eyes and Jade had to shake her head to stop her from acting on it. They couldn't risk so much as sitting up at the moment, if they made any sort of sound and gave themselves away those men would be in here in less than two seconds flat.

"I heard three of the gods were there," the older man stated. "Including the Emperor himself."

Gods? Jade frowned.

"May the Great have mercy," the younger man added, only for the older to give a bark of sharp laughter.

"Mercy? Boy, what god do you know of that grants mercy? No, those poor girls will be lucky if their deaths are quick. They should hand themselves in now, make it easier. The Dust Emperor is not known for his patience. Given that he's the God of Command he doesn't even usually have to bother practicing it."

The God of what now? What did that even mean?

"Their wanted posters have been plastered all over the city," the younger sighed. "It's only a matter of time before they're discovered."

"We should make a stop at the God of Feeling's temple," the older man said, though his voice was starting to fade, a sign they were finally leaving, "perhaps he'll convince the Emperor to make the killing blow quick."

"Was the God of Feeling there?"

They didn't get to hear the answer to that, the men now too far out of earshot.

"Is it safe?" Amelia whispered after a moment of silence passed.

Jade sat up, making it clear that it was.

"Did you hear that?" Amelia followed suit and glanced at the closed doors. "They were talking about gods. Like, real flesh and blood ones, weren't they?"

She nodded but didn't yet speak. There'd been parts of the story she'd left out last night since she'd been giving the abridged version. Like how supposedly her ancestor who fled to their world hadn't been mortal.

Now...

Jade swallowed the lump forming in her throat, suddenly even more uneasy about this whole situation. Even setting the whole god's part aside, there was another important bit of information they'd gleaned from eavesdropping.

Apparently, they'd accidentally appeared in the middle of a palace, in a restricted zone no less.

"I can't break us into a palace," she mistakenly said aloud, too unnerved to realize until it was too late.

Amelia blanched. "What?"

"They have our picture spread all over the place too," she continued, since the cat was already out of the bag anyway. "We can't risk going out during the day, possibly even the night, for a while which means I can't even go back to check on the security of the place."

"Jade, slow down, I'm not following."

"We need to get back to that hot spring," she stated, catching Amelia's gaze. "That could be the only way home."

"But you don't know that, not for sure." It wasn't a question, though it was obvious that she was hoping to be told something otherwise.

"No." She ran a hand through her long dark hair and cursed. "How the fuck did we end up here?"

"Question of the cent—" A coughing fit cut Amelia off. She heaved and doubled over, pressing the back of her hand against her mouth in a futile attempt to muffle the sounds. The fit turned into gagging, and then she was clawing at her throat.

"Are you okay?" Jade shifted onto her knees, leaning over her friend. Just as she was about to reach out and pat her on the back, a prickle at the corner of her eyes had her pausing. The prickle turned into a slight burn, and pretty soon it was difficult for her to keep her eyes open.

She blinked against the discomfort, feeling suddenly more tired than she'd ever been in her entire life. Her limbs began to lose strength, and she watched as Amelia's body slumped to a heap on the ground only a few seconds before Jade lost control of herself and toppled as well.

This wasn't right. Something was very, very wrong.

With a rising horror, she realized it was the air. There was something in it, something that sparkled like silver glitter in the beams of sunlight spilling through the single square window set in the ceiling. It twisted around them, flicking against their skin.

She'd fallen with her head facing the doors, and through the panic swelling within her, she watched as they slowly began to creak open. No matter how hard she willed herself to move, she couldn't so much as get her finger to twitch and was left with nothing else to do but stare as people appeared at the entrance.

At first they were little more than dark silhouettes against the light at their backs, but then one form stepped forward. It was only a single step, but it was enough for Jade to make him out.

Before she could help it, she sucked in a sharp breath, giving herself away and using up what little energy she'd been miraculously clinging to.

Eyes, a pale pink, trailed over to her, catching her gaze and holding.

The man from the hot springs had found them.

Her vision winked in and out; every time she focused she found he was closer than he'd been a second prior, until finally he was hovering over her.

He crouched down and glanced over at Amelia almost absently, attention quickly back on Jade. "Hello, little cat," he said, voice as smooth as honey. He reached for her, long fingers delving into her hair, nail skating over her scalp. "We have some unfinished business to attend."

Before she could so much as blink, his grip tightened and he jerked, tugging her up off the ground and back into a seated position by her hair. The pain was sharp, enough to have tears instantly stinging the corner of her eyes, though that was all the response her drugged body could manage to outwardly give.

He held her steady and slowly leaned in, bringing his face up against hers so he could breathe his next words against the curve of her ear.

"I'll have your life before the day is through," he promised, and when he pulled back, she got a quick look at his smile, wicked and cruel.

Then there was nothing but darkness.

* * *

"Jade!"

Someone was calling her, but their voice sounded muffled and far away.

"Jade! Wake up!"

She struggled to recall where she was, what she'd been doing before falling asleep, but her mind was a muddled mess and all she wanted to do was slip deeper into slumber and ignore the terror filled cries calling out to her.

Terror filled…

She frowned.

Why would someone be afraid—

It hit her like a freight train and she snapped into full consciousness, sitting up fast enough to give herself whiplash. Metal clanked with the motion, and with a sick twist in her gut she glanced down at the chains secured tightly to her right ankle. The rest of her limbs had been left unbound yet she somehow couldn't seem to find any comfort in that fact.

"Jade," Amelia's voice sounded strained, and when Jade looked up she realized why.

The two of them were in some sort of cell. The walls were made of iron bars and through them she could make out the rest of the dungeon. The space seemed to be pretty spacious as a whole, with more cells just like the one she was in. Straw and dirt littered the otherwise solid stone floor, the chill from the stone having already seeped through her clothes while she'd been unconscious. The smell was acrid and clung to her.

She'd been deposited in the back left corner, none to softly if the ache in her right shoulder was any indication, and secured by the single band of metal attached to a long rusted chain.

Her situation was uncomfortable, to say the least, but nothing like what her best friend had apparently been going through.

Amelia's blonde hair was knotted and shaggy, caked in a mixture of blood and dirt. Her dress collar was torn at the front, a couple of angry red welts visible across her collarbone, trailing over her left shoulder. Unlike Jade, she'd been bound by both of her wrists and attached to one of the bars of the cage with them held tightly over her head. The position forced her to balance on her toes, the stubs of them also muddy. Her shoes had been discarded across the cell.

There was a man standing in front of her, dressed in black leathers with an odd golden emblem stitched in the lower area, over his left hip. His hair was short and curled slightly at the edges, and when he finally turned in Jade's direction, she caught sight of his face.

He was younger than she'd expected, probably only a handful or so years older than Amelia and her. She wasn't sure she could call him handsome, but he wasn't ugly. Not that it made a difference given the current circumstances.

Like the knife he had pressed against Amelia's cheek, the tip of the blade already drawing blood so that a single drop spilled and rolled down the expanse of her face.

"Let's try again, girl," the man said on a purr, clearly enjoying the pain he was delivering. "What were you two doing in the Emperor's baths? How did you get there? Who let you in?"

Amelia whimpered.

The man gave a mock sigh. "Are you both Minor's or just your friend over there?"

"I already told you, I have no idea what you're talking about," Amelia said, voice shaking. Tears were spilling from her eyes despite the brave face she was trying so desperately to maintain. It wasn't fooling anyone.

While they spoke Jade took the time to take her friend's injuries in. There was already a lot of bruising over both of her arms and her lip was split in two different places.

How long had Jade been out for and why hadn't they bothered forcing her awake? Why start the interrogation on one of them when it surely would have saved time to torture and question them both?

There was only one reason she could think of, and that was that none of this really mattered all that much to them. Not really. This was more than likely just an excuse, an enforcing of the laws to keep others from breaking them the same way Jade and Amelia apparently had.

She'd seen her grandfather do it on multiple occasions—punish someone for something small, something obsolete, just to ensure no one else tried to get away with it later on.

Small crimes led to big crimes, he'd tell her. Let no one get away with anything. That was the rule they abided by. That was how they'd maintained control over the Emerald syndicate and the other Legends.

Jade had always considered it bullying. Her grandfather could wrap his actions up in nice little excuses all he wanted, but she knew the truth.

He liked the bloodshed, the fear it brought, as well as the sounds the injured party made.

He got off on it.

Kind of like how this guy right here was getting off on hurting her friend. She recognized the look in his eyes, blood hungry and a tad manic. Those were the ones to look out for, the ones who pretty much only lived for pain and discovering the many ways in which to deliver it.

"Making such ridiculous lies isn't going to do you any good," the man said to Amelia then, dancing the blade across the curve of her right ear. "If you don't spill the truth, your friend will once she wakes up. Might as well be the one to tell us everything before she gets the chance; it could be the only way you get to walk out of here alive."

"I already told you, we don't—"

"A puddle. Right," he scoffed. "Except the Water God is dead and has been for over a hundred thousand years and there's no way a measly Minor would be able to contain enough power to pull something like transportation off. Your lies are terrible. It's actually kind of a disappointment."

Without any further warning, he slashed the knife down across the center of her ear, nicking it enough that blood instantly swelled.

Jade saw red.

She eyed the man and the six armored guards who were with him. They'd crowded the cell, and even though a couple of the guards were less than a few feet from where Jade sat, none of them seemed to have noticed she'd woken yet.

Best to inform them.

She started off careful, easing herself up while trying to keep her right leg from moving too much. She didn't want the chain to rattle again and give her away. Her gaze remained latched on the nearest guard, assessing, noting his build and stature. Trying to find a weakness in his stance.

It didn't take long to spot. He was favoring his left leg.

Jade glanced down at the length of the chain attaching her to the side of the cell. It was long, probably long enough to allow her to move right up to the door at the end. It was open, with a guard standing just within the entranceway.

Her mind raced through a possible escape plan. If she could knock these guys out, then she could figure out a way to unlock her binds and Amelia's. After that, it was just a matter of running before reinforcements could come.

Simple.

In theory.

If the past couple days had been any indicator however, nothing in Jade's life seemed to want to work out.

Still, there was no other option but to try.

She shot into motion, swooping down and lifting the chain as she rushed forward. Her target heard the commotion and turned, but she was already upon him, whipping out the heavy metal so that it slapped hard against his right leg.

He let out a grunt and dropped like she'd expected and she twisted, flipping in the air so she could bring her knee cracking against his jaw.

The other guards didn't even wait for his body to hit the ground, coming at her.

She leapt into the air, kicking out with her left leg, conscious of the chain attached to her right. If she accidentally tripped herself, not only would it be embarrassing, it could cost her and Amelia their lives— lives that were so obviously already teetering on the edge.

Why the hell did the magic puddle have to deposit them here? Why couldn't it have been Disneyland or, like, a world filled entirely with fried shrimp?

Jade kicked at one of the guards, landing in a crouch a few feet across the cell. Lifting her right leg a few inches and pulling had the chain going taut just as another guard was coming toward her. He tripped and went sprawling.

"Gonna be real with you guys for a second," she said, straightening while the remaining guards moved in, "I really thought you'd be better at this. You call this fighting? My grandpa fights better than you and he's seventy-nine."

"Your grandfather is the head of the Emerald syndicate," Amelia reminded, somehow managing for the words to come out light despite the obvious pain she was in.

Jade sent her a mock glare. "Way to ruin my insult."

"You've got guts, girl," the man closest to Amelia said, drawing her attention his way. As soon as he had it, he grinned at her, flashing teeth that were just a tad too pointy at the ends. "But so does your friend. Should we see them?"

Before Jade could react, he slashed the knife in his hand across Amelia's stomach. The blade tore through the thin layer of the brown dress she was wearing, and while he hadn't pushed too deep, a thin line of red appeared across the skin of her now exposed upper torso.

Jade didn't wait for any other attacks to come, the sound of Amelia's sharp cry ringing in her ears as she shot forward. Her target was now the man with the knife, and the guards were mere nuisances getting in her way. It was simple enough to evade and dodge their blows, with only a few slipping past her defenses and hitting their mark. Not that she noticed when they did.

As the heir to the Emeralds, she'd been taught the importance of both a heavy hand and a silver tongue. Talking your way out of a situation and possibly keeping an ally was often the smarter play, in the long run it would provide more benefits than planting another body in the ground would. Obviously this was not one of those occasions.

Jade felt the chain yank at her ankle just as she was about to reach the man with the knife. She let out a short scream of frustration, shooting her arm out as far as it would go in the process. When she snatched the end of his long black sleeve, she had the pleasure of seeing surprise in his eyes before she tugged him forward and grappled with him over the knife.

Four of the guards were already groaning on the ground, some with broken bones—at least two wrists and one guy's ribs—but the two remaining were instantly on her, forcing her off of the guy with the knife.

Not before she'd grabbed it from him, however.

Switching the handle around in her grip, she swung back, puncturing the fleshy left thigh of one of the guards holding her. He screamed, and let go.

She was already repeating the process with the man on her right. Twisting around, she adjusted the weapon, so that she was palming the heavy hilt, and slammed the metal against the nearest guard's temple with all the force she could muster. The attack was swift, and before he could register what had happened, she kneed him in the groin and shoved him face first into the iron bars of the cell.

Jade moved in a flurry of motion, jabbing the remaining guards with both the sharp and blunt end of the knife over and over again. She allowed her instincts to take control, for her body to rely on muscle memory as it delivered blow after blow. The few hits she took herself would bruise later, but she barely felt them now, too hyper focused.

To keep herself in shape, she'd joined a mixed martial arts club in college and had stuck with it ever since. Sometimes they had tournaments and events. She didn't enter very often, because laying low was smarter, but every now and again when she felt that particular itch she couldn't scratch any other way, she gave in.

There was a big difference between friendly sparing matches at the gym and the training fights she used to undergo weekly with her grandfather. She hated to admit it, but there was something invigorating about getting to completely let loose, to just be and not have to worry about taking things too far or accidently hurting her opponent.

Now her hands were slicked in blood and the room was filling up with grunts and groans and that unmistakable tang of copper. She breathed it deep and swept through the guards with an easy grace, back in front of the man who'd tortured Amelia within moments.

The fight had probably only lasted a handful of minutes, if even, but by the time Jade pushed the man against the wall her body was singing in a mixed rush of adrenaline and anticipation.

It didn't last.

Just as she was about to deliver the finishing blow, something akin to a heat wave slicked across her back, straightening her spine. She was only turned partially away from the door, but before she could so much as cock her head, the new threat was upon her.

Amelia screamed a warning too late, and Jade had just enough time to allow her body to go slightly lax in preparation before a heavy hand was gripped tightly around the back of her neck.

She was shoved the few feet toward the bars, her cheek pushed roughly against them, the cold metal biting into her already swollen flesh. Refusing to cry out in pain, she bit the inside of her bottom lip and ended up reopening a crack on the outside that had just begun to seal.

"What is going on here?" a deep voice asked from behind her, his grip on her neck steady and strong.

She tested it a little, tried to press back if even to relieve a millimeter of space between her and the bars. A mistake.

He must have taken her movement as resistance, fingers tightening and spreading to cover more, the tips of his thumb and forefinger pressing just beneath her jawline. It was the only place he touched her, and yet she somehow felt like his presence had turned into a heavy cloak pinning her in place.

"Emperor," one of the guards spoke from where he was still sitting in the corner of the cell, nursing a broken arm, "she attacked out of nowhere—"

"She was locked in this cell," the man at her back, the one they kept referring to as Emperor, reminded coolly. "I hardly call that 'out of nowhere'. And what, exactly, were you all doing?"

Emperor. The guy with the pink eyes.

Shit.

The sound of soft steps prevented the guard from responding, and Jade watched as he hung his head as another man stepped around the corner and in to view.

With her head pinned the way it was, she was forced to stare in the direction of the doorway, giving her a great look at the newcomer, and the way the guards— who must have accompanied the Emperor—outside the cell stepped out of the way for him.

"Koya," the Emperor addressed him, "is this how you train the royal guard? To lose to a Minor? One who's been drugged *and* chained, no less?"

"Forgive me, Emperor." He bent his head further, the move clearly meant to equate to a deeper bow.

His hair was a deep blue, the shade so dark that it appeared black anywhere the light didn't touch. He was dressed fancier than the others—though not nearly as much so as the Emperor—in an outfit made of obsidian velvet and leather. The golden emblem she'd spotted on the guards was also stitched over his left hipbone, but that wasn't all the detailing his uniform got. There was also a trail of gold over his right shoulder, a trail that appeared to be a depiction of stardust.

"See something you like, little cat?" the harsh edge had returned to the Emperor's voice, and for a moment Jade stupidly wondered who'd pissed him off again before it hit her.

Hadn't he called *her* that back at the barn?

"What? Refusing to speak to me as well?" The Emperor leaned in closer, bringing his heat with him so that she felt it pressing to her back a second before his body followed. He sidled himself all the way against her, fitting them together like puzzle pieces. Though it started gentle enough when he shifted forward a bit more it forced her flush against the iron bars.

As much as she hated feeling trapped his warning was clear. She might want to cuss him out and try her luck attacking, but survival instincts told her she wouldn't win.

A sliver of fear trickled through the anger and indignation, bringing a chill to her. She'd known from the first time she saw him that this man wasn't weak, that he could be a serious threat. But she hadn't realized it would be this bad.

Initially, she'd run, sure, but she'd honestly thought he would give up the chase and call his men off. What would be the point wasting time on nobodies like her and Amelia? Surely he had more important things to do with his time.

And yet...Not only had he continued to track them, he'd also apparently spread news of them all over the damn city.

So far, the only good thing she was seeing from any of this was that, hopefully, they were near the hot springs they'd come from and could figure out a way back to first, it, and then home. Preferably soon too, because wherever here was, she wasn't really a fan.

"I'm not sure you've fully grasped what's going on here," the Emperor continued, practically breathing the words into her ear.

He was taller than she'd thought before, hovering over her by a good five or six inches. When he pressed into her, she could feel all the corded muscles that made him up, even between the materials of their clothing.

"Frankly, I couldn't care less about you and your friend sneaking in for a show," he told her, confirming her earlier assumptions that he was doing this to make a point and not actually because of the supposed rule they'd broken. "Still, I can't just let the two of you get away with it either, now can I? We gods aren't known for being just."

That's what the men outside the barn had been talking about. Gods. Those stories told by her father and grandfather had contained all sorts of creatures and impossibilities, but Jade had taken it all with a grain of salt.

Right now, he just looked like a man—a powerful one, sure, with strange colored eyes and an army behind him, but still...a man. But then, what did a god look like? How was she supposed to recognize the difference?

"God?" Amelia's tiny voice may as well have been a lightning strike in the cell for how it hit Jade.

Since the Emperor's arrival, Jade had completely forgotten about her best friend who was still hanging from her wrists. Her legs were visibly shaking now; staying on her tiptoes had to be a torture all on its own.

Jade tried to shake her head to tell her friend to stop but couldn't so much as budge in the Emperor's grip.

Amelia's gaze wandered toward her. "What's with the men in your life constantly trying to call themselves a god?"

Jade's eyes went wide just as Amelia started laughing. The sound was delirious and weak.

She scanned her over and found out why fairly quickly. The gunshot wound had reopened at some point and had been bleeding profusely all this time. Jade hadn't noticed it before because the lighting in the cell wasn't great, she'd been all the way on the other side, and with Amelia's arms up the way they were the wound wasn't in her line of sight.

The blood soaking through the brown dress and the droplets she tracked that were currently rolling down one of the iron bars to form a small puddle on the ground clued Jade in to just how much she'd lost.

"Amelia," Jade managed to get the word out without screaming it, only vaguely aware that more of that fear had slipped past her defenses and was slowly filling her up. "Amelia, snap out of it."

"Come on, it's a little funny, right?" Amelia's words were starting to slur. "He kind of hot though. Too bad about being so full of himself."

"Amelia."

"What? It's true, he's totally you're type. Trust me," her eyes moved pointedly to where Jade assumed his junk was located. "Too bad you can't see him from where..." Her eyes narrowed. "Wait. Is he hurting you? Look, asshole, you better step back. The second she's able to she'll beat the shit out of you. Don't you know who that is? She's the only granddaughter of the Emerald syndicate."

"There is no Emerald syndicate here," Jade stated. Which meant no one was going to come and save them. They were on their own. "Someone needs to stop the bleeding, she's about to pass out."

"Is there a reason I should care about that?" the Emperor asked.

A bit of that earlier fury slashed through the thick layer of fear. Not enough for her to do much, but still, she desperately clawed for it, focused on it.

"You said you didn't care about any of this at all," she bit out, "so why should it matter if you order them to save her instead of let her die? You wanted to punish us to make a point to everyone else? Okay, you did that. Look at her."

He hummed, and she got the impression he was doing exactly as she suggested and taking Amelia in. "Yes, she does look pretty bad. At least the Grazer, unlike these guards, knows how to do his job properly. You on the other hand," he pressed in closer, clearly enjoying it when she winced in pain as the bars jabbed into her ribs, "seem rather unmarred in comparison."

"So beat me then," she said. "Have them beat me, but let her go."

He grunted. "I was only mildly curious how the two of you snuck in in the first place. Then you interrupt me again by causing a scene down here. I don't think I'll be doing you any favors, little cat. You've certainly done nothing for me and I don't see how you ever will. Therefore," he moved back so quickly she actually stumbled, almost falling to the ground entirely, "I think I'll just kill you both now and be done with it."

Jade turned and dropped the rest of the way to the cold hard ground, tipping her head all the way back so that she could meet the stony look in his eyes.

They glimmered like pink pearls down at her, filled with boredom—like this was a mild chore that broke up his otherwise perfect day. Like killing them would be the same as having to take out the trash.

She'd seen that look in her grandfather's eyes a million times before.

But never aimed at her.

Her brain scrambled to come up with a way out of this, but she was drawing a blank. He didn't know them, and she didn't know him. There were few greater weaknesses than not knowing ones opponent.

Even though they were inside and it would do them no good, Jade felt the spark of her power flicker to life around her. Sometimes, when she was feeling an intense enough emotion she lost control and it got away from her, but those times were few and far between now that she was an experienced adult.

This time all the fear and anxiety and anger within her swelled to the point it needed an outlet, and she wasn't going to bother holding that back when it may in fact be her last moment of life anyway.

The sky burst open, seen from the tiny windows set high in the walls. The rain came immediately, the sounds of the downpour settling some of her nerves with its familiarity.

Not for the first time, Jade found herself cursing the fact that making it rain was all she was capable of doing. Unlike her grandfather, who had powers far more amazing and useful, this was the epitome of what she could do.

Her powers were supposedly meant to advance.

They just...hadn't.

The Emperor glanced at the window and dismissed it. "Really? Showing off your meager power,

Minor? Your fighting skills are far more impressive. Too bad you won't get the chance to use them ever again."

Jade bit the inside of her cheek, hard. The taste of blood on her tongue still wasn't enough to get her brain to think up a way out. Even if she did somehow manage to slip past the Emperor, she couldn't do so with Amelia in tow. Not to mention Koya who was still by the door…

This was it.

She was going to die here.

She was going to die in some random world in some dudes filthy dungeon surrounded by worthless guards she could have taken when she'd been only ten. She bested them all here, and for what?

"Take care of this," the Emperor said then, absently and already turning away from her.

Koya moved to obey his command, walking towards the entrance to the cell, hand already dropping to the sheathed sword tucked inside his belt.

Jade opened her mouth to say something, but her mind was still blank, and all she ended up doing was giving a shaky exhale.

Just when she was about to give up for real, it hit her. The Emperor was leaving the killing to Koya, which meant…So long as the Emperor left quickly, there was still a chance. Jade just had to beat Koya and then—

She frowned, thought process cut short when she realized something had already thrown a major wrench into that plan.

The Emperor had stopped moving, had in fact angled his body slightly back her way. His head was cocked and there was a slight frown furrowing his brow.

"Emperor?" Koya obviously found something odd about this as well.

Suddenly he sniffed, nose aimed in Jade's direction.

"Emperor?" Koya sounded shocked now, which had Jade's hackles rising even more.

Sure, it was weird that the dude was sniffing the air like some hunting dog, but it didn't seem like the type of thing that should elicit that intense of a response. Koya was looking at the Emperor now like he'd grown a second head.

"What…" the Emperor took a single step toward the window, then seemed to rethink that and moved again in Jade's direction instead, "what *is* that?"

Jade held herself very still when he dropped down in front of her, resisting the urge to shuffle back into the bars to renew some distance between them. Whatever was going on, she didn't like the look in his eyes.

They'd glazed over some, and his cheeks had flushed, giving him an almost drunk appearance. The change had come over him so quickly, she would have missed it if his face wasn't literally a mere few inches from her own. His red lips pursed, and he sniffed again, taking a long drag of the air around them this time before his mouth popped open on a small gasp.

"That smells—"

"Smells?!" Koya's shocked expression cut through his words but the Emperor didn't seem to hear him at all.

"—amazing," he finished, and before Jade had the chance to process what he was talking about or why, he shot forward.

With his teeth.

She felt them dig into her neck, piercing skin. His lips latched on, his tongue lapping over her flesh, the rest of his body surrounding her, caging her in against the bars in a far more aggressive way than he'd bothered doing earlier.

Jade tried to push him away, struggling beneath him, but the pain and the sudden dizziness that accompanied it had her weakening rather quickly and it wasn't long before the hands she'd been shoving him with were instead twisting up the material of his silk shirt and clinging for dear life.

At the thought of that, life, she grunted, head lolling to the side some to take in the look of her horrified best friend. Chained as she was, there was nothing Amelia could do to help, and a part of Jade was glad even, all things considered.

Amelia was screaming but Jade barely heard it over the rushing sound in her ears. Every time the Emperor sucked on her neck the sound increased, until it was like war drums pounding behind her skull.

Koya had entered the room at one point, was staring down at them with a look of pure horror painted across his handsome face.

The look had Jade grinning in her almost delirious state, because, honestly, it was kind of funny. She wondered what his Emperor would do if he glanced up and noticed it right now? Would he kill the other guy, or finish her off instead?

As the room spun and everything around her began to wink in and out of existence, Jade managed one last comforting thought.

She was pretty sure she knew where they were now, at least.

Hell.

They'd ended up in hell, and she was about to die here.

The darkness swallowed her up before the ironic laugh could completely slip past her cracked lips.

Chapter 4:

Someone had their lips on hers. She was groggy, not entirely awake, and her head felt light. But it was impossible not to note the tongue delving deeply into her mouth, or the way it invasively stroked against her insides, as if trying to feel all of her. It wasn't necessarily a pleasant kiss, more brutal and demanding than anything, and she found herself pressing against the assailant weakly.

A strong hand banded around both of her wrists, forcing her arms up and pinning them to a wall. She made a sound of protest that was quickly swallowed up by another fierce kiss that stole her breath and left her reeling. Her head pounded and she winced, wondering vaguely if she'd been drugged before the fleeting thought vanished in a puff of smoke and she was back to thinking about nothing but the man in front of her.

Who was he, and why wasn't she more freaked out right now?

Maybe it was the exhaustion, but try as she might she couldn't get her body to obey her commands to move again, to shake his hold loose and shove him away. Growing up in the syndicate there'd been more than one man who'd tried something like this on her when her grandfather wasn't looking.

Some had ended up with permanent scars.

Sharp teeth nipped at her bottom lip and she tasted blood, the salty copper spilling onto her tongue, which was then lapped up by her assailant. He groaned and shifted closer so that she felt the full weight of him against the length of her body.

With a start, she realized she was lying down.

Fingers suddenly dropped to the button of her jeans, struggling to undo it.

Jade tried to pry her eyes open but they wouldn't cooperate either, remaining tightly shut despite the final rise of panic at the center of her chest.

"Stop," the word was barely a whisper, rough and low and filled with so much desperation she winced at the sound, but at least she'd gotten it out there. At least she could say she'd said no.

Surprisingly enough, the hand between them actually paused, the mouth which had dropped to the side of her neck unlatching and pulling back slightly. He didn't go far, she could still feel the hot puffs of his breath against the now damp skin, but he'd stopped.

For now.

"Little cat," the man purred out then, and timbre coaxing and sweet. "You smell so good. Did you know? Like cake."

Getting that one word out had been hard enough, there was no way her battered throat could take another. The most she could manage was to emit a sound of protest. For good measure, she shifted as best she could beneath him, her meaning clear.

Her mind was struggling to catch up but she couldn't recall anything before this moment, before the feel of him on top of her and the taste of his lips.

There had to be more, a lead up of some kind, some reason she was here now instead of....Where had she been before now? What had she been doing?

"Don't hurt yourself," the voice told her then, and there was a teasing note to it as he finally released her captured wrists and stroked the hair off her forehead. "Relax. I'll end it here."

Did she believe that? Trust it?

Plush lips pressed to the rise of her cheek, tender and almost convincing. "Sleep, little cat. Sleep."

Jade wanted to fight against the command, but no sooner had that conviction come to her than she felt herself slipping back into the darkness.

* * *

Jade groaned and winced when doing so caused her throat to ache. She shivered, pressing closer against the solid surface her cheek was propped up on and shifted her legs, trying to get the feeling back into them. Everything hurt, like she'd been hit by a truck, or worse, like she'd just gone three rounds with Master Key, her grandfather's favorite soldier and the current underboss of the Emeralds.

She'd let him have the damn syndicate if it meant the two of them would leave her alone, but no. No matter how much she begged, no matter how many times she explained all the ways Key would make a better boss than she would, neither of them seemed keen to listen.

Was that why he'd beaten her up? Had they gone a few rounds after yet another failed attempt by her to convince him to get her grandfather to give him the coveted crown?

"Key," her voice cracked and she reached up and pressed her fingers against the center of her throat, "bastard. Water. Now."

They'd done this dance so many times it was practically second nature, despite the fact it'd been almost a year since their last jaunt. When she'd run, she'd had to cut contact with everyone who was a part of the Emeralds, even him. Even if it sucked doing so.

When no reply immediately came, her brow dipped into a slight frown. He'd never beat her and leave her alone. His presence was a constant, considered—at least by her—to be part of the aftercare. She endured his punches and kicks, and he stuck around after to make sure she was all right. It was almost the only alone time the two of them got. She hated that she cared so much about it, yet...

"Key?" Why did her neck hurt so much? She grimaced after every word spoken, fingers inching over to where something was sticking to her and pulling at her skin. When they danced over the edges of what was clearly a bandage, her frown deepened.

"Dust," a male voice shattered the quiet.

A voice that was most definitely, one hundred percent, *not* Key's.

Jade's eyes snapped open so fast the room momentarily spun, but then they settled on the man seated directly across from her and everything stilled and became hyper focused, from the way the edge of the plush mattress on the bed cradled his body to the single drop of blood on the tip of his left boot.

He was in tight black pants and had a mint green long sleeved shirt on, the collar open to expose swaths of tanned skin and a peek at toned flesh.

There was a small candle cradled almost delicately in his right hand, the tiny flame bright and dancing with every one of his soft exhales. He held it close to his face, almost like he couldn't get enough of its sweet fragrance.

Cherry blossoms and a hint of something woodsier, maybe mahogany or teakwood.

"My name is Dust," he continued, leaning forward slowly, until his elbows were propped on his knees, "but you can call me Emperor."

It hit her all at once, the events of the past few days, like someone was forwarding through a movie at maximum speed.

Jason. And the puddle. The hot springs. The barn. The cell. Someone called the grazer and a knife. Koya. Amelia chained.

And the Emperor.

"You bit me," she accused, hand slapping against the side of her neck so hard she saw stars from the pain. Stupid of her. The bandage was covering the wound he'd caused, and with another start, she realized she'd been tended to. Gone was the dirt that had been caked under her nails, and she was no longer dressed in the clothes she'd worn through the puddle portal.

Jade wasn't sheepish by any sense of the word, having grown up around men who were constantly taking their clothes off for the heck of it. But there was a major difference between being naked and conscious and being stripped while unawares and helpless.

The dress she was wearing wasn't her style—if it could even be referred to as a dress. Made entirely of black lace, the thing clung to her like a second skin, with a low v neckline, and a hem that stopped mid-thigh. At least there were sleeves, the material stretching all the way down her arms and covering half of her palms. Even in the dim lighting of the room they were in, however, Jade could tell the outfit was practically see-through.

"It appears it doesn't last long," the Emperor mumbled then, practically sneering at the candle he'd been holding so lovingly only moments ago.

Or had she been mistaken? Perhaps she'd seen wrong.

"Pity." He snuffed the flame out and dropped the candle onto the floorboards, not even bothering to watch when it hit the ground and rolled under the bed.

"Who changed my clothes?" she asked, tearing her eyes off the small object to look back at him. She was sitting on the floor, on top of a thick fur blanket. The fur was a mixture of golds and browns and whites, and she hated admitting it, but it was the softest thing she'd ever touched in her entire life.

Still, it was a far cry from the comforts of a bed where he was currently seated, watching her like she was some fascinating specimen in a jar.

The room they were in was a decent size, with her sitting against the wall in the middle between two large bay windows. Moonlit streamed in from them, alerting her to the fact she'd been unconscious for a while this time around. Across from her, a large fireplace was set, and there was a steady fire going in the hearth. On either side of that, there were doors, each closed and identical looking.

A small table with only two chairs took up one portion of the room, and on the other, there was the bed.

Once her gaze rounded back to him, the corner of the Emperor's mouth twitched upward in a mock smile.

"I did. Since I was the one who bit you and got blood all over your shirt, it only seemed right that I be the one who get you out of it."

"Would have preferred you leave my clothing on, thanks."

He quirked a dark brow. "You're bolder than you should be given your current circumstances, little cat. Would you like another moment to rethink your tone?"

"Pissing off powerful men is sort of my M.O." She lifted a single shoulder in a half shrug, carefully settling a mask of disinterest over herself. On the outside, she needed to appear calm. Maybe it would keep him talking, give her time to come up with a plan—yeah right.

"Ah," his words were spoken lightly, but the edge shimmering behind his pink eyes was undeniable, "that's right. Your friend mentioned something about that, didn't she? Something about gods in your life."

Jade's blood ran cold, all the feigned relaxation evaporating in a puff of smoke the second Amelia was mentioned.

Amelia, who'd been chained and bloody the last time Jade had seen her.

"Where is she?" she asked.

The Emperor let out a sigh, the kind of sound one would make to a teenager they were trying to explain a simple math problem to who just wasn't grasping it. He stood and slowly made his way toward her, dropping down into a crouch before her that mirrored the move he'd made not so long ago, just before he'd bitten her.

"Let's make a few things clear, here and now, shall we?" He reached out and gently took a lock of her long hair, smoothing the strands delicately between his fingers before he began to twist it around his pointer. "No one demands anything of me, least of all you. You're only still breathing because I've allowed you to continue doing so. That could change." His grip tightened. "And most likely will. I suggest you enjoy breathing while you can. From here on out, I am the only god you have to listen to. Understand, little cat?"

"Gods aren't real." Part of her screamed at the other to shut up, but she'd been taught to stand her ground and it was hard to shake that type of teaching, even in a situation like this.

With a monster holding her hostage by a strand of hair.

"Maybe not where you're from," he said, "but I assure you, here, we are very, very real."

She swallowed the lump in her throat and took another risk. "And where is here, exactly?"

The corner of his mouth tipped up again, and it was a vicious smile, the kind that foreshadowed countless horrors to come.

Jade couldn't help it. She shuddered.

He liked that, she could tell by the way he split into a wide grin, his finger slowly unwinding the strand he'd just bound up tightly. "This is Orremos. You're currently within the Celestial Empire, in the Parallel Province, which is where I call my home." He cocked his head, silent for a second before asking, "Where did you come from?"

At least he believed she wasn't from around here. Finally.

"Earth, Thailand. But I'm technically from New York. Bangkok just happens to be where we were when—"

"You fell through a puddle," he stated.

"Yeah." *Did* he believe her?

"Did you bleed?" he asked, almost absently, turning his attentions to the lock of hair he still held.

"What?"

"Before the puddle?" he elaborated. "Where you injured?"

"I—" A gun had gone off and she'd been grazed. She'd almost forgotten, after everything that had happened since. "Yes. I was. Why?"

"That explains the puddle."

"It does?" How?

He clucked his tongue. "Your blood must have opened the portal. Poor little cat. Doesn't even know how her power works."

"Excuse me?" she couldn't stop the heat from reentering her tone and it unfortunately didn't go unnoticed.

With one sharp tug he had her rocking forward and slamming into him. Her hands braced themselves on his thighs, her head smacking against his chest just beneath his chin. When she tried to quickly pull away, his arms banded around her, pinning her in place with her mouth practically pressed against the material of his shirt. The position made it hard to breath, but her struggles went unanswered.

"I've been far too hospitable to someone who doesn't deserve it, it seems. Perhaps I should have you tossed back into that dank cell. Or, better yet," he lowered his mouth and she felt the threatening press of his teeth against the uninjured side of her neck, "maybe I should just take what I want from you now in one go and be done with this whole ordeal."

"No." The thought of his teeth ripping into her again, of the pain that had brought...

"No what, little cat?"

She ground her teeth but there was no way around this. "Please."

Suddenly, she was tumbling backwards, falling onto the soft furs. Before she could fully catch her breath his body followed, pinning her down between himself and the solid ground. His body was a heavy weight over her, and he settled himself there, as if preparing to remain that way for a good while.

His ears were pierced, she noticed, catching a glimpse of the right one and all the gold there. Rook, orbital, upper lobe, standard lobe, and forward helix—she ticked them off in her head. The gold jewelry he wore glittered brilliantly in the firelight.

She hated gold.

She could feel all the hard lines of him fitted against her, could see the individual dark hairs of his curved eye brows with his face hovering just over hers like it was. When he exhaled, his warm breath fanned across her cheeks, and when he inhaled and groaned, she watched as his eyes rolled back in some twisted form of pleasure.

Then there was something else. Something lower. Something...that was getting bigger.

Jade gasped and tried to shove him off of her, only to have her wrists taken in one of his hands and slapped against the floor above her head. He held her still, waiting for her struggles to die off and end.

"Shh," he lowered his voice as he lowered his head, running the tip of his nose up the length of her neck, "relax, little cat. I have no intentions of taking it all the way tonight."

The word tonight didn't go unnoticed.

One moment he was talking about killing her in some grimy cell, and the next he was at full mast on top of her? What the actual fuck was going on here, and what was wrong with him?

She was remembering before now as well, when she'd woken with someone on top of her just like this. It didn't take a genius to guess it'd been him.

"What did you do, when you undressed me?" she demanded, part of her afraid of the answer. Her memories only stretched so far, and were fuzzy at best. More than anything else, the taste of him stood out, a rich tart flavor, almost like black cherries dipped in dark chocolate.

"Only stole a few kisses," he admitted right away. "It was hard to help myself, since you smell so sweet. I was curious."

"Only," she parroted dully. "Forcing yourself on someone isn't attractive."

"Who says I'm trying to attract you, little cat?"

"My name is Jade," she corrected, sick of the weird nickname.

He grunted against her jawline. "I don't recall asking."

She bristled. "No, why would you. You just want to—"

"What?" He pulled back slightly, just enough to be able to stare down at her. "What is it you think I want to do to you? I'm in a surprisingly good mood, so I'm more than willing to play. But there will be stakes, of course."

"I don't want to play any games," she told him, certain that was the correct answer. For her safety, anyway.

"What do you want?"

"I want to go home."

"No."

Her mouth dropped open momentarily until she could regain her composure. "What?"

"I said," he leaned in close again, bringing his plush lips up to the curve of her ear, "no. It's unfortunate for you that your portal opened up in my hot spring the way that it did, but how you feel about that isn't my problem. There's something I want from you, and until I get it, you aren't going anywhere."

"Are you talking about my blood?" She didn't want to but had to ask, "Are you a vampire or something?"

Was that what this was? Why he'd been making out with her even though he didn't appear to be even remotely interested in her at all?

Well. Aside from down there, anyway.

She was trying hard *not* to think about his cock though.

He snorted. "A vampire? Those don't exist."

"Then why did you bite me and drink my blood?"

"It wasn't your blood I was after," he said. "It's your magic. I can smell it." He sniffed loudly at the curve of her neck. "Why do you smell so good? Do you wear perfume?"

"No," this was weird, "and even if I did, it would have worn off by now. After the impromptu bath, the sleeping in a hay barn, and that lovely trip to your dungeon."

He chuckled against her skin. "I was considering cutting out your tongue earlier, but I've changed my mind."

Jade went still beneath him. He's said it casually enough, but there was no mistaking the truth in his words. He'd been thinking about cutting out her tongue, and now he was telling her as much without batting an eyelash.

God, vampire, whatever, one thing was crystal clear.

This guy was a sociopath.

The Emperor ground his hips into her then, rubbing his thick length against her lower abdomen.

She sucked in a sharp breath, eyes widening and snapping back to his.

"I don't like being ignored," he explained. "Where did your mind go just now?"

"I'm debating if I can beat you in a fight," she lied, mostly to hear his response. She needed to test the waters, get an understanding of what exactly was going on here and why. He hadn't killed her outright, had instead changed her and brought her to a room, which meant she really did have something he wanted.

Her power?

As far as she knew that wasn't something she could give, or that he could take.

He grinned down at her, flashing a smile that showed his teeth for the first time. With his freehand, he brushed the hair off of her forehead, in a gesture that could easily be misconstrued as caring.

"Would you like to attempt it?" he asked, voice like honey.

He was enjoying this for some reason.

Jade knew better. Even if by some miracle she managed to best him here, there must be guards at the door and down the hall. Then, if she set all that aside, there was still the issue of not knowing where Amelia was being kept. She didn't even know the way to the dungeons, so even if her friend had been left there—which she doubted—it would do Jade no good.

"I was taught to bide my time against an opponent who is physically stronger than me," Jade told him. Did stroking his ego have the same effect on him as insinuating she wanted to punch him?

"You are admittedly fascinating," he said, "but it's unclear if that's because of your magic and what it does to me. It could have nothing to do with *you* at all."

"What does it do to you?" Did she really want to know? She was torn.

Almost casually, he began lightly rubbing his hard length against her, twisting his hips so subtly that if he hadn't been pressed so close she might not have noticed right away. As it were, his movements were impossible to miss, and though his expression never altered, she felt her cheeks begin to flame.

"I'll tell you a story, little cat." He rested an arm on either side of her head, propping himself up so that he could easily stare down at her, all while his hips continued their lazy movement. "Once upon a time—Is that how stories begin where you're from?"

She nodded.

"Once upon a time," he continued, "there was only one god, the Mother. But she grew bored, and, tired of cultivating the universe on her own, decided to end her very long existence. Energy doesn't simply vanish, you see, it has to go somewhere, become something. The Mother's energy was dispersed, reformed. This was called the Great Beginning, and from it sprouted everything you see around you. The first beings to arise from the ashes were the Preeminent, nine gods, all with their own powers and purpose. These gods formed a new way of living, structuring what would otherwise be a chaotic world."

"Let me guess, you're one of these gods."

"I am."

"Bullshit." She rolled her eyes. "More like a pathetic man with a complex."

To be honest, she wasn't sure why she said it. Even she knew it was stupid doing so. But she'd been reminded of all those times her grandfather had forced her to sit with him in front of the fireplace. He'd drone on and on about their heritage, about what had given them greatness and made them better than everyone else. She hadn't been allowed to leave until she could repeat it all back to him, down to every last detail.

Which was probably what freaked her out here the most.

Because those stories, the ones she'd always thought where made up delusions to help bolster her family's image in the eyes of their subordinates…What if those hadn't been stories at all?

What if they had been real?

What if gods were real?

What if there was one on top of her right now?

He went still above her, and she knew before he spoke that she'd made a mistake.

"Just because I'm being gentle with you, doesn't mean you should forget your place." He pressed the pad of his thumb against the wound on her neck, ignoring her soft cry of pain as he brought his face closer to hers so the tips of their noses grazed. "Beneath me."

The pain was sharp, shooting up her neck to spark beneath her scalp. She reacted, grabbing onto his wrist with both hands in a poor attempt to pry him off, the heels of her feet scraping against the wooden floorboards as she struggled to slip out from underneath him. Stars winked behind her eyes and his face came in and out of focus.

She'd been injured more times than she could count, was covered in scars, and yet this was going to go down as one of the worst pains she'd ever felt. One of the trainees had bitten her thigh once during a sparring match overseen by Key. It'd left a mark and had burned like a motherfucker, but that had been the most of it. Maybe it was because this time it was her neck.

Rage and fear burned through her, igniting her nerve endings, followed swiftly by a heady frustration. She was powerless against him.

For now.

Silently, she promised herself she'd get back at him. There had to be a way, and she would find it.

Whether she wanted to be or not, she was the granddaughter and sole heir of Owen Blakely, kingpin of the Emerald syndicate, and she would not lie down and take disrespect from anyone.

Not even a terrifying god with pink eyes and a wicked smile.

"I call you little cat, but it's the adjective you should pay attention to. You're a house cat, a stray or a pet—I haven't quite decided yet—while I'm an eclipse tiger. You don't stand a chance against me. Your only hope is that I don't grow tired of you too quickly."

Jade had to do something. Anything. She just wanted to make it stop, and maybe prove a point in the process. So, even though she knew it was stupid, she couldn't help herself from taking the bait.

"You talk too much," she snarled, then before he could react, she jabbed a fist against the center of his throat.

He shot back, finally lifting off of her enough she could pull herself free. She debated kicking him in the balls, but opted not to go full-on suicidal, and instead landed a blow at the center of his chest, effectively sending him sprawling onto his back.

She practically tripped over the fur on her way to the door, already preparing herself for whatever guard was standing on the other side.

Of course, she hadn't anticipated it being locked.

She swore at her incompetence and abandoned the brass knob, spinning around just in time to brace.

The Emperor practically crashed into her, not caring this time around if he crushed her beneath his weight, pinning her between himself and the door. His hand went around her neck, fingers pressing painfully against the wound as he squeezed.

Her ribs were starting to hurt and the lack of oxygen made the room begin to darken almost immediately.

"Let's try this again when you're feeling more amicable," he growled, tightening his grip further.

The last thing Jade saw before slipping into oblivion was the slight glow of his eyes, the color darker and as vibrant as the sky at sunset.

Chapter 5:

The first time Jade woke, her mind was foggy once more, and her head was pounding so hard that it was hard for her to move, let alone pry open her eyes. Instead, she kept them closed, focusing on inhaling and exhaling, trying to regain some semblance of balance. She knew what she was experiencing this time, the aches and the exhaustion coupled with the sharp pain in her joints and at her neck a result of not just the Emperor, but of having used too much of her power.

If he was to be believed, falling through that puddle had been her doing. She still didn't understand it, but if she took that into account and added it to how she'd summoned power to fight off his guards and then again when she'd been about to die in the dungeon, it made sense that she was experiencing magic burn.

The burn had kept her incoherent and weak for days when she'd been younger, bedridden and vulnerable. Key had always been ordered to remain by her side when that had happened—the one good thing her grandfather had done for her after being the reason she was in that state in the first place. It was always because he'd pushed her too hard in training, refusing to listen when she'd begged him to let her stop and rest.

It'd been a long while since she'd experienced it, since she'd kept her magic locked down in college to keep a low profile, and then had fled that day her graduation party was being held at the estate. While on the run, she'd only used when necessary, not wanting to risk drawing attention and giving their location away somehow.

It helped that her power to summon rain wasn't exactly something useful.

The pain Jade felt was so intense, it took her a moment to realize she'd been woken by the sounds of a conversation.

"With all due respect, I don't agree," the voice was familiar, but she couldn't place it at first.

"I do not need, nor want, your agreement, Koya," another stated, the wall against her back rumbling with each word.

If she had the strength to move, she would have shot away, but as it were, Jade was unable to so much as twitch her pinky let alone separate herself from the god cradling her against him.

She must still be in that room on the floor with the Emperor. How much time had passed since he'd choked her?

"You say you know who Valued her line," Koya, the initial speaker, said. "What if this is all part of a plan? She could be an assassin."

The Emperor grunted. "What a poor assassin she'd be. Look how dangerous she is." He stroked a finger down the length of her arm, but she gave no reaction. "All lax and unconscious in my arms. A half hour ago she tried to escape; that went well for her, as you can see. No. She's no assassin."

"Normal people aren't trained to fight the way she is," he argued. "She took down those guards with ease. Something isn't right here. Emperor, I beg you, don't—"

"What?" The change in the air was apparent as he lost his temper, everything seeming to thicken around them. "Don't give in to my base nature? Don't wish for things I don't need? Need according to whom, Koya?"

"That's not at all what I meant, Emperor. Forgive me. I worry for you, that's all. We don't know enough about this girl or her friend. Killing them—"

"Won't solve my problem, only get rid of my possible solution. No. I have better uses for her, whether she was sent here by Master Mist or not."

"It can't be a coincidence."

"Of course it can. You heard her friend's testimony. They were being hunted when they fell through the portal. The little cat must have accidentally accessed her power while on the run and, not knowing how to use it, subconsciously called for a way out of their predicament."

Jade had been wishing for an escape when Amelia and her had been shot...When her blood had been spilled...Was he right? Was that what happened?

"Her magic was born here, thus it brought her here," he continued, unaware of her thoughts. "It's simple, really. Nothing to be concerned about."

"*If* that's what really happened." Koya didn't sound convinced. "How can we be sure they're telling the truth? Her training—"

"She was raised in something called a syndicate," the Emperor stated. "That's interesting. Find out more about that from the girl."

"And what about her? The other one could be faking. Feeding us false information on purpose while you're distracted with this one. You smelled her blood, and okay, she's no Minor, but that doesn't mean she wasn't trained as well."

The Emperor was quiet a moment, as if thinking, and then, "You would like me to test her?"

"Them," he corrected, then seemed to realize his tone was too demanding and softened it, "Emperor. This one is too weak to make much of a difference to you anyway, and we aren't yet sure about the rumors."

"You have men on it, correct?"

"Yes. They're searching for the truth now. Once they find out if the vial is real they'll return and inform us. If it turns out that it isn't, then keeping them alive would have been for nothing."

"If it turns out that it does exist, and yet you've killed this girl, how would you make it up to me, Koya? Do you really think your body would be enough?"

"Forgive me, Emperor."

It was hard to follow, but Jade was getting the impression that they'd figured out she had magic and Amelia didn't, yet Koya didn't trust it. She didn't even want to contemplate what possible things the Emperor could have in store for her, so she didn't allow her mind to go there.

"Let's do it," he surprised both Koya and Jade by saying. "Let's run a test, see if the other one's been lying about her skillset. If it turns out she has and is just as dangerous, we'll kill them and be done with it."

"Emperor…"

"You're right," he sighed. "Getting my sense back isn't worth the possibility of Mist's return."

"He died…," Koya was clearly confused.

The Emperor snickered. "How often do dead gods remain that way?"

"Do you really think…"

Jade struggled to hear the rest, but the darkness was tugging her back down, forcing her mind to blank until for a time there was nothing but the solid feel of the Emperor around her, holding her, almost gently.

And then for the millionth time since she'd entered this damn realm, there was nothing at all.

* * *

Jade came too with a hiss, trying to pull away from the sharp burn at her wrist, only to have something tighten around her waist.

She blinked open her eyes, feeling a lethargy she hadn't upon waking the first time. The fire was still going, though the flames had died down some, casting a warm glow across the floorboards to the tips of her bare feet. She was still on the furs on the ground, but this time she wasn't alone. The second she processed who was holding her, she stiffened, even going so far as to halt her breathing as if that would somehow help her go unnoticed.

Her back was against the Emperor's front, his legs up at either side of her, caging her in. He had his right arm wrapped around her waist, keeping her close, while his left held her wrist aloft.

When she risked shifting her eyes in that direction she felt bile rise up the back of her throat.

He'd bitten her again, the mark ugly and red, with blood welling from the puncture wounds. That was why her wrist hurt and probably what had woken her in the first place.

Her mind struggled to recall something, something important, but there were only bits and pieces, fractures of a conversation between him and Koya she wasn't all together certain hadn't merely been a dream.

The Emperor hummed and the vibrations of his chest rattled through her where they touched. A second later he dropped his chin to her left shoulder, strands of his dark hair tickling her cheek.

"It only works when you use your magic," he told her quietly, disappointedly. "Otherwise your blood is just that. Regular mortal blood. Useless." He let go and her arm dropped like a dead weight, slapping against the curve of his thigh.

Jade pulled away, tucking in on herself as best she could, uncaring how the move would come off. So what if she seemed weak at the moment? People who knew when to put their pride aside were the ones who lived the longest. She'd tried her hand and had failed. Now she'd need to utilize a different tactic if she was going to make it out of this room.

Preferably in one piece, and not drained dry.

"Are you thirsty?" he asked, still using that same soft and coaxing tone. "You asked for water before. Would you like some?"

She nodded, opting to concentrate on one issue at a time. Right now dealing with the fact she was parched seemed like a good start.

He picked up a cup that was out of her line of vision and brought it up to her lips. When she hesitated, his fingers splayed against her hip bone. He didn't need to take the subtle threat any further.

Jade gulped down half the contents of the ceramic cup, the cool water soothing her at an unexpected level. She slumped back against him once she was finished, eyes actually drifting shut momentarily. Vaguely, she wondered if he'd drugged it, but logically she knew it was just her body catching up with her.

She'd been through too much these past days, hadn't had the chance to properly take care of herself or recover. Hell, she couldn't even recall the last time she'd had a drink of water or a bite to eat.

"You're past the worst of the burn," he told her, clearly understanding why she'd been out this whole time and knowing it wasn't simply his doing. "I'll keep the comments about how pathetically weak you are to myself."

How kind of him.

"My friend—"

He shushed her. "We'll get to that later. I tried to tell you a story but you didn't want to hear it. This time you'll tell me one."

"What?"

"Describe where you're from." He rested his left arm on his upturned knee, the thumb on his right hand beginning to draw lazy circles against her hip. "Tell me everything."

"I..." Jade frowned, trying to figure out if there was something specific about her he wanted to know. He'd made it fairly clear that she was nothing more than a passing fancy, something new and shiny he could play with, possibly break, and then discard. With that in mind, she doubted very much he cared to know details like what she majored in in college and what her favorite foods were.

Power. That's what he seemed to care about. That's why she was here and not already dead.

Her power came from her bloodline.

"It skipped over my father," she tentatively began, carefully reading the feel of his body for signs of disinterest or annoyance. Being choked into unconsciousness once was enough. "My grandfather wasn't very pleased about that. It made it harder to find my dad a match with the proper lineage."

"Explain," he ordered.

"There are a few families like mine," she told him. "They have gifts, can do things. We're told it's because we're the descendants of gods."

He made a derisive sound. "They were Valued by gods, there is a difference."

"Valued?" Jade wanted to resist the inkling of interest she felt, but these were questions she'd had her entire life. Questions that didn't have answers in her world.

It wasn't hard to figure out whoever had graced her family with these powers—in however way they'd done it—that person had started in Orremos. Earlier, the Emperor had insinuated that she'd opened the portal in the puddle herself with her blood. That was a fair assumption. She had been bleeding and a drop could have easily fallen into the murky water. If that were the case, then to believe she was the only one capable of opening gateways into this world was hubris.

"They came from here," she said, only partially aware she did so out loud, still too tangled up in her own thoughts.

"Yes," he agreed. "The god who Valued your familial line was one of the Preeminent. Over five thousand years ago he slipped through a portal into your world and vanished. The rest of us were aware of his death some time later, but we had no idea he'd Valued a mortal before his demise."

"So, you're saying he gifted these powers, right?"

He nodded as best he could with his head tucked against the curve of her shoulder and managed to shift even closer, despite the fact she would have bet money they were already as close as humanly possible.

"When a god Values a human, he bestows on them a bit of his own magic. It's not done lightly, or often, and can even leave the god weakened for a while. Doing so also creates a bond between them, one that stretches an eternity, passing from generation to generation. Even those without ability, like your father, have a connection to him. Or, did, until his death. Now the power continues on through you but without a tether. That's probably why it's weakened with every spawning."

She made a face at that word choice, but luckily he couldn't see.

"How powerful is your grandfather?" he asked, and though nothing outwardly changed about it, she got the impression there was more to that particular question than met the eye.

Should she lie? There wasn't really a point to; no matter how strong her grandfather was, he was nothing in comparison to a bona fide god. The Emperor hadn't done much by way of proving to her he actually was one, and yet...

There was something about him, an energy that flickered off his skin and seemed to fill the entire room. Clearly he wasn't human.

"He's the strongest in a while," she ended up confessing. "The other Legends—that's what we call ourselves—they follow his orders."

"Ah," she could hear the wicked smirk in his voice, "is that what your friend meant back in the dungeon? Does your grandfather think himself a god?"

Before she could come up with a reply she felt his hand back at her throat. He didn't squeeze, merely rested his fingers around her neck, careful not to press against the wound beneath the bandage. Still, she felt herself clam up.

Pathetic. Since when was she this afraid of pain?

She was in the process of trying to convince herself it had more to do with not wanting to pass out again and be vulnerable, than with the actual affliction itself, when he spoke against her ear.

"I assure you, little cat, no one, god or man, is stronger than I, and certainly not a mere Minor." It was almost as if he'd read her thoughts just now. "If you've been placing all your hopes on a valiant rescue from your grandfather, put those dreams to bed. There isn't a creature alive who can take from me that which I am unwilling to give. Tell me you understand."

She tried to bob her head, but when all that got her was a slight tightening of his hand, opted to say out loud, "I understand."

"Good." His arm returned to rest on his leg and she took a shaky breath. "I was going to make you apologize for attacking me, on your knees no less, but you've behaved so well since waking, and really, you can't be blamed for trying your luck the once. Once," he reiterated firmly, "little cat. That's all I'll give you."

He didn't have to add that he thought she should be grateful for even that much, it was easy enough to pick up on her own.

"What do you want from me?" she sounded meek even to her own ears, but she couldn't be bothered by that now. Because he was right, there wasn't a way anyone else could come and rescue her, which meant she needed to rescue herself.

And she couldn't do that locked up in this room.

"If I tell you," he asked suggestively, "will you give it to me?"

She almost shuddered, only managing to hold herself still at the last second. "Honestly?"

"Of course."

"It depends. What do you want me to give you?"

He took her chin between two fingers and tilted her head so that their eyes could meet over her shoulder. When he grinned, his eyes lit up and a dimple formed on his right side. "Freedom."

Jade pursed her lips in confusion.

"We'll get to that soon enough. Unfortunately for you, whether or not I'll let you live to see another dawn is yet undecided." He pressed his nose beneath the curve of her jawline. "Would you like to know what you can do to persuade me to be in your and your friends favor?"

She wanted to hit him *so* badly. Of all the hot springs in all the worlds, why did it have to be this guys?

Hitting him the once hadn't gone all that well for her though, and she knew from experience that she needed to wait for the right moment before even considering to attempt another try at it.

Now that she was starting to get her barring back, Jade was pretty certain that conversation she'd overheard had actually happened and wasn't just a dream. Which meant Koya wanted her and Amelia dead, and the Emperor was only just toeing the line in the opposite direction. It also meant that wherever Amelia was right now, something more had happened to her. It had to have, she wouldn't have talked otherwise, and they'd known things they wouldn't have if her friend hadn't spilled.

Which meant as badly as Jade wanted to risk it all and tell the Emperor to go fuck himself—because that's the sort of pride one developed when raised under the assumption that they were top of the food chain, like she had been—she swallowed that urge.

"Tell me," she said, hoping that whatever it was, whatever he wanted from her, it wasn't going to be that awful.

The corner of his mouth tipped up and he reached out and took her chin between his thumb and forefinger. "Tell you, what?"

"Please," she was less capable of keeping the edge out of her tone that time around, but even though his eyes flashed for a second, he contained his annoyance, that mocking half smile never slipping from his face.

"I've gotten some more explanation about what a syndicate is since our last discussion," he told her silkily, maybe even somewhat impressed. "From the sounds of it, you should be familiar with having to prove yourself and how important people like us go about gathering that proof."

She searched his dark gaze, easily picking out the viciousness there. This was a predator, a monster, the type of person who drew pleasure from others pain. Even if she hadn't figured that out for herself firsthand, that much would be apparent just looking at him as closely as she was.

Another look she was familiar with, but not one exclusively reserved for her grandfather.

There were a lot of guys in the Emeralds like that. Girls too.

She thought about the night she'd walked in on Key, standing over the beaten and bloody body of his best friend. The look in his eyes...

She'd started devising her plan of escape not soon after.

That was the night Jade had realized with perfect clarity that while she might enjoy a little bloodshed here and there, while she liked that electric feeling of knowing she was stronger or smarter than somebody else...She didn't have that black spark that people like her grandfather and Key did.

She was no monster.

Still, that didn't stop the glimmer from entering her eyes now, or the thrill that raced through her, the anticipation.

Yes, she knew exactly how people like them needed to prove themselves.

"Who do I have to fight?" she asked.

The Emperor grinned, and she felt like little Red Riding Hood lost in the forest.

At the whims of the wolf.

Chapter 6:

Jade went to the cage willingly. And it was a cage, it couldn't be considered anything but. It had been set up in a part of the palace unlike the others, reminding her of the warehouse back home that her grandfather used to train and test new recruits. She'd started going with him when she'd been thirteen because he'd wanted her to see everything about the business firsthand, even the seedier underbelly of it.

The Emperor and his guards had brought her to a separate building a bit of a ways off the main portion of the palace. They'd walked down yet another white pebble path and though she'd tried to be subtle, it was obvious she'd been searching for signs of the hot springs.

Eventually she would need to find it again in order to have even a slight chance of getting out of here.

But not now. Right now she needed to stay focused on surviving long enough to make it out of this room.

The cavernous space smelled much the same as warehouse as well, like blood and sweet—maybe even a hint of piss. There were stains seeped into the dirt ground, and bits of torn cloth and pieces of broken chains dangled randomly from some of the bars that made up the cell. It was large too, with more than enough room for two dozen men to duke it out.

Which was most likely a bad sign.

Things only got progressively worse when the door to the building opened at her back and two soldiers dragged in a semi-unconscious Amelia.

"What the hell are you doing?!" Jade had let them walk her into this place and lock the iron door behind her but now she spun on the Emperor, glaring.

He was at the front of the room, seated on a long leather chaise, legs sprawled out before him, ankles crossed. Absently, he picked at the fruits on a silver platter a servant held out next to him.

Koya was nearby, standing just over his left shoulder, arms crossed behind his back. His expression was closed off but the hatred he felt towards her was pretty apparent none-the-less.

Her grandfather wouldn't have been caught dead lying down at one of these things, too intent on upholding his intimidating vibe. He'd stand the entire fight, watching closely, sometimes even walking around to peer down at a particular gang member as he fought.

The Emperor was lax, nibbling on fruit as if he hadn't a care in the world, and yet…

Jade was still afraid of him.

And it wasn't just because of how bad her friend looked or the fact they were trapped here and at his mercy.

The cage door opened and Amelia was tossed uncaringly inside.

Jade tried to catch her, but her deadweight took them both down with a hard thump. She dragged her friend over to the corner and propped her up against the bars, swiveling on her feet so that she could face her. The move also blocked off the Emperor's line of sight, something she knew she couldn't maintain, but hoped would be at least a mild comfort for her friend.

Amelia took a shaky breath and then blinked up at her, coming to. "Hey."

Her entire right eye was practically swollen shut, and there was more blood on her lips than there'd been before. At least the gunshot wound had been tended, though not very well. Her dress was in serious tatters now, and scrapes and bruises littered her bare arms and legs. There were cuts on her knees, but no other knife wounds that Jade could find.

They'd beaten her some more, but not a ton.

"Sorry," Amelia said while she was inspected. "I sort of caved and spilled."

"It's fine," Jade shook her head, "don't talk."

She sounded awful when she did, like she'd swallowed a bucketful of gravel and chased it with rubbing alcohol.

"Can you move?" She checked Amelia's fingers, was relived to find that nothing appeared to be broken.

"Just tired," she confessed. "Haven't been able to sleep."

"They've been keeping you awake?"

Amelia shook her head slightly. "I'm just too afraid to shut my eyes for longer than a few minutes." Finally, she seemed to come to herself enough to notice where they were and a flash of fear crossed over her face. "What is this?"

"Don't worry," Jade reassured, placing a comforting hand on her shoulder. "Just sit here and stay out of the way."

"The way of what?"

There was no point in trying to sugarcoat anything, the doors were already opening again and she could see from the corner of her eye that there were a lot of people entering this time around. It'd be obvious what was about to happen in a moment.

"You remember that story I told you about when I was fifteen? The first time I stepped into the Abyss?" That's what her grandfather called it. A nifty name for a shithole in the middle of nowhere. That was where he took all his strongest new recruits. Where the real test was conducted.

Jade didn't like to talk about her time with the Emeralds, but one night their sophomore year she'd gotten so wasted the words had simply tumbled past her lips and in a slur of sentences. Luckily, Amelia had been the only one there to hear any of it, but that was what had outed her to her best friend.

Amelia had known she was the granddaughter of a gangster after that.

Yet things hadn't changed between them.

"I'm going to get you out of here," Jade promised, but Amelia was still hung up on her question, brow furrowed deeply.

"Don't fight these people." She gripped Jade's upper arm, nails digging a bit into her flesh in her panic. "We don't know anything about them."

"I've beaten some of them before," she reminded, only to have tears well in her friends eyes.

"You caught them off guard. What if...Jade. I can't be here alone. I can't."

"Relax," she took her hand and squeezed. "Nothing is going to happen to me. I won't leave you. Besides, it's not like I have a choice. It's either this or he kills us anyway."

"Jade—"

The cage door opened again, and nine men entered. Some of them stared down at her crouched in front of Amelia and sniggered. Others grunted and looked away, as if she wasn't worth their time. Even though word about her taking down the guards before had more than likely reached them, it was obvious by the smug or bored looks on their faces that none of them considered her to be much of, if any, threat.

That was going to be a mistake.

They were bigger than her; one even so broad she was certain two of her could stand side by side in front of him and not cover his entire width. They wore black pants and shirts with cut sleeves to show bulging arm muscles and flashes of tight abs when they shifted and the thin cotton material opened at the overly large armholes.

"You are all here because you've done something to displease the Emperor," Koya's voice carried over them then, causing some of the men to finally tense and show a modicum of seriousness. "This is your one and only chance to gain his pardon. There is only one rule. The last one standing wins."

Several guards stood against the walls, facing the cage. One of them stepped forward and slipped a large knife from his belt, tossing it between the bars.

The weapon landed with a loud smack against the center of the floor.

Jade felt her hackles rise, eyes snapping to the Emperor's. She wasn't able to contain her surprise but he didn't so much as blink at her.

This was a fight...to the death.

People had died in her grandfather's ring, of course—it happened. But it wasn't *necessary*. As long as someone was knocked out and unmoving, that was good enough. At least in the regular matches, the ones only meant to prove and test their skills.

Jade had never had to partake in anything darker than that. She was protected, after all. The Heir. No one would mess with her in the same ways they would the others.

She thought about the first time she'd killed and couldn't hold back the shiver. That feeling had stuck with her for weeks, sticking to her insides like old chewing gum. She'd ended up painting her nails red just so she could stop picturing the dried blood beneath them that had been washed clean forever ago.

Amelia clutched at her arm tightly. "Jade..."

Her friends fear was palpable.

Jade felt it as well.

She made a point of wiping the shock from her face, resetting it into a glare as she held the Emperor's gaze defiantly. There was no way out of this, which meant the only way was through.

"Jade, you can't," Amelia croaked behind her.

"Wouldn't be the first time."

Her friend sucked in a sharp gasp. "Still...There are a lot of men."

She almost snapped at her, her frayed nerves getting the best of her, causing her to loosen her hand on the tightly wound control she clutched at. What exactly did Amelia want her to do instead? Cry? Beg? Offer to suck their dicks in exchange for their lives?

Koya didn't give her the chance to voice those crude questions, raising his arm in the air in a signal that the fight was about to begin. When his eyes met Jade's they were smug.

The bastard didn't think she was going to make it out of here.

Admittedly, she had her doubts as well.

His confidence that she was about to die made the monster her grandfather had so carefully crafted twitch, however.

Jade grabbed onto it and held. She needed to set aside all empathy. This wasn't her world, these weren't her people, and if it wasn't them it was going to be her.

Like hell she'd let that happen.

She thought of her grandfather and of Key and even of the Emperor still watching casually like this was a chess match after a hearty lunch.

All men who thought they could control her. Who thought they knew her well enough to puppeteer her to their whims.

"Ready?" Koya didn't even try to hide the smirk. "Begin!"

Jade was going to wipe that smirk clean off.

II.

Captured

Chapter 1:

Jade couldn't feel her right arm. It hung limply at her side, blood running down like a river from the deep gash against her upper arm. The blood loss wasn't the problem, it was the dislocation of her shoulder that was causing her to slip up, costing her precious seconds as she dodged and weaved between the remaining two opponents.

The others had been reduced to slowly cooling bodies on the packed dirt ground.

A droplet of sweat rolled down her forehead, into her eye, and she blinked against the slight sting. Darting to the right a split second before one of the men's meaty fists swung through the air, right where her head had been a moment prior.

She almost lost her footing, slipped in a puddle of blood, but caught herself with a hand against one of the iron bars that surrounded the cage they were currently fighting in.

If one could even consider this fighting anymore. This was survival, pure and simple.

Jade had managed to keep her friend Amelia from the thick of it, mostly by picking off men who got too close to them and leaving the rest to their own devices. By doing this, she'd been able to wait things out, watch as they killed each other, most of them too certain that she wasn't a high enough threat to bother with right away.

Every minute or so, one of the men separated from the pack and attacked her, but she easily dealt with them, grateful that they hadn't gone for what they'd viewed as the weaker link first.

She could have taken them if she'd been alone, she was sure, or at the very least, could have held on for most of it before their combined strength in this confined space may have overpowered her. But with Amelia here as well? She'd stood no chance against eight men. At least, not when they'd been alive.

Although, admittedly six bodies did make it more difficult to move about.

As she twisted around, fending off the remaining two men—one of which gripped the single weapon they'd been provided—she also had to keep mindful of the sprawled limbs. If she tripped and twisted an ankle the two standing would be on her faster than she'd be able to defend herself and she knew it.

There was also the matter of their audience. There were too many distractions here, too many pieces that Jade was forced to focus on all at once.

Amelia, huddled in the corner crying.

The man with the busted nose on her right who was three times her size.

The man on the left who was a more manageable height, but was clutching the knife in front of himself.

The bodies.

The Blood.

And the Emperor.

He'd watched the spectacle silently. The only indication he was even invested at all had been when her arm had been twisted and yanked so hard that her shoulder had popped out of its socket. Then he'd leaned forward on the leather chaise lounge he was languishing on. The fruit platter he'd been eating from finally forgotten.

Jade had caught the look in his eyes, the change in them. Those eerie soft pink had hardened, a flash of anger and intensity strong enough she'd almost lost her breath.

She didn't know him well enough—or at all—to know where that anger was directed, however. If it'd been her grandfather giving the look, it would have been placed on her. He would have been furious that she'd allowed anyone to get the better of her in the ring. If it'd been Key, the underboss of the Emerald syndicate which her grandfather headed, it would have been at her opponent for daring to take it that far against the heir.

The Emperor…Honestly, she couldn't think of a reason he'd have to be angry at anyone, given the situation. He was reason they were all here. He'd orchestrated this whole circus act and made them the dancing monkeys.

If anyone had the right to be pissed, it was Jade. Maybe even the guys she was fighting against.

Koya, the Emperor's right-hand man, had mentioned at the start of this that they'd wronged the Emperor somehow. What kind of crimes had they committed to deserve this, she wondered?

The man with the knife dove for her then, and she ducked beneath his swinging arm, slamming her fist into his stomach on the way.

Unfortunately, the other guy was waiting for her behind the one with the knife, and he caught her in the side with a knee. The attack was harsh enough she may have felt ribs crack. Jade went down, landing on her scraped and bloodied hands, practically falling on top of a dead body with glassed over brown eyes.

She hissed and shoved off him, more frustrated than anything. This was taking too long and she was the one running out of energy too quickly. Perhaps these men had been kept in a better state than she had, one with proper food and water. There was no way of knowing how long Jade had been unconscious before she'd woken in that room with the Emperor all over her like some creep.

A sexy creep.

Ew. She mentally cursed herself for going there. Must be all the hits she'd taken to the head, that was all. Had to be.

Jade threw herself back into the match, raising both arms to block just as another swing came her way. She let the man without the knife drive her back, let him believe he had the upper hand until she came against the iron bars.

When he threw another punch, she grabbed, yanking his wrist with all her might and ducking down at the same time. The sudden change in tactic threw him off guard and his momentum went against him. His head smacked against two of the bars with a loud clanging sound.

Jade slipped from between him and the bars, twisting on her heels. She latched onto the back of his thick neck, nails imbedding into his flesh. Before he could recover from the head injury, she slammed him forward again, and again, putting all her strength in the move until the bars were left sticky with blood and bits of skin every time his face was pulled away.

She would have kept going, if not for the sudden sound of alarm to her right.

The man with the knife had turned his attentions on Amelia and was advancing. He didn't appear to be happy about it, his mouth twisted in to a grim frown, but his personal feelings about this ordeal weren't going to stop him.

Jade dropped the man in her hold, too distracted to even note the way his body slumped to the ground. There was too much distance between her and the man with the knife; she wasn't going to make it there in time to completely protect Amelia.

"Block!" Jade yelled just as the man swung the knife down in an arch.

Amelia lifted her arm, fortunately listening to the order out of instinct. The blade sliced through her forearm, blood spraying everywhere, and she let out a scream.

Still. It was better than the slash against her throat the man had been aiming to deliver.

It was also all the time Jade needed.

She pushed off the ground, landing a jump kick that sent the man slamming into the bars, hard enough he lost hold of the knife. She hit the ground the same time the weapon did, and she rolled, slapping her palm over the hilt to drag it back toward her.

The man recovered, turning on her with a snarl, only to halt when he saw her crouched a few feet away with the blade held expertly in her grip.

Jade had been trained in Kali from a young age. Holding the knife felt more second nature to her than tying her shoes. It'd been unfortunate that she'd been unable to go for it until now, because it certainly would have saved her a lot of time if she had, but protecting Amelia had been her first goal.

Now that it was just two of them left?

"Might as well have some fun with it," she said to herself, quietly and under her breath.

He heard anyway, it was apparent in the way his gray eyes momentarily widened in shock.

Slowly, Jade rose, resituating her body in to a fighting stance.

Amelia gasped in the corner, but Jade didn't risk glancing her way. She knew what the sound was for anyway.

She probably looked like a nightmare come to life at the moment.

Jade was covered in blood and ached all over. Her ribs burned every time she inhaled, and her right arm was still dangling useless at her side. Her clothes had been soaked in crimson and grime—probably even piss at this point—and her shirt had almost been torn clean off her by some guy. She'd killed him soon after.

Without wasting a second more, Jade attacked. She shot forward, sliding in the blood and then turning at the last second.

The feint had the man stepping after her, only to end up in empty air. He almost lost his footing, but it didn't matter that he remained upright.

Jade jabbed the knife forward, stabbing it into his fleshy side and pulling it free quickly. She'd only pressed the blade in a little, leaving behind a wound that wasn't too deep but would bleed and hurt like a bitch. She twisted, swinging her arm to deliver a similar blow to his other side before he could react. Then she dropped down behind him and slashed it across the side of his left thigh.

He freaked out, stomping and turning, hands pressed to his sides as he backed away.

Jade blew him a kiss.

He lost it. Wounds all but forgotten, he raced forward, cracking his knuckles across her jaw. His fingers dug into her hair at the top of her head and pulled as he let out a war cry.

Jade shifted the hilt of the knife in her palm and then brought it against his wrist. This time she pressed deep, but couldn't be sure if she'd managed to cut anything important. Not willing to risk it, she switched tactics, pushing up off her knees.

The attack hadn't been enough to get him to release her, so with his arm still in her hair and extended, she had the perfect shot at his armpit. She drove the blade in to that spot, turning the tip of the knife toward herself as soon as it'd entered. Then she yanked, severing the Axillary artery.

Warm blood sprayed into her face and she jolted backwards the same time he did. She heard him hit the ground as she was rubbing the gore from her eyes, no doubt smearing it over her face even more in the process. Once she felt like she could see again, she blinked.

The man was squirming on the ground, but he wouldn't last long. Already his motions were slowing.

Now that he wasn't a threat, Jade gave him her back, quickly dropping next to Amelia.

"Holy shit." Amelia was staring at the guy, eyes wide as saucers. There was a mixture of fear and wonder there that had Jade's heart leaping uncomfortably in her chest.

She so hadn't wanted her friend to ever see her like this.

What if she thought she was a monster now? What if she was afraid—

Amelia suddenly flung herself into Jade, knocking her onto her ass in the process and causing her to hiss in pain.

"Sorry!" Amelia pulled back some, but didn't completely let go. "I can't believe we survived that. I can't believe you killed him by stabbing him in the armpit!"

"There's an artery—"

"Don't care about the details," she stopped her. "Just glad we're alive."

"For now." Koya stepped up to the side of the cage. It was clear in his gaze that he wasn't as pleased by this outcome as Amelia was.

Jade tensed. "If you say some bullshit about the rule being only one person is left standing, I swear the next person I kill will be you."

"Says the captive."

"Even caged, a tiger is still a tiger," the Emperor's voice trickled to them. He stood, the move languid, and made his way over, eyes locked on Jade appreciatively the entire time.

At least he was no longer referring to her as a house pet. It wasn't much of a comfort, but beggars couldn't be choosers and as much as she hated it, that's what she was right now.

"Let us out," she demanded when he stopped only a foot or so from the iron bars.

He clucked his tongue. "Drop the knife first."

She hadn't even realized she was still clutching it. Having the weapon was a false safety net, she was smart enough to recognize that.

Jade tossed it to the other side of the cage with a clatter.

"You were very pleasing to watch," he told her, sidling closer. "I was not disappointed."

"She's a bigger threat than we realized, Emperor," Koya pointed out.

"Yes," he agreed, and Jade bit the inside of her cheek to keep from snapping at them, "but her skills also make her a more interesting asset."

"She's not a thing for you to use, a-hole," Amelia said.

The Emperor smiled. "Interesting that your friend has so much faith in your ability to protect her." His stare briefly landed on Amelia. "A smarter person would be terrified. You are at my mercy, currently locked up with several corpses. Unless you'd like to spend your night in there, you'll keep that tongue of yours in check."

Amelia clearly wanted to argue, but smartly pressed her lips into a thin line instead.

"What do you say, little cat?" His eyes searched her intently. "Are you an asset or a liability?"

Jade was still on the ground, with a now shaking Amelia next to her. They were trapped in a cage, and as far as she could tell their only way out of any of this was to get on the Emperor's good side.

The only problem was she wasn't yet certain he even had a good side. The type of person who could so callously pick at fruits while people killed each other in front of him, *because* of him, wasn't the same type she'd expect to have a conscience. He didn't care that they were stranded or that they'd gotten here accidentally.

In order to survive this she needed to discover what he did care about, and figure out a way to use that to her advantage. Which meant playing along for a while longer.

"If there's something specific you want," she found herself saying, unable to get the bite out of her tone none the less, "then spit it out. I'll do what I have to if it means getting us home."

"For now, I just need you to do one thing for me," he leaned in closer to the bars, "we can get to the rest later on."

Jade swallowed the lump in her throat. "What?"

He grinned. "Sleep."

"I'm not—" she'd been about to say tired, but just like that, her lids were drooping shut and her body was going lax to the point she felt herself tip over.

Amelia cried out, but Jade couldn't respond.

She was getting so sick of being unconscious.

Chapter 2:

The room was different from the last one.

A pallet bed had been situated on the ground, next to a massive window with a window seat. From the floor, Jade could see the inky night sky in all its splendor; bright stars winked and flickered down at her. For a moment, she simply took it in, her body lax and motionless on the plush bedding.

She knew this peaceful calm wouldn't last and wanted to soak up as much of it as she could. Plus she'd always been a sucker for stars and the sky and the things in it.

None of the constellations outside were familiar, but that didn't frighten her. Instead, she felt a pinprick of excitement at having something new to discover. She'd long since memorized the ones back home.

If Jade had gotten her wish, she'd have studied astronomy. Her job would have been as an atmospheric scientist. It wasn't flashy, but she would have been doing something she liked and would be able to afford to pay her own way through life.

Her grandfather had shot that dream down immediately. Even when she'd tried to spin it, explaining that it might help her develop her powers further if she understood how the weather worked and how it affected the world. He hadn't bought it, had given her the same old spiel about how she was destined to take over the family business.

So she'd settled and gone through the motions. She'd gotten her boring degree in business management, had met with the board of several of their front companies—all ones that made money and allowed the Emeralds to pass as law abiding tycoons. She'd fallen in line. Like she always had.

Until the day after her graduation. She'd snuck away from the party that was being thrown in her honor to find her passport which she knew her grandfather kept locked in his study. After putting in four years for him, playing the part of dutiful granddaughter, with nothing but a future she didn't want before her, Jade had decided to do *one* thing for herself.

She, Amelia, and a couple other of their friends had agreed to go on a backpacking trip through Europe. They were only going to be gone for the summer, so she'd make it back with plenty of time before she was meant to start working at Em-Com, the company she'd been told to start with. She'd get into a ton of trouble later, but she'd considered the risks and had decided it was well worth it

Only, her passport hadn't been the only thing her grandfather had kept hidden from her. There'd also been a file, one with her father's name printed on the tab in black sharpie. It'd captured her attention for reasons still unknown to her, though maybe she'd thought he'd kept photos of her parents there since he'd taken all of hers away years prior.

There had been a photo. But it hadn't been one she'd ever wished to see.

Ever since her grandfather had shown up at the funeral and announced himself as her new guardian, Jade had been told her parents death had been due to a car accident. Some drunk driver had gone out and swerved into their lane, causing them to crash into a semi-automatic. The impact had supposedly killed them both instantly.

Lies.

All of it.

Lies.

That's what Jade had dedicated her life to. That's what she was always rolling over for, putting her mind and her body through hell for. Her grandfather and the lies he'd told.

She barely recalled leaving the estate, but must have snuck out since no one came after her right away. She'd managed to make it to Amelia's a half hour drive from there by taking a taxi and the two of them had fled in the middle of the night soon after. Amelia didn't have family, had grown up raised by her aunt who'd paid for school but was never around. She'd been planning on leaving anyway, moving cities to start a new life.

It'd been two days before she'd finally asked Jade what had happened. She had to have been curious, but instead of pressing she'd allowed Jade the time she'd needed to process. That's the kind of friend she was.

Letting out a sigh, Jade turned her attentions to the matter at hand. They needed to get back home, and she couldn't get them there if she was in bad condition. She didn't feel nearly as awful as she had back in the cage though. Without looking down, she could tell that her injuries had been bandaged and her shoulder had been reset. There was a soreness there when she shifted, lifting herself into a sitting position, but no sharp, unbearable pain.

Taking that into count, she'd probably been out for at least a day this time.

The comforter over her was thick and made of a silky white material. She'd been changed into another nightgown, this one made of a similar silk, the feel of it like water on her skin. Since she didn't smell like sweat and was no longer caked in dirt or blood, it was easy to guess she'd also been bathed.

Jade turned to look out the window again.

A well of hopelessness threatened to open up inside of her and she fought it back, trying to keep the tears from prickling the corner of her eyes.

She was used to feeling more like a *thing* than a person—to her grandfather, she had always been the heir. To the Emerald syndicate members she had always been a figurehead. He'd dressed her up and made her smile for the camera at more events than she could count. Before leaving for college, her face had been splashed all over the papers and business news websites. She was considered an heiress and one of the most sought after bachelorette's simply because the Emerald syndicate had a good front in Em-Com, the communications company the mafia her grandfather led hid behind.

At least she'd been the one to put all of those clothes on. No one had ever changed her before, or bathed her.

She held in a shudder at that lost thought, not wanting to go there.

Jade felt like she'd been reduced to a doll, a pretty little plaything. The Emperor had wanted to see her fight? So she fought. All he had to do was threaten Amelia, and she knew she'd jump into the ring again with no hesitation. Power over someone like that was scary.

What would he ask her to do next?

Whatever it was, she already knew she wouldn't say no. Couldn't. That made her feel…

"I know you're there," finally, she broke the silence, not wanting to give her mind anymore chance to spiral. She had to keep it together, at least on the outside. In front of him.

She'd become aware of his presence over by the door almost as soon as she'd opened her eyes. It was hard not to; he brought a certain air to any room he was in, a thickness and sharp sense of trepidation. Her nerves were fried and despite having slept for what must have been at least twenty-four hours, Jade was exhausted.

The room was massive, though with the only light source being the vibrant night sky out the window there wasn't much she could see. There was a rather large king sized bed a little bit behind her, centered, and against the wall. Across from her there was a floor desk with a cushion for a seat. All around it were shelves with books and scrolls. The shelves had been organized to create a sort of nook around the desk, so she couldn't see what lay beyond the left of them.

The door was all the way across the room. She knew that with perfect clarity because that's where he was, where he'd been lurking this entire time.

Fabric shifted next to the closed door and then the Emperor appeared from the shadows, his gorgeous face slipping under the moonlight a second before the rest of him followed. He'd changed clothes as well, was now wearing a loose black silk robe that was untied at the front, exposing swaths of tanned flesh and the plains of toned abs. His pants were of the same material and hung low on his hips, her gaze frustratingly lingering there even though logically she knew it shouldn't.

She couldn't let him get to her. So what if he was sex on a stick? He was a monster, an asshole.

A god.

So what if that put him a step above her grandfather? She'd dealt with powerful men—powerful assholes—all her life. Sure, she knew how to play the game, knew it was best she sit pretty and fold whenever he pushed, but those blows to the head in the ring really must have damaged her because she found irritation welling despite her best efforts to contain herself.

"Is this what all powerful gods do?" she asked, her tone flat despite the accusatory words. "Spy on sleeping women?"

He'd risen to his feet and was slowly making his way toward her, stalking forward lazily as if he had all the time in the world. A single shoulder lifted in a partial shrug. "Sometimes it's sleeping men. It depends really."

She didn't bother hiding the twist of disgust that passed over her, not due to his preferences but because he really didn't seem to find fault in watching people against their will. Not that it came as a surprise, all things considered.

She tried not to think about how he'd held her before the cage incident. How he'd kissed her...Key had done many things to her while training her and controlling her life, but never that. He'd never touched her sexually at all, even when it'd been obvious she'd wanted him to.

Great. She'd *definitely* been hit too hard.

"How are you feeling, little cat?" he asked, letting her get away with her judgmental look. Maybe he felt bad for almost getting her killed in the cage.

Maybe he wanted her to think that.

It was most likely option two. Jade would put money on the Emperor not having a drop of empathy inside of him. Even now, after having asked a seemingly thoughtful question, he stalked forward like she was prey and he was the semi-bored hunter with nothing better to do than catch his next meal.

"Can we skip the false pretenses?" She rubbed at her suddenly throbbing temple. "I don't have the energy for it. Just tell me what I'm doing here—what you're doing here—and what comes next."

He clucked his tongue, disappointment visible. "That takes all the fun out of it, doesn't it?"

"I'm not here to have fun," she reminded.

"No," he agreed, coming to a stop at the edge of the mattress she was on, "you're here because of a mistake. But your pain is my gain."

She bristled when he dropped down, situating himself snuggly behind her. His legs came up around her sides, arms wrapping around her front, one at her waist, the other across her chest.

Like he had a *right* to her.

She shouldn't. She knew the situation. And yet…

"Get off," she practically growled, clenching her hands into tight fists on her thighs to keep from attempting to forcibly remove him. That never worked in her favor.

Instead of listening, the Emperor tucked his nose against the curve of her neck and breathed deep. After letting out a resigned sigh, his arms amazingly loosened. They didn't completely fall away, but she felt him lean back, putting space between them.

"I can't smell you at all," he said a moment later, after they'd been seated in silence for a spell. "I had you dipped and bathed in so many different oils, and yet…nothing. Not even a hint."

"That explains why I'm getting a headache," she mumbled, rubbing at her forehead a second time. She'd smelled it when she'd woken, the heavy scent of rose and lemon and bergamot coming from her skin. It was far too intense for her liking.

"Do you have a strong sense of smell?" That piqued his interest.

"I wouldn't call it any better than the average person." She considered what he'd said. "Do you...Do you have a problem smelling?"

"Yes," he admitted, but before she could pick that apart and even begin thinking up ways to possibly use it against him, he came forward again. His arms tightened and she felt him press flush against her back. "Until you."

"What?" She frowned, but suddenly things starting making sense.

Back in the dungeon, after he'd ordered her and Amelia killed, he'd suddenly sniffed at the air and changed his mind. Koya had been shocked by his usage of the word smell.

Then again, when she'd woken in the other room, he'd been so put off by that candle...

But what the hell could she have to do with his messed up senses?

"I told you what you are, a Minor who's ancestor was Valued by a god, well, I can taste the god in your blood. I'm very familiar with his particular brand of power, you see, because five thousand years ago I'm the reason he fled."

That brought up so many new questions, but she held them in, afraid to derail them just when it seemed like she was about to be told why she was still alive.

"We had a disagreement which led to a war," he continued. "It ended with him all but banished from his home world."

"And you?" she couldn't help but ask. "What did it leave you with?"

"A curse." He traced the line of her jaw. "That bastard took my sense of smell with him when he left. I've spent centuries unable to smell a single thing, and do you know what else that means?"

The Emperor took her chin, this time pulling at her bottom lip with his thumb.

"Taste," she whispered.

"When you lose your sense of smell, it diminishes your sense of taste as well. Everything has tasted bland, muted. Life, as you can imagine, has been rather dull. Until you," he repeated. "The only way to break a gods curse is with magic belonging to that specific god. Your power is his power, which means you'll be able to do the one thing I've been unable to. Are you willing to?"

That's what all of this was about, the reason for everything that had happened thus far.

He wanted her to fix him, and Koya thought she was too big of an unknown threat to be worth the trouble.

It was annoying that it'd taken him this long to explain things, but Jade wasn't about to look a gift horse in the mouth. Because at least with this, knowing exactly what it was he hoped to gain from her, she could twist things to her advantage.

She could get what she wanted in return.

"Do I have a choice?" she asked anyway, testing the waters.

He laughed. "You only have what I'm willing to give."

She sighed. "What do I need to do?"

"Go to the Shivering Sanctum, the territory of Master Mist, and retrieve an item from his abandoned palace. When a god dies, his palace becomes a fortress, locking itself and preventing all others from entrance. Only those with a power or blood link may enter."

"Like me." It made sense now, the reason he was playing this cat and mouse game with her, why he kept switching between being gentle and domineering. He needed her help, and he was planning on demanding it from her.

That's why he hadn't told her anything about Amelia since she'd woken. Why he'd separated them in the first place. He was going to use her friend as a hostage.

It was a good play, predictable, but good.

Jade hated him.

"What's the item?" There was no point in drawing this out any further. The sooner they finished this talk, the sooner he could send her on her way and, hopefully, this could all be over.

He seemed pleased with her response, leaning back a second time to give her some space, though he kept hold of her waist. "A vial, no larger than your pointer finger. It'll be silvery-blue glass, and in a safe place. That's what I need. Bring it to me."

"That will cure your sense of smell?"

"For the most part."

"And?" she prompted. "What do I get out of it?"

He quirked a brow. "Your life?"

"Not good enough. This thing seems pretty important to you. I need incentive."

Most of his earlier ease was gone now, but instead of threatening or attacking, he merely bit out, "What do you want?"

"Guarantee's that once I cure your curse, you'll let my friend and I go home." She considered adding on more, like that they had to be unharmed when he did so, but didn't want to push her luck. Besides, they were already injured. Hopefully wherever this Shivering Sanctum was, it wasn't far, and she could go there and be back within a couple of hours and they could be on their way.

She thought about Jason and the rest of her grandfather's men who would no doubt be waiting for her. Her disappearance must have been reported as well. Her grandfather might have even made a trip there himself by this point. The idea of jumping out of one hellhole just to end up in another…

Whatever. She'd cross that burning bridge when she came to it.

The Emperor was watching her closely now and something about the look in his eyes made her uncomfortable.

"All right," he surprised her by agreeing without a fight. "You take care of my curse, and I let you go home."

"And my friend."

"Her too."

"I want her *alive*," she emphasized, still seriously put off by how easily he was going along with this.

"She isn't dead," he assured her. "I'll even let you see her before you go. There? Does that satisfy you?"

There was no way of knowing if he was going to keep his word but...There was no way of ensuring he would either. She was at a major disadvantage here. Truthfully, she was fortunate that he was willing to humor her and offer terms at all. He could have simply used Amelia's wellbeing as a threat and forced her to cooperate.

He might betray her, he might not. Either way, right now, she had no other choice but to accept what he was offering. Maybe another way out would present itself to her while she was searching for this cure. Surely the house of a god had to be filled with something useful.

Mind made up, Jade held out her hand, ignoring the way his eyes filled with humor at the offering. "Deal."

"All right, little cat," he took her hand, practically dwarfing it with his own, "we have an understanding then."

When he made no moves to get up, she quirked a pointed brow. "Well?"

"Oh, you won't be going now," he chided, expression taking on a darker look, a hungry one. He leaned in close, turning her easily so that she was sitting with her side pressed into him, his mouth hovering less than an inch away from her own. "You'll take more time to heal first, and then, once I'm certain there will be little risk to your person if you go on this journey, I'll let you leave."

"Don't act like you care," she told him, anger flashing.

He cupped the back of her head, holding her still. The smile he flashed her had her spine straightening and her heart all but freezing in her chest. It made her recall that while he might need her alive, he definitely didn't need her *intact*.

"I feel like you still haven't quite grasped this world, little cat. Perhaps it's the god part you're stuck on? Are you mistaking me for someone like your grandfather? Or that Key person you spoke of? Men, Jade."

Had she wanted him to use her name? She'd been so wrong. It was somehow worse hearing it come from him than the nickname he called her by. It was spoken intimately and possessively, in a way she hadn't been aware it could be. With that single syllable, he had even her blood recognizing the ownership he claimed.

Bile rose up the back of her throat as a wave of heat flashed through her, settling low, between her legs.

She hated him and herself for that reaction, because it made no sense.

"Mere men," he continued. "I am a god. You compare me to no one."

Jade was stiff as he gathered her into his lap, readjusting them both so that she was being cradled like a lover would. His hand delved into her hair, nails skating lightly over her scalp in a suggestive gesture.

"I'll show you what it means to be a god, little cat. I'll have you too afraid to even consider defying me. And then," his thumb hooked beneath her chin, tipping her head up so she was forced to meet his gaze, "I'll make it so you purr for me every time I enter a room. But fear first. Let's teach you the difference between a man and a god."

She was pretty sure she'd stopped breathing at one point, the alarm bells clanging too loudly within her to be sure. She'd thought he'd had an intimidating aurora before; she hadn't even known the half of it.

He must have been holding back, because now...

He hadn't even done anything yet and already she felt tears at her eyes, threatening to spill. This time, she didn't bother trying to stop them. Pride was nothing in the face of this. It was clear there was something going on, something visceral, maybe something to do with his power and how he wielded it, because Jade wasn't the type to bow easily, or to cry.

Gently, the Emperor brushed one of the lone drops off of her cheek, but then he spoke again, and all softness was gone.

"Jade," his voice was different, hypnotizing and deep. She felt it claw all the way through her and hooked into her insides like fangs. His pink eyes seemed to heat and glow. "Make it rain."

Her power rose within her on its own, as if a separate being. It swelled and collected until it burst at the seams, pouring out of her on a gasp that had the sky outside cracking open. Rain pelted against the glass, heavy and unstoppable. It blocked out the view of the stars and the sky almost immediately.

"Good girl," he praised, smiling all the while, even though she'd gone white as a ghost in his arms. "Now, offer me your neck."

Horrified, Jade found herself doing just that, tilting her head to the side, exposing the section he'd already taken a bite out of. The wound was still bandaged, but had yet to fully heal, and she winced some when he pealed the protective layer off and flicked it absently off the bed.

"My power comes from my voice," he told her, "but there is so much more my mouth is good for. It can bring you pain."

He bit her.

His teeth found the old puncture wounds and reopened them, blood pooling into his mouth as he gave one long pull.

She felt the skin tear and the pressure as he sucked. The pain of it helped her regain some of her agency, and she finally started to struggle, pushing and shoving at his bare chest to no avail. A cry escaped her, and the tears were more forthcoming now.

Even though he was careful not to open the injuries up further, and didn't yank this time around, the red hot agony was still excruciating, so much so, that she actually sobbed in relief when he unlatched his jaw.

"Shh," he hushed her, the hand at the back of her head turning coaxing. He stroked her hair comfortingly and rocked her some in his lap as if she were a child. "It can also bring you pleasure."

This time, when he lowered his mouth it was on the other side. His lips pressed but there was no teeth, just his tongue lapping at her skin before his mouth gave one long suck that had her hips jutting against her will.

She gasped, more mortified by that reaction than she was about crying. There was no way...

"Would you prefer the pain?" he asked against her throat, clearly sensing her resistance. "I don't have a preference. As long as I get what I want."

"Which is?"

He inhaled deeply and moaned. "I can smell you again. You're right. Next time I won't add anything to the baths. Your blood though," he moved back to the wounded side, "smells divine."

She pressed a palm to his chest when he went to place his mouth over the wound again, stopping him. "Not pain."

He grinned. "Pleasure then."

"If all you want is to smell me—"

"And taste you," he interrupted, licking the underside of her jaw before she could pull away.

"I'm not food." Maybe he was right. Maybe the fear of him hadn't been instilled in her enough. Even she thought she was mildly crazy for talking back at a time like this.

"But you are decadent, and it's been so long since I last enjoyed anything like this. Your power is weak. It hides in your blood, only activated once you use it. Even then, it only lingers so long before fading. I can smell other things if they're close, but nothing as strongly as I can you."

So it only worked a little?

"Is that why I'm weak in comparison to my grandfather? Dormant power?"

He hummed in agreement, leaning into suck on the spot just below her right ear.

She squirmed, but forced herself to remain focused. Answers. That's what she needed, and right now he seemed willing to give them.

"The vial, what's in it?"

"Pure power," he said. "We don't yet know why he had it, what he hoped to use it for, but Master Mist extracted some of his own power before the war was through. With it, I'll be able to smell and taste everything again, not just you, little cat."

He trailed kisses all over her, down her neck and across her jaw. He moved in lower, to the base of her throat where he sucked and lapped like a kitten to milk.

The thought would have made her laugh in any other occasion, but here, with a literal god clutching at her like she was the most important thing in the world, there was no chance at finding humor.

He'd gotten her to do things simply by telling her to. The God of Command. Now she understood what that meant. He could get anyone to do whatever he wished, whenever he wanted. If she'd refused to help him find this vial, if she refused in the future, he could simply order her to do it.

And she would.

That was a terrifying realization, one that had her blood going cold and any inkling of the attraction she'd been feeling fizzling into nothingness.

He didn't like that.

The Emperor had her on her back in a flash, kneeling over her with a hungry look in his eyes. His robe had fallen open even more, one sleeve starting to slip down his arm. In the moonlight, the studs lining his ear glimmered. His hands were resting on her knees, but the touch was light.

"Spread," he ordered, the word delivered sharply.

Jade felt herself reacting to the command, widening her legs to give him more room between them. She opened up to him even as the breath caught in her throat and her cheeks stained red in a mixture of embarrassment and resentment.

"Please," she wasn't above begging at this point, that fear palpable, "don't."

The Emperor paused, meeting her gaze. He was quiet a moment, the only sound in the room her frantic breaths.

"Be calm, little cat," he urged, though he didn't use his power when he did. "My clothes will remain on. I don't need to force a woman to take my cock. They do so willingly. Besides, that's not what I'm after." He stared between her legs then, look intensifying to the point it was a wonder he didn't cause her to spontaneously combust. "I just want a taste."

She trembled when his palms slid down her thighs, and squeezed her eyes shut when his thumbs pushed the lacy material of the short white dress up, exposing her lower region to his view. She hadn't bothered to check before, but she was bare underneath.

"You're wet," he pointed out, clearly pleased. "I don't recall commanding you to be, do you, little cat?"

Before she could come up with a response, he dipped his head and gave one long lick across her seam.

Jade jolted, gasping and suddenly clutching at the thick comforter beneath her.

With a chuckle the Emperor pressed down on her hips. "Keep still. You don't want to bust open one of your stitches."

Stitches. Right. From injuries *he'd* inadvertently given her.

"Stop," the word was breathy and all together unbelievable even to her ears. Still. She shouldn't want this—*didn't* want this. Her body was reacting because it'd been a long time since she'd last slept with someone, that was all. It had nothing to do with his hot kisses or the predatory gleam in his eyes.

She was *not* attracted to this sadist who took pleasure in tearing at her neck like some animal.

As if to help drive that conviction home, Jade reached up and pressed against the wound, hissing at the shooting pain. That's what he did to her. Hurt her. Locked her up. Tortured her best friend.

Some of the fire below died down.

She should have known the Emperor would figure out what she was doing.

"Keep trying to refuse me," he told her, an edge to his voice that hadn't been there before, "let's see how long you last."

"Don't—"

His tongue shot into her opening, lapping at her and delving deeply. She tried to resist the urge to moan, forced herself to keep her hips still beneath the heavy palms of his hands. Within seconds though she was certain he could feel her shaking, certain she was fooling no one.

He fucked her with his tongue, curving to hit that spot inside her just right before moving to suck lightly at her clit. He circled that tight bud, eyes glittering up at her knowingly as she clenched her thighs. He nibbled and sucked and stroked, sometimes with slow lavishing motions, and other times turning rough and desperate.

All the while, Jade resisted, clawing at the sheets until her knuckles went white.

Until he penetrated her with a finger, and her entire world crumbled and all the reasons she shouldn't want this went right out the damn window.

His finger was thick and long, and he shoved it deep, stroking her silky walls skillfully. When he hooked upwards, catching that spot with more pressure than his tongue had allowed, she lost control of herself, hips jerking off the bed. The motion pressed her clit more firmly against his mouth.

"That's it," he pulled back only long enough to speak, the words harried and sharp. "Come, Jade. Come for me."

She exploded, stars winking behind her eyes, blackspots dancing across the wooden ceiling above her. She gasped and twitched, her pussy clenching around his finger. The waves of pleasure seemed never ending, and it was a long time before she came back to herself. Before she realized that he was still down there, between her spread thighs, rubbing his cheek against the inside of her thigh lazily.

Risking a glance down, a rush of bile rose up the back of her throat quickly killing any lingering buzz.

There was a smug look on his face, a taunting glimmer in his pink eyes.

All at once she understood why.

The sound of his voice when he'd ordered her to come just now...

He hadn't used his power to make her do it.

He hadn't needed to.

Chapter 3:

"Are you ready to go?" the Emperor asked her the next day from his perch on the window seat.

She was still seated on the bed on the floor, her hands clasped tightly in her lap. Part of her wanted to snort at his question—what happened to the guy who said she'd need time to heal?—but she held her tongue.

"What's wrong?" He shifted to the edge, leaning down toward her. "Afraid I might touch you again?"

Last night he'd given her another earth shattering orgasm, this time with only his fingers. The tears had been flowing more freely by that point, the self-hatred within her at a staggering height.

He'd know too, knew that she hated how her body was reacting to him, how she felt betrayed by her own flesh every time his skillful fingers tweaked her clit or pumped between her folds.

He'd liked that.

Afterward, when she'd just barely come back down, he'd mumbled something about how the effects hard worn off, rubbed his hand on the comforter to clean it, and…left.

Just like that.

She hadn't seen him again until he'd walked in about an hour ago, carrying a metal tray with fruits and cheeses. The try sat in front of her mostly empty now. She'd almost forgotten what it was like not to have stomach aches, and even though her body still felt sore and leaden, she wasn't nearly as injured as she'd expected to be upon waking.

"Little cat?" the Emperor dropped down to the mattress, kneeling next to her. His left hand captured the back of her head and pulled her toward him, stopping her face with only an inch between them. He didn't appear to be angry at having been ignored, only curious. "What are you thinking about?"

"My side doesn't hurt that badly," she blurted. She'd seen the gash from the fight. It'd been pretty deep. Surely the stitches should be pulling at her and she should be in serious agony right now without painkillers.

"Ah." With his other hand, he traced one of her eyebrows, then brushed the pad of his thumb over her full bottom lip. "You should be healed by now. Nothing more than a bruise."

"What?" That was…impossible.

"Haze, the God of Feeling, keeps my medicinal cabinet fully stocked. There's a lovely balm in there that can heal even the most life threatening injures as long as it's applied soon enough." His thumb pressed against the divot above her upper lip next.

"The God of Feeling?" How many gods were there? He'd said nine before, right?

She now knew of three: Master Mist, The Dust Emperor, and Haze.

Master Mist was dead, so that meant there might still be eight alive. Aside from the one currently staring at her like she was the most fascinating thing ever, that left seven others that she'd need to avoid.

The Emperor's mouth was on hers so sudden she actually cried out in surprise. Her hands automatically went to his chest, struggling to keep him at bay even as his tongue pried her lips apart and forced its way inside.

There was that taste again, dark chocolate covered cherries, and Jade's fingers inexplicable tightened in the material of his thin black shirt.

The kiss started off just like all of his other advances, violent and demanding. But then the harsh strokes of his tongue slowed, his firm mouth pressing lighter against hers. The hand cupping the back of her head turned coaxing, his other going to her chin, tipping her head to give him a better angle.

He explored the cavern of her mouth, licking and sucking, humming throaty, pleased sounds now and again that she swallowed without thought.

Because she was kissing him back.

The Emperor pulled away and the heat in his gaze seared her, causing her heart to leap in her chest. Despite how delicately he'd just unraveled her, his anger was unmistakable.

What had she done to piss him off this time?

"The only god you ever have to think about," he snarled, low and threatening, "is me. Understood?"

She nodded her head, though didn't manage much motion with his hands holding her the way they were. It wasn't a battle worth attempting, even though she really just wanted to tell him to stuff his orders where the sun don't shine.

Now that the tender moment had passed, reality was seeping back into her thoughts. Being sex starved was one thing, letting the man do whatever he pleased was another.

"You mentioned leaving," she said, forcing her voice to remain even. "Yes. I'm ready to go."

His grip on her tightened, nails curving slightly to dig into her tender scalp.

She remained unflinching, not wanting to give him the satisfaction, though she wasn't even sure he was aware of what he was doing.

A second later he relaxed, arms dropping to his sides, heat leaving his eyes almost as quickly as it'd come. He sighed and rose to his feet, peering down his nose at her. "We should, before I change my mind and decide to keep you here, in bed with me, instead."

Jade stood as well, stepping back and off of the mat to put space between them. The bare soles of her feet hit the cold wooden floor and she felt the chill shoot up her legs, shivering slightly.

"There are boots over there," he lifted his chin toward the end of the large bed. At the foot of it, her boots and clean socks were carefully set out. He moved to the door, waiting while she put them on.

His sudden haste made her nervous. Surely he hadn't meant those words just now—that he was considering not letting her leave...

Had to be another scare tactic.

At the door he pulled a key from his pocket, a large brass looking thing, and inserted it into the lock. The sound of it clicking open had anticipation thrumming through her even though she knew freedom was an illusion at this point.

"I do this for you, get the vial, and you immediately let my friend and I go home," she said as they stepped into the hall, needing confirmation before she let things go any further.

Wanting to be sure that he really hadn't changed his mind after that cryptically spoken statement.

"That was the agreement," he told her, "yes."

"I need more than that."

He paused and turned toward her, eyes narrowing. "Getting bold again, little cat?"

She was intensely aware of the fact that they were not alone in the hallway, and she bristled at the underlying threat. She held her ground anyway, spine straight, head tipped upward defiantly. Sure, he could toss her back into the room, but she was betting on him wanting the vial more than he wanted her to bow before him.

"I'll be risking my life to get something *you* need," she pointed out. "I just want to be sure that you're going to follow through and give me what I need in return."

He grunted, the corner of his mouth lifting in a partial smirk before he caught himself. "You'll hardly be risking your life," he corrected. "But understood."

She forced herself not to retreat when he took a step closer, putting them toe to toe.

"Don't worry," he said. "I didn't forget the terms of our deal. After you have the vial, you and your friend will find yourselves safe and sound," he leaned down, momentarily distracting her when his mouth hovered mere centimeters from hers, "at home."

He headed away then, leaving Jade no other option but to follow behind. When they made it to the end of the long hallway, the four men who'd lined either side of it fell into step at their backs.

"Don't mind them." The Emperor must have picked up on her nerves.

Jade pulled her gaze away from the nearest guard, settling her expression into one of mild curiosity when she turned his way.

The Emperor wasn't fooled.

"You could take them," he told her, easily picking up what she'd been thinking. "But it isn't them you have to worry about."

Right. Because even if she did put down all of his guards, she didn't stand a chance against him. If she wanted to even the playing field, she first needed to come up with a way to keep him from talking—not easy. Gaging him was the only thing that came to mind, and she somehow doubted she'd ever get close enough to pull something like that off.

No, her only play here was to go along with his wishes and hope for the best. Hope that whatever weird sexual tension had been between them before didn't happen again.

Jade couldn't let it.

"Here." The Emperor stopped them suddenly in front of a wooden door. Instead of opening it himself, he stepped back, waving a finger at it.

Though it was suspicious of him, Jade didn't bother wasting time considering if it were a trap or not. She shoved the door open and stepped inside, sucking in a sharp breath the second her eyes landed on her friend.

"Amelia!"

She was lying on a thin mattress on the floor, a thin wool blanket tossed over her. Her hair was matted and caked in blood, and there was bruising all over her arms. She'd been asleep when Jade had entered, but at the franticly spoken sound of her name her eyes peeled themselves open.

"Jade?" Amelia blinked in an attempt to focus, the corner of her mouth turning up before she winced from even that small movement. "Thank god you're all right."

She dropped onto the makeshift bed and scooped her up, careful of her injuries. Some of the major ones had at least been bandaged, but she could see red already seeping through, and knew they hadn't bothered doing a good job.

"Let's leave gods out of this." Jade wanted to rage. Wanted to hit someone.

"Careful, little cat," the Emperor warned her from the doorway, where he watched them from beneath hooded lashes. He'd propped a shoulder against the doorframe, his arms and ankles both crossed casually.

She couldn't help it, she glared at him, all the earlier fear she'd felt vanishing in a bitter puff of smoke.

"You can't just leave her like this," she stated. "Her injuries need tending to. She almost died."

"At least here she'll be more comfortable if she goes."

If she hadn't been holding Amelia, Jade would have shot back onto her feet at that. "We had a deal."

"The two of you broke into my home, and now you're expecting good treatment?" He quirked a brow at her. "Is this how things work in your world? Are thieves and trespassers welcome with open arms? What would your Emerald syndicate do to someone who showed up unannounced the way you have?"

"You used some of that healing balm on me," she reminded. "Give it to her too."

She purposefully avoided answering his question. Because they would have done the same thing. Her grandfather and Key. They would assume the invader was a spy sent from a rival organization or an undercover cop. They'd try to find answers, discover the truth, but they wouldn't try that hard. Not if the threat were minor.

Two random girls appearing in a bath? That constituted as minor.

Didn't meant they'd let those girls live.

The Emperor smirked. "Keeping *you* healthy benefits me."

"Keeping my friend alive benefits you more," she snapped. "Just because you got her to tell you about where we're from, don't think for a second you actually know either of us. I've only gone along with all of this for her. If she goes, you lose all leverage."

"And you don't know me," he told her blandly. "Clearly." He let out a heavy sigh and straightened from the doorway. "Do we need another lesson, little cat?"

"Stop calling me that. And stop using the same threat every damn time I speak my mind." She squeezed her eyes shut and blew out a breath, trying to stabilize herself. She couldn't let her emotions get the best of her, no matter how strongly she felt about Amelia's treatment. "Fine. Yes. If someone showed up the way we had, the Emerald's wouldn't treat them kindly either. That isn't the point though."

She reopened her eyes, latching onto him with a renewed determination.

He cocked his head. "Isn't it?"

"No." Diplomacy. That's what she needed here. That was the angle she needed to go with. "The point is that you and I have a deal, and you're close to breaking your end of it. If she's left like this, she'll die before tomorrow morning. I don't know where this Shivering Sanctum is but I'm guessing it's not conveniently located down the street. You can't uphold your part of the deal if she dies before I make it there and back."

"I could always just take the vial from you, if that's the case," he said.

"I could always smash it on the ground," she countered.

For a dangerous moment, he was unreadable. She couldn't tell if he was pissed off by her threat or if he found her amusing. The not knowing made him scarier than he'd been prior. It made her realize what even being pinned beneath his muscular body hadn't been able to make clear to her.

She couldn't beat him in a fight, sure.

But she might not be able to beat him mentally either.

"Koya." His sudden barked order had Jade's heart leaping in her chest. If he noticed, he didn't show it, though his gaze remained steady on her the entire time, even when the man from the dungeons slipped into the room and bowed. "You'll be accompanying her on her mission."

"Yes, Emperor." Koya kept his head down.

"If anything happens to her," finally, he set those eyes elsewhere, locking them on Koya instead, "you'll pay the price."

"Yes, Emperor."

He turned back to Jade, but only long enough to wave between her and Amelia. "You have five minutes, that's how long it will take for the physician to get here. Once he is, you and Koya will be setting off. When the two of you are traveling, think of it as having me by your side. If you try anything, I will know of it, and your friend here will be the one who suffers."

Without waiting for a response, he turned on his heels and exited.

Koya immediately followed, closing the door behind him with a soft click, giving them some false semblance of privacy.

"What does he mean, going?" Amelia asked. Her voice was thready and weak, but there was color in her cheeks and her breathing was even, indicators there was no immediate danger. Her wounds had been bandaged in time to stop severe blood loss, at least. "You can't go anywhere here, Jade. It isn't safe."

"I don't really have a choice." She heaved a sigh. "Besides, worry about yourself, okay? Look at you."

Amelia snorted. "Look at me? Check a mirror, babe. You've seen better days."

"Worse than that time Adam Carson dropped an entire bucket of purple paint on my head?" They'd been painting props for a drama class because one of Amelia's other friends was performing and had asked. Jade had walked a little too close to the ladder and Adam had lost his balance with the large canister.

It'd taken days to get all the purple out of her hair, and her clothes had been ruined and trashed.

"Like ten times worse," Amelia said. "Though, at least he let you change your clothes and ditch the bloody rags. Red's just not your color."

Jade grunted. "Tell my grandfather that."

"Will you really have to kill people?" she asked quietly. "If you go back?"

They may have both been raised in the States, but they came from two different worlds all the same. Amelia claimed to understand what Jade's life had been like before she'd managed to convince her grandfather to allow her to go to college alone, but she didn't really. Couldn't. How did a spider explain to a butterfly how it made its web?

"Try not to think about what happened in the cage," she said, knowing that's what had been on Amelia's mind all this while.

While she'd been letting the Emperor touch her and kiss her…make her come…

"I'm sorry, Amelia." She felt sick. "This is all my fault. You're going through this because of me."

"Don't be stupid." Amelia pulled an arm out from beneath the scratchy blanket and took her hand. "If there's anyone to blame it's your grandfather. Or that asshole that chased us down the alley and got me shot. I really hate that guy. In fact, him. When we get out of this and get back home, I totally give you a pass to kill him. I'll look away. I know a good place to hide the body and everything."

Jade laughed, hating that she also had to reach up and quickly brush away a few tears that managed to slip past her defenses. "I promise I won't be long. I won't leave you here."

"I know that." She hesitated before asking, "What is he making you do exactly?"

"Go to some dead god's old residence to steal something," she waved, "no big."

"I mean, if we take out all those other words and just leave steal, then yeah, I agree. Stealing is something you can totally handle."

"Hey!"

Amelia sobered some. "Jade. Tell me, honestly. What do you have to do?"

"Steal something," she repeated, but blew out a breath. "It's complicated. Apparently my family was gifted powers by some god from here or something like that. That's why the Emperor needs me to go. But it's really no big deal. Like you said, I make a good thief, and once I'm back you and I can go home."

"You actually believe that?"

"There's no reason for him to keep us here." Jade wasn't sure which of them she was trying to convince, but forced herself to smile reassuringly anyway. "We broke some rule about trespassing, and we were punished. Since he can use me, he's going to, but after that—"

"We'll serve no purpose," Amelia cut her off darkly. There was no missing the fear in her soft honey brown eyes.

"That's why he's going to let us leave."

"Or that's when he'll kill us."

"Try to think positively, Mel."

"You're used to this sort of thing, to being kidnapped and beaten, but me...Don't take this the wrong way or anything, but I grew up in a normal family with parents who worked a nine to five job and always paid their taxes."

"If you're trying to tell me you regret becoming friends—"

"No," Amelia forced herself into a seated position despite Jade's protests, or the way her body clearly fought against her, "that's not what I'm saying at all. I'm trying to point out that even I, someone who has lived an incredibly bland and uneventful life, can see how this is likely to all end." She cupped Jade's hand between both of hers. "You don't have to lie to try and make me feel better."

"I'm not lying," Jade confessed, her words barely a whisper. "I'm hopeful. I've got to be, because the alternative…"

Amelia's shoulders sagged and Jade pulled herself together, forcing all those dark notions aside. This was the last conversation the two of them were going to have until she got back; she needed to leave her friend on a positive note. Had to do that much for her, at least.

"Hey," she waited until Amelia met her gaze once more, "if I have to fight our way out of here, I'll do it. You know I will. I'll kill them all if I have to. You and I will be going home, and a week from now, we'll be laughing over chestnut latte's at Mike's about how unreal this whole experience was. Okay?"

"Okay." Amelia gave a shaky half smile that didn't reach her eyes. "But, Jade? When we get home, we can't hang out at Mike's anymore."

She was in the process of frowning when the reason why hit her. "Right. My grandfather."

"Love how you've got someone after you no matter where you go." She'd tried to make it sound like a joke, but the waver in her voice gave her away.

"We can separate as soon as we're back," Jade offered. "As long as I'm nowhere near you, the Emeralds will leave you alone. It's not you they're after."

"Hell no." Amelia's expression tightened. "I'm not ditching you when you need me the most. We'll figure something out when we get home."

"We just have to actually get home first," Jade finished for her.

The door opened on creaky hinges, abruptly putting an end to their conversation.

Koya appeared and he moved to the side to allow an elderly man to enter the room. "The physician," he told Jade, then, "You and I head out now. The goodbyes are over."

She stood but frowned, trying to peer over his shoulder into the hall. "Where—"

"The Emperor has better things to do than see a thing like you off," Koya stated, stone faced.

Jade debated whether or not she felt offended, opting to pay it no mind. Wasn't the goal here to do all of this so she could get the hell away from the Emperor and his eerie eyes and overly touchy hands in the first place?

She'd known him less than a day and already she wanted as much distance between them as possible.

Which meant the fact she was leaving Amelia behind, alone in this palace with him, made her uncomfortable.

"Now, Minor." Koya clearly lacked patience.

"It's all right," Amelia said, even as she flinched away from the physician's withered hands when he reached for her bandaged arm. "I'll be fine. You taught me self-defense, remember? I got this."

Jade had taught her a total of three moves, none of which would be very useful against a god.

"When we get home I'm going to teach you for real," she promised.

"Deal." Amelia held up a thumb.

Get the vial and get home.

That's what Jade needed to focus on.

Get the vial, get Amelia, and get the fuck out of here.

Chapter 4:

"Um," Jade stared down at the leather straps Koya had just slapped into her open palms, "yeah, this isn't gonna work for me."

Attached to the other end, a large all black horse blew out an indignant hot breath. She would have sworn he shook his head at her before turning away as well.

Koya heaved a sigh of frustration. "Do they not have horses where you're from?"

"Sure they do," she handed the reigns off to a stable hand when the boy came for them, "but I was born in the city. They're sadly not as common. I'm guessing you guys don't have cars here." She glanced pointedly around at the dirt paved roads, as well as recalled the ones she'd traversed on during her failed escape. "This might be a setback."

"Already? Are you doing this on purpose?" Koya's presence wasn't nearly as threatening to be around as the Emperor's, but there was still an unmistakable air of darkness to him. He held himself stiff, the uniform on his body pressed and wrinkle free. The outfit was a mix of a tunic made of black silk, and pants the same dark shade tucked into boots. The gold and pink threads that made up the emblem at his hip also adorned the shoulders, and the end of the thin fabric that made up the belt synched around his waist.

Now that she was close to it, she could make out what the emblem design was: a rising sun with a serpent wrapped around it.

"I'm not trying to do anything," she told him, exasperated by the accusation. "I seriously just can't ride a horse. You're going to have to come up with another solution. How far away is this place? Can we walk?"

"Not unless you're comfortable leaving your friend here an extra three days," he stated. "The Emperor isn't well known for his patience; he might grow tired of waiting before then and decide to take his anger out on her."

She clenched her hands into tight fists at her side. "Okay, so not walking then. Any other ideas?"

The same servant who'd taken the reigns from her walked up to them again, this time bringing along another horse, though one much larger than the mare she'd been offered. The horse was a deep brown, with a carefully braided mane. The saddle over him bore the same emblem of the sun and serpent.

Koya didn't bother answering her with his words. The second the servant brought the horse to a stop, he reached out and grasped Jade around the waist. Ignoring her protests, he hoisted her up and over the creature, quickly planting a foot in the stirrup to bring himself up after her.

His body settled behind her with ease, and in the next instant, he was tugging her back against him. His muscled thighs caged her in, and his arms reached around to take the reins, also forcing her to cave in on herself in a poor attempt to avoid touching more of him.

"What the actual hell?" she growled, bracing as he kicked the horse into a sprint. "What's up with you assholes and touching? Is it too much to ask me? I could have gotten on the damn horse myself."

"If you're referring to the Emperor," Koya said, dipping his head low so as to be heard over the sound of pounding hooves and wild wind, "he doesn't need your permission for anything. If he wants to touch you, as you put it, that is his right. The same goes for if he decides you've outlived your usefulness. Don't make the mistake of thinking you have any privileges here just because he hasn't killed you for your stunt in the baths."

Why was she getting the feeling that Koya would have preferred that?

"You can heal him, that's the reason you're still breathing and not just another rotting corpse outside the palace walls."

"Right," she countered, "which is why I'm out here with you in the middle of the freezing night."

He snorted. "It's not even winter yet. You wouldn't last then."

"Not arguing with you there." She hated the cold, well and truly. Her grandfather had always used that against her during training.

She made a mental note not to bring up her discomfort with the weather again. Giving Koya, and therefore the Emperor, any more ammunition against her was like signing her own death certificate.

"He believes you've arrived here accidentally," Koya said, and the bitterness in his tone had her raising a brow.

"You don't?"

"I believe that if you're here for any other reason, I'll make you pay for the deception in blood."

"Lovely." She rolled her eyes. "Has anyone ever told you you've got a sparkling personality?"

"Has anyone ever told you you have a foolish tongue? We may both be Minor's, but I am far older and stronger."

That caught her attention, both parts. One, she hadn't realized he was a Minor. Two, he looked like he had three years on her at best. Since it'd already been explained that her family were all Minor's she knew for a fact that there was nothing special with their ageing process. There were no family myths about a great-great-great-whatever living past their prime or anything like that.

"Are you the Emperor's Minor?" she asked, quickly realizing she must have worded the question incorrectly when he stiffened even more at her back.

"The Emperor doesn't make personal claims lightly, or often. To say I am his would be too bold a declaration. I was Valued by him, yes. The God of Command took me in, gave me a purpose, when I had nothing and nowhere else to go."

That kind of loyalty was dangerous. Aware of it now, some of Jade's mood soured further. She'd been trying to keep her head up, to at least pretend things were all right and this wasn't an insane shit-show she'd somehow woken up in. But she'd seen men like Koya before, those within her grandfather's ranks, and those without.

Men who thought their entire being rested on another tended to be more willing to cross the line. They'd do so in the name of allegiance. They were the first to raise their hand when a dangerous mission came up, when a serious law needed to be broken. It wasn't as simple as mere adoration. It was devotion.

Devotion was a scary thing.

She hadn't taken his words lightly before, but now, Jade reconsidered his earlier threat. If only for her own wellbeing she needed to find a way to convince him she was telling the truth about showing up here. There was no telling what he thought her hidden agenda could be, but he even considering that she had one was alarming.

He could slit her throat while she slept in the night and simply tell the Emperor it'd been somebody else. If he was really as loyal a soldier as he insisted, which she bought one hundred percent, there was a good chance the Emperor would dole out a light punishment and be done with it.

If something happened to her, not only would he have no reason to keep Amelia alive, there also wouldn't be a way to send her back home.

Jade's blood was the key, it had to be. It was the only thing that made sense. Which meant she and it needed to get back to that palace intact.

"The Emperor is the leading god, created in the aftermath of the Great Beginning, formed from the dust and ashes of the Nothing Before. His eyes took the shade of the first dawn, his hair the color of the rich earth, his skin the warm sands of time. He rose, the others followed, and with them came the world as we know it. It is an honor to be given a task by the Emperor. It is an honor not to have been—"

"Killed on sight," she finished for him, pretty sure she knew where he was going with that whole spiel. He sounded like a nut job, but then, what did she know. She wasn't from around here. Maybe gods were real and the Emperor was one of them. Maybe that meant her family was once touched by one a couple thousand years ago.

Who knew.

Didn't really matter.

What did matter was what had already been proven to her.

The Emperor was powerful, the people here revered him, and her magic did something to him, healed him somehow. The only logical explanation for that last part was that he was telling the truth.

"Careful with your tongue," he said. "You won't be warned again."

Before she could reply back, he urged the horse onto a new path, suddenly shooting them into the midst of a thick forest. Most of the moons glow was blocked, and a darkness descended on them.

"What the hell are you doing?!" Jade asked, trying to discern even a single branch as they raced through what might as well have been solid blackness. Her heart leapt into her throat, her mind already playing all the ways they could run face first into a tree big enough to kill them on impact.

"I can see just fine," he told her, only this time when he leaned in it felt...different. His voice, though the same deep timber, was honeyed now, as if he were trying to coax her into something, what she couldn't be sure. His words came against the curve of her ear, and when he spoke, he was sure to lightly graze her with his bottom lip. "Afraid of the dark, are you? I'll be sure to remember that and make use of it later."

Yeah, definitely a good thing she'd stopped talking about the cold.

His right arm came around her waist then, hand splaying against her hip familiarly.

Jade slapped at him and struggled to pry him off. "Let go."

"What if you fall?" he practically purred. "Can't have that, can we."

"Why? Because it'll piss your precious Emperor off? Wouldn't want him to lose his new plaything so soon," she sneered. Now that she couldn't see him, and they were drawing further and further away from the palace—and the man who ruled over it—some of the fear from earlier was lifting. Jade felt herself returning, felt comfortable treating this man the same way she would any other who crossed the line.

"It's good you know your place," he said. "That pleases me."

"Like I give a shit. Get off."

He chuckled. "You didn't talk this way before. You're wilder than I first thought."

"Before?" She tried to glare at him over her shoulder, but barely managed to make out the tip of his chin and gave up. "Pretty sure I've been like this since we got on this horse. While we're on the subject though, I also happen to have little patience. If you don't get your paws off me, I'm going to make you bleed."

His fingers thrummed over her hip twice, as if debating, before he finally drew away. He returned his hands to the reigns and that she felt herself bump into his arm whenever her body shifted in the saddle, but that was it.

"This is going to be more fun than I thought, litt—"

"Jade," she practically screamed. "My name is Jade. I might have to deal with him calling me something else, but I sure as shit don't need to tolerate you doing the same."

He was quiet a moment, before, "Don't you?"

"No, no I do not. Because you're under orders not to let anything happen to me." She put all earlier thoughts about how he could probably find a loophole to that order out of her mind.

"Is that a threat?" his voice dropped low. "Are you threatening to harm yourself if I don't oblige?"

"Yes."

"You would do that?"

"Try me." She probably wouldn't, not when there was Amelia to consider, but he didn't have to know that. The thing about people with power, she had learned over the years, was that they absolutely hated even the idea of losing any semblance of it over someone else. If she was willing to cause herself pain, that made his threats of it almost obsolete. He wouldn't want that, wouldn't want to lose that edge.

Sure enough, she felt him pull back slightly, not by much, but enough for the cold wind to slip between their bodies.

Enough to give her the chance to breathe again.

"All right," he said, and it was hard to tell what he was feeling now, "Jade."

With nothing clever to say back to that, she kept her mouth shut.

The rest of the way the two of them rode in silence.

* * *

They rode the rest of the night and well into the day. By the time Koya finally stopped the horse, Jade was certain she wouldn't be able to stand, let alone get down on her own.

Fortunately, he didn't bother asking, slipping easily off the horse himself and reaching up to drag her unceremoniously down after him.

Jade's legs did in fact give out beneath her, and she made a big show of sitting in the grass, rubbing at her calves to try and get feeling back in them. All the while she shot daggers at Koya with her eyes, glaring while he led the horse over toward a small stream.

He was much more careful with the creature, stroking its neck, cooing to it softly. It was like he was a different person.

"You like animals, huh," she spoke before thinking better of it, silently cursing herself when his head snapped in her direction.

"If I liked animals, I'd probably be less averse to you," he stated, but lost most of the intensity in his stare when all that got him was a snort and guffaw from her.

"Come on," she said once he'd turned back to petting the horse, clearly pretending to ignore her, "you have to admit that was a bad insult. Surely you can do better, Mr. Minor."

"That isn't my last name. I'm not about to call you Miss Human."

"Correction," finally trusting she could stand, Jade lifted herself up, wobbling a bit but otherwise all right, "you'd have to call me Miss Minor, since we're supposedly of the same ilk."

"We are not." The disgust burned brightly in his smoky gray eyes. "I was Valued by the Emperor. You? Your family was touched by a deserter. A traitor. You're nothing in the grand scheme of things, not even worthy of licking my boots, let alone comfortably riding my horse."

"Comfortably?" She made a face. "Our ideas of comfort are vastly different. Also," she held up a hand and wagged a single finger, "this Nothing over here happens to be pretty important to your precious Emperor at the moment, so I'd bite my tongue if I were you."

This was…not fun, per se, but less stressful than everything else she'd been through thus far. At least this felt normal, casual even, if one could consider having a tet a tet with a blue haired surely man in the middle of a foggy field normal. Prior to this she hadn't been able to, but now…Maybe. At least until she got out of this hell hole world and back home.

"The key word there," Koya snarled, "is at the *moment*. As soon as you've lost your value, he'll toss you aside."

"I'm counting on it." She blew him a kiss and then burst out in laughter when his cheeks actually flushed. It was definitely due to a mixture of indignation and anger than anything else, but still. "Speaking of key's, you kind of remind me of him."

He frowned. "Him?"

"Key. He's…let's call him a friend. We grew up together. He's probably super pissed at me right now." Some of the ease she'd managed to scrape together died out. He'd be more than pissed, he was most likely going out of his mind. Like he had when she'd disappeared the night after graduation.

She'd walked with the rest of her college class, had accepted her diploma and smiled for the cameras. That night, she'd even had dinner with her grandfather and his men, Key included. But the next day she'd run right from under their noses.

Honestly, she was bit surprised that Jason had been the one sent for her instead. That he'd been trusted with a task like that, knowing that Jade would most likely run again at the sight of him—like she had. Actually, maybe that meant something. Maybe she should have thought of it sooner, but what if Key was more than angry with her? What if he was just point blank done?

If he felt betrayed over her disappearance…

She stopped herself. That didn't make sense. She'd made a point of calling him from payphones every now and again, and he always sounded relieved to hear from her, even if the calls didn't last more than a minute to avoid them being traced.

Why was she thinking about Key anyway? She'd done a good job of putting him from her mind along with everything else about the life she'd been trying to escape from.

"I had a meeting with a company today," she said, mostly just filling the void of silence since Koya had gone back to tending the horse. "It was a good one too. I was positive I was going to get the job. Guess that's out the window."

"Job for?"

She blinked at his back, surprised he'd even mustered enough false fascination to ask and play along.

Because he was playing along. There was absolutely no actual interest in his tone whatsoever.

"Body guard," she told him anyway. "The dream was to work my way up and eventually open my own private security firm. It's kind of the only thing I can do, really, when you take my upbringing into consideration."

"Why?"

"Oh, I'm the—"

"Heir of a syndicate," he glanced over his shoulder briefly, "yes, I know. But what is that, exactly?"

"Do you not have those here?" She shrugged and continued without giving him a chance to reply. "It's basically a very large criminal organization. My grandfather does a lot of seedy business, underground stuff, the whole works. He sells drugs, weapons, flesh— he claims not be part of that last one, but let's be real here."

"You don't sound too bent out of shape about that."

"I am," she corrected, "it's why I don't want to be a part of it."

"Pity." He turned just in time to catch her frown. "If you'd stayed, perhaps you could have done something to change things. Runners? They don't change anything."

"They do for themselves."

"No," he shook his head slowly at her and urged the horse back up the small rise toward where she was standing, "no they don't. A person only runs when they're afraid, too afraid to stand and fight. And, once a coward," he gave her a pointed once over, "always a coward."

She didn't have a snarky enough response to that, and was left with a lump in her throat and her hands clenched at her sides.

"Let's go," he ordered.

Jade glanced up at the darkening sky above them. "Hell no. It's almost night. We should stop and rest."

"That's what we just did."

"That's what the horse just did," she corrected.

"You want water?" He tugged a leather pouch from the end of the saddle where it'd been tied, tossing it to her. "Here."

She wasn't about to let herself go thirsty just to stick it to him, so Jade unscrewed the cap and chugged. Once she was done, she threw it back, albeit with a little more force than necessary, but still refused to take even a step forward.

"You drank, now let's go."

"Don't think so. I need actual rest. Besides, we can't just ride straight through the day and night. Even your horse needs to sleep." He'd seemed to care for the creature. Surely he wouldn't abuse it by making it carry the two of them again so soon after getting them off its back.

"We need to ride hard in order to make it by tomorrow afternoon," he said. "The Emperor gave us a schedule. We need to keep it."

"The Emperor can chill the fuck out for five seconds," she snapped. "I haven't eaten anything since that block of cheese you practically shoved down my throat this morning."

It hadn't tasted great either, no matter how hungry she'd been, which was saying something.

"Get on the horse, Jade," he demanded, cold, shoulders straight.

Like he was scolding a kid. Almost the exact same pose Key would make every time she tried to pass on those extra training sessions the two of them were forced to attend.

Actually...

"Or what?" her voice lowered suggestively, and she felt her muscles uncoil, become loose and lax in anticipation. These past two days had been well and truly the worst. A normal person would beg for the rest she'd been trying to coerce him into giving her.

Jade Blakely had never been normal.

"You going to hit me?" She practically beamed when his entire body went on high alert. "Oh, you want to don't you."

"Don't tempt me," he growled.

"Tell you what, I'll get on the horse if you can make me." She shouldn't be doing this, for a million different reasons, and yet...

She just wanted *some* relief. As a child, that kind of mindlessness, that separation from everything in her life that she hated, only came when she was on the mat. It only came when she was overworking her body—sometimes swinging her fists at another person, other times at a punching bag.

Jade wanted that burn, she wanted to feel something other than this cloying desperation that was tearing away at her insides.

Had she thought standing here tossing quips his way had helped? How wrong she'd been. It'd only buried her feelings a fraction, only enough for her to convince herself they weren't there for a split second of time that had already passed.

Koya dropped the reigns and took a threatening step closer to her. "I was made by the God of Command, you don't want to do this."

"Are you insinuating you've got some kind of mind control power?" That would suck. It would be hella cool. But it would suck. "We don't get specific abilities based off the god who Values us."

"How do you know that?"

"My grandfather's power is a lot different from mine."

"Doesn't mean anything. The gods have more than one gift each."

She cocked her head, trying to determine whether or not he was bluffing. Not about the gods part—it made sense that they'd have multiple powers. But did that really affect the kinds of things Valued humans could do?

"What does being the God of Command even mean?" she asked, though admittedly the question was mostly to herself.

As expected, Koya didn't tell her. Instead, he whipped out a hand, a neon red string seemingly twisting out from around his pointer finger. It flicked forward, lengthening so that the end was to her without him having to take a single step closer.

It caught around her left ankle, and she felt it synch a split second before Koya tugged. Her feet went out from under her and she hit the ground with a heavy thud, some of the damp earth seeping into the back of the thick wool jacket she'd been handed just before exiting the palace.

Jade cursed under her breath and sat up, reaching down to tug at the string. It felt strong, almost like metal wire, except for the way it moved. No matter how hard she tried, she couldn't untangle it from around her ankle.

Koya pulled, sending her sprawling back a second time. He dragged her unceremoniously through the dirt, only stopping once she was close enough he could bend down to lift her.

Or, at least try to.

She wasn't about to miss the opportunity to get back at him.

With a quick twist of her hips, she tossed her right leg over, flipping herself and landing a blow to the side of his head all in the same move. She got back on her feet and went to knee him in the face but he caught her and shoved her away.

Her arms came up to block his fist when he swung, her teeth clenching at the sharp pain that radiated through her when he made contact. She dropped low, dodging a second attack and came up behind him, delivering a cheap blow to the center of his back.

She'd been trained to win.

Not to be honorable.

Koya spun around to keep her in his line of sight, taking up a fighting stance. Above them, the sky had darkened, casting his face in shadows that almost hide the bright glimmer of anger in his eyes. "Get on the horse, Jade. Before it's too late to do things the easy way."

"I'm just starting to loosen up," she told him, smirking when he swore at her.

His gaze darted up to the sky. "You can't fight the Emperor."

"I'm not an idiot. That's why I'm fighting you." Because doing this was a hell of a lot better than simply rolling over and letting the Emperor do whatever the hell he pleased. Sure, she'd have to go along with it, for now, but that didn't mean she liked it, and frankly, she'd started to feel pathetic about the whole ordeal.

He'd been scary in person, but now with distance between them some of that fear had diminished and grown murky.

If nothing else, this little scrimmage would eventually make its way to the Emperor's ear. Hopefully it annoyed him as much as it annoyed Koya. Not enough to have him second guessing upholding his end of the deal or taking things out on Amelia. Just enough that he got the message that she wasn't anyone's plaything.

She'd do what she had to to survive. Nothing more, nothing less.

"You *are* an idiot," he corrected, frustration ringing clear. "You have no idea what's going on. You don't understand anything about this world, or about the gods, and yet you insist on being insolent. What is so special about you that you could possibly think yourself above them?"

"I'm sorry that you consider my not wanting to be a captive or allow anyone to torture my best friend as an affront."

"You—" The pale lighting that had kept things visible suddenly dimmed further, cutting him off. He sucked in a breath and looked up, and this time she caught a sliver of worry pinch his features.

Which was daunting.

If *he* was anxious, that meant she should be as well.

Clouds rolled in, cascading over the moon until it'd blocked out most of its glow. Darkness settled around them, thicker than she was used to, enough that it gave her pause.

Her eyes scanned where he'd been, struggling to find him to no avail. She titled her head, listening intently, but aside from the huffs of the horse a few feet away and the soft trickle of the stream, she heard nothing.

Was he standing in the dark, waiting for the clouds to pass like she was?

Maybe he was right, and after they did, she'd just give in and get on the horse so they could get out of here. She wasn't afraid of the dark, but it was unsettling being out here all alone with only him. Besides, he wasn't entirely full of shit. She had no clue what kinds of creatures roamed the night in this world.

She didn't really want to stick around to find out.

Jade had just opened her mouth to suggest they attempt to make their way to the horse when something heavy and solid slammed into her full force, knocking the breath out of her. She hit the ground for the third time in the past ten minutes, letting out a slight cry upon impact. Her bones rattled, and her shoulder blades hurt where they'd hit the dirt, but that was nothing compared to the feel of the body pinning her down.

He wasn't being careful about it either, didn't shift to allow her lungs room to expand, or seem to care that he was slowly but surely crushing her.

"What do we have here?" he said, and there was something off about his voice.

Her mind instantly flashed back to last night when a similar occurrence had taken place, but before she could dwell on it, her chest constricted painfully and she gasped.

"What's the use of fighting?" he drawled, and she felt how close his face was to hers by the puff of warmth that spread across her cheeks with every one of his exhales. "If it was pain you were after, you could have just asked."

Jade struggled to free one of her arms from where it was caught between them. As soon as she did she beat at him, trying to shove him off to no avail. How the hell was he so heavy? What the fuck did they feed people here?

"Get off," she managed between clenched teeth, tears pricking the corners of her eyes.

"You're kind of fucked up, aren't you, little cat?" He stroked the back of his knuckles down her cheek, no doubt feeling the wetness there. "Instead of going with the flow and making things easy on yourself, you insist on resisting."

"Don't," she sucked in a shaky breath, "call," stilled beneath him, "me," focused all of her strength, "that."

She shot upwards, slamming her forehead into his hard enough she saw stars and thought for sure she'd just killed herself. It did the trick though, to some extent anyway.

He hissed and reared back, giving her enough space to curl in on her side and suck in much needed oxygen.

She kept a hand pressed between her eyes, unable to keep the sounds of pain from slipping past her lips as she fought through it. Experience had taught her this type of agony had to be ridden through, and she waited, beneath him, as the sharp stabbing slowly turned into a harsh pounding.

"Was that worth it?" there wasn't so much as an inkling of discomfort in his voice. The bastard had recovered quickly.

"Yes," she hissed, pride momentarily getting the better of her. She groaned when another pang flashed behind her temples and curled even more in on herself.

It wasn't until he moved that she recalled he was still above her, having forgotten since they were no longer touching. He lowered himself back down though, angling himself slightly so that he settled curved around her back, managing to both cling to her and keep her in place at the same time.

She tried to turn but his hand shot out, settling beneath her jaw, gripping her firmly.

"Don't look," he ordered.

Their positions gave him a clear view of her, but prevented her from turning the couple of inches needed for her to see him. It was still very dark, but her eyes had adjusted and she could make out the long legs of their horse some feet away.

"Why?" she asked.

"Is there something about this face you like?" Oddly, he didn't sound pleased by that notion.

Despite their positions, she risked openly scoffing. "As if."

"What kind of features are you attracted to?"

An image of Key flashed through her mind before she could shake it away.

Koya pressed more closer at her back. "Who were you just thinking about?" he demanded.

"No one." For the life of her she couldn't explain why she lied. Koya was dangerous, sure, but not that dangerous. Not in comparison to others here. And yet…There was something off about him right now. She couldn't quite place her finger on it and that was making her feel all the more unsettled having him so near.

Ironically, even though she'd been the one initiating the fight earlier, now she wanted nothing more than distance between them.

She should have just gotten on the damn horse. Shouldn't have tried drowning out all this self-doubt and self-hatred with violence.

Violence wasn't typically the answer.

Typically.

"Key," he said then, and she realized that he'd been quiet while she'd gotten lost in her inner mussing. "It's that Key person, isn't it? That's who you were thinking about. I wonder what he'd think if he saw you now."

"What—" His nose suddenly buried in the curve of her neck had the words dying on her tongue.

He inhaled deeply, and she went ridged beneath him. "You know, this was how it had to be done before. The only way it could be. But now...with you here..." his sentence trailed off.

"You're not making any sense," she told him. Why was he speaking so cryptically all of sudden?

"I suppose to you I'm not. Don't fret. You'll understand soon enough." He sighed and then let her go, shoving onto his feet in one swift motion. "But not tonight. Tonight, we get back on task. Unless, of course, you haven't yet finished with your little tantrum?"

Jade stood, careful not to turn and face him even though she really wanted to. Brushing off the bits of grass and clumps of dirt from her pants, she forced herself not to rise to the bait. "No. It's too dark to spar anyway."

"I'm sure you could manage."

"Let's just go." It took her a second to find the horse again, but as soon as she spotted it she headed toward it. This time, she didn't wait for him to hoist her up, her pride having taken enough hits for one damn month, let alone just this night. She pushed herself up into the saddle and then pointedly kept her gaze straight ahead as he moved to follow suit.

As soon as he was seated behind her, his arm came around her waist, tugging her back against him hard enough her head hit his chest, reigniting the ach behind her brows. She hissed, but he mere chuckled against the curve of her ear.

"Still worth it?" he coaxed, only to have her emit a low growl through the pain.

"Yes."

He clucked his tongue. "Stubborn."

With one quick tug on the reigns, he had the horse shooting forward, driving them well into the darkness.

Grateful to have their conversation come to an end, Jade decided to take the risk of closing her eyes. It'd been days since she'd gotten any proper rest and she was exhausted.

They hadn't traveled very far before that exhaustion got the best of her. With the feel of his warmth surrounding her and the tight band of his arm keeping her safely on the saddle, Jade drifted off to sleep.

Chapter 5:

"This is it?" Jade stared up at the sprawling gates that encircled what appeared to be a dilapidated mansion. She could see in some parts that the roof had caved in, and all over the paved paths that led through and around various buildings that made up the residence weeds had grown through cracks and overrun the place. The bars surrounding were covered in spirals of ivy, parts both dead and alive, and a large oak tree creaked in the harsh mid-afternoon breeze.

Koya had woken her up from a deep sleep a few minutes ago, alerting her to their arrival. He didn't seem as surprised by their surroundings as she was, more focused on tying his horse up to a part of the fencing than anything else.

"It's been abandoned for over five thousand years," he said. "What did you expect?"

Oh right. She'd actually forgotten that part. She cocked her head, trying to see everything from a new perspective.

"I guess, considering that, it's actually in pretty good shape."

"It's the lingering magic," he explained. "Unless someone of his bloodline or magical line decides to destroy the place it will stand here until the end of time."

"What about all the other people who lived here?" she asked, trying to picture servants moving through the courtyard, or children playing in the large stone fountain in the center. The fountain was mostly destroyed now, with half the basin smashed, rocks spilling out. "What happened to them when the god died?"

"They stayed for a little while," he took a look himself now finally, "but not long. The second they stepped foot beyond the property line, the wards prevented them from entering again. They prepared to go first, packed and took their things along with them all at once. I believe a single grounds keeper remained, but he was human, and would have died long ago."

"Alone?" That was…sad.

"He made his choice." Koya stepped around her and motioned toward the gate. "Now make yours."

Jade rolled her eyes. Of course he couldn't be a decent person for two seconds. Just like that, the spell of this place, all the ghosts she'd been imagining, went up in a puff of smoke.

"What would you do if after coming all this way I refused to go in?" she asked, just to needle him. Upon waking, she'd paid him particular attention, relieved to find that in the light of day he'd returned to his old self.

His old, infuriatingly annoying self, but still.

That was a hell of a lot better than the scary vibes he'd been throwing off last night. Jade almost shivered thinking about it even.

"I would leave you here and ride back to the palace where your friend would be executed," he told her dryly, having clearly caught on to what she was doing.

She sighed. "You're no fun."

"We aren't here for that."

"Yeah, yeah, yeah." She waved at him and then turned back to the gate. The entrance was right in front of her, less than five feet away. All she had to do was give the thing a good push, step inside, and then go find the vial. She took the place in again and pointed out, "How am I supposed to find something as small as my pinky in there? All of the tenants of my apartment building could live here easily."

"It should be stored in the main building," he said, pointing past the fountain toward a larger portion of the manor. "Master Mist would have kept it close, most likely in his bed chambers."

"Would it be hidden?"

"Probably not. Taking a gods power like that would be deadly for most."

"How does one go about removing their power anyway?" The wound on her neck twanged—of course the asshole had healed the knife wounds but not that one—as if in reply and her eyes went wide.

"No way," she spun on him, "am I looking for a vial of blood?"

The Emperor had told her the bottle would be blue. He'd said nothing of its contents. He'd also been pretty forthcoming about having bitten her for her power. If this was about magic and breaking his curse, it made sense that that's what he'd need.

Still though...Ew.

"Whatever." She shook her head and turned back to the gate. It wasn't like she had an aversion to blood or anything, just that the concept of some ancient, long deceased god's blood being stored in some dilapidated mansion was out there.

"Make it quick," Koya told her the second she pressed her palm flat against the door, "we have a schedule to keep."

"You and that damn schedule," she muttered under her breath, not bothering to get into it with him this time. Truth be told, she didn't want to hang around this place any longer than need be either.

Jade wasn't sure she believed in ghosts, but she definitely hadn't believed in gods, and look how well that had turned out for her.

The metal creaked loudly when she pushed it open and she eased herself inside, eyes scanning the area, in case something was about to jump out at her.

The courtyard was covered in debris; and her boots crunched over piles of leaves as she made her way across toward the large main building Koya had pointed out. The roof was still mostly intact here, the rusty red shingles only slightly smashed in places. The two front doors were painted blue, with chips and peeling strips of paint curling off of it. The one of the right was ajar, giving a good view into the darkness within.

The sounds of her steps as she ascended the stone echoed loudly, cutting through the otherwise stillness of the place.

At least there was comfort in the knowledge that no one else could get in here. Although…she glanced over her shoulder back at the front where Koya stood on the other side of the gate. She hadn't felt anything when she'd passed beneath the awning. What if all of this was a lie and she'd fallen into a trap?

Cutting those thoughts short, Jade forced herself to shove open the door and enter the building, pausing beneath the threshold only long enough for her eyes to adjust to the slight gloom.

Whether or not this was a trap didn't matter.

Amelia would be killed if she didn't go through with this.

The warped floorboards creaked beneath her, and even in the dim light she could see old footprints in the thick layer of dust. The walls might have once been white, but were now tan and water-stained in various places. Cobwebs hung everywhere, and when she passed the first room, a single glance inside had her quickly walking past.

The wall inside had caved in and aside from a single rotting desk, the room had been overrun with plants and vines.

Where the hell was she supposed to find the bedroom?

Halfway down the hall it branched off, with a small walkway to the right leading to a large set of stairs. Some of the steps were cracked, and half the railing was missing—broken from a piece of the ceiling crashing onto it.

Hoping she could avoid that deathtrap all together, Jade kept moving forward, passing another three rooms. The rooms were open spaces without doors, all three housing broken furniture and the same aged walls. It was clear that no one had been here for a really, really long time. If it weren't for the fact it was day and sunlight managed to find its way through the busted windows, she might have been freaked out.

At night this place would really look like a haunted house.

Shuddering, she picked up the pace, relieved when she finally came to a door. It wasn't locked, though the handle did stick a bit, but when she pushed it open she was disappointed to discover it wasn't the bedroom she was seeking.

The kitchen had a stone hearth, still blackened from use even though it'd been sitting there for centuries. Any food that had been left behind was long rotted and gone, so there was just dusty silverware and a couple overturned chairs.

"This is going to take forever," she complained. No wonder Koya had insisted on their tight schedule. There were still a handful of hours until nightfall but she wasn't confident that she'd find the right room before then.

Jade searched the entire lower floor—all four wings of it—never once finding a bedroom. By the end, she'd lost three hours and ended up in front of the crumbling stairwell anyway.

"He said it'd be easy," she mumbled to herself, hands on her hips as she inspected the stairs, trying to come up with the safest way up them before she actually set foot on one. Best to have a game plan to avoid fumbling around and possibly falling through one of the broken boards.

There were about twelve steps in total, with a landing between them that looked solid enough from what she could see of it. The fourth step was completely gone, and part of the second, so Jade stuck close to the right, practically hugging the wall as she eased her way up. She didn't want to spend too long on any one step, but also didn't want to rush up them.

When she reached the middle landing, she inhaled and slowly placed her foot on it, testing her weight. It creaked a bit, but not any more or less than any of the other spots, so she felt safe enough to continue onward. The upper half of the staircase had miraculously gone unscathed, a massive relief after how cautious she'd just been.

The stairs led to another hallway. Directly across from it a large room with wide open doors led to a sprawling view of the mountains in the distance. Sunlight streamed through, highlighting dust motes and the balcony that stretched outside.

Jade moved closer, peering into the room to find that, despite how open it was, things within the room looked a lot more preserved. There was a low desk to the right with a couple of stone knickknacks carefully sorted over the surface. The opposite side housed what had probably once been a long silk screen, though it was in tatters now, more a frame than anything. Through it, she could see a shelf which housed a couple empty flower pots.

She tried to imagine what else had once filled the room. Chairs? A table? Was this a study? Maybe the god who lived here once spent his mornings out on the balcony, overlooking the tiny village surrounding the massive place and the mountain range in the near distance.

What had this world been like, five thousand years ago?

There was so much about this whole situation that was fascinating, and if not for the fact she was trapped here, being held captive against her will, Jade might have actually enjoyed exploring. She'd always been the curious sort, and there was no doubt that as far as hiding from her grandfather went, there was no better place than another damn realm to do it.

If things were different, and Amelia was up for it as well, she might even consider staying for a while…Of course, that was completely out of the question with the Emperor breathing down her neck.

As well as other things…

She cleared her throat, embarrassed of herself and where her thoughts had gone and turned, opting to go left down the hall instead of right. She didn't want to think about what happened to them the other night *ever*.

As soon as she was home again, she needed to hit up a club and get laid. With someone *human*. Clearly she'd gone too long without and that paired with the stress of everything going on had made her momentarily weak willed. She needed to think of the Emperor as just another asshole to be avoided, the same way she'd always needed to avoid those thugs who tried crossing the line whenever Key or her grandfather weren't looking. She'd beaten most of those men bloody and blue, and the Emperor...

Even thinking about how he'd touched her had her thighs clenching tight and a wave of heat rushing through her. She ground her teeth against her body's reaction and cursed herself. Who cared if he was the hottest man she'd ever seen? He wasn't even human. Or a semi-decent person.

In fact, really, she couldn't recall ever hating someone as strongly as she did him. If it came down to it, she'd choose her grandfather's service over being the Emperor's unwilling captive. Just because he was good with his tongue and his hands didn't change that.

Yes. One-night stand the second she was out of here.

Key's face swam in her mind and she paused on her way down the hall.

Maybe she'd go with her grandfather's men initially after all...

She snorted.

As if.

Key wasn't interested in her, never had been. As soon as they'd hit puberty he'd kept his distance, at least when it came to anything but the extensive training he'd been tasked with ensuring she attended.

That was part of what made leaving so easy for her. Knowing that she could never have him anyway, that she wasn't actually abandoning him, a man who had no real attachment to her other than duty. If things had been different, if he'd even so much as hinted at being interested…Maybe she would have stayed.

Really, now that some time had passed, she was grateful that he hadn't. Grateful that she'd gotten out and had managed to, for the most part, put those childish feelings to bed. She'd casually dated throughout college, nothing serious. But it wasn't because of Key. It was because of the fact getting serious with someone meant putting them under her grandfather's radar.

It was true she still thought of him often, more often as of late since coming here, but that was all it was. Lingering thoughts of a one sided first love.

Jade kept going and at the end of the hallway she finally found what she'd been looking for. The door was ajar already, and when she eased it open and stepped inside, she grinned.

A large four poster bed was pressed against the wall next to the door. The blankets had somehow been preserved well enough she could make out that they'd once been blue. They were moth ridden but that was to be expected.

The room itself was massive, but like most of the others, empty aside from the few pieces of heavy or built into the wall furniture that couldn't be moved when everyone else left this place. For a moment she worried that the vial might have been taken like most other things, but the only thing she could do was search anyway and hope.

She moved deeper into the room, eyes scanning her surroundings. There was a large hole in the far wall that appeared as though it'd been built and not made accidentally after the mansion had been abandoned. For now, she ignored it, giving it and its dark cavernous recess a wide berth.

On the other side of the room was a wall of shelves. There were so many odds and ends scattered on them that it took her a while to make it through. Some of the items were familiar, like a tea cup made of the same material as her namesake, and dagger with a golden handle and a blade only as long as her palm.

Jade hesitated, eyeing the weapon for a long time before finally giving in to the urge to pocket it. She swiped it off the shelf, coughing as she inadvertently disturbed a cloud of dust and slipped it into her back pocket.

One shelf was packed with glass containers but she sorted through each and every one and none of them were the right color or contained anything that could be even remotely considered blood.

Out of the single bay window, she could see that the sun was starting to set; she'd been in here for hours. Her muscles were starting to cramp and her neck injury was burning slightly. The thick bandage would at least help prevent any dust from infecting the wound, but it wasn't enough to make her grateful to the Emperor.

"Bastard could have healed all of me," she grumbled, moving on to the next shelf.

Jade shoved a chipped glass out of the way and paused.

There.

She almost hesitated before picking up the small glass vial, afraid she was somehow hallucinating out of desperation. It felt solid and smooth in her fingers though, the cerulean blue color becoming more distinguishable as she rubbed the caked layer of dust off on her shirt. Holding it up to the light, she could make out the red tinge to the thick substance inside.

"Thank god." She felt a tension ease out of her all at once, the relief like a live thing sweeping through her. Then it hit her, what she'd said, and her nose scrunched in displeasure. "No. Not god. He didn't do shit."

Now that she'd gotten what she'd come for—finally—she needed to make the trip back and get out of here. With any luck she could beat sunset and she and Koya could be on their way to shelter. He'd mentioned something about staying in the nearby village tonight instead of traveling and she was all for it.

The spot between her shoulders hurt from being on the horse and in an upright position all this while. Not to mention her tailbone.

They'd get a good night's sleep somewhere warm and safe, and then they'd head back to the palace.

Back to the Emperor.

She wished she could skip that part. Give Koya the vial and have him trade Amelia off without ever having to see the Emperor again. The part of her that had been raised by the syndicate scoffed at the idea of leaving without taking some sort of revenge against the god, but fortunately self-preservation won out. Maybe later, if she was still angry about everything that had gone down here, she could try convincing herself it'd been just a bad dream. A nightmare.

A seriously fucked up nightmare.

That decided, Jade slipped the vial into her pocket and turned toward the door.

The sounds coming from the hole in the wall were so quiet at first she was already halfway across the room before she heard it.

She came to a standstill, the hairs on the back of her neck prickling as she slowly angled her head in the direction of the darkness. As soon as she had, the floorboards beneath her quaked as something within that deep black moved.

It sounded a lot like something heavy being dragged across the ground, and she risked another step closer to the door, trying to gauge how long it might take her to make a run for it.

A snout poked out first, almost as wide as the pillow still resting on the bed, and covered in pale pink feathers. Aside from those it appeared incredibly reptilian, and Jade's breath caught in her throat as more of the creature emerged until a large snake-like head hovered less than twenty feet away.

The creature had circular inky eyes the size of dinner plates and in them she saw her reflection.

Saw how pale she'd gone.

More of the creature slithered out, its serpentine body completely encased in that light layer of feathers. She would have pegged it for a weird feathered snake even if not for the tips of wings that popped out next.

That was all she stuck around for. The sight of them, folded over its back, massive leathery appendages tipped with a hook-like claw at the very top, sent her running for the door without another thought.

The creature came after her; she heard it crashing through the doorway, busting through the walls in the process, but she didn't risk looking back to see the damage herself.

Jade ran faster than she ever had—faster even than she'd run from Jason and the rest of the Emerald goons. Her thighs burned and the injury on her neck may have opened up, she wasn't sure. Didn't care. When she made it to the stairs, she took them with a lot less care than when she'd taken them up, tripping onto the middle landing and slamming her left shoulder into the wall hard enough to let out a hiss of pain.

Part of the wood cracked beneath her boot, but she was already leaping off of it, scrambling down the rest of the steps. She landed with a thud on her knees at the bottom, scrambling up, unaware of the layers of dust sticking to her or the harsh sounds of her coughing as she raced through a thick cloud of it.

Behind her, the creature continued to destroy the mansion in its attempt to catch her. Its impossible size was the only thing slowing it down enough she was able to get away, but it wouldn't be a problem once they made it outside.

She needed to get to the gate, then the magical barrier would keep the creature from being able to leave and she'd be safe.

Jade burst out onto the porch, feet clattering down the steps. She was far less interested in the scenery this time as she pushed herself as hard as she could across the courtyard.

Koya saw her coming, and she saw him frown and take a step forward a second before something caught his attention over her shoulder.

The main building exploded as the creature freed itself, the sound of impossibly large wings flapping and the wind slapping against her back causing another rush of fear to spike through her.

The gate entrance was still open and even though Koya was standing in front of it, Jade didn't slow.

"Move!" she yelled, but he was too busy being fascinated by the winged beast hot on her trail.

She didn't bother asking again, wasn't about to take the chance. Instead, she crashed into him, falling to the ground and rolling some feet before coming to a stop on her back. She'd taken him down as well, was aware he was sitting up a little ways away, but she remained where she was, sucking in oxygen to appease her burning lungs.

The relief that she was safe had just started to sink in when the creature burst over the gate, flying directly over head.

She screamed and shot up, but the creature had lost interest in her and kept flying, heading away without a backward glance.

"Wow," Koya said after a long stretch of silence passed with the both of them merely staring after the beast. "I thought for sure Pearl was dead."

"*Pearl*?!" Jade's head whipped in his direction to find he'd gotten to his feet and was dusting himself off.

"Yeah," he pointed in the direction of the creature, "the amphiptire that just flew by. That's Pearl. She's been trapped in there since Mist's death. Wonder how she survived without food this long."

"You *knew* that thing was in there?!"

"Sure—" He didn't get another word out.

Jade's fist connected with his face. At the last second, she twisted, so that her knuckles dug in and tore flesh upon impact. It was a cheap shot.

But he deserved it.

The only one who deserved it more was his fucking Emperor.

Koya hissed and stumbled back, hand going up protectively. His cheek was bleeding and he furiously swore at her. "I thought she was dead!"

"Like that would have made a difference," she countered. "You would have sent me in there anyway."

"Those were our orders!"

"You could have given me a heads up!" She ran her hands through her hair, frustration and anger boiling over. She wanted to hit him again. Repeatedly. Until he bled so much he was unrecognizable.

Forcing herself to still, Jade closed her eyes and inhaled through her nose, slowly releasing the breath through her mouth a second later.

"You can't kill him," she reminded herself. "You don't know the way back to Amelia."

"You couldn't kill me anyway," he sneered, but quieted when her eyes popped open and she growled at him. Instead, he cocked his head, and once she'd calmed some mentioned, "He's right about you. You've got a bloodlust."

Jade didn't ordain that with a response. Mostly because he wasn't entirely wrong. It was part of the reason she'd realized she needed out of the Emeralds.

Before it was too late for her.

Before things like coldblooded murder, kidnapping, and doping people up against their will didn't bother her any more.

"At least tell me you got it," Koya said gruffly a moment later.

Jade's hand instantly went to her pocket. Thankfully, the glass hadn't broken during her tumble. Pulling it out, she held it up for him to see. When he reached for it, however, she snatched it back, returning it to her jeans for safe keeping.

"No way," she told him.

"Don't trust me?"

"I don't trust any of you people."

He snorted but didn't argue, moving toward his horse which was amazingly calm even after a dragon-snake-bird-thing had flown over them. "Let's go. We're only an hour's ride from the village and I'm exhausted."

Jade moved after him, but as soon as she was up on the horse a realization hit her. With a frown, she twisted to face him as he settled behind her. "How the hell did that thing get past the barrier?"

"Oh, that?" He shrugged and took up the reigns. "That broke the second you entered. Bringing Master Mist's magic back, even the miniscule bit coursing through your veins, destroys the magic creating the barrier. Now anyone can come and go as they please."

He snapped the reigns and turned them onto the road.

Jade's eyes narrowed. "Anyone?"

"Yeah." He was doing a good job of avoiding her gaze, and continued directing the horse despite how awkward their positions currently were with her still turned toward him.

"Stop the horse."

He shook his head.

"Koya."

"So you can hit me again? No, thank you." His cheek was still bleeding.

She spun around and seated herself more comfortably. Not because she was letting this go. She wasn't. She'd find a way later to make him pay.

Because if the barrier had been broken the second she'd entered, that meant the bastard could have gone in with her to help her search for the vial.

"Asshole."

If he'd thought she was bloodthirsty before, he should be grateful he couldn't read minds. If he could, he would have a gotten a front row seat to all the ways she thought of murdering him as they traveled toward the village.

Chapter 6:

It felt amazing to be able to sleep lying down. So much even, that Jade had little to no qualms about doing it right in front of Koya.

As soon as they'd been brought to the tiny room in the inn Jade had undone the bed roll and sprawled out. The aches and pains she'd collected over the past few days stretched and settled, and she'd sighed and promptly passed out.

Now, with her vision bleary and her throat dry, Jade forced herself to rise, sitting up on the pad and glancing around until she caught sight of Koya sitting in the corner of the room diagonal from her.

He had his legs pulled up to his chest and was currently poking the end of a long stick into the flames at the center of the room where a fire pit was set into the floor.

The heat and crackling of the logs must have been what had roused her.

It was late afternoon, but there was still sunlight streaming in through the single window and the sliding wooden doors which he'd left open. They looked out on a small backyard and then a dense forest. Sounds of people could be heard—villagers going about the rest of their evening—but Jade didn't see anyone.

"Got any food?" she asked, turning her attentions back to Koya, noticing that he appeared drawn and tired.

His dark blue hair was in disarray, as if he'd been running his fingers through it while she'd slept, and his eyes, typically spitting with anger or derision, looked dulled and lackluster. There were still some dirt stains on his clothing from when she'd slammed into him, but aside from that, his uniform was put together.

No one would be able to guess he'd spent the last forty-eight hours riding across the country.

Koya picked something off a plate nearby and tossed it at her.

She caught it with ease, inspecting the hard roll before taking a hearty bite. The crust was flaky and the inside was soft and still warm. It wasn't a turkey dinner or anything, but it'd certainly do the trick of keeping her hunger at bay.

"Did you get any sleep?" she asked, not sure why she was bothering. Except for the fact if he was this exhausted he might end up passing out while they were on the road, and *that* would be a disaster. She glanced outside at the setting sun. "I guess you're waiting. We're staying the whole night here, right?"

He snorted. "I can't believe you slept. Have you no survival instincts?"

She rolled her eyes and took another bite. "If you were going to kill me and take the vial, you would have done so already. There's no reason for me to torture myself over something as obvious as that."

"What if I was just biding my time?"

"Then I guess I'd be dead now?" She shrugged. "Not sure what you want me to say here."

She wasn't about to tell him that her training had also included sleeping with "one eye open". If he'd so much as approached her, she would have woken instantly. But letting him believe that she was letting her guard down around him was a good way to get him to do the same.

"And you're so certain I won't betray the Emperor and kill you against his wishes?" Koya sounded funny, not his usual self, but also nothing like those couple of times when he'd spoken to her in an odd silky voice in the dark.

No, there was something else going on here, something Jade needed to figure out, and quick, before she lost control of the situation and he really did try something they would both regret.

"You're loyal," she said, pretending to lose interest in the roll, letting her arm hang over her upturned leg. "You wouldn't do anything he didn't want you to do."

"I had a purpose before you got here," he told her tightly. "Without purpose…what's the point of remaining loyal?"

"Are you talking about being his second in command?" She frowned.

He watched her silently for a moment before, "You know absolutely nothing about this world or how things work here."

"Well, yeah. I'm not from here. Hence my trying so desperately to leave."

"I've been with the Emperor for over a decade. His curse—" he stopped himself abruptly, causing Jade's ears to perk up.

He'd been about to spill something he shouldn't.

But what?

And how did she get him to tell her?

"It's got to be terrible," she lowered her gaze to the fire, pretending to be pensive. "I can't imagine not being able to smell anything. I have this massive candle collection back home. And what about on Christmas? The smell of Christmas trees is one of my favorites. Always puts me in the holiday mood."

Not that celebrating was a big family thing, in Jade's childhood. She got a present or two from her grandfather each year, and they had dinner, just the two of them, Key, and the dozen or so guards. But...

She hadn't had a proper, intimate holiday with family since her parents died.

Still. It remained her favorite holiday because her grandfather was usually busy the whole season with one thing or another—the cold brought the desperation out in people, and criminals lapped that shit up—which meant she always had more freedom.

In high school that'd meant getting to spend more afternoons at school partaking in activities and hanging with friends. Going to the movies or the mall on the weekends.

Her friendships had all been superficial, most of them kids of other members of the syndicate, but it'd still been nice to laugh and stuff their faces with too much junk food.

It'd been nice to pretend they were normal.

It'd been especially nice knowing Jade wasn't the only one doing it.

She hardly spoken to any of them since, but she hoped wherever they were, they'd gotten out of the life and escaped the control of their parents.

Like she'd been trying to do before this shit show.

"What is Christmas?" Koya asked, snapping her out of her memories.

"Oh, right. I guess you wouldn't have that here considering your nine god pantheon." Opting not to get into the religious aspects of it all—because who had the time for that when her sole purpose here was to get answers out of *him*—she went with the abridged version. The consumers' version. "It's a holiday where we put a tree in our house, pile presents underneath it, and then open them on the morning of the 25th. You're supposed to spend it with the people you care about the most. I'd planned to spend this year with Amelia and our other friends."

Her real friends. The first ones she'd ever made on her own, with no connections to the Emeralds.

"That sounds…"

"It's weird, I know. But the food is good."

"Scent is attached to memory," Koya said then, stoking the fire absently, "but not being able to taste is what really gets to him."

"That makes sense," she grabbed onto that string and held. "I love food. Life would be kind of bland if I wasn't able to enjoy it."

"He's lived a very long time, and has the metabolism of, well, a god. Partaking in drink and food was one of his only true vices. It kept him going, in a way." His gaze hardened. "Master Mist knew that."

"Why did he curse him? I wasn't told." At his glare, she held up her hands. "It's just that that's a really cruel thing to do, that's all. I was wondering why he took it that far."

She wasn't lying. A curse like that was meant to torture the recipient. It didn't cause any actual pain, wasn't life threatening, and yet...when cast on someone who apparently lived for trying new tastes, it could certainly make them want to die. Having the thing you care about most taken from you was horrible. This was a bit unorthodox, sure, but the results were the same.

"Master Mist was trying to overthrow order," Koya informed her. "He wanted to lead."

"Yeah, I don't see the Emperor stepping aside for anyone."

"No." The corner of his mouth twitched but he stopped the smile from fully forming. "He didn't take the betrayal well at all. The two were close before, the Emperor, Master Mist, and Haze were the first three gods to come into existence. Though the gods are cruel and without mercy, they cared for one another in their own twisted sense of the word. Until Master Mist tried to take his power.

"By the end of the thousand year war, Master Mist was finally defeated, but in the process he lost the family he had raised. In a last ditch attempt at revenge before fleeing the world like a coward, he used almost what was left of his power to curse the Emperor."

"For him to have gotten the upper hand like that..." Jade let the sentence trail off, knowing he would get where she was going with it. Not wanting to come off too interested, yet just interested enough that he would keep talking.

Koya's free hand tightened into a fist. "He lied and claimed he wanted to meet to settle a truce. The Emperor, thinking he'd already knocked Mist down enough, willingly went and was ambushed. The curse is a small one in the grand scheme of things—many of us would be saddened, like you said, but we would survive. But the Emperor..."

"Is an ancient being who pretty much only took pleasure in taste," Jade finished for him. So many memories were routed in taste and in smell. It was also the easiest way to tell if something was spoiled. If life had been dull before, not getting to at least take pleasure in a bite of chocolate or a coffee would have made it ten times worse. "That sounds lonely."

She tried to ignore the pang of pity in her chest. He didn't deserve it, no matter how sad his story was.

"You're not immortal," she said, eyeing Koya. "So how do you know all of this? Did he tell you?"

"Everyone knows," he stated. "It's no big secret. The story is passed down, written in scriptures and told in the Dust Temples. People place food as offerings at his alters. He only gets to try them once in a while, but—"

"Wait." There. That's what she was after, she was sure of it. "What?"

He blinked at her then seemed to realize what he'd said and straightened defensively. "Nothing. Forget it."

"Does it matter if I know? You said everyone already does."

The look he gave her spoke volumes.

They knew about the curse, but they didn't know about this. This secret that Koya was holding for the Emperor.

"The Emperor has a way to break the curse," she guessed, grinning when she saw the truth of it in his eyes. "Even if it's not permeant. I'm not the only way."

Which meant…

He didn't actually need her.

Confusion swept through her, and Koya saw it.

"It isn't the same," he snapped. "You're a permanent solution."

"You mean this vial is." She patted the glass still in her pocket.

"Yes," he corrected himself.

"Which is why he was so willing to trade my friend and my life for it." There was still something she didn't understand, however. "You don't like that. I get that you're loyal, but is that the only reason you're going along with this?"

Because he'd been trying so hard to hide it, but it was impossible not to have figured out that Koya had a part in however the Emperor got around his curse.

It explained the hatred he'd shown her. He thought she was taking his place, removing his purpose and importance to the Emperor whom he doted on.

"I don't want to get any closer to him than I've already been forced to," she found herself saying. "You can keep him, your precious Emperor. I just want to go home. Whatever you think of me, I'm not a threat to you."

He grunted darkly. "You're a fool if you believe that. Maybe we're both fools. I'm a Minor, but I'm also a human. I've seen the things he's done, the ways he's chosen to direct his fury at being cursed…The new…hobbies he took up to take the place of tastings and cooking. I know what he is. The gods are not kind or just. They're devils. But they're in charge here. And—"

"You're in love with him." She was an idiot for not seeing it sooner.

He bristled under her gaze, hand stilling with the end of the stick still in the fire. It caught flame a moment later and he swore, quickly smacking it against the ground in an attempt to put it out. Afterward he glared at her as if the whole thing had been her fault.

Jade rolled her eyes, though inside she'd gone even more alert. He'd been dangerous before, when he'd been loyal, now…

"Does he know how you feel?" she asked, willing to take the risk of prying and setting him off. She needed to know where they all stood. Maybe there'd be a way she could use this to her benefit.

"It doesn't matter." He slumped back against the wall.

"So he does, but he doesn't reciprocate," she guessed. "Been there."

He snorted and she had flashbacks to being in high school, sharing stories about her crush around the lunch table. Koya was a Minor with supernatural abilities, and yet he was in here moping about one-sided love just like everyone else. It was grounding, in a sense.

Jade shifted into a more comfortable position, glad for the distraction, even if the topic was a dangerous one that could lead to him losing his cool at any moment. At least this felt normal. It was ironic how desperately she'd been grasping at those straws when they came to her. How badly she wanted to feel, even for a second, that her life was back to the way it had been.

Her life had never been normal, and she'd always been on the run from something or someone. It was laughable that she was trying to convince herself otherwise here, and yet, she couldn't seem to help it. It was pretty much the one comfort she was able to find amongst the chaos. The one thing that at least felt familiar and made sense.

Even if she'd never lived a normal, regular life she knew what one was supposed to look like. That was enough to build her fantasies around.

"I have," she continued once she'd resettled, opting for a friendly tone in the hopes it would help open him up. "There's this guy back home, Key. I've had a crush on him for forever. But he's never looked at me like anything more than a sister or a responsibility."

He also wasn't a Minor. Meaning, despite how high his rank in the syndicate was, her grandfather would never approve of their relationship.

"I've always been controlled," she said, thoughts deviating before she could realize. "There's always a man in the shadows thinking he knows best. Trying to tell me what to do, where to go, how to be. The Emperor wants to do the same thing to me that my grandfather did."

"Is that why you're pretending you're not attracted to him?" Koya surmised.

Startled, she blinked at him. "I'm not doing that at all."

"Lying then." He shrugged a single shoulder. "Even to yourself."

"Just because you think he's the greatest thing since sliced bread, doesn't mean everyone does."

He quirked a brow. "I can assure you, *everyone does*. Men and women are constantly throwing themselves at him. You haven't seen it because—"

"I was beaten and locked up my whole stay at his palace?" she interrupted.

"You're an intruder and a possible threat," he pointed out. "What makes you think you should have been treated any differently? Why? Because you claimed you came here accidentally? What proof do you have?"

"I don't need proof," she argued. "All I need is to be let back into the hot spring. If my blood is the key, then I can easily send myself and Amelia back without causing any trouble to you or your Emperor. I know this, you know this, and he knows this too. The only reason he wouldn't let me is because he realized he could use me a little longer."

This was not at all where she'd intended for this conversation to go. She needed to get them back on track.

Jade sighed. "If you know he doesn't like you, why do you stick around? Why not get over him?"

"Was it that easy for you?" he asked. "Were you able to get over this Key guy?"

No.

She glanced away and he chuckled darkly.

"I didn't think so. Advice is always much easier to give than it is to take."

"I don't still have feelings for him," she said after a moment of silence between them. "I just think about him sometimes."

"Don't let the Emperor hear you say that," he warned, and there was a layer of sincerity in his voice now that hadn't been there before.

"Why not? He won't care, and I won't still be around once we get back." She made sure to keep her posture lax, though she went on alert, searching him for any tell. If the Emperor was planning on betraying her, Koya would probably already know about it.

He was a professional though. It wasn't hard for him to remain a closed book, making it impossible for her to read anything other than his exhaustion.

"It's not just your attraction you're lying about I see," he drawled, back to stoking the flames even though they really didn't need it. "The Emperor wants you. He hasn't looked at anyone the way he looks at you."

"That's jealousy talking," she told him, even though her chest tightened. "You're seeing things that aren't there."

"And that's fear talking," he countered. "You're ignoring things that are. You can't pretend for much longer, Jade. He won't let you."

"I'm going home soon," she repeated, less inclined to conceal her doubt now. She held his gaze, desperately trying to convey the look of a lost soul, someone he should take pity on.

He wavered, she saw it in his eyes, but only for a heartbeat. Then his gaze hardened all over again and his expression returned to being enigmatic. "That's true."

"Why do you say it like that?"

"Like?"

"Vaguely. Like it's a lie." It couldn't be a lie. It couldn't. An idea came to her then. "Tell me where the hot spring is located. If I know where it is, I can get Amelia and get to it."

"Why would I do that?"

"Because you don't want me here either."

"The Emperor is going to let you go home, Jade," he said, a bit more believably this time.

"Okay, so then it shouldn't matter if you tell me, right? He's going to let me go there anyway. What can it hurt if I know the way sooner rather than later?" She needed to convince him, now, before it was too late.

He was already melancholy over thoughts of his one-sided love. Vulnerable.

As shitty as it was, she needed to take advantage of that vulnerability before she missed the chance.

"Think of it this way," she leaned forward a bit, lowering her voice even though they were alone. People had a tendency to open up more if they felt they were being let in on a secret. "It's a failsafe. If anything should go wrong, I can get myself home, meaning you'll once again be the only one near the Emperor."

She didn't bring up his earlier comment about how everyone else in this world seemed to throw themselves at him. That wouldn't help her case.

"He'll never know you're the one who told me," she added. "I'll make it seem like I got lucky finding it."

He seemed to think it over before, "If something goes wrong, it will probably be your execution. I'm not seeing how that won't benefit me more than you getting to flee and keep your life."

"I won't go down easy." She refused to die here, in some foreign world at the hands of some egotistical god. End of story.

"Forget it." Koya closed his eyes and propped his head back against the wall, settling in and putting an obvious end to the discussion.

Jade wanted to press him further, but knew when to back off. She just had to hope that she'd planted the seed correctly, that it was swirling through his mind and eventually would get the better of him. As much as she hated it, she needed his help. This world was too foreign for her to beat it on her own, and his feelings for the Emperor could tip things in her favor.

Or out of them. But she didn't want to bother contemplating that prospect.

Outside, the sky was turning gray, the spaces between the trees of the forest already pitch black. The sounds of villagers moving about had also quieted.

Koya's breathing evened out, indicating he'd fallen asleep despite his earlier reprimand. Clearly he didn't think she was much of a threat. Could be that's why he'd gotten them the one room in the first place, to let her know in no uncertain terms that he didn't view her as anything but the Emperor's new plaything.

That he wasn't scared of her and had no reason to be fearful for his life in her company.

Jade was tempted to get up and beat him with the stick just to make a point, but refrained. She wasn't an idiot, no matter how much her pride tried to urge her into being otherwise.

She was too close to the end of this for that anyway. One more day's ride, one more night, and they'd make it back to the palace.

Her eyes wandered to the flames.

For a long while, she merely stared, lost to the silence and stillness of the room.

Chapter 7:

Jade was on fire. A small furnace was surrounding her, engulfing her, and there was something in her mouth. Tongue and lips and teeth.

Was she making out with someone right now?

Consciousness surfaced, and Jade tried to tip her head to the side, to pull away from the intrusion but was met with resistance. A hand tightened in her hair, holding her still, tugging and causing her to cry out at the brief, sharp pain.

As soon as she did, the tongue stroking against the roof of her mouth delved deeper. The kiss was hungry, aggressive and raw.

Familiar, somehow…

In her sleep addled mind, Jade conjured the first image she could, picturing Key sprawled out on top of her in her bedroom back at her grandfather's mansion. Even in her current state, however, she knew logically that was impossible. Key didn't like her, and his kisses certainly wouldn't be familiar considering they'd never so much as held hands before.

And if it wasn't Key…

Jade's resistance grew stronger. Her heels kicked at the floor to free herself from beneath the heavy weight pinning her down, hands going to his sides in an attempt to shove him off.

All the while, whoever it was ignored her, rewarding each one of her struggles with another lash of his hot tongue or a deeper press of his lips. His hips settled between her spread thighs, body against her core in a way that had her sucking in a breath.

He swallowed that with as much greed as he did all the sounds of protest she made, groaning in turn.

She tried to twist her head free a second time, but his hold was unbreakable, and all she managed to do was smear her mouth against his harder. He seemed to take it as an invitation to travel further, and his lips drifted to curve of her jaw.

Self-hatred washed through her when her heartrate spiked. She didn't want it to, but she felt her body reacting, knew that if he touched her lower, she'd be wet and ready. Just from a few kisses *while she'd been asleep*.

She didn't even know who this was.

When he sucked on the sensitive spot there, she gasped, hips jerking off the floor imploringly.

Suddenly, he froze above her, hands and mouth stilling so quickly it took a minute for her mind to catch up to the fact she was no longer being kissed.

"Are you receptive to this body, little cat?"

Her eyes popped open, any lingering sleep blasted away by the familiar nickname. It was like being doused in ice water, and what she'd foolishly thought was a bad dream burst as reality came crashing back in.

Except…She expected to find the Emperor cradled between her thighs. Instead, Koya's face hovered mere inches above hers, cast in shadows, yet still unmistakably him.

The fire had gone out some time ago, so that not even an ember flickered to give light. The door had also been closed, blocking out the moon and the night sky. A small window set high up was the only source of light, and just barely. In the dark, the sounds of their breathing intensified, and without the fire, she was forced to admit that his body heat was helping chase away the chill she'd somehow managed to sleep through.

"Answer the question," he said tightly, and while the edge of displeasure confused her, she was too busy collecting her emotions to care much about his.

"Get off." She didn't bother trying to push him away, but did test out her legs to see how much movement she had, how restricted he was keeping her with his body draped over top her. "Move."

"Do you want it?" he asked, ignoring her. None too gently, he ground his hips down, rubbing the thick length of himself against her stomach. He was hot and heavy.

The hands still at his back curved, and even though the material of his shirt was between them, she pressed her nails against him pointedly.

"Get. Off."

"I'm trying to." Despite his crass words, his tone never wavered.

"What exactly do you have to be upset about?" she demanded. "You're the one taking advantage of me here."

"Are you saying you don't want this?"

"I've been saying that from the start," she snapped. Over his little display of power, she pulled her hand back and placed it instead at his throat, gripping hard enough she felt his intake of breath. Though she couldn't actually make out his expression in the darkness, she stared where she imagined his eyes were, hoping that his vision was somehow better than hers and he could see the rage in her own. "I'm not sure how you think doing this will solve your problem, but I can assure you, it won't. It's just going to make me want to kill you."

She kept the rest of that statement, "more than I already do", to herself.

"My problem?" He canted his head.

"When I told you to get over him," she said, "I didn't mean do it by getting on top of me. I'm not interested. *You're* not interested. Move."

"Does it feel like I'm not interested?" He rubbed against her a second time and her hands went to his hips to still him.

"You're thinking about the Emperor." Even if he wasn't, she had no interest in playing this game with him. She was also getting sick of his weird Jekyll and Hyde personality. By day, he was surly and rude. At night, he was flirty and dramatic. "What's wrong with you?"

"Is that projection?" he asked. "Were you thinking about the Emperor just now?"

Jade bit her tongue when he lowered his head back down, settling his face snuggly between her shoulder and the curve of her neck. From the tiny window, the clouds shifted, finally exposing the vibrant full moon. More light filtered into the room, not that it mattered. She wasn't sure she wanted to see this.

Talking to him wasn't doing her any good.

The stick he'd been using to stoke the fire had been discarded on the floor at the side of the diminished flames. She tried to gauge how far it was, and estimated it was probably just out of reach.

She needed something though. She couldn't just lay here and take whatever he had planned.

"I'm pleased," he mumbled against her neck, planting a soft kiss there that had her frowning all over again. "You should think of him often."

"That is completely different from what you told me earlier."

"It's good this body isn't suitable for you," he went on, as if she hadn't spoken. "I'm rather fond of it myself, and would have hated to have to cause it harm."

"What the fuck?"

She gripped his hips and tried to push him off one last time, hoping he'd at least take the hint.

Slowly, he pulled away, lifting onto his forearms so that there was finally some space between them, even though he kept himself securely above her. Before she could feel even an inkling of relief from that, however, he tilted his head, eyes catching the dim glow of moonlight.

Pink eyes.

Jade froze.

"Ah," he clucked his tongue down at her, the corner of his mouth twisting in a half-grin, "I forgot. I told you not to look."

She shoved herself out from beneath him and scuttled back until she came up against the wall. It only put a few feet's worth of distance between them, but that was better than the mere inches that'd been there before. Her heart was racing in her chest and her mind scrambled to make sense of what she was seeing.

This world hadn't made sense from the get-go, so at least it was easier for her to process.

"I was hoping to keep this a secret a little longer," Koya—no, not Koya, just his voice, and his mouth—said.

"You're the Emperor." It sounded crazy to her own ears, but Jade knew it was the truth even before he sat back on his haunches casually and nodded.

"I knew the eyes would give it away," he told her. "They always do. It's the one thing I can't change when I put on this little puppet show."

"Puppet..." What a crass way of putting it. "You possess him or something?"

"Were you confused, little cat?" He sat back, resting an arm over his upturned knee as he watched from the dark. The clouds outside moved, covering the moon and casting them back in a thick darkness.

Jade held her breath, straining to hear any telltale signs that he was taking advantage and moving closer.

She went over all of the things that she'd spoken about with Koya, trying to pick and choose which conversations were had with the real him and which had taken place with the Emperor in disguise.

"It only works at night, doesn't it?" That made the most sense. The first time a change had come over Koya, the two of them had entered the forest on their way off of the palace grounds. He'd gone from cold and aloof to handsy all at once. Then, in that field when she'd lost it and had started a fight... "He tried to warn me."

"I'll have to have a talk with him about that," the Emperor drawled, and his voice sounded like it came from the same location she'd last seen him in.

"Why?" she asked. "Why are you doing this?"

"Before you, this was the only way," he told her, and she recalled something similar being mentioned cryptically before. "Because he's my Minor, we're connected. That connection allows me to reach out with my power and take control, for lack of a better term. When my mind is connected to his body, I have access to his senses."

"You can smell and taste again." She pursed her lips. "Is it really that important to you? So much so you'd hurt someone that loyal?"

"Hurt him?" he clucked his tongue. "Hardly. Koya does this willingly. I might be the God of Command, but possession is no easy feat. If he wasn't willing, I'd burn through power just trying to get a foothold. It wouldn't be worth it in the end."

It hadn't seemed like Koya had wanted him taking over in the field, but what did Jade know.

"Do you do this every night?"

"No." He sighed. "Typically, I do this once a month. Usually I have to store enough power to counteract the curse—even in Koya's body, it lingers, trying to prevent me from using my senses. It's thanks to you that I've been able to do this so many times in a row. And even then...you're the only thing I can smell, little cat."

"Did you like food that much?" Koya had explained it to her, that it'd been the Emperor's only pastime, but Jade still struggled to grasp how this of all things was what Master Mist had chosen when he'd gotten the upper hand. "Why didn't he do something worse?"

"Worse?" his tone darkened, sending a chill down her spine before she could help it. "Clearly you've never experienced something like this before, or else you wouldn't be asking me such a foolish question. How do you torture someone who can live forever? What's worse in your mind? Should he have cut off my arm? A leg? Turn me into a beast? You're smarter than that. If your grandfather wanted to punish someone, he wouldn't just lash out the first chance he got, would he?"

Her grandfather would never act rashly. Everything he did, right down to what time he took his breakfast every morning, was carefully planned out.

"He'd find the persons weakness," she mumbled, thinking back to the lessons he'd given her in preparation for her to one day take over the syndicate.

Even though it typically changed hands through bloodline, times were different, and her grandfather had known it would be difficult for her. Others would fight for the position, protest against her—a female with little experience—taking control. He'd warned her that it wouldn't matter that she could take them all on in the ring and beat them to a pulp.

What happened in the shadows, whether or not she could survive a surprise attack, that's what counted.

And that's where control came into play.

"My grandfather's collected the secrets of all of those closest to him," she found herself saying, mostly to herself. "Collateral. To help keep them all in line." It was not a very good basis for a friendship, but then, was there anyone who really wanted to be friends with a crime boss?

People didn't hang around her grandfather because they wanted to. They did it because they needed to. For some personal gain, be it greed or desperation. Or, if they were like Key, because there was nowhere else for them to go.

"He'll exploit those weaknesses without a second's hesitation," the Emperor said appreciatively. "There's only one God of Command; others need something more than their voice to make the masses do as they please. Your grandfather knows this, and Mist knew it as well. He didn't just want to debilitate me—he went for the jugular."

"Because your sense of smell was that important to you?" Koya had told her the Emperor liked food, liked to cook…Jade had just taken that explanation because she'd been too focused on finding the vial and getting the hell out of here. But now… "No. There's got to be more to it than that. What aren't you telling me?"

He chuckled, and she startled when the sound came from her left instead of ahead of her. When had he moved? She hadn't heard so much as the fabric of his shirt rustle.

"Curious, little cat?" His fingers caressed the side of her face, ignoring her when she jolted from the sudden contact. When he gripped her chin and turned her head toward him, there was nothing but a blurry outline of his form in the dark. "Come to me. Bring the vial. And maybe, if you're very good, I'll tell you what you want to know."

She clenched her jaw. "The only thing I want is to go home."

He sighed. "Yes. That too."

Suddenly, the smell of burnt cinnamon tickled at her nose and she frowned. She'd smelled that scent before. Back in the cage after the fight with his men.

The Emperor leaned in, brushing his lips lightly against hers, momentarily distracting her from her thoughts. Briefly, she caught a whiff of salt and birch wood, which was odd, because Koya didn't smell anything like that, and even though the Emperor did shouldn't he smell like the body he was in?

"Sleep, little cat," the Emperor whispered, in that deep, rumbling tone that indicated he was using his power, his lips a mere breath away from hers. "Sleep, and then come to me. Come home."

Unable to resist the given command, Jade slipped away.

Chapter 8:

Jade didn't wake up again until the next day. She was back on the horse, Koya's arms on either side to keep her steady while he steered them on the path at an even pace. The sun was bright in the sky above and the breeze brought with it a soft hint of walnuts and freshly turned earth.

"I'm getting really sick of that," she said, voice loud and clear, not bothering to hide her irritation from the man at her back. "He can't just go around forcing people to sleep—"

"What did you and the Emperor talk about?" Koya cut her off, and there was an edge to his tone that was unusual enough to have her tipping her head back to try and get a look at his face.

His expression was pinched, his coloring a bit off.

"Why are you nervous?" She felt her body tense in preparation.

For a moment, it didn't appear as though he was going to answer her, but then he heaved a sigh and leaned in ever so slightly. "We're being followed."

"Since when?" She was glad she'd woken up.

"A half hour or so. They came from the last village we passed. There's a chance they're simply heading to the Everyday Sanctuary, but I won't know for sure until we pass that road up head."

"How likely is this chance?"

"Fifty-fifty." He paused again before adding, "You aren't thinking this could be a daring rescue, are you? You can't be that foolish."

"Nope," she agreed, too concerned about their possible tail to bother being offended, "not that foolish. Even if I do want to get away from you and your insane Emperor, Amelia is with him. I wouldn't leave her behind."

"Even if it could mean your one chance at escape?"

"Yes." There was no question about it. She hadn't gone through all of this to protect her friend only to give up at the final hour.

No matter how terrifying the god who awaited her was.

"You're lucky then," Koya's hands tightened on the reigns as the sounds of hooves finally began to echo at their backs, "because I can assure you, there's no way whoever that is plans on aiding you."

"What's the Everyday Sanctuary? What makes you think that's where he's going?"

"That's where most that travel this road end up. The sanctuary is home to Restless, the God of Intention. The two of you have met before; he didn't help you then. He won't help you now. Although, it's most likely the person behind us is just an average citizen hoping for the aid of a god or merely going for prayer."

Jade thought back on all of the faces she'd met since arriving here. There were only two others, aside from Koya and the Emperor, that she could recall looking powerful. Both of those men had been at the hot springs the day of her unfortunate arrival.

"The one with the scar?" she took a jab in the dark. Restless was a name that suited him.

"That's the one," Koya confirmed. "Word of advice, avoid him."

"He can't be any worse than your Emperor."

"He stays in check because of my Emperor, and no other reason but. He hates humans, and Minors even more so."

"So, I'm guessing that means he doesn't have any of his own."

Koya grunted. "And risk having his power used against him? No."

"Can a Minor betray their god?"

"Of course."

This time it was her turn to grunt. "Turns out we're still human after all." Apparently, no amount of magic could change that. "Tell me about Restless' power."

"He can read intention. Figure out what it is someone truly desires, what their hopes and dreams are. How far they're willing to go to achieve them."

She hummed in understanding. "That's why he has trust issues. He knows how twisted people are inside."

"Sounds like you know a thing or two about that as well."

"My grandfather made sure of it." She didn't want to talk about this anymore. Especially since there wasn't really a point. "This is the longest cordial conversation you and I have ever had."

"Don't get used to it."

"Wasn't planning—" His body shoved forward, forcing her hard against the front of the horse. The pommel jammed hard into her ribs, but she didn't have much time to care because in the next instant, he was slipping from the saddle and taking her with him.

The two of them hit the ground, just barely avoiding the horses hooves as the creature picked up pace and raced away from them. Everything hurt as Jade struggled to sit up, eyes going wide when she spotted the reason for their fall.

An arrow was sticking straight through Koya's upper chest, on the right. The bloodied metal tip had pierced the space just below his clavicle, and that wasn't the only spot he was bleeding. He'd hit his head when they'd fallen, knocking himself out.

Jade swore and looked up, catching sight of the rider who'd up until now had been tailing them quietly.

The person sat atop a large white horse, their body wrapped in black, leaving only a strip bare over his eyes so he could see. He had a bow in hand, another arrow already notched and at the ready.

"I hate this fucking world." They were on a wide road, with dense trees on either side, so she debated whether or not she'd have enough time—and the upper body strength—to pull Koya into them before whoever the asshole hunting them let that second arrow loose.

Deciding to give it a try, Jade scrambled to hook her hands under his arms. If anything, she could use the damn guy as a shield. Bastard had helped hold her hostage, so it wasn't like she owed him anything, she reminded herself as she began the painstakingly difficult task of moving him. He must weigh a ton.

An arrow whizzed by her head, missing her face by a mere inch or so, and only because she'd kept her eyes on their attacker, giving herself enough time to duck out of the way.

Cursing, Jade's struggled increased, and she dragged Koya's body through the dirt. Their attacker was fast approaching, and she still didn't have a plan for how to handle him once he got there.

Fortunately, she made it, dropped the dead weight between two trees with thick brush that instantly swallowed him up. Of course, if she didn't handle the guy after them, he'd obviously know where she'd put Koya and be able to kill him too but...Whatever. One thing at a time.

Shoving her hand into the greenery, she felt around his pant leg until her fingers brushed against cool metal. Good thing she'd paid attention to where he always kept his dagger.

Jade slipped the blade free and spun just in time to avoid another arrow to the face. She forward rolled back into the road, making it as close to the other side as possible. With any luck, if she kept him away from Koya, the blue haired a-hole might wake up and be able to help her.

The rider, less than twenty feet away now, dropped down from his horse without bothering to pull the creature to a stop. As soon as he'd dismounted, he readied another arrow.

She had experience with guns which fired bullets at a much more rapid pace than an arrow. Still, this was clearly no ammeter shooter, and it was just as deadly a weapon.

Adjusting the hilt of the short blade in her hand, Jade rolled out of the way of another arrow and then lifted her hand.

The second she snapped her fingers, power poured out of her like the release of a floodgate. She felt it zip through her veins, sparking to life so that the air around her popped and crackled.

The rain came instantly, heavy sheets pounding down from the sky so thick it made seeing through it impossible.

She heard the attacker swear, a deep guttural sound and word she didn't recognize but was obviously an expletive. Not wanting to give him any more time, she planted her feet against the solid ground and pushed off, darting through the rain straight for him.

The tip of the blade swished forward, slicing through water smoothly before finding its mark. She'd managed to catch him off guard, felt the knife cut deep into his side, and even had enough time shift around behind him.

He tried to move away, but between the sounds of the rain blocking his hearing and the rain forcing his eyes closed, he miscalculated. Instead of stepping forward, he retreated back, incorrectly assuming she was still at his front.

Jade stabbed the blade above his lower back, feeling a momentary resistance before a rush of warmth spilled out over her hand. She twisted and then helped him when he tried to move away, shoving him forward and using his own momentum against him.

He hit the ground on his knees, hard enough she heard the impact.

With another snap of her fingers, the storm stopped as swiftly as it'd begun. She gave him a wide berth, despite the fatal injuries she'd delivered, circling around to his front.

He was drenched, the thin material of his black robes sticking to him, giving him more of a form than he'd had previously yet still withholding any truly telling details. She would need to remove the mask first, but wouldn't risk getting too close just yet.

Besides, she'd need Koya awake for there to be any chance of identifying their attacker.

That asshole better not have bleed to death already. She also needed him to get back to Amelia. They'd gone a different route than the one they'd used when leaving the palace, so she had no idea where they were or where to go from here on her own.

"I swear you better not have just cost my best friend her life," Jade stated, mostly under her breath, though the words were technically directed at the attacker still heaving on the ground.

He had one hand pressed against the wound at his side—the one he could reach—and the other was clawing at the earth, mud squishing between his fingers. He was at least twice the size of Jade, and his eyes were filled with hatred when he finally glanced up at her.

They were copper, like pennies set into his skull, with thick black eye brows arched over them.

"You shot at me," she reminded, coming to a stop in front of him. "Pretty sure if anyone has the right to be pissed off here, it's not you."

He said something to her, but the language was completely foreign to her ears.

"Sorry," she shrugged, "I'm not from around here."

"I would have taken you alive, fool," he ground out, this time in smooth English.

"Why didn't you say sooner?" She tapped the flat part of the knife against her thigh, uncaring about the blood stains left behind.

He noticed.

She wanted him to.

"You didn't give me the chance," he told her.

She snorted. "Again, you shot at me." She pointed with the tip of the blade toward the area she'd stashed Koya. "You shot my ride."

"Your captor," he corrected with a sneer.

"We're all captives of something," she said. "At least mine has a face this time. He better still, otherwise you're going to be seriously sorry."

"I hope he's dead."

"I need him," she crouched down so that they were eye level, still carefully keeping six or so feet between them, "which means no, you really don't."

"I'm going to die anyway."

"That's true. Right now you're bleeding out. I give you another ten minutes, if you're lucky. A lot can happen in ten minutes. If you're given the proper care you could even make it. Otherwise...I'm sure I don't need to tell you there are a lot of things worse than death." She pictured her grandfather's face whenever he threatened someone, the way his shoulders would go slightly lax, but obviously coiled. How his eyes would be hard as ice, yet his mouth would loosen and curve at the edges.

People didn't like oxymoron's. It confused them. Unnerved them.

Intimidation was an art form. To utilize it to its full potential meant mastering that delicate balance between friendly and unfriendly, caring yet uncaring. The person needed to feel like what they said and did didn't really matter. They had to feel like this was all a pastime, a game. If they answered correctly, maybe the person interrogating them would be merciful—because they didn't really care one way or the other. Torture or not. Kill or not.

Jade felt this persona settle over her like a well-worn cloak. Her grandfather had trained her in this the same way he'd trained her in hand to hand combat. The same way he'd taught her everything else that she'd need to know if she were to someday become the kingpin of one of the world's top criminal organizations. Since leaving that life behind, she'd tried hard to keep herself in check, to not use these types of tactics, or anything else he'd taught her that wasn't absolutely necessary.

Mostly, she hadn't wanted to be that bitch in college who threw her weight around and therefore had no real friends.

But it'd been a year since she'd graduated, and this wasn't a young adult heaving on the ground across from her. His eyes alone were enough to tell he was at least in his mid-thirties.

Those eyes also made it obvious the very second he noticed the change in her. A flash of fear was apparent before he could get a handle on it.

"What?" she teased. "Afraid of a little girl?"

"You aren't a girl," he said, "you're a Minor."

"Sounds like you mean monster."

"It's one in the same."

"And yet, you were going to take me alive, remember?" She hid her own unease well, focusing instead on fostering his. To do so, she couldn't let anything affect her. "Why bother, if you think so little of me?"

"What I think doesn't matter," he snapped.

She had him.

"Whose thoughts do then? I assume someone sent you here for a reason. What could it be?" Knowing what little she did about this world, there were only two suspects that came to mind. Two other gods had been present when she'd come through the portal. But that didn't mean anything. She was most likely wrong in her assumptions and needed him to clarify before she could even risk voicing such things.

The Emperor had also plastered posters of her face all over his town. It was likely others had seen her and were aware of her existence as well. She kept being told about how powerful he is, but Jade better than most understood the danger that came with having power.

Hell, wasn't the whole reason she was considered useful now due to the fact the Emperor had gone to war with another god?

"How can I help screw over the Emperor?" she asked, when her first question went unanswered for too long. Maybe she could lead this conversation in the correct direction if she gave a little leeway. Besides, it wasn't like she gave a shit about Dust either. If not for the fact she needed Koya's help, she wouldn't care about his currently bleeding body. "Time is ticking. There's still a chance to convince me and have me help save you."

"My wound is deep," he disagreed. "The likelihood of survival, even if you patch me up now, is slim."

"That's still better odds than zero."

He watched her for a moment, breathing heavy, blood pooling out around him to seep into the already soaked dirt. "His curse can't be lifted. It would be bad for us all."

"The Emperor's?" She cocked her head. "What's the big deal? So what if he can't smell?"

"You know nothing, Minor."

"Yeah, I get that. So fill me in." She'd known there was more to this whole curse thing, and this might be her only chance to get answers. "He doesn't just want his smell back because he likes food, am I right?"

He man snorted. "Food?"

"He said he was a cook."

"The Emperor doesn't cook," he practically snarled. "He has cooks. Servants do everything for him, and if his curse is broken, we will all be his servants once more. The world has been a better place with the God of Command in check."

"You're talking about his power; that thing he can do with his voice." With a few words, he'd made her fall asleep. "What does his sense of smell have to do with that?"

"His power needs strengthening," the man said. "His voice only reaches so far. Without the ability to create dust, he is severely weakened."

"Dust?" Was that why he'd been named that? What the hell was this guy saying?

"Yes, it comes from him, only he can create it, but it's delicate, difficult to manage. He needs to be able to smell it in order to ground himself and produce the correct effects."

"I'm not sure I'm following." He made dust and needed to smell it to do so?

The man was clearly frustrated with her. "You've been to his palace. Did you see candles?"

"Yeah." Considering they didn't have electricity here however, that hardly seemed like anything of note. "So?"

"Did he use one on you?"

"A candle? How does someone use a candle on someone else?" No sooner had she said, though, did she recall that time she'd woken in the room after he'd bitten her. He'd had a candle in his hand, had been staring at it almost lovingly.

She could smell it...

And she'd been turned on.

"What the actual fuck." Her hand tightened around the handle of the knife, and she momentarily lost her composure.

"He did," the man chuckled at her. "His voice has the power to make you do things. His dust can make you feel things. Emotion, that's the most dangerous thing of all, just ask the God of Feeling."

As pissed off—and frankly, violated—as she was, that last part captured her attention and held.

"God of Feeling?" She eyed him. "Bet he's not too keen on the idea of another god messing with something he should have control over, huh?"

The man's expression darkened.

"Got ya." She grinned. Whoever this God of Feeling was, clearly he was this man's benefactor, but... "What could he want with me, your god?"

"You're the only living link left to Master Mist," the man said, though it was clearly a struggle now, either because he didn't want to divulge his secrets, or because his blood was forming a puddle around him. "The only thing that could break the curse is you and that vile in your pocket."

"Why not just kill me and destroy the vile?" Not that she was giving him any ideas or anything. "Makes more sense than a kidnap attempt. Unless your god needs leverage for something. Another secret, perhaps?"

"Mind your business," he growled. "You should be more concerned about yourself. You're heading straight for your end. The second the Emperor has that vile *and* you he's going to—"

The man never got to finish his sentence.

A dagger identical to the one still clutched in Jade's hand sailed through the air and stuck straight through his neck.

The man gurgled and dropped to his side, brown eyes going dull in a matter of seconds.

Jade gave a sigh of annoyance and stood, angling her head toward the direction of the throw.

Koya was sitting up in the brush.

"Was kind of in the middle of a conversation here," Jade said before discarding the knife she held and clicking her tongue. "I should have known you'd have more than one weapon on you."

Without a word Koya glared and struggled to his feet.

Jade didn't offer any help.

Chapter 9:

Koya didn't say much the rest of the trip, barely even mumbling a thank you when she helped him pull the arrow free and somehow managed to get their attackers horse to come to her. They were riding the white creature now, Koya's own horse long gone, with the palace in sight.

They were close, and with each step nearer, Jade felt her insides twist just a bit more.

What had that guy been about to tell her? Had Koya woken up and killed him immediately, or had he been trying to keep her from hearing what the man had to say? Asking point blank would get her nowhere, only rouse his suspicion, so she kept it to herself.

She couldn't even be pleased that she finally had information about the Emperor. What good did knowing how much more terrifying he could be do her? There was no way to stop him that she could see, and if anything, the realization of what he'd been up to in that room with that candle made her livid.

Angry people made mistakes.

Amelia couldn't afford for her to do that.

Jade's hands tightened into fists in her lap.

The wooden gates creaked open, and with a start, she realized she'd zoned out the last mile and now they were here.

That sick feeling grew even more.

She should be hopeful; she got the vile which meant she'd upheld her part of the deal. The Emperor was either going to uphold his, and let her and Amelia go home, or he was going to kill them. Either way, there wasn't much she could personally do about it, which meant dreading the moment she'd see him again was pointless.

And yet…She couldn't will the sensation away. Something wasn't right. Those words spoken by the now dead attacker wouldn't leave her be. She was convinced he was about to tell her the one thing she needed desperately to know.

That, or the lack of sleep and proper meals was finally getting to her and she was being paranoid.

Koya led the horse back to the stables where three servants waited. They tipped their heads to him slightly at his approach, but it was nothing like the deep bow they would have given the Emperor.

Two of them rushed forward to help him when he stumbled off the horse, catching him and righting him despite how he tried to push them away.

Jade rolled her eyes and dropped down on her own, making to move around the creature before the final servant lifted an arm to stop her. She quirked a brow at him, silently waiting for an explanation.

"The Emperor has ordered your presence immediately upon your arrival," the servant explained, and when Koya went to step to them, turned to shake his head curtly at him. "Not you. Only the girl."

"You should probably go get that treated." Jade motioned to Koya's injury, which they'd bandaged with his shirt earlier.

"Don't act like you care," he replied.

There wasn't time for a witty retort; the servant had already turned and started down the path, obviously assuming Jade would follow.

What choice did she have, really? Disobeying meant putting Amelia in danger.

The servant led her across the palace grounds, to an area she hadn't been before. Although, considering she'd been confined to the same two rooms for the entirety of her stay previously, that made sense.

She did her best to search around for any sign of the hot springs as they walked, but the Emperor had probably ordered this particular path for a reason. It most likely came nowhere near his bathing spot—The sound of trickling water had Jade tripping. She caught herself before she actually fell, but even if she had, it wouldn't have mattered. She didn't care about embarrassing herself, not when the unmistakable smell of salt and rose—the same one she'd caught whiff of when they'd come through the portal—was saturating the air.

Holy shit. Was he really going to keep his word? Was the servant really leading her to the hot spring?

It felt almost too good to be true, and Jade's defenses rose even as she fell back into step behind her guide. The stone path curved to the left ahead, and as soon as they took that turn, the familiar sight of the bath house came into view along with the entrance to the hot spring.

There were guards peppered around, all off to the side with a hand on the hilt of their sheathed swords. None of them so much as glanced at her as she passed, remaining stiff and still to the point it was almost as if they weren't breathing. Still, she counted the ones she could see, mapping out where they stood—even though she doubted the Emperor would allow her to as easily escape as she had the first time.

She wouldn't have to escape though, not if he planned on upholding his end of the bargain.

The vial felt heavy in her front pocket and she barely resisted the urge to touch it. The ground beneath them sloped and then they were near the embankment where she'd fought off the guards that first time.

Pulling her gaze away from the steaming body of water, she turned and instantly spotted the Emperor standing on the dock.

Amelia was only a few feet behind him.

Jade pushed past the servant who had come to a stop at the foot of the steps of the deck. The man let out a startled yelp, but she hardly noticed, too focused on getting to her friend and ensuring she was all right. Her feet pounded across the wooden boards of the deck, and then down to the end of the dock.

The Emperor let her pass him, simply watching as she snatched Amelia's hands in hers.

There were two guards up here as well, but Jade paid them no mind, instead noting the healing cuts and the angry looking bruises that still peppered over her friend's fair skin.

"Are you okay?" Jade asked, voice low even though she knew there was no keeping the words from being heard by the man at her back. "Did anything else happen while I was gone?"

"No." Amelia gripped her hands tightly and shook her head, sending tendrils of blonde hair—recently washed hair—flowing around her heart shaped face. "Nothing happened."

"I took great of her," the Emperor interrupted. "You should be pleased, little cat."

"Seeing as how you possessed a dude to keep an eye on me, not torturing my friend any more than you already had is the least you can do." She kept one hand in Amelia's but let the other go so she could angle her body in his direction.

They were standing at the center of the dock, the edge only a couple feet away. Briefly, she wondered if she'd be able to jump before he could stop them. She'd have to bleed first, and though there was still that tiny dagger she'd taken from Master Mist's place, she didn't see how she was going to pull off unsheathing it and cutting herself before he could stop her.

No, she had to play by his rules. As much as she hated that fact.

"He did what now?" Amelia asked, tucking herself more closely against Jade's back.

"I've heard you were attacked on the road," the Emperor said, ignoring her comment all together. His eyes scanned her from head to toe before settling on her face once more. "You appear unharmed."

She couldn't tell how he felt about that, whether or not he was relieved or indifferent.

Yeah. Intimidation tactics sucked.

"Koya wasn't so lucky." She watched for any signs that he cared at least about him, but he didn't so much as bat an eyelash. "Aren't you curious if he's okay?"

"Not really."

She blinked at him, a bit caught off guard by the honesty. "He's loyal."

The Emperor shrugged. "He serves his purpose. But there's one less thing for him to do, now that you're here. Where is the vial?"

Jade's fingers twitched at her side and her hesitation didn't go unnoticed.

"You've come all this way, little cat. Don't disappoint me now. Your friend wants to go home, shouldn't you let her?" His gaze hardened. "Or have you truly developed a fondness for my right hand man during your short time away?"

She was smart enough to openly scoff at that concept. "Not if he paid me."

"I'll take that as a definitive no," this time, it was obvious he was pleased by the news. He held out his hand. "The vial then. You're safe in these walls, but the fact you were attacked means word has already gotten out about what I plan. I can't risk things going sour, not now that I'm so close."

"Why would another god try and stop you from breaking your curse?" Jade asked. On the way here, she'd already decided to pretend like her conversation with their attacker had never happened. If Koya hadn't overheard any of it, that was her best option. There'd be no reason for the Emperor to try and enter their world and come after them if he thought she knew nothing about him. Her admitting she'd gotten some explanation about his power, his real power, would only cause more trouble to her.

Sure, she'd like to get revenge for the fact he'd most likely used that candle on her, but that wasn't what was most important. Getting home, that was the end goal.

But she had to make her ignorance believable.

"What did the man on the road tell you?" the Emperor stiffened slightly.

"Just that he worked for some god," she made sure her voice was nonchalant, yet laced with a bit of curiosity. "The God of Feeling, I believe. Who is he? Did you piss him off like you pissed of Master Mist?"

"It's unimportant." His curled his fingers slightly. "The vial, little cat."

Jade pulled the small glass container from her pocket, but didn't hand it over right away. "You're going to send us home?"

The Emperor slipped a small blade from his own pocket, holding it up when she took a defensive stance. "Take it. It's for you. Cut yourself and bleed into the spring."

Jade had to let Amelia go entirely and step away in order to reach for the knife, sure to keep the vial in her other hand. He made no move to take it, however, simply allowed her to pluck the tiny knife from his fingers and retreat again.

"Leave the vial on the ground," he ordered the second there was space between them. "Then you can proceed."

"What? You think I'll take it with me?" She made a big show of lowering and clicking the bottom of the glass against one of the wooden planks. "And have you chase after us? No thank you."

The Emperor remained where he stood, as if the vial wasn't now right there for the taking.

He was really going to keep his word, wasn't he. Jade couldn't believe it, but all signs were pointing to yes.

Before he could change his mind, she dragged the knife across her palm, slicing deeply enough blood welled instantly. She turned and extended her hand over the edge of the dock, making a fist and squeezing. Five heavy red drops plopped into the water below and for a second nothing happened.

Work, damn it.

Almost as soon as she'd had the thought, the water sparked. The area around them changed, going from clear to translucent before the scene of an upside down alley could be made out clearly. It was the same one they'd vanished from a week ago, and they had a clear view of blue sky and stretching brick walls on either side.

"Holy shit," Amelia stepped forward, leaning over to stare down. "It actually worked."

"All you have to do is jump through," the Emperor said.

"Together," Amelia took Jade's hand, linking their fingers. She obviously had the same thought, about this maybe being too good to be true. "Quickly."

Jade didn't have to be told twice. She made to move, just one step off and they'd be gone from this place for good. One step.

She and Amelia moved in sync, feet momentarily hovering over the edge.

"Stop, Jade," the Emperor's voice came suddenly, dark and deep.

Commanding.

No.

Her body locked into place against her will.

No. No. No.

Amelia, free from the Emperor's power, toppled forward, unable to stop herself the way Jade had. She dropped, hand still latched onto Jade's.

It forced Jade to her knees, but even then she couldn't move so much as an inch forward or back.

Amelia dangled, most of her body now in the portal, but she clung to Jade's hand, grabbing her wrist with her other. "Jade!"

"Let go," the Emperor suggested, glancing at Amelia. He didn't order her, didn't use his power. "You don't want to be half in and half out like that when the portal closes. It would be a messy sight, I assure you, and I'd rather not have my favorite hot spring completely ruined."

A rush of fear skated down Jade's spine at that, and she took in her friend, and how only her upper body was above water level, outside of the portal.

"We had a deal!" Jade turned on the Emperor.

"And I'm holding it," he said.

"I'm not leaving without you!" Amelia put all of her weight behind trying to pull Jade down, but Jade's body merely buckled into place, resisting.

Suddenly, the view of the alley began to grow smaller, the edges closing in.

"Let go!" Jade tried harder now to free herself, watching in horror as the portal started to close with her friend still halfway inside of it. Amelia wasn't paying attention though, hadn't yet noticed the danger. Her head shot to the Emperor. "Make her go, please! I don't want to see—" she couldn't even say it, it was that horrifying a notion.

He'd implied she'd be sliced in half.

Jade believed him.

"Make her go!" she practically screamed.

He grinned at her, the bastard. Fully pleased by her panic. Almost getting off on it even. He locked gazes with Amelia, and then in that same riveting tone ordered, "Release her."

Amelia followed the command.

"Jade!" she screamed as she fell, just in time, with the portal snapping shut and vanishing less than a heartbeat later.

Jade stared down at the spot, seeing nothing now but her own wide eyed reflection staring back.

"What just happened?" she hadn't meant to say it aloud, but the words whisked past her lips, breathy and disbelieving. This wasn't making sense. Why would he… Slowly, she forced herself to sit up, to turn to him. "Why?"

"I'm keeping my end of the deal," he told her.

"You said you would let us both go home." She wished she could scream it, but it was like all of her energy had been zapped. She really shouldn't have believed him, even at the end there. Especially at the end there. Now she felt blindsided and hollow which was idiotic because *of course* he couldn't be trusted.

"And so I have." He closed the space between them, lowering down to a crouch in front of her. "I just sent your friend to her home, safe and sound, as promised. As for you…" He held her gaze as he reached out, not needing to look himself to find the vial and pluck it from the ground. He pulled the stopper off and then took the discarded knife, pricking the tip of his finger. He added a single drop of his blood to the contents of the vial.

Jade stared at it when he held it out to her, confused.

"Drink," he said, his power thrumming through his tone, even stronger than before. "Drink, Jade."

Her hand lifted of its own accord, her breath catching she took the tiny bottle and brought it to her lips.

"Wait, don't—" She wasn't sure who she was talking to, him or herself, but either way, the words fell on deaf ears. She pressed the glass to her mouth and tipped.

The liquid was warm and bitter, possibly the bitterest thing she'd ever tasted in fact and she gagged a little as it slid across her tongue. She swallowed it and dropped the empty vial to the dock, shock at what she'd just done causing her to freeze in disbelief.

The Emperor eased closer, pulling her in so that her head was resting beneath the curve of his chin. He hummed, the sound filled with approval and pleasure, and skated his fingers gently through her hair.

For once, Jade didn't even care that he was touching her. All she cared about was what had just happened. Why would he make her do that?

Then the Emperor's hot mouth was lowered to the curve of her ear, the warmth of him flickering against her suddenly chilled skin.

In fact, it was freezing. Why hadn't she noticed before just how cold it was out here?

She found herself nuzzling closer to him, just to gain some of his heat and chase the ice away.

If she were in her right mind, she would have noticed how this seemed to please him more. If she were in her right mind, she'd pull away and shove him into the hot spring so she could run.

But she wasn't in her right mind, and she was both very aware and unaware of that fact all at once.

The Emperor's arms tightened around her, cradling her closer. "Welcome home, Jade."

No. This wasn't her home. He couldn't possibly mean…

Before she could finish that thought, her body was consumed by an internal ice storm so intense she actually gasped. The pain followed quickly, like shards were tearing at her insides, ripping her apart.

Jade cried out, only partially aware when she started to cling to the Emperor, when her body began to jerk and twist completely out of her control.

It was seemingly never ending, the cold and the pain, the mixture sweeping everything away from her so that all that was left was the agony she was in and how desperately she wanted it to end.

Through it all, she thought she heard his voice calling to her, but it was as if from a million miles away, and all she caught were single words here and there, fractions of full sentences that were probably important, though she couldn't even recall why.

Promise.

Kept.

Welcome.

Home.

Jade screamed until her voice went hoarse.

And then she screamed some more.

III.

Command

Chapter 1:

It was hard to hang onto consciousness. It didn't help that no matter if she was awake or not, Jade felt floaty all over, like her soul had left her body and the only thing keeping her tethered to earth were the thick leather straps chaining her to the bed.

They were at her wrists and her ankles, she felt the pull of them whenever she tried to move—which wasn't often, and usually just because she was either freezing and wanted to pull up the blanket or her skin was on fire and she wanted to get rid of it.

Maybe she didn't even have a blanket.

She couldn't be sure.

Sometimes, when she managed to pull herself out of the darkness, *he'd* be there. Pink eyes hovering close, always close, watching her. If he touched her she'd moan, unsure if it was in pleasure or discomfort, only aware of the way her skin prickled beneath the pads of his fingers.

Time didn't exist. Jade was lost to a void of sensation that both battered her body and stroked the flames lying dormant within. As soon as she pinpointed a thought or a feeling it abandoned her, leaving her crying out in the nothingness.

She couldn't even recall how she'd gotten here, what her name was. Whether or not she'd ever been anywhere else or if this was all she'd ever known. Just pain and heat and cold and the occasional spark of pleasure.

And an ever-watching pink gaze.

* * *

"She's adjusting nicely," the Emperor's voice drawled in the darkness, and Jade shifted, groaning at the way her body ached.

A hand stroked against the curve of her jaw, another down the length of her arm. She was propped up against something solid and warm, the smell of roasting chestnuts and cinnamon cloying at her senses.

"It's been over a week, Emperor," Koya stated, and he didn't sound nearly as pleased as his leader.

Jade tried to pry her eyes open to see them, but it was too much effort and she quickly gave up, tuning in to their conversation instead. She felt out of sorts, but not nearly as discombobulated as she had been feeling. When she shifted, the bed creaked, and the arms around her settled more firmly on her, as if afraid she was going to try and sit up or move away.

She would have laughed at that notion if she'd had the energy. As it were, she'd barely even managed that much movement.

"Awake again, little cat?" the Emperor asked, his face close enough that she felt his breath fanning across her cheek. "Don't fret. I've got you."

Yeah, that was the problem.

At least Amelia had gotten out.

Thinking about her best friend and how she'd managed to make it through the portal leading back to their world had a tear slipping past Jade's defenses. She wasn't sure if it was out of relief for Amelia, or hopelessness for herself. She'd been a fool for trusting the Dust Emperor, even for a second. All of the signs had been there that he'd needed more from her than simply the vial of Master Mists' power.

He'd tricked her into going to collect it, dangling the hope of release in front of her like a carrot and she'd fallen for it.

The Emperor collected the drop of water as it rolled down her face, and though she couldn't see, she got the distinct impression he brought the teardrop to his mouth. A second later, a sigh escaped him, his chest rumbling beneath her in satisfaction she didn't quite understand.

Maybe the bastard just liked making people cry. That was seriously likely. She'd already decided he was a psychopath. It was clear in the way he treated the people around him, even the ones who were loyal like Koya.

If he wasn't so annoying and rude, Jade might even feel bad for Koya. His one-sided love didn't appear as though it was ever going to become anything more for him, and she understood that feeling, how gut-wrenching it was.

How badly the person feeling it wanted to cast it aside, to no avail.

Key had probably been sent after Jason reported how she and Amelia vanished through a puddle in the middle of a dirty alley. She wondered if he'd been there when Amelia had finally come back through. Wondered if he'd interrogated her and if he'd at least attempted to be kind while doing so.

Key wasn't a bad person. Jade had seen him beat people close to an inch of death, had seen him murder, in fact, but he wasn't evil. Not like her grandfather.

Not like the Emperor.

"Can you access her magic that way now?" Koya asked, piquing Jade's attention so that she tuned back into them once more.

"Yes," the Emperor replied, pleased. "The contents of the vial unlocked whatever had been blocking her magic. She's potent now, even a single tear has my body thrumming. I can smell you, Koya, smell what you ate recently. Were you out in the gardens earlier?"

"Just before you summoned me, Emperor," Koya confirmed, sounding awed. "That's amazing. But..."

Silence answered his hesitation, and Jade imagined the Emperor giving Koya a questioning look.

"Forgive me," Koya cleared his throat, "but why is she still alive?"

"Why?"

"Couldn't you drain her and be done with it? You've waited so long to regain your power, and you said her blood was the key to breaking the curse."

"It is," he confirmed, but before Jade could panic, added, "but it isn't the only way."

"Emperor?"

"Any bodily fluid will do," he explained, and Jade somehow managed to scrunch her nose in disgust at that wording. He noticed, of course, chuckling down at her. "Oh, not a fan of that, little cat?" He leaned in and pressed his lips to the corner of her eye, the touch soft and promising. "You will be."

"I don't understand," Koya confessed, and it was impossible not to note the edge of hurt in his tone.

There was no way the Emperor didn't know exactly what he was doing to his second in command. No way for anyone to misunderstand. He knew, he just didn't want to bother even pretending to care.

"You don't have to understand," the Emperor said tightly. "Your only purpose is to serve. Unless that no longer appeals to you?"

"Of course not, Emperor. Forgive me."

"How many times do you expect me to? That's twice now you've had to ask forgiveness in this conversation alone. Don't push your luck, Koya."

"I'm sorry, Emperor."

He sighed, clearly annoyed, but ended up explaining, "My power has been dormant for so long, it'll take time to coax it out and break through the curse. I've tied Jade to me, so there's no fear of escape, which means there's no reason for you to want to rush things. I'll take my time with this, with her, and you will cease your complaining."

"You suck," the words slipped past Jade's lips before she could help them, crackly and weak. She'd meant to only think them, hadn't thought she was capable of speech.

Apparently, neither had the Emperor, for he stilled at the sound. "Leave us."

Koya's retreating footsteps and the door opening and shutting echoed through the room before silence settled over them.

The Emperor pressed the pad of his thumb against the closed lips lightly. "How do you feel, little cat?"

"Awful." There was no point in denying it. He had to know already anyway. She bet she looked even worse than she felt, in fact.

"Should I make you feel better?" There was a hint of something she couldn't place in his suggestion, something that had her shivering and her body going on the alert all at once.

"No." Whatever he intended, it couldn't be good.

"Are you certain?" He pulled away, easing her back down so that she was lying on the bed.

Jade finally managed to crack her eyes open, catching the blurry sight of his large form looming over her as he resituated himself. She blinked a couple of times, trying to get her vision to focus, and he waited patiently.

That only made her more nervous.

He looked better than ever, she noted as soon as he came into clear view. His skin was golden in the nearby candlelight, and his dark hair was silky, short strands falling over his eyes. He cocked his head at her while she inspected him, settling himself more securely over her so that his hips were resting between her legs and his arms are propped up at either side of her face, blocking the rest of the room out so that all she could focus on was him and him alone.

"You're doing so well," he told her, voice quieter, intimate now that it was just the two of them. "Better than I'd hoped, even. You'll make a full recovery soon, and then the real fun can begin. Until then—" he ground his hips down, rubbing the thick length of himself against her core, grinning when she gasped, "—there are other ways to pass the time."

"You need help," she said.

"That's true, and you're giving it to me."

"I hate you."

"Hate is a strong word," he told her.

"You haven't given me any reason *not* to hate you, or are you forgetting about how you had my friend and I tortured upon our arrival here? Or how we were hunted through the streets? Or how you tricked me into getting that vial for you just so you could use it on me?"

Not to mention the touches, like the ones he was giving her now, lazily circling his hips so that she couldn't ignore the fact that he was hard even if she wanted to. Ignoring that her body was responding was even more difficult, and that's what had her anger growing.

He was playing her. Like he had been from the start. And just like then, she was powerless to do anything to stop him.

"It's a pity you haven't figured it out on your own," he said, continuing when she frowned. "I did us both a favor, little cat. You came to be here because you were running from something in your world." He smirked, just an upward tip of the corner of his mouth, but there was so much intensity there it took her breath away. "Thanks to what I've done, the only thing you'll have to run from is me. Your grandfather? This Emerald syndicate? You need not fear them any longer."

Yeah, because they weren't trapped here with her. She wanted to yell but refrained. All it would do was cost her energy.

"You want me to be grateful that you're holding me hostage?" she asked because it was preposterous.

He sighed, disappointed. "You'll know what I'm saying eventually. You'll come to appreciate what I've done for you. You might even thank more for it with that pretty mouth of yours. I can think of a few ways I'd like to receive your thanks…"

"Stop."

"Why?" He searched her expression as he spoke. "I like your body. I like your magic. I even like the way you talk back, I think your defiance has grown on me. I always get what I want, Jade, you know me well enough by now to know that much already."

"I don't know you at all," she disagreed, mostly to be difficult, because he was right and she hated that.

"Don't you? Should we start from the beginning? It seems appropriate since you're no longer the same woman you were when you first stepped through that portal. I'm the Dust Emperor, you can call me Dust. I rule this world and everything in it. That includes you, little cat." He gripped her chin when she tried to look away, forcing her still. "You're mine."

She snorted. "Dream on."

"Careful what you say," he warned, "I can make this a nightmare just as easily as I can make it a fantasy."

"And I repeat," she stated, "I hate you."

"Do you?" He ground his cock against her once more, and even with the clothes between them he must have been able to feel the way she heated for him. "If I reached down right now what do you think I'd find?"

She wanted to argue, but it wasn't like she was about to tell him her earlier theory about how she was just really horny after not getting any for a while. Instead, she clenched her jaw shut tightly.

"You're wet for me," he said. "You find me attractive."

"I find you insufferable," she corrected. A second later she let out a startled yelp when he nicked her under the curve of her jaw, shocked when he held up his hand to show her the ring he was wearing, and the tiny metal thorns decorated across the band.

He made a big show of licking off the drop of blood before he forced her head to the side and licked the scratch.

The pain was minimal, barely even present amongst all the other things she was feeling, but his point was made nonetheless and she found herself tensing beneath him again.

"Magic is fickle," he told her, his mouth still pressed against her, though he moved it down to kiss lightly at her pulse, "and curses are complicated. I could do as Koya suggests, of course, bleed you dry, take my fill now and hope that it'll be enough. But why risk it? Why, when I have better options available to me? Options that'll gift me with so much more than just the return of my full power?" He shifted to the other side of her neck, kissing her a second time. "I've wanted you from the moment I saw you, Jade. The moment I recognized that fire crackling behind your eyes. We have something in common."

She couldn't for the life of her imagine what that could be.

He glanced down at her. "We both want to escape our fate."

Sure, she hadn't wanted anything to do with the Emeralds or the man responsible for her parents' deaths. She'd been on the run from her grandfather and the life he expected her to lead. But that didn't mean she preferred being *here*.

"All you did was remove me from a cage and place me in another," she pointed out tightly. "I will never be grateful for that. It's true I don't want to be the next leader of the Emeralds, but that's not the only thing that turns my stomach." She held his gaze. "I don't want you."

She'd expected the anger she saw flash behind his eyes, but not what he did next. His mouth was on her faster than she could blink, his tongue forcing its way inside to flick and tangle against hers. The kiss was brutal, demanding, and he shoved a hand through her hair and angle her head to his liking, sucking and nipping at her to the point it was hard to catch a breath.

He bit her hard enough to draw blood and then lapped it up, delving his copper-tasting tongue back into her mouth afterward. The Emperor devoured her, ignoring her struggles and attempts to shove him away. After a while, he grew tired of that even, and without breaking the kiss, he captured her wrists and pinned them above her head.

"Little cat," he moaned against her and that cinnamon smell coming off of him turned sharp, "Jade. Make it rain."

Her power exploded out of her at the command, the skies opening up outside instantly. The sudden downpour helped drown out the sounds they both made as he continued to fuck into her mouth, ignoring her gasps and struggle for air.

Chapter 2:

The creepy bird was staring at her.

Jade eyed it from where it rested on the backing of one of the wooden chairs around the table in the center of the room. The creature appeared to be a salmon-crested cockatoo, and if this were here world, Jade would probably think it was pretty but...

"What's up with that thing?" she asked finally. "And why is it giving me such a bad feeling?"

"Probably because you two didn't have that great of an introduction," the Emperor guessed. He'd arrived with the bird in tow less than ten minutes ago and had taken a seat on the bed. "Don't worry, out of the two of you, Pearl is the most well-behaved. You have nothing to fear from her."

Why was that name familiar...

Jade's eyes widened and her head snapped in the Emperor's direction. "Pearl as in the monster that chased me out of Master Mists' manor?!"

"She isn't a monster," he chided. "She's an amphiptere."

"You have a pet dragon." She grunted. "Why am I not surprised?" Of course he'd have something like that.

"She isn't a dragon either." He frowned at her, and it seemed like he was actually taking offense to her mislabeling Pearl. It was the most caring she'd ever seen him and it threw her for a major loop.

"How does she change her form?" Magic, obviously, but Jade was hoping there were more specific details. It was interesting, even if a part of her still worried Pearl would transform into that same winged snake-creature and try to swallow her whole.

"All of her kind can," he explained. "It's just part of their nature. Many creatures in Orremos contain power of their own. Do you not have anything like it where you're from?"

"Magic is scarce," she told him. "Most people don't even believe it exists." They certainly would if they saw Pearl.

"You should eat something," the Emperor slid the plate closer to her across the mattress and changed the subject. Even though there was a perfectly good table, he hadn't let her move from the bed, and now that Pearl had taken residence there Jade found she wasn't too put off about that fact.

At least she was still in the black silk robe and was no longer in chains. The last time she'd woken her wrists had been undone but not her ankles, so that was something at least.

Though it didn't elude her that she was satisfied by the smallest, and stupidest, things now, and what that most likely meant.

He was training her to be grateful for scraps, grateful for any kindness, no matter how minuscule or small. It was a tactic she'd seen Key use on prisoners from rival organizations they were hoping to sway and use as spies, so she recognized it for what it was. And yet...

Knowing what was happening and *stopping* it were too different things.

The Emperor watched her closely, perched on the edge of the bed turned toward her. He'd been gone most of the day and had only just returned to find the food he'd had delivered over an hour ago still mostly untouched before her. His hair was damp, and he was dressed in a teal and pink robe cinched tightly at his waist, making her wonder if he'd come from a dip in the hot spring.

"Jade?" he called her out of her inner mussing. "Eat."

She sighed and leaned back against the headboard. "I'm not starving myself," she said, knowing that was what he was thinking, that she was doing this as an act of rebellion. "I'm honestly just not hungry."

"Your body burns through calories while it adjusts to the influx of power," he told her. "You should be starving."

"I'm not lying."

He eyed her a moment longer, then gave a short nod. The plate had an assortment of fruits and sliced meats and cheeses, as well as a couple pastries. Straightening, he reached for one of the small tarts and took a bite.

Then he leaned forward and pressed his mouth against hers.

Caught off guard, she opened, and he slipped the bit into her mouth and planted an almost chaste kiss on her lips before pulling back. She frowned but chewed and swallowed. Still, when he made to take another bit she snatched the tart out of his hand and nibbled on it with a scowl.

He laughed. "Even if you don't feel like it, eat something. It's probably the stress that's killing your appetite."

"Caused by you," she muttered and his gaze hardened.

"Would you like the restraints back on?"

She shoved the rest of the tart into her mouth.

A silence settled over them as she continued to pick at the plate, finding that the more she ate, the more she realized he'd been right and she was in fact hungry.

The Emperor busied himself by waving his left hand around in weird patterns, almost like he was rolling a ball in his palm even though there was nothing there. Jade found herself watching anyway, curious to know what he was doing. It didn't take long for her to realize what she'd thought had been empty air wasn't.

Tiny grains of sand glittered, the grains multiplying and clumping together until there was a golf ball sized lump hovering above his hand. After he played with it a moment longer, he waved his other hand over it, then clasped them together a moment. When he separated them, the ball had solidified, and he set it into a tiny brass dish on the side of the bed.

"Next time, if you find you aren't hungry when you should be, light this," he said, pointing to a book of matches also set on the end table.

"What did you just do?" She'd seen her grandfather turn metallic objects into gold with a single touch, but she'd never seen anyone make something seemingly out of nothing before.

The Emperor held out his hand palm up for her. As soon as he had her attention, he did something, and tiny grains of colored sand, this time ruby red, appeared as if from thin air. "They come from me," he explained. "I need my sense of smell to know if I've got it right, which is why breaking the curse was so important. Without being able to smell the slight cherry scent, this could be the recipe for madness just as easily as it could be for lust."

That gave Jade pause, and she glanced at him suspiciously. "Lust?"

He chuckled and curled his fingers. The grains were gone when he opened them again. "Don't worry, I don't need to use magic on you for that." He winked at her, and it took all of her willpower to resist picking up the plate and cracking it over his skull.

She thought back on what that man had been telling her when she and Koya had been attacked on their way here. "You can make any feeling, just like that?"

"Any feeling I've experienced myself," he confirmed. "Candles make it easier, but I can leave the substance in its natural form. People call it dust. You may recall when you and your friend were hiding in that filthy barn there was an odd smell a moment before you passed out."

She'd known he'd been the cause, but... "You couldn't smell then."

"My power has been limited to verbal commands for thousands of years, it's true, but I kept stores of dust during the war, some to be used against my enemies, others for safekeeping. I brought some with me that day."

"Should I feel special?" He was basically telling her he'd used some of his special stash to capture her, after all.

The corner of his mouth curved up. "The second you used your power on my men I knew what you were. How valuable you were."

She'd known it'd been stupid to use her magic that day, but they hadn't had any other options, and Amelia had just been shot...

"I suppose not," he surprised her by saying. "You're already used to people using you; you can recognize the signs a mile away. There's nothing for you to be grateful for because I didn't start off doing any of this for you."

She snorted. "Start off? Don't tell me you've changed your stance since. *None* of this is for my benefit."

He'd mentioned something similar earlier and though her interest was piqued, she refused to give in and ask him to elaborate. What she needed to be focused on was figuring out a way out of here.

She was back in the room with the large window, but instead of the mattress on the floor, she was on the large bed. She'd been there this whole time, and if what he said was to be believed, that had been half a month already. Master Mist's magic had messed with her body, had changed her somehow, she could feel it.

When the Emperor had ordered her to make it rain yesterday, the rush of power had practically blindsided her. She'd never felt that strong before, and the storm had lasted much longer than the measly ten minutes she'd once managed.

But she knew better than to think that boosting her abilities had anything to do with helping her out. It was all for him, so that the Emperor could break his curse. And once that was done...

"It could be," the Emperor said.

"If I repeat what I told you yesterday, are you going to force yourself on me again?" She made sure the bitterness was clear in her tone.

He grunted. "I'm not going to make out with you again, if that's what you're referring to. That test is done. It was...not as satisfying as I'd hoped. I have another in mind."

"Test?" Was that what it'd been? Her eyes narrowed. "You were just using me after all. All that talk about wanting me—"

"Was the truth," he interrupted. "I want you, and I'll have you."

"No," she shook her head, "you won't."

He pointedly glanced at the chains still attached to the bed, stilling when she snorted a second time.

"I'm not an idiot or an optimist. I know where this is headed. You can command me to sleep with you at any time, and I'll do it. That's just my body though. You'll never have *me*." Even if her body betrayed her—and she already knew that it would—and he turned her on, there was a big difference between wanting someone physically and wanting them mentally.

Jade would never fall for the Dust Emperor.

"If that's what you're hoping for," though for the life of her she couldn't figure out why he would be, "then give up. You can skip all of these false pleasantries," she waved at the now empty plate, "and pretend worry for my wellbeing. Skip playing the nice guy, it doesn't suit you."

"You're goading me on purpose." He canted his head, inspecting her, but instead of the anger she'd anticipated, there was only a glimmer of interest in his pink gaze. "It seems I'm not the only one conducting tests in this room. All right, little cat. We'll see which one of us is victorious in the end."

She forced herself to remain still when he leaned toward her, brushing his mouth lightly against the underside of her jaw before bringing them to her ear.

"Don't worry, Jade. I promise not to gloat too much when I win."

A sudden knock on the door had him scowling, and he pulled back but didn't get off of the bed, barking out for whoever it was who'd interrupted to come in.

A slight woman who appeared to be around the same age as Jade entered, her head bowed low. Her black hair was tied back in a thick braid, and she was wearing a tan dress with pink detailing. At her hip, the familiar gold symbol of a sun and a serpent had been stitched into the material.

The Emperor sighed and stood, adjusting his clothing as he motioned for the woman to approach. "This is Kyo," he told Jade. "She'll be your attendant for the day." He didn't sound pleased about that at all.

Something about it put Jade on edge.

"Why? Where are you going?" And why did she care? This was an opportunity. The maid didn't look to be very strong. Jade could most certainly take her and—

"If you try anything while I'm away," the Emperor warned, "I'll kill Kyo and her entire family line."

Jade blinked at him, waiting to see if he was being dramatic. When he didn't waver, her mouth parted slightly. "You can't be serious. That's a bit extreme, don't you think."

"Not at all," he disagreed. "To be clear, you might think you're well enough to move on your own, but you aren't. The second you try to crawl out of that bed you'll see I'm telling the truth. You're still very weak. Vulnerable." He frowned, the concern on his face impossible to miss. "I don't like leaving you, but I've put off meeting with Haze long enough."

"Haze?"

"The God of Feeling."

Her hands tightened in the sheets.

"Ah," the Emperor noticed her reaction, "Koya wasn't sure, but I had a feeling that assassin he killed had spoken to you beforehand."

"He was trying to kidnap me," she corrected, not really sure why she bothered.

He seemed just as interested in the reason as she was, however. "Why are you telling me that?"

"Maybe because I have no idea what this other god could want me for?" At least with the Emperor she knew enough, even if he'd started speaking cryptically about wanting her. There was always the chance she'd wake up tomorrow with him slitting her wrists and draining her after all, but there was also the chance that she wouldn't. With someone else? She knew nothing.

"Better the devil I know."

"I hope you mean that," he said. "Don't do anything stupid while I'm away, Jade. I'll hurry back as quickly as I can but…"

She made a big show of leaning back against the headboard again. "Please. As if I don't already know you've set at least two dozen guards in the hallway. As you've already mentioned, this isn't the first time powerful men have tried to use me."

When she'd first announced where she wanted to go to college—on the opposite side of the country from where Blakely estate resided—her grandfather had been livid that she'd even had the gall to suggest it. He'd ordered her locked in her rooms until he deemed enough time had passed and had set guards around to secure all of the exits.

Another time, when she'd been around thirteen, there'd been an attack and she'd been locked in there to hide. The guards set then had been there to protect her.

It was hard to tell in this situation what the Emperor intended his guards for. Were they there to keep her safe, or were they there to keep her a prisoner?

"It'll be at least another week before you've recovered enough to protect yourself properly," he said. "Keep that in mind." Then he turned to Kyo. "You are the only one allowed to enter this room. Failure to bar anyone else from doing so will result in death. Is that understood?"

"Yes, Emperor." She kept her head down.

He turned back to Jade and then hesitated. When she quirked a brow, silently urging him to get to the point, he exhaled in mild annoyance. "I need a booster before I go. I'll give you the chance to choose how I get it this time. Consider it an early reward for behaving in my absence, which I know you will be doing. Won't you, little cat?"

Hitting him over the head with the plate was sounding like a really good idea again.

"Well?" he prompted when she didn't respond. "What's it going to be? Should I cut you and drink your blood, or would you prefer we go an easier route? I seem to recall you're not a fan of pain."

She wasn't sure she agreed that what they'd done yesterday was easier, but whatever. There was more to this than simply him trying to offer her a choice. This was another one of his tests. A means to see how much she was willing to bend when push came to shove. If she chose to let him bleed her now, there was little doubt in her mind that he'd punish her for it later, and he was right, pain wasn't her thing.

But the idea of willingly kissing him like before…

The Emperor took a step closer. "Time is running out, Jade. I suppose I'll just bite you again and be—"

"No." She planted a hand on his chest when he bent over her, stopping him. When she tipped her head back to meet his gaze, his mouth was hovering right there. This was conditioning, she was aware of that, but there was no around it. He'd cornered her.

Without another word, she pressed her lips to his, tentatively at first, unsure. But the second they touched, a rush of warmth flooded through her, and the smell of rich cinnamon wafted over her, invading her senses. He wasn't using his power, hadn't uttered a verbal command, and yet her body reacted as if he had.

As if it wanted to touch him and be touched by him.

She forced the fear that caused down, opting to deal with it later when she was alone, concentrating instead on the kiss and the way he opened up for her. Unlike yesterday, he didn't invade her mouth or press forward.

The Emperor held himself back, allowing her to advance and pick the pace. He stroked his tongue lightly against hers, welcomingly, when she flicked it into his mouth, and the tingle that caused had both of them moaning.

The spot at the center of her chest seemed to pulse, and she frowned, pulling back slightly. It felt a lot like the sensation she had just before using her power. Like something inside of her was filling up, readying.

"Power," the Emperor whispered down at her, reaching forward to cup her chin and ease her face back toward his. He kissed her again, softly, without tongue, as if just for the enjoyment of it and not so that he could collect what he needed. "Yours calls to mine and mine calls to yours. It's because of the contents of the vial."

"Because of the drop of blood you added." He'd said something to Koya about tying her to him...Had this been what he'd meant? She pulled back a second time. "You're manipulating me again."

His look turned steely, like she'd insulted and infuriated him all at once, and the good mood he'd seemed to be in only a moment prior went up in a puff of smoke. He straightened, staring down his straight nose at her. "Believe what you must, little cat."

The Emperor turned and rounded the bed, steps no longer at ease, and Pearl flew to him, dropping onto his shoulder as if sensing he was about to depart. He practically rushed to the door, as if he couldn't wait to get out of this room and be away from her, stopping only for a second to remind the maid that no one else was allowed in before he exited the room. He slammed the door after himself.

Jade would have rolled her eyes at the childish nature of the move if not for the way her chest was currently cinching tightly. Had he done something to her with that drop of blood? Was that way she didn't recoil from his touch? Why the kiss just now had set her skin on fire in a way no one else ever had?

Chapter 3:

Jade sat at the table in the center of the room, staring out the large window. The pallet mattress that had been there before had been removed, and she was debating whether or not she wanted to go over to the window seat when Kyo entered with lunch.

The smell of rich herbs and broth tickled at Jade's nose as a large bowl of soup was placed carefully before her, and her stomach growled. Inadvertently, her gaze wandered over to the side table by the bed where the ball of dust still sat in the small copper dish. She hadn't needed to use it since the Emperor's departure yesterday.

She'd need her strength if she had a hope of getting out of her, so Jade was glad that she could eat again without problem. The first sip of the soup had her sighing in contentment as the flavors of chicken and salt exploded on her tongue. She'd always been partial to chicken and was happy to know that this universe still had them. The other meats she'd eaten so far had been…questionable. Tasty, but questionable.

Was Amelia skipping her meals due to worry or was she all right? Jade hated the idea of her friend suffering anymore for her sake. And now that she'd taken the contents of that vial and her powers were growing…

A melancholy swept over her and any semblance of a good mood vanished. If she did get back home, her grandfather would discover her power and use it for his benefit. She'd thought it impossible to escape him before, now it truly would be. At least in the past, she'd had a chance of him changing his mind and letting her go because she'd been weak and a poor choice for leadership. He'd only insisted because she was his last remaining blood heir.

A fact he'd made happen himself.

He deserved to be alone and have the Blakely reign end with him after what he did to her parents.

Jade felt disgusted at herself for caring about him even a little all of this time. For all of those nights she'd struggled to fall asleep because she'd felt guilty she hadn't measured up and made him proud. Or all the times she worked herself until her body was shaking and her vision was fuzzy in an attempt to earn his approval. He'd been hard on her, uncaring, strict...But she'd tricked herself into believing he wasn't a monster because he'd been all the family she'd had left in the world.

Had Key known?

She stopped that line of thinking short. If she went there she'd fall apart and she couldn't afford that right now, not when she was finally starting to ground herself once more. Her mind needed to stay clear for her to come up with a plan out of here, and with no telling when the Emperor might return, she needed to keep herself focused.

Starting with collecting information. Up until this point, Koya had been the only other person she'd been left alone with, and he hadn't been very forthcoming with information. But Kyo might be different.

"I have a question," Jade said, keeping her tone light and friendly and her attention on the soup to appear less threatening.

Sure enough, Kyo perked up from where she stood a few feet away from the table. "What can I help you with, my lady?"

"I'm sure you've heard," everyone here had to have, "but I'm sort of new to," she waved a hand in the air, "all of this. I've been told that the story of the Great War is pretty well known. Can you tell it to me? Specifically the parts involving the Emperor? I know that he had a disagreement with another god, Master Mist, and that they went to war because of it. But that's all I know."

Kyo hesitated, nibbling on her bottom lip before she seemed to decide it wasn't a big deal to comply. "It was well before my time, my lady, so all I have is the stories I've heard since I was a child. Those stories are always changing, and there's no way to know for certain if they're accurate, but it's said that the argument was over a human child."

That was…surprising. Jade frowned. "How so?"

"Apparently, the Dust Emperor came upon a small boy drowning at sea, and in a rare moment of mercy, he commanded the boy to swim to shore. The boy did as he was ordered, able to only because of the Emperor's power for he didn't actually know how to swim. Except, once he made it to shore, Master Mist appeared furious. He'd been trying to drown the boy on purpose as revenge for something—that part of the story is unclear. He demanded the boy back into the water and of course, terrified, the boy refused."

"Why didn't the Emperor simply use his power to make him go back in?" Jade asked. "He hardly seems like the type who would bother with saving someone if it meant going up against a fellow god. Seems like the type of thing he'd find a waste of time."

Her grandfather never would, that was for certain. If someone couldn't benefit him in one way or another they were useless in his mind. It wouldn't have mattered if that boy lived or died. He would have merely shrugged in mild apology to Master Mist, ordered the boy back into the waves, and walked off without even staying to watch him drown.

"He might have," Kyo said, "but the boy happened to be the son of one of his high priestesses. The priestess was loyal to the Emperor, more so than any of the others. He had a fondness for her and didn't want to see her hurt over the loss of her child. Then there was also the fact that he'd been openly screamed at by Master Mist, a god of lesser station than him."

"Ah," that last part made sense at least, "hid pride wouldn't let him sit back and take that."

"The Emperor refused to comply with Master Mist's demands and instead took the boy back to his temple, reuniting him with his mother. He thought the matter settled, but less than a day later, both the priestess and her son were found dead in their bathing chamber. Drowned."

Master Mist controlled water. Jade had picked up on that well enough, understood that though her grandfather didn't have anything to do with liquid, her power was similar enough in the sense she could control the rain.

"He murdered them." It was a sad story, even if Jade should have been hardened against such feelings by now. Though he'd attempted to keep that part of the business away from her for as long as possible, by the time she'd turned thirteen, Jade had come of age in her grandfather's mind and had been let in on the darker happenings in the Emeralds.

If she thought about all of the deaths and beatings she'd either heard about or witnessed, she'd go insane.

"Yes,' Kyo confirmed. "The Emperor was furious. An attack on his people was a sign of war, and he didn't take it lightly, even when Master Mist tried to backpedal and claim he was only taking back what had been stolen from him first. He truly believed the boy's life was his right. Out of the seven other gods, only two sided with him. Still, the war was brutal and took many human lives. The Emperor was the most powerful of them all, but Master Mist was a close second."

"And then he cursed the Emperor and fled." She didn't need details of the actual war. Her purpose here was to understand what had happened and how she could use this story to her advantage.

"Master Mist claimed he wanted to surrender," Kyo told her. "Not much is known about what the message he delivered saying as much, or why the

Emperor trusted it, only that he did and he went to meet with him. He was caught off guard and the curse was placed before he had a chance to defend himself. After, he managed to deliver a fatal blow to Master Mist, but the other god opened a portal and fled."

"If no one actually saw him die, why are they so certain he's dead?" She'd been taught not to walk away until a kill had been confirmed. Seemed odd that people that powerful wouldn't want to do that as well.

"For a couple of reasons. For starters, only Master Mist could open portals into another world," Kyo explained. "Then there's the link between all of the gods. They sensed the moment he passed on. That, paired with the fact that in all this time he hasn't returned, is proof that he died in the other world."

"In my world." The story matched up with the one passed down the generations. That a god had come and blessed them with power before dying and taking any remaining secrets with him. Master Mist had escaped, Valued her ancestor, and then succumbed to his injuries.

"What do you mean he's the only one who could open portals?" That part caught her attention and held.

"Something about his ability allowed him to slip through bodies of water and enter another realm," Kyo said. "While powerful, none of the other gods can do that. Some have tried to find a way, but none have been successful. Perhaps it is the universe's attempt at keeping things in check."

"Right," Jade nodded, thinking that over, "we don't have gods where I'm from. That must be because they can't invade our world." If they ever did…She shuddered. "Which gods have tried?"

"I can't be sure, my lady," she said apologetically. "Though there is rumor that Young Shadow and Restless have."

"Who?"

"I apologize," Kyo dipped her head, "that's the God of Chaos and the God of Intention, respectably, my lady. I believe you've encountered the latter. He was visiting the day you and your friend came through a portal in the hot spring."

Jade thought back to that day. There'd been two others standing on the deck. "The one with the pretty face or the one with the scar?"

"The one with scar, my lady," Kyo told her.

"How did he get it?" She wasn't sure why, but she was curious.

"It's believed that he got it during the war from Master Mist."

Restless the God of Intention. Jade filed that information away in case it became useful later on. Ideally, she'd find an escape before she came into contact with another one of the gods, but considering how poor her luck had been as of late she wasn't holding her breath.

"What about this other god, the one the Emperor is meeting with right now?" Jade asked.

"Haze, the God of Feeling," Kyo said. "He was also here that day."

"He was the pretty one?" That was surprising.

"Yes, my lady. Although that's subjective. Many believe Restless to be the more attractive of the two. Though neither hold a candle to the Dust Emperor."

Yeah, right, whatever. Jade waved her off. "If he was here that day, doesn't that mean they're friends? Why would he try to kidnap me?"

"I'm not sure you can consider any of the gods' friends with one another, my lady," Kyo thought it over, "but I suppose they're close. The three spend more time together than they do with any of the other gods. That's probably why the Emperor risked leaving you here during your change. He needs to get to the bottom of this as soon as possible."

"The change?" She clucked her tongue. "Is that what people are calling it."

"It's what it's called, my lady." Kyo frowned at her. "It's the process that takes place after a human has been Valued by a god. It's slow and I've been told very painfully. Typically, the god stays nearby for several weeks to ensure their Valued is safe."

"But the Emperor didn't Value me," Jade argued. "It was Master Mists' power I took, and I was already Valued to begin with."

"Yes," she nodded, "that's why you're recovering so much faster than anyone has in the past. Your body was already primed. I was informed that you were also Valued by my master, however. He told me so himself before he left and he would not lie about something so serious. Up until now, Koya is the only human blessed by the Dust Emperor in the last thousand or so years."

"He didn't—" The drop of blood. That must be what they were referring to. His power must have been in that single drop. "Can he control me because of it?"

Kyo stared at her like she'd sprouted a second head. "He's the God of Command, my lady. He can control anyone. And now that the curse is in the process of being broken, that also means he'll be able to control people from afar."

The magic she'd seen him weaving with his hand the other day. That allowed him to create balls of dust that could be dispersed and used by others. If he wanted to force an entire room to fall asleep, he could do so without having to utter a word. Hell, he could do it without having to even be there—like what had happened with her and Amelia that day at the barn. His power was already scary, Jade could understand why the thought of him breaking the curse had others on edge.

"Aren't you worried about that?" she asked Kyo, curious over what the maid's response might be. "It sounds like he'll be unstoppable."

"He is the leader of the gods," Kyo said. "It is only right that he be unstoppable." She wrung her hands, something clearly on her mind.

"It's okay," Jade urged, "tell me. I won't get mad."

"I know this is a horrible thing to say to you, my lady, considering everything you've been put through against your will since your arrival, however…the Dust Emperor isn't as bad as he seems. He is vicious, that must is true, but all the gods are. They're vicious and bright, like a burning flame we're all desperate moths to dance around. But he isn't pure evil. A devil wouldn't have saved that boy from drowning."

She'd heard what Jade had called him before he'd left, and it had obviously stuck with her if she was bringing it up now.

"He saved him because he didn't want his priestess distracted." Jade was ninety percent positive about that.

Kyo didn't agree. "With all due respect, my lady, that is not the only human he has saved."

"Right." Jade didn't need to hear any more of this. "Well, we clearly have different opinions on the matter. Let's change the subject."

"What else would you like to discuss, my lady?"

She was tempted to ask where the hot spring was located, but the Emperor's warning echoed in her mind and she refrained. Funny, that Kyo didn't seem to recall the threat he'd made to her life yesterday the same way Jade did.

"Do you know what happened to me while I was unconscious?" She had a fuzzy recollection of waking now and again. When she had, the Emperor had always been there, either at the side of the bed or holding her. There'd been pain though, enough that she was always quickly dragged back into the dark.

"No one was allowed into the room," Kyo said. "Even your meals were delivered at the door. Only the Emperor was with you. But his power has increased, and the curse has started to break, which leads me to believe that the two of you were in here working on dismantling that."

"While I was asleep?" He'd told her that he'd been experimenting.

"You will need to ask the Emperor yourself, my lady, I'm sorry."

Finished with lunch, Jade eased the empty bowl away and pushed herself out of her chair. She had to move slowly, her entire body still ached and her legs felt wobbly, but she made it around the table on her own before Kyo rushed to her side, catching her before she could fall.

"Thank you," she said, pointing toward the window. "I'd like to sit there if you would help me."

"Of course, my lady, I'm at your service." Kyo held her steady as they moved toward the window seat, not letting go until Jade was comfortably sitting with her back propped against the wall. "Is there anything else I can help you with?"

Jade blew out a breath, eyes closed as the pains receded and turned to a dull thrum she could manage. This whole healing thing sucked; she couldn't imagine what others had to go through, the ones who'd just been Valued. If she saw Koya again, she might try asking him how his change had gone.

No doubt he'd spout some bullshit about it all having been worth it to please his emperor.

"Tell me about yourself," Jade suggested. If she asked any more questions about the gods, she risked Kyo growing suspicious of her intentions. Right now, she was too weak to even attempt escaping, and even if she wasn't she wouldn't risk the other girl's life.

She wasn't her grandfather.

She wouldn't toss someone aside simply because their life didn't directly benefit her somehow.

"What would you like to know about me, my lady?" Kyo seemed surprised to have even been asked.

"Anything," Jade smiled softly at her, "whatever you'd like to tell me."

The rest of the afternoon passed as Kyo told her stories of her childhood and her hometown, and though the aches in her bones and the anxiety she felt never completely disappeared, Jade found herself laughing with the other girl, feeling for once like she wasn't quite alone.

Chapter 4:

She was in the process of drifting off in the tub when she felt someone enter the bathroom. Used to Kyo by now, she didn't so much as stir at the person's approach, too caught up with enjoying the heated water lapping at her skin.

The past three days had been quiet, with only the maid as her company, and some of her nerves had settled. Though there were still aches and pains, for the most part, Jade had recovered and could now move freely on her own. After drawing the bath for her, Kyo had gone to prepare supper, leaving Jade alone to rest and relax.

She'd always enjoyed being in the water back home, but it was almost like the experience was heightened now, the sense of belonging she felt, of rightness, having tripled somehow. If she had a say, she'd stay in the tub until her skin was past the point of pruning.

Hands lightly began combing her hair back from her face, carefully untangling the knots that had been made when she'd washed it a few minutes prior. The feeling was so nice, so soothing, that Jade felt herself going even laxer.

"Do you like that, little cat?"

She jolted at the sound of the Emperor's voice, trying to sit up straight and turn to see him.

He stopped her, wrapping an arm around her front to pull her back against the tub. Once he was sure she wouldn't move again, he went back to stroking those long fingers through her hair, humming in approval when a sigh slipped past her parted lips against her control.

"Let me attend to you," he said, though his tone lacked command. "I've been told you were good in my absence. So well behaved. Perfect."

She scowled, a sliver of irritation slipping through the otherwise blissful feeling she'd been experiencing. "I'm not a child."

"No," he chuckled and she felt him lean forward a bit so that he could press his cheek against hers, "you're definitely a grown woman. My woman."

"Can we not start a fight the second you get back?" she asked, because his claims made her uncomfortable. "I was finally starting to feel less awful about this world. You're making me hate it all over again."

"Not my intention, I assure you." His right hand came around her and he traced the length of her neck with his thumb before trailing it over the rise of her collar bone. "You don't seem bothered by my seeing you naked, however."

She snorted. "As if I'm not already aware you've seen me naked before?"

"Do you remember what happened at the beginning of your change?" he asked cryptically.

"Only bits and pieces," she admitted.

"You cried a lot," he said.

"And I was cold." That she recalled. It'd taken her a while to, but she did now. There were fuzzy memories of her shaking so hard she thought her bones were going to break. He'd stripped her then, held her tightly beneath a mountain of blankets through the worst of it, until all she'd been able to feel was the heat from his skin and the darkness enveloping her once more.

"I drank your tears," he told her. "I held you close." He tipped her head back so that their eyes could meet. "But nothing else happened."

Even though she couldn't remember everything from that time, she believed him.

"No," she said, holding his gaze, "you'd want me to be awake for that. You'd want me to be aware."

His grin was fast and fierce. "You know me so well, little cat."

"I don't know you at all," she disagreed, pulling her chin out of his grasp so she could look away. She didn't want to talk about this, it was a dangerous path that led to things she was better off avoiding for as long as possible. "You were gone for a long time."

"Did you miss me?"

"No."

"Should we put that to the test?" His hand skated over the surface of the water before sliding back toward her breasts. He chuckled when she grabbed his wrist to stop him from touching her. "I hurried back as fast as I could."

"I don't care," she told him.

"You're angry with me."

"Yeah, but that has nothing to do with you having been gone and everything to do with all the other crap you've pulled."

"I'll make it up to you."

"Not possible."

He sighed and suddenly he was leaning over the tub, wrapping both arms tightly around her in a hug. "I missed you, little cat. So much."

"You missed my blood," she corrected. "My tears too."

"I missed your mouth," he said, brushing a finger over her pursed lips. "The taste of you…" his tone turned suggestive and Jade's heart leaped in her chest.

"What happened with Haze?" It took all of her effort to keep her voice from giving her away, from cluing him in to the fact she wasn't as unaffected by him as she was pretending to be.

"He denied having anything to do with attacking you."

She frowned. "He could be lying."

The Emperor shook his head and she felt his hair tickle the side of her cheek. "I summoned Beautiful Liar, the God of Truth, and Haze agreed to let her use her power on him. She confirmed his claims."

"If it wasn't him that means the guy Koya killed was either set up, or he gave me false information on purpose." He'd seemed sincere when he'd been talking to her, so her money was on the first and not the latter. "Were you able to figure out who was actually behind it?"

"Not yet," he said, "but I will. If they came for you once, they'll do so again."

"Why? It's too late to stop you, you've already broken the curse."

"I'm close," he confessed, "but it's not fully broken yet."

She hated the slight twist of fear she felt, hated that the idea that another god out there wanted her made her want to stick closer to the Emperor. What she needed to do was get back to planning her escape. If she were no longer here, no one could do anything to her. And they couldn't follow either.

Only Master Mist could open a portal, and Jade was able to do so because she was Valued by his line. Once she was back home, she'd be free from the Emperor and the gods.

Perhaps she could make a bargain with him…Things hadn't turned out well for her the last time, but he had kept his word when it'd come to Amelia. The second his curse was fully broken, he wouldn't need her anymore. He could kill her, but he could also let her go home. He didn't need her willingness, but wouldn't that make it easier for him? Speed up the process? She doubted he wanted to stay cursed longer than he had to.

Before she could open her mouth to suggest a truce of sorts, the Emperor broke the silence first.

"I've already bled you, tried your tears, and tasted your mouth," he said silkily. "You're well enough now for the final test."

"What—" She was swooped up out of the tub and into his arms without warning, and she yelped and clung to him as he carried her from the bathroom without even bothering to dry her off. She protested on the way, but he ignored her as he so often did, his hold tightening wordlessly against her struggles.

He tossed her onto the bed, yanking on her left wrist before she could sit up and move off of it. The chains that had bound her at the beginning of her change were fastened, and even though she knew it would do her no good, she fought him, trying to kick and punch him to no avail.

The chains at the head of the bed were attached to the legs, stretching up over the top of the mattress with leather cuffs at the end that tightened around her wrists. It was a similar situation with the chains at the end, though they were slightly longer, giving her a bit more leeway. Not enough, and they forced her legs spread apart, but she could bend her knees, though that did her little good.

No sooner had he snapped the last cuff around her ankle, than the Emperor was on her, settling his heavy body between her thighs, pressing her down into the mattress with his hard form. His hands grabbed her face, holding her still so his mouth could take hers, his tongue burrowing in deep in a repeat of the bruising kiss he'd given her before leaving.

"It's not enough," he groaned, breaths harried. "I need more."

Jade tugged at her bonds and glared. "Untie me."

"I can't. You need them."

"I—"

"You need an excuse to keep hating me," he cut her off, smiling almost wistfully. "We both know it. You want me," his hand trailed down to her abdomen, but no further, "here, but not," then he tapped her forehead, "here. Keep fighting, little cat, I understand. If you need me to be a monster, I can do that."

She blinked at him, a flood of embarrassment and anger twisting in her gut, momentarily snuffing out the heat she'd been feeling despite the way he'd tossed her around like his own personal doll. Even she hadn't realized that she was turned on whenever he was in the same room. She hated the fact that he had.

"You are a monster," she stated, needing to regain some semblance of control here.

"I know."

"You are," she insisted. "All you've done since I've gotten here is treat me like a pet! I will never—"

His hand dropped down, reaching between her legs. He pressed the pad of his thumb into her and she bowed at just that slight breach, arms tugging at her bonds so that they rattled against the headboard.

Dust chuckled, lowering himself closer to her side, and propped his head up on his palm almost lazily. He glanced down at her spread thighs and danced his fingers across her folds, tweaking her clit and retreating without applying the kind of pressure she needed.

His thumb sunk in up to the knuckle and he twisted it, causing her hips to jerk. The move spun his hand and he cupped her ass, his middle finger playing between the crack before he found her other tight ring of muscle.

"Don't." Jade had never done anything like that before, and she was already struggling against giving in. She didn't want him touching her. Didn't want—A keening sound slipped past her lips the second he pushed his thumb in as deep as it could go.

At the same time, he prodded at her second entrance, not forcing himself in, but teasing her.

"I can get your power any number of ways, Jade," he cooed. "From you blood, your tears, your spit, your..." His gaze dropped to the wet place between her legs and she jerked against her bonds again, causing him to laugh a second time. "I guess you've already figured out which method I prefer. But I'm not opposed to bleeding you if I must. I'll do anything to get what I want. Anything. Even if that means I have to wring your body dry."

He hummed in disappointment and tapped that finger against her clenched muscle one last time before he pulled his hand free completely. "With that in mind, taking you there won't do me much good. Although," he pondered it, obviously putting on a show, "I bet I could make you come hard enough to satisfy my needs if I put my cock here." His finger returned to her ass, though he didn't slip his thumb inside her pussy again.

"Don't," she repeated, wishing she could close her legs and push him away. Wishing that her body wasn't currently on fire and thrumming like a livewire.

"What's wrong, little cat?" He leaned over her some more, bringing his face a little closer. "That perfectly plump mouth of yours says no, but your eyes are telling me a different story."

"It's not real." She needed to hold onto that. Needed to remember. "You did this."

He grinned, wolfish, the self-satisfaction practically wafting off of him. "I didn't command you to want me. Not yet, anyway."

"The blood," she argued. "The drop of blood you added to that damned vial."

"Ah," he pretended to feel bad, morphing his expression with ease into one of concern, "are you worried about that? Don't be, I did it for you, little cat, to make things easier on you."

"So you admit it?" Her anger flared and she momentarily forgot that she was naked and on display. That he was in control and she should be careful because of it. "Bastard. You're making me feel this way, it isn't——"

"Feel what way?" Interest piqued, he trailed his hand up the plains of her stomach, stopping to plant his palm between her breasts. He splayed his fingers, touching as much of her as possible, and watched the way she squirmed from it. "Answer the question. How do you feel, Jade?"

He used his power, and her lips pried themselves open despite her attempts to keep them shut, the words pouring out of her against her will.

"Like I'm on fire," she said, "like I…" she fought against it, but for all her struggles, all he did was quirk a single brow. "…I need you."

"Need me?" He feigned ignorance. "Need me where?"

She squeezed her eyes shut, trying to block him out. But it was no use. He was everywhere, all around her, clawing on her outsides and her insides. Forcing her to bend to his whims. A tear slipped out and rolled down her cheek, and she felt him lean and collect the lone drop with his tongue.

He didn't pull away after, his mouth kept close, his warm exhales fanning against her damp face. "Tell me where you need me, little cat. Tell me, so I can make you purr."

He'd said something similar once before, hadn't he? In the beginning.

I'll make it so you purr for me every time I enter a room.

"Dust." His name felt foreign spoken in her voice, but she wasn't reprimanded for using it. He merely hummed, allowing her to continue. Jade turned her head so that they were eye to eye once more, wanting him to see the truth of her next words more than anything. "I hate you."

He took her chin in a firm hold, gaze hardening some. "Tell me what you want from me, Jade."

His power twisted around her, conjuring all sorts of images in her mind of the ways she could want him. All the ways he could make it worth it.

"Touch me," she found herself saying, words breathy and low. "Make me forget."

He frowned, and this time his confusion was real. "Forget what?"

"The things I was running from before I got here." Like her grandfather, and Key, and the Emeralds. And the future they all wanted to shove down her throat despite all of her protests.

She must have said that last part out loud without realizing, for the Emperor snorted.

"I'd like to shove something down that pretty throat of yours as well, little cat," he skimmed his fingernails down the length of her jugular, "but you don't seem all that concerned about that at the moment. No, you're too concerned with before. I should remind you of your present and what you really need to be concerned about."

In one swift move, he'd settled himself over her, kneeling between her spread thighs with his face hovering a mere inch above hers. He planted a soft kiss on the tip of her nose, the move so out of character that her mind went blank for a second, distracting her from the fact he was undoing the sash around his waist and stripping over her.

It was the first time she'd seen him fully naked since the hot spring, and the first time from this angle. Jade's breath caught in her throat as her eyes roamed over him, taking in the broad width of his shoulders and the way his waist tapered down, all the corded muscle between his pecs and—

Her eyes widened at the size of his cock, jutting proudly between his legs, already swollen and hard. The thick rosy head leaked precome under her attention, the pearlescent drop rolling partway down his shaft.

"Have you done this before, little cat?" Dust asked, all sultry and smooth sounded, and she nodded her head before she could think better of it, mind still caught on the sheer size of him and how he could possibly think all of that was going to ever fit inside of her.

Before she knew what was coming, he'd moved, shoving through fingers into her pussy with little care for how much it might hurt.

She let out a cry and tried to pull away, but the bonds kept her trapped there as he drove them in deeper, forcibly stretching her tight walls before she was ready. More tears welled at the corner of her eyes, but when she gathered enough strength to look at him again, there was nothing but anger burning in his.

He scissored his fingers then pulled them out and slammed them back in a second time, twisting them inside of her as if trying to feel everything at once. "I shouldn't even be giving you this much," he muttered, though it was hard to tell if the words were meant for her or merely for himself. "I could make this hurt far more than it is. I can make it hurt every time, in fact. Remember that, Jade. Remember this," he splayed his fingers inside of her as far as they would go and she saw stars borne from a mixture of pain and pleasure, "I control what you feel and when you feel it. I control whether it hurts or it doesn't."

Dust pulled his hand free and brought it to his mouth, greedily licking her juices from his digits, holding her gaze all the while. Around them, the air seemed to crackle and pop, and his skin took on an almost glittering sheen, like golden grains of sand beneath a bright summer sun.

He situated himself between her thighs, and she felt the wide head of him settle against her entrance, a wave of fear gripping her and wiping clean any pride she might have been clinging to up until this point.

"Wait—"

He didn't. With a single snap of his hips he thrust himself inside of her, not gently, but rough, and with all the force he could muster. It had her body sliding up half an inch, restricted by the bonds keeping her in place.

The leather dug into her ankles and wrists, cinching, but the pain was nothing like the sting of where he filled her, stretching her poor inner walls wider than they'd ever been before. It was hard to breathe, and she gasped, trying to recall the breathing techniques she'd learned as a kid to help stave off pain, the ones she would have sworn were second nature to her prior to this.

But it was hard to think with him fully seated inside of her, lowering his body so that he was lying on top of her with his arms at either side of her head. He shifted and she winced.

She'd slept with men before, but no one had ever been this rough with her, this cruel. It was impossible not to note that the pain was on purpose; he wanted her to feel this, their first time, because he wanted the message to be clear.

He could hurt her, just like he had the very first time they'd met when he'd jabbed his teeth into her neck in that dank cell.

"Shh," his voice turned soothing and he planted soft, feather-light kisses up her jawline, over to the other side, and then against both cheeks, "breathe, little cat, it'll get better, I promise."

He'd still around her, careful not to move anything other than his head as he lavished her with his mouth, and even though there'd been no power in his words, Jade found her body listening.

Slowly, her tensed muscles eased and the sharp burn shifted to something else, something electric and pleasing.

"There you go," he brushed sticky strands of hair off her forehead, "give in to it, little cat. Give in to me." He eased his way out of her, his cock rubbing against her inner walls on the wall out causing her to gasp. Just before he was all the way out, he slammed forward, pounding into her with the same momentum as before.

It hurt, but not nearly as much.

The chains rattled as he took her like that, slow and torturous strokes out, brutal and rough strokes in. He set the pace and he kept it, immune to all of the pleading sounds she made or the way her body writhed beneath him. He took her the way he wanted to, eyes locked onto her face all the while as if he was memorizing all of her expressions, feeding off the way she parted her lips.

It went on for a while, just like that, him slowly emptying her and quickly refilling her, that spot deep in her gut growing in intensity until it felt like she was about to burst from all the tension there.

Before she could, he thrust back in and stilled a second time, dropping his mouth hungrily to hers. He nipped and bit at her lips, slipping his warm tongue past her defenses to flick against the roof of her mouth and tangle against hers. He sucked and pressed and licked her, practically feasting on her with his heavy cock still buried deep between her folds.

The flame in her lower region died down some, the intensity evening out so that she wasn't as close to tumbling off the edge.

As if sensing it, Dust began to move again, rocking his hips against her leisurely, teasing her with his unhurried movements until she was moaning beneath him and it was impossible not to note the pleading edge to the sound she made.

He chuckled against her lips, finally disengaging their mouths so he could stare down at her once more. "Jade."

His power danced over her skin and her eyes fluttered.

"Jade," he smiled, that mischievous smirk he gave right before he did something self-serving, "make it rain."

She didn't bother with snapping her fingers. Her magic burst out of her with a single breath, the skies outside bursting instantly, the heavy rainfall pelting down over the roof, blocking out what little light the darkening sky had been providing.

At the same time, Dust stopped his teasing. He braced his arms again and went for it, pounding her into the mattress with the force of his thrusts. He didn't slow or hold back, pummeling her with his cock at a pace impossible for her to keep up with. His mouth pressed against her again, and everything about what he was doing screamed that he was marking her, claiming her.

Jade should hate it.

But it all felt too good for a thing like hate to stand a chance. His solid weight pinning her down, the way he rammed into her, the curved head of his cock stroking against that spot just right, the taste of his tongue as he fucked her mouth in the same frenzied way he was fucking her pussy...

It was all too much. Too much and not enough, and for the first time in a long time Jade didn't care about anything other than this feeling and how she could hold on to it. How she could make it grow.

The rain continued to pour and the smell of it drifted in through the open window, the cool breeze licking against her sweat-slicked skin yet another pleasurable feeling that had her bowing up to meet one of his thrusts. Her inner walls squeezed around him the next time he went to pull out, and they both moaned, the sounds mingling between them.

"Come, Jade," he ordered, the sound of him battering her flesh with his own filling the room, creating a war beat with the rain. "Come for me."

Jade exploded. Her walls clenched and unclenched around him as he continued to take her, the orgasm hitting her hard enough she momentarily saw nothing but blackness, her whole body feeling as though it were coming apart at the seams and stitching itself back together again.

She'd slept with men before.

But it'd never felt like this.

There was magic in the air, she could taste it, like ripe berries and moss and rainwater. It seeped from her pores, surrounding them, connecting them so that suddenly it wasn't just his cock still fucking her that she felt, but the hastening rhythm of his heartbeat and the core of power that rested in the center of his being, like molten lava.

She felt all of him, around her, inside of her, felt him so intensely that just as over-sensitivity was starting to kick, she knew the very moment he was about to hit his release.

Dust dropped his head to the curve of her neck and bite down, muffling his roar of pleasure as he came. He continued to pump into her, coating her battered and sore inner walls with his come.

His orgasm seemed to last ages, but after a while, he finally stilled over her, his hips settling with him still buried deep inside. When she tried to shift beneath his weight, he growled, mouth still latched onto the place between her neck and her shoulder.

Now that it was over and she was starting to come down from the high, the little aches and pains were making themselves known. Her ankles and her wrists had been rubbed raw from the leather cuffs, and the muscles in her thighs burned from being forced into this position for so long. Where he'd bitten her hurt as well, though the stinging sensation was minor and slowly fading. He might not have even broken skin.

"Dust." Her voice sounded off amongst the silence of the room, reedy and unsure, practically overshadowed by the continued rainfall, but he heard her.

Easing himself up onto one forearm, he peered down at her, giving no reaction when she gasped at the sight of him.

His eyes were glowing, the pink so bright it was almost as if they'd been backlit by something. He blinked, and the light winked in and out, hypnotizing her in the otherwise sheer darkness of the room.

She couldn't look away even if she'd wanted to, stunned into submission even as she felt him harden deep within her, and alarm bells rang in her mind that she couldn't possibly go through that all again and survive.

He started moving, keeping her locked in his gaze, her tiny gasps urging him on. He took her slow and steady in short strokes that had them both panting all over again.

It burned and her bruised pussy protested but Jade couldn't speak, couldn't look away.

Wasn't sure she even really wanted to.

Dust fucked her well into the night, up until the rain finally stopped as the sun breached the horizon.

Then he used his magic to command her to make it rain again, and started from the beginning.

Chapter 5:

Jade stared at herself in the foggy glass. The mirror in the bathroom showed a stranger, a too pale girl with hickeys on her neck and across her collar bones, bright red lips from rough kisses, and messy hair.

She'd lost weight since coming here, not enough to be noticeable to someone else, but to her it was glaringly obvious. Most likely due to the fact that a third of her time here had been spent unconscious thanks to the guy in the other room.

The guy she'd just had the best sex of her entire life with.

For almost two days straight.

She squeezed her eyes shut and leaned against the stone countertop. The bathroom here was modeled similarly to the ones back home, only without electricity, candles lit the room. The toilet still flushed and there was running water, and Jade had long since stopped trying to make sense of this world or anything in it. In a realm where magic was abundant anything was possible.

Even her being inexplicably drawn to her captor.

Maybe that was it. She straightened and considered the possibility she had Stockholm syndrome. Even though she couldn't remember all of it, he'd apparently been the only one with her while she was going through the change, which was a painful, vulnerable process. Could she have subconsciously latched onto him? Or was it the drop of his blood in the vial?

When she'd brought it up just before he'd penetrated her, he'd sounded insulted, but could she trust he'd tell the truth about something so important? What about what he'd claimed he was chaining her to his bed for her benefit?

She snorted, dropping her gaze to the filled basin of water in the center of the sink. No matter where she looked, it seemed she could escape herself; her reflection peered back almost mockingly with a tired and lost expression.

Defeated.

Jade needed to get out of here.

Okay, there was clearly something seriously wrong with her, she inwardly admitted as she stared herself down. She didn't like Dust, but she was incredibly attracted to him physically. He was an asshole and a dictator and so much like the men she was around back home—

Shit. Was that what this was? Was this the result of latent granddaddy issues? Was it the story Kyo had told her about how he'd supposedly gone to war all for the sake of a little boy? Or maybe it had to do with Koya's loyalty. Loyalty like that wasn't granted for nothing. He was also a dick, but Koya had his reasons for being that attached to the Emperor.

Although…he was probably a bad example since he was in love with him…

Jade gripped the edge of the sink hard enough her knuckles turned as white as the marble.

"What are you doing?" Dust quirked a brow when she jolted at his sudden appearance. He was standing in the doorway, which meant she'd been so lost in thought she hadn't even heard him open it and come in, and had thrown on a black silk robe that matched the one she was currently wearing. His eyes dropped to the filled basin and his brow furrowed. "Don't tell me you're in here trying to escape?"

For a moment she didn't follow, then it hit her what he meant, and she turned her attention back to the water. She hadn't even considered...

"Would that work?" In her excitement, she forgot who she was speaking to, bracing herself when she heard him approach, expecting anger.

Instead, the Emperor wrapped his arms around her and settled his chin on her shoulder, the move docile and sweet in a way that had her mind blanking and her heart clamoring in her chest.

Yes. Definitely granddaddy issues. That was the only explanation. He was cruel to her one minute and caring the next. The Emperor made him seem attainable in a way her grandfather never was.

She'd long since realized she would never measure up in Owen Blakely's mind. She'd never be the granddaughter he really wanted, the heir that could make him proud.

"Little cat," Dust cooed then and she met his gaze in the mirror over the sink, "where did you go?"

"My grandfather must be so pissed right now," she said, not really even sure why she bothered.

He hummed, the vibrations from his throat tickling her shoulder. "You sound concerned."

"Not for him."

"Ah." His arms tightened around her waist subtly. "You're worried about how you'll avoid him if you ever make it back to your world."

There was no use in denying it, he knew her stance on the matter, and no amount of amazing sex was going to change her mind. This wasn't her home, wasn't where she belonged.

Not that she belonged where she'd come from either.

Jade didn't think she'd ever actually belonged anywhere.

"You shouldn't waste energy fretting over something that will never come to be," the Emperor told her, burying his face against the curve of her neck and inhaling deeply. "I'll never let you go. You'll stay here, by my side. Your grandfather won't be able to touch you ever again."

"Why?"

"Because I won't let him."

"No," she shook her head, and he glanced up, meeting her gaze in the mirror once more, "That's not what I'm talking about." It was now or never. Now, before the disturbing thoughts she'd been having before he'd walked into the bathroom consumed her. "What if we make a deal?"

He was silent for a long time, merely staring at her unblinkingly. Then he straightened, his expression enigmatic as his arms dropped away. He stayed close though, looming at her back, watching her reflection. "Deal?"

"Once your curse is broken you won't need me anymore," she said. "Let me go home then. You'll have gotten what you want and I—"

"There seems to be a misunderstanding here, little cat," he interrupted.

"You mentioned you were close to breaking the curse," she rushed on, not liking the sudden edge in his eyes. "I'd prefer you not bleed me dry, of course, so if we have to go other…routes," she tried to ignore the way her inner muscles clenched at that prospect, "then so be it. What will it take? Another day like today? Two? Three?"

"You're saying you'll lay with me as many times as I want until the curse is broken?" he asked darkly.

She should have headed the tone, but she was lost to the desperate sensation clawing at her chest telling her this was it, her final chance to reason with him before it was too late.

"Yes," she nodded, "it's just sex. I'll stop resisting and help you end the curse once and for all and then after you let me go home—to my actual home. In my world. Alive." She could already picture him killing her and tossing her corpse into the hot springs through a portal and calling that even.

He nodded and she held her breath while he seemed to consider it.

She should have known better.

"No."

She frowned, the sinking feeling in her gut feeling a lot like hopelessness. "Why?"

"Here's the thing, Jade," he wrapped his fingers around her elbow and turned her so that she was facing him, "you haven't seemed to grasp what's really going on here. Allow me to enlighten you."

He planted his hands on either side of her on the counter and recovered the inch of space between their bodies so that she was caught between him and the sink. "You will help me end my curse because that is something that I want. Something, but not everything. Once the curse is broken I'll have the power to control the whole damn universe, let alone this world. Do you really think a place exists where you could hide from me?"

"I wouldn't have to if you would just let me go."

"Little cat," he clucked his tongue at her, "you'll stop resisting? I like the way you resist. I like the look on your face whenever I break through one of your walls. Whenever I make you realize you want me."

"I—"

"—Want me," he finished for her. "You want me, Jade."

"You're hot," she admitted, "that's all. There are plenty of hot men in the world, whether it be this one or mine."

His mouth thinned into a sharp line, his irritation apparent. "Whether that's true or not, I'm the only one for you. You aren't going anywhere. I'm keeping you, and that's final."

"You don't get a say on how or where I live my life," she snapped, pushing that hopeless feeling aside. It wouldn't do her any good to feel sorry for herself. Fighting was the only option. "My grandfather thought he could control me and look where that got him. He might not be a god, but he's every bit a domineering asshole as you are. Resisting?" She snorted derisively. "I'm not resisting, I'm refusing."

"Let's see for how long, Jade." The Emperor scooped her up and tossed her over his shoulder, carrying her back into the bedroom.

He didn't bother with the chains this time, pinning her down with his body as he took her well into the night.

* * *

Jade was seated at the window seat, staring out at the forest below when the Emperor set a bowl of water before her. She was back in the robe after two days of being out of it and felt cranky and exhausted.

She'd really set him off with her suggestion of a deal, and the two of them had been tangled in the sheets since, as if he somehow believed he could fuck his way into her heart and make her want to stay that way. Because it was obvious that her words had affected him, that he'd taken her seriously when she'd pointed out that she'd managed to escape her grandfather.

The Emperor settled down across from her, adjusting the bowl so that it was perfectly centered between them. "You've adjusted to the change. We should see what you're capable of."

She eyed him suspiciously. "You want me to, what? Bleed and open a portal?" Wasn't he afraid that she'd take the chance and run?

"Portals can't be opened anywhere. There are specific areas where the veil between worlds is thin. Apparently, my hot spring is one of them."

"Lucky you," she muttered, but he continued.

"You happened to fall through there, but you could have come through any number of places. It all depends on where the thin spots attach. If you went back through the portal in the spring—which you won't be doing, ever—it would deposit you back at the same place you left." He tapped the side of the wooden bowl with a finger. "The likelihood of this specific spot also being a thin area is slime. But even if it was, you couldn't fit through this tiny bowl, now could you? And it wouldn't bring you to the same location."

"So even if I find another portal, it could lead anywhere." She could end up in the middle of the Amazon rainforest or at the bottom of the Pacific Ocean.

"Exactly." He sat back, satisfied that she understood. "I've cordoned off the hot spring and ordered over a dozen guards to watch over it around the clock. Even if you did figure out where it's located on the grounds, it wouldn't matter. You'll never get to it, Jade. And if I discover that you've tried—"

"You'll what? Bleed me to death?"

He pursed his lips. "I have no intentions of killing you, that should be obvious by now. You're mine, and I don't discard my things lightly. I tend to obsess over them instead."

"Is that what this is?" she demanded. "You're playing with me because right now I'm an interesting new toy, and once you're no longer amused that's when you'll toss me aside? I'm not an object, Dust, I'm a human being."

The tension left him suddenly and he smiled at her. "Again."

"What?" His mood swings were so hard to follow.

"Say it again," he reiterated.

"I'm not a toy or a sex doll, I'm—"

"Not that," he waved her off. "My name. Say it again."

She clamped her mouth shut. Was he this happy over a little thing like that? She'd said it accidentally, in the heat of the moment, and now she was regretting it because pleasing him was the last thing she wanted to do.

"Say it again, Jade," he insisted, "or I'll make you say it."

She heaved a frustrated sigh. "Fine. Dust. I'm not a toy, Dust. You can't just fuck with me whenever you feel like it, Dust. I have my own thoughts and wants, Dust."

"Tell me."

"What?" She wished he would stop being so cryptic about everything. Whenever he got like this it was too hard to keep up and she hated being thrown for a loop. He already had her on edge as it was.

"What are your wants?" he asked. "Aside from going home, of course."

She waited for him to add something else, curious if this was another trap of some sort, but when all he did was continue to watch her patiently, she shrugged. "Why does that matter? According to you, I won't get anything I want anyway."

"You can't leave me," he corrected. "I've said nothing about anything else. How can I, when I'm not even aware of what it is you're hoping for?"

She smiled sardonically. "You can't give it to me anyway, so what's the point?"

"Try me."

"I'd rather not."

"Tell me, Jade," this time, his voice filled with power, a warmth that spilled from him and encased her like a heated blanket in the middle of the winter. It coaxed her and comforted her all at once, made her feel like she had to do as he said. Made her want to. "Tell me what you want most. What you've always wanted most."

"Myself," she said, the word slipping past her lips. "I just want to be me. I want to figure out who I am and where I belong. I don't want to be chased anymore."

He canted his head, but if her confession surprised him he didn't show it. "Have you ever belonged anywhere?"

"No."

"What about your parents?"

"My grandfather killed them."

His eyes widened a fraction before he seemed to get a hold of himself and his expression went blank once more. "How?"

"He ran them off the road. Made it seem like an accident. My dad died instantly when their car hit a tree." Her grandfather had kept the medical records in his safe as well, and she'd made the mistake of going through them. Thinking about what she'd read there now had her stomach clamping and breakfast threatening to make a return appearance. "My mom was rushed to the hospital. They say she was partially conscious and kept asking for my dad. She was in bad shape, in a lot of pain. The nearest hospital was over a half hour away and even though she made it there she died on the table later that night."

She'd suffered, that much had been clear. She'd suffered needlessly, scared and alone, with the knowledge that her husband was already dead.

"She used her last words to accuse my grandfather of causing the accident," Jade added, "but the police covered it up and removed it from the report because he had them on his payroll. I spent my entire life believing a random drunk driver had killed them, that they'd both died upon impact with no time for pain...When I found out the truth..."

"You ran," he concluded.

"I was able to hide for a year. Amelia came with me and we traveled a lot to avoid staying in the same place for too long. They found me just before I came here. That's who I was trying to get away from and why I accidentally opened the portal."

"And if you hadn't gotten away from them?"

"They would have brought me back to my grandfather and he would have forced me to act as his heir. Typically only someone with power can fill the role of leader, and I have it. He was always frustrated at me that I wasn't powerful enough." She chuckled humorlessly. "I suppose that'll no longer be a problem for him."

"You'll never have to see him again," Dust told her, then before she could argue a second time asked, "How would he force you?"

It wasn't like there was anyone here she cared about that he could use against her, so Jade couldn't see a reason not to be honest with the Emperor. "He'd use my friends as leverage most likely. Either threaten to get them fired from their jobs or worse. Kidnapping, torture, and murder aren't out of the question. He's done all of that and more to others in the past. I wouldn't want to risk my friends so I'd go along with whatever he told me to do. That's how it worked before I left. He governs through fear and intimidation."

"You hate him."

"He killed my parents." She more than hated him.

"Do you want revenge?"

"In order for that to happen, I have to let him find me," she said. "Not only do I hate that idea, I'm also not strong enough to stand against him. Even with power," she held out her arms indicating herself, "he'll still win over me."

"Because he knows what you care about."

"Isn't there anything you care about?" He'd sounded like he was judging her just now and she didn't like it. Her grandfather used to judge her like that too.

Dust thought it over. "Not especially."

"Not even Koya? He cares about you."

He shrugged. "Koya has been tedious as of late. He says I'm addicted to you because you're the first thing I was able to smell and truly taste in centuries. He's probably not wrong, but that doesn't mean I need to hear it over and over again."

"It doesn't bother you? Doesn't it make you feel like you've lost some semblance of control?"

"No," he replied. "It changes nothing. I accept all parts of myself, Jade, even the parts my logical mind might fight against. Does it make sense that I'm obsessed with you to the point I'm even willing to take my time to cure myself? Of course not. But it's a fact and there's no changing it, the only thing I can do is make peace with it and move on. I want you. I have you. I'll keep you. It doesn't matter if the reasoning behind that is because you've ensnared me with your scent or because I genuinely like your company. The only thing that matters is that I do."

"We're very different people." As if she wasn't already aware of that.

"Yes," he agreed, "you're torturing yourself over how badly your body wants me instead of accepting.

Things would be so much easier for you if you did. You could be, if not happy, at the very least content here with me. I can make it so."

"I want to go home." He wasn't going to change her mind that easily.

"Why? So that you can be captured by your grandfather and forced into a life you don't want?"

"It's different," she insisted. "There, I still stand a chance. There's a possibility I can make it through the portal and escape before they see me. There's no hope for that here at all. But aside from that, my situation, with you, isn't much different. You say you want to keep me? What does that even mean? You'll lock me in this room until I'm old and gray and die lonely and bitter?"

"Would you like to leave this room?" he asked.

"Of course," she snapped. "Who wants to stay locked up?"

He nudged the bowl closer to her, reminding her that it was even there. "Make the water move, little cat, and I'll let you out."

"What?" She stared down at the water, frowning. The only thing she'd ever done before was make it rain. Her grandfather had tried to get her to do more before and it had never worked.

"You're stronger now," Dust reminded, as if able to read her thoughts. "You can do this. And as soon as you do," he stood with a flourish and bent to place a chaste kiss on her cheek, "I'll let you wander the palace grounds to your heart's content."

Even with an incentive like that, it was easier said than done.

Chapter 6:

She couldn't do it.

She spent hours focused on the bowl of water, recalling all of the steps her grandfather had taught her about controlling her magic, but nothing worked. No matter how much she focused, how much energy she summoned to the surface, she couldn't get it to do what she wanted.

With a growl of frustration, she shoved the bowl off the seat, the sky opening up out the window as she lost control and called the rain instead.

The wood clattered on the floor and rolled toward the door, leaving a puddle in its wake.

Jade closed her eyes and inhaled, trying to calm her nerves before she totally and completely lost it. Acting out like that was childish and would get her nowhere. Now, not only did she feel like shit she also had a mess to clean.

"That was real mature of you." Koya was standing by the doorway and shook his head at her mockingly when she noticed him.

"What are you doing here?" Up until this point, the only two people she'd been allowed to see had been the Emperor and Kyo. To say she was happy to see Koya would be a lie, but the glimpse of a courtyard through the open doorway caught her attention.

She wanted to go outside.

Damn it.

"I brought you lunch," he explained, holding up the tray with a spread of cheeses and meats slices before walking over to set it on the table.

"Where's Kyo?"

"She's busy somewhere else," he said. His dark blue hair was combed nicely and his black uniform was crisp as always, but there was something about his face that clued her in to the fact he wasn't as put together as appearances seemed. "I can't stay long, the Emperor doesn't know I offered to bring your lunch in Kyo's stead. That thing we spoke of before, while we were out of the palace? Okay."

Jade had no idea what he was talking about at first until it hit her that he must be referring to the time she'd asked him to help her locate the hot spring. "Seriously? Why?"

And more importantly, how could she trust him?

"It's become clear the Emperor isn't going to get rid of you," he explained, sounding disgusted by that fact. "If I help you, he can never know. If you're caught it's your funeral and you swear to leave me out of it."

"You'll trust me to keep my word?"

"You'll trust me to actually lead you to the springs and not just kill you in the woods somewhere?" he countered.

Not really, but it wasn't like she had a lot of other options at the moment.

"What about the guards?" Even if she made it to the hot spring, she couldn't get near it so long as it was being watched.

"Leave them to me," Kyo said and she narrowed her eyes.

"Seems awfully convenient. You're willing to risk betraying the Emperor just to get me out of the way?" She felt a little bad for him, really. "You do realize that it won't change things between you, don't you? He isn't going to magically fall in love with you once I'm gone."

"I know that." But he obviously didn't like being reminded. "I can't kill you outright, there's too great a risk that your body might one day be discovered no matter how well I hide the corpse."

Lovely.

"This is the best way. I don't want you around him, he's changing and I don't like it." He crossed his arms. "What do you say? Are you in or what?"

There was the chance this was a test set up by the Emperor to see what she'd do in a situation like this—she wouldn't put it past him—but it didn't matter one way or the other. She'd made it clear from the beginning and throughout their time together thus far that she wanted to leave. If this was all a lie and he got pissed at her for agreeing now, it wouldn't come as a surprise. And if it wasn't...

Maybe there really was a chance she could get out of here. Initially, she'd been plotting on memorizing the palace grounds when she was finally allowed out of this room. If she could discover where the hot spring was, that was one less thing to worry about. She'd simply have to figure out a way to distract the guards and she'd be home free.

If Koya was to be believed, he could help her bypass both of those steps, which was a good thing, considering she'd had absolutely no luck with moving the water in that bowl at all. Not even a ripple.

"I'm in," she said. "Tell me where the hot spring is."

"It's west of here," he explained. "Take a left out the door and head down to the main level, then cross the courtyard and take another left. There's a large statue of a dog, when you come to it, go past it, there's a small path that you wouldn't notice if you didn't know to look. That'll take you straight to the area you need to be. You should recognize the building you ran away from when you arrived. The hot spring is there."

Jade concentrated on memorizing all of that since they couldn't risk writing it down and she didn't think he'd bother trying to find another chance to sneak in here and see her to tell it to her again. "And the guards?"

"I'll handle them when the time is right," he stated. "Be warned, if you try to make it there before I give you the okay, you will be caught and I won't go down with you."

He wanted her to wait...

"You'll help me once the Emperor's curse is completely broken," she figured.

"He's close. Probably only another couple of days or so if—" he stopped himself abruptly, mouth scrunching up in displeasure.

No doubt he'd been about to talk about her and the Emperor having sex.

"He should just bleed you and be done with it," he mumbled, though not so under his breath that she couldn't easily make out the words, which she felt was probably done on purpose. A sound she couldn't hear caught his ear then and he titled his head, silent for a second before, "I have to go. Await my signal. Don't be rash, we could only have the one shot at this and if you ruin it—"

"Yeah, yeah," she said. "I get it."

He snarled at her but turned on his heels and quietly snuck back out of the room.

Less than a minute later the door opened again and this time the Emperor strolled in. He glanced between her and the bowl on the ground, then grabbed a cub of cheese off the tray and walked over to her. Wordlessly, he pressed the morsel against her lips.

Jade took the offering and chewed, watching as he bent and retrieved the bowl next and brought it over to the table to refill it with the half-empty pitcher of water.

Without turning back to her, he held out a hand, the other working on setting the refilled bowl near the edge of the table closest to where he stood. When she placed her palm against his, he tugged her forward and resituated her facing the table with him pressed against her back.

"Should I help you, little cat?" he practically purred, his fingers dancing down to the tie at the sash holding her robe together. He untangled the note before she could reply, and the next thing she knew, his fingers were dipping between her folds, stroking across her sensitive flesh. He rubbed at her clit, gentle strokes that didn't supply enough pressure, and had her breaths quickening.

Her conversation with Koya was all but forgotten as her skin heated and arousal flooded through her. Part of her wanted to push him away and deny the effect he had, but the other more rational part acknowledged it was far too late for that.

He knew very well what he did to her, that's why when they were together he was constantly touching her. It was as if he wanted her to get used to his touch, whether that was merely a hand on her knee, or the feel of his chest beneath her cheek when he held her close. Little touches, subtle touches. And not little or subtle ones. Like the ones he was giving her right now.

Jade leaned back into him for support, grabbing onto his arm and clinging as he worked her into a frenzy.

"Concentrate on the bowl," he said then, voice low and coaxing. "Think about making the water move."

She couldn't even concentrate on remembering her own damn name at the moment and he wanted her to do what? She shook her head, biting the inside of her cheek to keep from mewling when one of his long fingers trailed lower and pushed inside.

"Do you want my help?" he asked, and she nodded before she could even really consider what he meant by that. A second later, his tone changed, the steady thrum of his magic circling them, causing her breath to catch in her throat even more. "Use your power to move the water in the bowl, Jade."

At the command, her body seemed to act of its own accord. She felt the burst of magic shoot out of her, the feeling similar to how she called the rain and yet different at the same time, more like she was throwing something instead of summoning something. Shoving something outside of herself in a steady stream.

A ripple skated over the surface of the bowl before three perfect drops of water separated and floated, rising into the air to hover a couple of inches.

As soon as it happened, the Emperor flicked against her clit, sending her over the edge and she gasped and came, jerking against him, watching in amazement as the drops continued to float even when her mind went blank and all she knew was pure bliss.

She came down from the orgasm slowly, little by little, with his fingers continuing to play her gently the whole while, almost to the point of over-sensitivity. The clearer her mind seemed to get, the lower the drops dipped, until they touched the surface and burst, mixing in with the rest of the water.

The Emperor made a disappointed sound, but when she turned her head toward him, he was staring down at his hand as he pulled it away from her, brow furrowed. "It doesn't work if it's my fingers," he said as if to himself. "Let's try again."

He let go of her for a moment to shove the bowl to the other side of the table, careful not to dislodge the tray of food in the process. Then he lifted her by the hips and set her down where the bowl had been, pushing her shoulder until she was lying down, splayed out before he settled between her spread thighs.

"What—" she was going to ask him what he meant, but he was already answering, clearly impatient to get things going.

He was wearing more than rob, and it was taking him longer to remove the long-sleeved pink silk shirt. He spoke as he undressed, tossing his clothing aside with little care for where any of it landed.

"The exchange," he told her, "when I make you orgasm and use your magic at the same time the effects are heightened because you're blissed out. More power seeps through, and more of my curse is broken. But I need to have contact with—"

"I get it."

"—and apparently my fingers aren't enough," he continued anyway. "You need to come on my cock."

"How romantic." They both froze at the same time as soon as the words slipped past her lips. She slapped a hand over her mouth, eyes going wide. She had no idea why she'd said that. It'd been meant as a joke and had at least come out sounding sarcastic but still. The last thing she needed was to put foolish notions in his head.

"Is that something you want?" he asked her, and she immediately shook her head.

"Absolutely not."

He watched her for a minute, possibly trying to figure out if she was lying. Thankfully, he dropped it altogether, hands undoing the ties on his black pants. Then he was naked and slipping his cock inside of her, pressing in deep.

Her eyes rolled back and she moaned loud and long. Her body slipped an inch up the table and he grabbed onto her thighs, yanking her back to meet his hips as he pounded forward, taking her in steady pumps.

"Look at the bowl, Jade," he commanded, and she did as she was told, tipping her head back to stare at the bowl only three inches or so from the top of her head. "Picture the water lifting out of it. Think of how it felt a moment ago when you used your power on those droplets. Concentrate on that and the feel of me inside you. Nothing else. There's only this, little cat. You, and me, and the magic we make."

Jade stared at the bowl, unable to see inside at this angle. The wood clanked slightly against the surface as the table rocked beneath them, the legs creaking with each inward thrust. The smell of burnt cinnamon and rain and the unmistakable hint of their mutual arousal filled the room and she focused on it. Focused on all of the sensations right down to the way her toes were curling and how her inner walls squeezed him tight whenever he pulled his cock free of her.

She felt the pressure building low as well as in the center of her chest. This was typically the part where he'd order her to make it rain, but she knew that wasn't the case this time. She needed to lift the contents of that bowl.

Jade exhaled and imagined what it might look like if the water flowed upward in a spiral, picturing some of the ice sculptures she'd seen back home on TV and in magazines. She held out a hand, holding her palm near the side of the bowl without touching it and pushed that tight ball of energy in her chest up her arm and out.

Water snaked its way into view, twisting slowly as it rose, quacking when she let out an elated sound. It made it almost six inches into the air and would have kept going if Dust hadn't noticed.

He shoved his cock in deep and reached down to press his thumb roughly against her clit.

The second orgasm felt like being hit by a truck and her back bowed off the table, her mouth parting on a partial scream as pleasure exploded inside of her. She moaned as he continued to thrust, chasing after his own release, and when he found it his grip tightened on her thighs and he gasped as he came inside of her.

Spent, they both panted through the wake of it, regaining their senses little by little. The Emperor recovered first, opening his mouth to say something before the water over her head caught his attention. He laughed.

Jade tilted her head again to see, sucking in a breath.

The water spiral had frozen and was now a solid swirl of ice.

"I..." She'd done that. She'd been thinking about ice and now it was ice. "I've never been able to do that before," she finished dumbly.

Dust lifted her off the table and back into his arms, hugging her close before kissing her. "That's just the beginning," he promised.

And she hated it, but the pride in his pink eyes had her heart soaring.

Chapter 7:

Jade held her hands above the water of the fountain, concentrating. In her mind, she pictured the liquid rising, forming into a shape, morphing the same way clay could be molded. The now familiar crackle and pop of magic as it burned through her had her lips turning upward slightly, and she called on more power from that well deep inside of herself.

The water lifted into the air, not all of it, but just enough that she could play with it as she pleased. The form came together quickly, much faster than she'd been able to make it even just yesterday, and she added details here and there for good measure before willing the entire thing to the flat edge of the fountain and turning it to ice.

"What is that?" Dust asked, tilting his head as he inspected the sculpture. It was roughly three feet wide and three feet tall, and he brushed a finger lightly over the highest part curiously.

"It's a swan," Jade told him. "You guys don't have swans here?"

She'd discovered that was the case with most animals. It seemed this world shared a lot of foliage with hers, but when it came to the creatures that roamed the Earth, they varied. So far, aside from chickens, dogs, cats, and horses, there weren't many similarities. Even most of their bird species were strange.

As if to prove that point, Pearl squawked at Jade from her perch on the Emperor's shoulder. She might have looked like a salmon-crested cockatoo from back home, but Jade recalled the dragon-like form Pearl could just as easily take on when she felt like it.

Jade turned back to the sculpture. She'd done a pretty good job of it if she did say so herself. The neck was delicate and curved with the bird's head tucked against its breast, and she'd even added ridges for the feathers of the folded wings and a sharp point to the tail. It'd gotten easier in the past week she'd been practicing, and she was loathed to admit it, but that was mostly due to Dust and his attentiveness.

"We do not," he answered her question then and stepped back from the sculpture. With a flick of his fingers, he silently ordered her to continue to the next step. He'd been training her not only to control water and freeze it but also how to turn it to steam as well.

This part didn't take nearly as much concentration, and with a mere snap of her fingers, Jade melted the sculpture, turning it first back into its liquid form which splashed into a puddle on the rim of the fountain, before heating it to the point of boiling and then past that. A waft of steam twisted into the air, the whole process taking less than a minute to accomplish and she smiled at herself a second time.

Used to be she could only make it rain, now look at her.

"You've improved," Dust hummed and folded his arms, turning a satisfied smirk her way. Even Pearl let out another sound on his shoulder, one that sounded an awful lot like agreement though Jade knew the bird didn't actually speak any human languages. "There's still a long way to go, but you're going well."

He'd told her before that with the amount of power she had at her disposal, she should be capable of lifting lakes and raising the seas. She wasn't quite sure she believed him—and didn't understand why she'd ever need to do either of those things—but the concept of being that strong was appealing.

It meant no one would be able to control her, didn't it? If she were capable of feats like that, she would be free from fear of both her grandfather and the Emperor using her as they pleased. Although...

In the time since she'd woken up after drinking the contents of that vial, Dust hadn't really done much of anything to her that she didn't ultimately—even if she refused to confess as much—end up enjoying in one way, shape, or another. The sex, for one, didn't just make him feel good. She felt empowered each and every time, like that well of power within herself had strengthened and grown and she could move oceans if she had to. Since he'd let her out of the room, she'd been allowed to roam as she'd pleased, though she'd made a point of not exploring too close to the statue where Koya had told her the path leading to the hot spring was.

She didn't want to tip the Emperor off that she still planned on escape, because, sure, the conversation was good—Dust was actually a very intelligent and eloquent speaker—and she liked the way he made her feel physically, but that wasn't enough to get her to want to stick around. Right?

Right.

It didn't matter that there wasn't much to look forward to once she made it back home. This wasn't it. This place with its odd creatures and its pantheon of ruling gods. This wasn't where she belonged.

"You're going through a lot of trouble teaching me," she said. It wasn't the first time she'd brought it up, but he always seemed to grow angry whenever she did.

Sure enough, he sighed and frowned at her. "Is it so hard to believe that I want you prepared for the next time something happens? Have you forgotten how you and Koya were attacked outside the palace?"

"You haven't let me step foot off the palace grounds," she reminded. "So I'm not sure why that matters."

"Because eventually I will," he stated, expression darkening further. "I don't intend to keep you holed up here forever, Jade."

"What exactly do you intend? You've never said." They'd been getting close to one another recently, and she'd overlooked just how much because it'd been better than the alternative. It was better than being chained to a bed or thrown into the dungeons. It was better to have him smiling at her and praising her than it was having him sneer and threaten to tear into her neck.

But how much of this was real and how much was simply another trick?

And why was she hoping that he was being honest? That he was training her for her own benefit and not so he could use her for his own means?

"Haven't I?" He shook his head. "I don't know how to be any clearer than I already have been."

"I don't know," she suggested, "maybe by using your words? You haven't told me anything. Why are you helping me, really? Because your curse—"

"The curse is broken," he snapped, giving her pause.

"What?"

"It's been broken for weeks," he said.

"Since when?"

"Since the night you first froze water."

He'd kept that from her. She'd had no idea. It'd been over twelve days since then and she'd been under the impression that his curse was still intact. There were many reasons she could think of why he'd want her to continue believing that, but one rang louder than the rest.

She glared at him. "You wanted to keep fucking me."

His hands fisted at his sides, though he didn't deny it. "You wanted me to keep fucking you. It's why you never asked about the curse, why you were comfortable assuming."

"That isn't true."

"Isn't it?" he disagreed.

For their first time, he'd kept her chained to the bed and had claimed it was for her benefit. Was this similar? He'd kept it a secret because he'd known how she would react when she found out?

With self-hatred.

It pissed her off even more that, if that were the case, he wasn't wrong. Anger toward herself was already brewing, swirling in her gut so she thought she might be sick. At least when she thought they were sleeping together to break the curse, she could convince herself she was doing what she had to. But now…

"Nothing bad will happen if you admit it, Jade," he urged her then, clearly noting the way she'd tensed and paled. "It's okay to want me."

She vehemently shook her head. It wasn't. It wasn't okay.

"Why?" His frown returned, though the edge of frustration never abated.

"Because it's a trick." It had to be. Jade hadn't fallen for him, she'd fallen for the moments of kindness he'd shown her. She'd fallen for the way he wrapped her in his arms at night and the feel of his warmth and the steady sounds of his soft breaths as he slept. She'd fallen for the way he made her feel, like she wasn't powerless or worthless or a mistake—the way her grandfather had always made her feel.

"You want me to pretend this is all in my control," she found herself saying, "but it isn't. I won't forget the things you did before, the way you treated me and Amelia, the lies you told." All of that pain and fear and doubt, she clung to it now, trying to remind herself it was there.

Trying to ignore the fact that the way he looked at her now was different from the way he'd looked at her then.

"I haven't used my power on you in days," he said, which was true. Even when they were tangled up in one another, close to release, and he whispered that she should make it rain he hadn't used magic to make her. She'd done so on her own.

She'd been more than willing to obey.

And that terrified her.

She took a step back and his anger flared at the move. Before either of them could get in another word, however, a soldier appeared at the Emperor's back.

The soldier cleared his throat to get their attention and then bowed low, obviously seeing that he'd walked in on something he shouldn't. "Forgive me, Emperor, but there's been a commotion in the greeting hall."

"What kind of commotion?" Dust asked, his fury never dimming.

"A servant of the God of Intention is here and demanded an audience," the soldier explained. "We've tried to calm him down, but he insists it is an emergency and he must speak with you at once."

The Emperor stared at Jade for a long moment, a range of emotions swirling in his gaze, too quick for her to identify any of them. Then took a single step back, the move almost a mirror of the one she'd made before the interruption.

"Lead the way," he ordered the soldier, and then with one final look, he turned and left Jade standing there alone.

She glared at his back as he disappeared around one of the many small buildings that made up the place. All of the exits to the palace were carefully guarded, and soldiers peppered the way, it wasn't like Jade could do anything while on her own. Sometimes she brought Kyo out with her, but other times she wandered the grounds alone and the Emperor had never said anything against that.

Another false sense of control, most likely. He wanted her at ease so she didn't realize what was really going on. He was trying to get her to be relaxed and comfortable so she wouldn't think about leaving. So she'd give up any plans for escape.

Turning back to the fountain, Jade decided to spend the rest of the afternoon practicing. No matter his true motive, Dust had helped her, and the more she improved the better chance she had at doing what she really wanted, whether that be escaping or not.

There was nothing particularly spectacular about the fountain. It was circular and probably around ten feet in diameter, with crystal clear water and a statue of a serpent wrapped tightly around a blazing sun. It was the symbol of the Emperor and was on just about everything here from the uniforms to the decorations on the walls.

Jade thought about the green panther that symbolized the Emeralds and how it was also on everything back home. There was even a massive statue of it carved from stone in the foyer of the Blakely mansion. Its mouth was open in a perpetual snarl and its fangs had been filed to a point sharp enough that someone could cut themselves on them.

She would know, since an eleven her old her had done just that one day after school when the curiosity had gotten too great for her to resist. She'd even gotten a drop of blood on the beast's stone tongue which, to this day, was still there. Either no one had noticed—impossible, considering how many maids her grandfather had on staff—or no one dared bring it up to the master of the house for fear of punishment.

She'd kept the secret to herself and not even Key knew she'd done it. Later when it'd been noticed that she was wearing a band-aid she'd lied and claimed she'd gotten a papercut.

Jade shoved the memory aside and looked at the water she'd been playing with, scowling the second she realized she'd inadvertently been forming that same panther out of water and had already been in the process of turning it to ice.

With a growl, she swept her hands to the side, shattering the sculpture so that pieces plopped back into the fountain, sending up a spray of mist.

Changing her mind about continuing to train, Jade turned and rounded the fountain, heading down a random path in the opposite direction of where the Emperor had gone. It wasn't long before she caught the sound of voices and made her way toward where she thought they might be coming from.

There were a lot of people who worked for the Emperor, considering the palace itself was massive. Most of the buildings were also attached with wooden walkways, meaning there was a lot left out to the elements. In order to get to the main kitchen, Jade needed to cross two courtyards and pass by the laundry building and one of the maids' buildings where they slept and spent their free time.

She wasn't anywhere near that area right now, however, and was a bit of a way away from the more crowded parts of the palace. There shouldn't be anyone else out here aside from the occasional guard, which only had her more curious about who she was overhearing.

The path took a left, trailing around another set of buildings, but the voices sounded like they were coming from straight ahead, so Jade stepped off of the dirt and onto the grass. She made her way slowly toward the tree line, angling her head to peer between the branches, aware that if she was discovered she'd look like a creep. It was better than the alternative though, which was to go back to stewing over the Emperor and her feelings for him.

She shifted closer, trying hard not to rustle the leaves too much. She was just in the middle of deciding to give up and stop being so nosy when she finally caught sight of the two men talking.

The man with the scar on his face was turned toward her, giving her a good look at him and his stern expression. He was dressed in a crimson, long-sleeved shirt tucked into snow white pants and knee-length boots, and he was saying something to the guys standing across from him.

Though he was turned away, she recognized Koya, especially since he was in his black uniform. He had a hand resting on the hilt of his sheathed sword, and his words were sharp as he delivered them.

"I don't care what your plans are," he stated coolly. "My loyalty is with my Emperor."

"And yet," the man with the scar—Restless, Jade recalled being told—growled back, "here we are. You're the one who came to me asking for help. Loyalty? Our definitions must be different."

Koya had gone to another god for help? Help with what? There was only one thing that came to Jade's mind and she didn't like it at all.

"You were supposed to stop us before she made it back here," Koya hissed, inadvertently confirming Jade's suspicions. "Now you're saying you won't even follow through with our second arrangement?"

"I hear she's powerful," Restless said. "She could be an asset."

"She won't work with you," Koya stated, and it was clear by his frustration that this wasn't the first time he was saying as much. "She just wants to go home. She wants nothing to do with this world or the people in it!"

"Is that why you're so panicked about her staying?" Restless called his bluff. "Admit it, she's caught feelings for the Emperor, and we all know how Dust feels about her."

"It's an addiction," Koya disagreed, "nothing more."

"It's an obsession," Restless corrected. "The kind that only has one cure."

"Yes," finally, they seemed to agree on something, "separation. Which is why I'm trying so hard to get rid of her. But I can't do that alone, that's why—"

"You convinced her you'd help her find the hot spring," Restless crossed his arms, "and told her that there would come a time when you'd tip her off and distract the guards for her. That's all well and good, but you want me to do all of the actual work. Why should I?"

Koya was silent a moment, possibly stunned. "What do you mean? Stopping the Emperor before his curse is fully broken is in your best interests as well!"

Restless snorted. "Fool. His curse is already broken."

Well, at least Jade hadn't been the only one who hadn't known.

"And since that's the case," Restless continued, "getting rid of the girl will only put me at risk of Dust's ire. You're too young to know, but when he's at full power he's not only dangerous, he's frightening. Even to us other gods. He once destroyed an entire village because a man dared pluck a single rose from his garden. What do you think he'll do to us if he finds out we got rid of his woman?" He clucked his tongue. "You're on your own, but some advice? Give up. It isn't worth it."

"If you don't kill her who—"

"No one," a deep voice cut off Koya's sentence and everyone froze.

The two of them had tucked themselves off to the side of one of the storage buildings that wasn't often frequented, probably thinking that was the best place they could be alone. They'd been wrong.

The Emperor stepped from around the side of the building, having overheard most of what had been said between the two. The air around him heated like a furnace, and if Jade thought the anger he'd displayed toward her earlier was bad, it was nothing compared to the ferocity he was now showing.

It was all she could do to remain still and not step back and risk exposing her presence. Something told she so didn't want to be caught by him lurking and listening in on this conversation.

"It isn't what you think!" Koya said at the same moment that Restless cursed.

"Kneel," the Emperor's voice took on that note of power as he forced out the command.

Koya dropped to his knees, wincing at the sudden impact.

Dust turned his attention on the other god. "While I appreciate you sending your servant to inform me of this meeting, know that I will not allow you to go unpunished for what you planned to do to Jade."

"I'll await your judgment," Restless replied, not seeming the least bit put off by the threat. He must have seen it coming and had already decided this was the lesser of two punishments he'd receive if he'd instead gone through with his and Koya's plan.

It shouldn't surprise her that Koya had hoped to murder her before she left, despite his comments otherwise. He'd probably hoped Restless would do it and then they could toss her body through the portal using her blood. When the two of them had fought before while they'd been out searching for the vial, Jade's powers hadn't been very great, but her fighting skills had been on par with Koya's. He'd most likely feared going head-to-head against her and losing.

Restless had changed his mind after discovering that the Emperor's curse was already broken and had tipped Dust off. That must have been the emergency that he'd been called away to.

"Confirm that you sent the assassin after Jade to try and prevent her from returning with the vial," Dust said and Restless nodded.

"I did. Though, he was given orders not to kill her. At the time, I was hoping to kidnap and use her as a bargaining chip instead. Clearly, that didn't pan out."

"Clearly," Dust drawled.

Restless might know his place, might be aware that the Emperor was the more powerful of them, but he didn't act like someone who was afraid. He stood his ground and spoke without hesitation. Being a god as well must mean he didn't have to fear death at the Emperor's hands.

Jade didn't quite understand their dynamics, but since they were friendly with one another, that must be why.

"Leave," Dust told him then, motioning toward the set of guards who'd arrived with him and had remained ten or so feet away. "They'll escort you out. Do not return until invited."

"Of course." Restless didn't bow, he merely turned on his heels and followed orders.

"I can explain," Koya said the second they were alone.

"There's no need," the Emperor told him. "I already know everything. You were hoping Restless' man would kill Jade before bringing me the vial because you didn't want me to be cured."

"You wouldn't need me then!" Koya's grip on his sword tightened.

"You're my second in command," he reminded. "That position has nothing to do with whether or not I have my full power. What you're referring to is your body. I would no longer need to possess you once a month just to smell something and keep from going mad. That's true. I'm cured now and you were right, I don't need you the same way I used to. But I would have kept you around at the very least."

"Emperor—"

"Enough."

"She doesn't love you!" Koya yelled. "Not like I do! She was going to leave! You should have seen how happy she was when I told her I would help her!"

Jade really wished he hadn't said that. There'd been a chance at least that the Emperor hadn't arrived in time to hear the part about her being partially in on the plan. Now...

Not bothering to stick around to hear anymore, Jade quietly pulled back and then raced down the winding path. She headed straight for her room, mind racing through all the possible excuses she could give the Emperor when he was done with Koya and came to confront her.

Because he would confront her.

It was just a matter of when and how.

Chapter 8:

He found her pacing in the room less than an hour later. She'd sort of hoped for more time, though she didn't know what for.

When he entered, he brought with him that same heated cloud that he'd carried when confronted Restless and Koya, and it caused a shiver to skate down her spine and her shoulders to stiffen.

The Emperor stormed into the room, slamming the door shut behind him as an afterthought. The second he spotted her he growled, a deep animalistic sound that had her freezing in place without meaning to. He was upon her a moment later, grabbing onto her wrist to tug her against him.

His hold was bruising and she flinched away, but that only made his fury grow.

She struggled as his arms banded around her, mostly out of panic than anything. Logically, she knew she needed to handle this a different way, but it was hard to think with him touching her.

"You aren't even going to pretend to not know why I'm upset," the Emperor said a second later, realizing that she'd yet to verbally complain.

"I know you're angry about Koya and—"

"You were there?!" He shoved her away so fast she stumbled, falling against the end of the bed. "Why? Did you follow one of them to their secret meeting in the hopes they'd help you escape sooner? Was that the plan?"

"No, I didn't—" Why was she cowering before him? Who cared if he was a god or in charge here. She was Jade Blakely. She pushed herself onto her feet. "You knew I intended to leave. This isn't new information and you shouldn't be this shocked."

"What?" He actually appeared taken aback.

"You thought pretending to be nice to me would somehow change my mind?" All that time spent trying to come up with a plan to lessen his anger had been moot because the words spilling out of her mouth right now would most definitely do the opposite and she knew it. Still, she couldn't seem to stop them from flowing, unloading all of the things she'd been thinking to herself since she'd woken up in that bed.

"You let me walk around the palace and think that I can't see it for what it is? You've removed the leash, but you still have me in a cage. I'm no one's pet, Dust, and I never will be. You're no better than my grandfather."

The Emperor flinched as if she'd slapped him. "You're comparing me to him? The man you hate most?"

"Why not?" she snapped. "I hate you too!"

"Liar."

"If you hadn't put that stupid drop of your blood in that vial I would never welcome your touch and you know it!"

"My blood?" He laughed, but the sound was dark and twisted. "This again? You still believe that? That I somehow messed with your emotions by feeding you that single drop? You're either naïve or you're purposefully lying to yourself."

"You would say that." Although…A sliver of doubt crept past her defenses.

"All that blood did was link our power," he divulged. "It did nothing to you that it didn't also do to me. Can't you feel it? My magic? It's in the air, seeping from my pores because I'm so damn angry with you I could—"

"What?" she stopped him. "Hit me? Toss me back in the dungeons and set the Grazer on me?"

He froze. "You really think I'd do that to you? Now? After everything?"

"What's the difference between now and when I first got here," she stated. She knew though. She knew because she didn't feel the same about him as she had then, and if he was to be believed, she couldn't blame that on the blood anymore. She couldn't use it as a crutch to protect herself or her bruised ego.

If he was to be believed.

"I don't trust you," she said. "How can I?"

"Perhaps I should teach you another lesson," he replied, voice low and throaty. The edge of anger there was daunting, but before her mind could come up with a single response, he'd already moved, tossing her over his shoulder in one swift motion that left her gasping in surprise.

The Emperor carried her over to the bed, tossing her down with all of his frustration. When she tried to crawl away, his hand grabbed onto her ankle and pulled, until he had her ass hanging off the edge of the bed, her legs spread wide around him. His glare was enough to have the breath catching in her throat.

"You tried to run," he growled.

"No, I—" She hadn't. Not yet anyway. "That's not—"

"You dare deny it?" He grabbed at the chains at the foot of the bed, fighting with her as she tried to pull her leg free from him.

"Stop!" She slapped him, hard.

For a moment, everything went still.

The Emperor hovered over her, the leather cuff in his hands partially wrapped around her right ankle.

Outside, thunder boomed a second before the skies split open.

His head tilted toward the window where the downpour pinged against the windowpane. Then, slowly, he eased off of her and stepped away.

Jade's heart thumped wildly in her chest as she waited, unsure what he was going to do next. She'd reacted without thinking, her only thought that she wasn't going to allow anyone to tie her up anymore. She was over being confined. Restricted. It wasn't because of pride, however, it was because, secretly, a part of her had been yearning for more from him. Had hoped that it wasn't all an act and that maybe she really could believe him.

But someone who loved her wouldn't chain her up.

"Dust—"

"I won't force you," he said quietly, his words spoken so low they had to compete with the rain. "I told you from the very beginning, I don't force women to sleep with me. I meant it then, I mean it now. If you don't want me, well and truly, I won't force myself on you."

"But you won't let me go either," she whispered.

He searched her expression, silent a moment. He'd only just opened his mouth to give a reply when the door burst open, interrupting.

Koya raced into the room, sword already drawn. Behind him shouts could be heard from the corridor, accompanied by the sounds of pounding footsteps. He must have been arrested and on his way to the dungeons. He'd slipped his guards and instead of running, he'd come here.

He was across the room with his sword raised faster than she could blink, his intentions clear. He swiped the blade down between her and Dust, forcing the two of them apart to avoid being cut. Then he swung on her a second time, hissing when she rolled off of the bed to evade.

She hit the floor with a heavy thud that sent tendrils of pain shooting through her body, and before she could rise he was rounding the bed after her. Jade scuttled backward when he swung a second time, the whoosh from the sword sending a gust of air at her face, the tip just missing her chin.

The two of them were so distracted by each other they both forgot all about the fact they weren't alone.

Jade was only halfway to the exit and her hand slipped on the polished floorboards. The second cost her and this time when he swung the best she could do was raise her arm to protect herself. The blade sliced through her forearm instead and she cried out, pulling back and clamping down on the wound to staunch the bleeding.

Koya lifted his sword over her again but before he could deliver another blow, something metallic and shiny punctured his throat. He stilled, confusion written all over his face for a dreadfully long moment. He coughed and blood burst past his lips, thick and crimson, and then the metallic item was pulled back out and he dropped to his knees.

Jade's wide eyes traveled up to the Emperor, who stood over Koya with a butter knife gripped tightly in his right hand.

He'd stabbed Koya through the neck with that.

She glanced down and saw that blood had also sprayed all over her front, and when she licked her lips, the taste of copper had her sucking in a breath and rushing to her feet. She slipped again, this time in the pool of blood that had already seeped from Koya and formed around his head.

When she looked into his eyes, they were empty.

It was true, Koya had been trying to kill her just now.

It was also true that Koya had admitted to having tried to kill her in the past.

But he'd also been in love with the Emperor.

And now he was dead.

He'd loved the Emperor and now...

Mindlessly, Jade ran.

She bolted out of the room faster than the Emperor could react, turning right and barreling past three guards who were rushing toward her room. They didn't stop her, merely got out of her way as quickly as possible and watched as she kept going.

The Emperor called after her, but she didn't turn back. Outside the rain was falling so hard that the second she stepped out from under the surrounding awning she was drenched, but she didn't slow then either. Without any inkling of where she was going, Jade trusted her feet and kept running.

She could hear Dust screaming her name all the while, sometimes close, sometimes far, but she tried to block him out, not wanting to risk him using his power on her.

She didn't even really understand why she was fleeing like she was, only that there was a panic clawing at her insides screaming at her to escape before it was too late. Before she ended up like Koya, so obsessed with the Emperor that even her own life didn't matter.

Because he had to have known when he'd come to her room that that was the fate he was seeking. Koya wasn't stupid, and he knew the Emperor. Knew Dust would never allow him to live after something like that. But he'd come anyway, because even the chance of taking her out and getting her away from the Emperor had been enough for him.

It wasn't until she heard the sounds of fighting that Jade realized with a start that she'd been heading toward the hot spring. She'd passed the statue already and was on the other side of the path Koya had told her about. Even with the heavy rainfall, it was easy enough for her to recognize the building she and Amelia had climbed over to get to the town.

Jade slowed, headed toward the right where the hot spring was, something tugging at her chest, calling for her wordlessly.

She spotted the bodies before anything else.

Guards were discarded on the muddy ground, their weapons dropped carelessly around them. The fighting was ongoing, but out of the dozen or so men, only two remained to fend off their attacker.

Jade was about to turn around and run back the other way, but something about the attacker's movements seemed familiar and that feeling in her chest, the one that coaxed her closer despite the obvious danger, continued. She frowned, tilting her head as the attacker moved between the two guards, slashing at them with two short blades which he held in each hand.

Golden blades.

Like the ones she'd had custom made for Key on his twenty-first birthday…

"It can't be…" the words slipped past her lips before she could stop them, and even though it was impossible between the sounds of fighting and the rain, the attacker somehow heard her.

His head snapped to her direction, his mop of sandy blond hair wet and falling into his face and over his ocean blue eyes. The distraction cost him and one of the guards managed to nick him in the right thigh. He cursed and twisted, slashing one of the golden blades straight through the guard's gut, ending him instantly.

"Jade!" he called to her as he fought with the final guard, throwing up both blades to block a swing of the other man's heavy sword. "Jade!"

"Key!" She was already halfway to him when she noticed one of the other fallen bodies moving.

The guard had already been on the ground when she'd arrived but he must have been bidding his time. He moved stealthily behind Key and the one he was fighting with, grabbing up a discarded sword in the process.

Knowing she wouldn't have enough time to warn him, Jade reacted, summoning her magic and tossing her hands out toward the hot spring. A wave rose up and wrapped around the guard just before he was able to reach Key, and as soon as she had him encased entirely, she turned the whole thing to ice, sealing him within.

"Jade!" The Emperor's voice cut through her concentration and she faltered, losing control of the ice. It toppled, shattering onto the ground, spitting out the now still guard in the process.

He didn't so much as twitch.

Key killed the final guard and in the next moment was standing in front of her, heaving and sopping wet. His gaze traveled all over her body as he grabbed onto her wrist tightly enough it hurt. There was wild desperation in his expression, a mixture of relief and worry.

He'd never looked at her like that before.

"Thank god," he said, and then something caught his attention over her shoulder and he started pulling her toward the hot spring. "We have to go!" he yelled. "Now!"

"What—"

"Jade!" Dust was running toward her another dozen guards at his back. "Jade stop!"

"Come on!" Key tugged her into the water, holding her upright when she tripped so she didn't fall in. "Think of home," he ordered, and when she frowned he pointed to the slash on her arm. Blood was dripping from the wound into the water around them, and he'd somehow gotten them deep enough it was up to their waists already.

She glanced back over to Dust, noting the panic on his face.

"Jade," Key shook her, "think of the alley."

The alley?

Oh. Right. The alley back in her world where—

The ground opened up beneath them and before she could even realize what it was that she'd just done, she dropped.

The last thing she heard before the portal closed over her head was Dust yelling her name.

IV.

Obsession

Chapter 1:

It was too nosy.

And crowded.

She should be grateful, because the fact her grandfather was meeting her here, in public, meant he was trying to contain his rage. It would be harder for him to lose his composure and lash out at her with witnesses around. But still...

The entire airplane ride she'd been sick to her stomach, her mind racing over all the possible ways she could get out of this. Funny, considering she'd hoped escaping from Orremos would be enough.

That had been before Key had come through a portal to try and find her, however. Of course her plans hadn't panned out after that. As soon as they made it back to their world, she'd been whisked off into a car and driven straight to the airport. He'd asked her questions on the way, mostly about her health, but she'd only partially mumbled out answers, too shocked to do much of anything else.

Shocked because she hadn't meant to leave, and shocked because she had.

It'd taken over twenty hours for their flight to arrive, and then she and Key had stopped at a hotel for the rest of the night. She'd somehow managed to sleep, and he'd let her for as long as he could before he'd had to wake her to bring her here where they were meeting with her grandfather.

Jade had filled the sink with water out of habit—the past couple of weeks she'd been practicing how to use her powers—and now she peered down at her reflection. A memory of the time the Emperor had caught her doing this crossed her mind and she shoved it away.

Mostly because it didn't make sense, the way she was feeling, how much it hurt whenever she thought of the way he'd shouted her name at the end there just before she'd slipped through the portal.

He hadn't used Command to do it. He could have, but he hadn't.

And now here she was.

A clipped knock on the door had her straightening, catching sight of herself in the mirror over the sink. The restaurant bathroom was a single, fortunately, which meant she was in here alone, giving her extra time to stare at herself and the noticeable bags under her eyes. She looked exhausted.

Defeated.

She clenched her hands into fists on the granite countertop. "You've got this, Jade."

She'd somehow managed to survive a world filled with gods. She could handle Owen Blakely. Besides, she wasn't the same woman she'd been a couple of months ago. For good or for bad, Orremos had changed her. Dust had changed her.

She flicked the lock and pulled open the door to find a concerned Key standing out in the hall. His hand was lifted as if he'd been about to knock a second time, and when he saw her, his eyes roamed her face and down her form the same way he had when he'd first seen her at the hot spring.

She'd been given a change of clothes and was back in a pair of tight black jeans and a lilac blouse. Her makeup was impeccable because, despite how she'd prefer to show up looking like the hot mess she felt, she had to be somewhat presentable in front of her grandfather after all of this time to lessen the blow. The vibrant red lipstick and the gray eye shadow she'd applied was the best he was going to get, but it was something.

Key had given her the makeup bag before sending her here, and she shoved it against his chest now, returning it with more force than was necessary.

He frowned at her. "You've been like this since I found you," he said quietly, an edge of irritation in his tone. "Shouldn't you be more grateful that I rescued you?"

Rescued.

It was an odd word.

Odd because Jade didn't feel like she'd been rescued, even though logically, he was right.

Wasn't he?

Key was dressed in a three-piece all-black suit, his sandy blond hair styled off to the side, the right swoop of his bangs just falling over his eye. He was tall, taller than her by a foot or so, but shorter than Dust by at least two inches. Everything about him was familiar and yet...

He may as well have been a stranger to her, for all the connection she currently felt.

"How did you find me?" she asked, mostly in an attempt to distract herself from the hollow feeling in her chest. She'd wanted to since the beginning but hadn't found the opportunity; there'd always been one or more Emerald guards around. Now, it was just the two of them, the sound of the busy restaurant filtering down the hall toward them the only indication that they weren't actually alone.

"Your friend Amelia," he replied. "When she came through the portal, I was there. She explained what had happened and told us how you believed the two of you had gotten there. It took us some time because your grandfather wanted to be sure, but once it was confirmed through some of your ancestors' logs that world travel was possible, he sent us a vial of his blood. That's what I used to open the portal in the alley to get to you."

Jade's family, as well as all the other Legends— families with magical abilities—kept extensive reports about their powers and the things they could do with them. This was because it was ever-changing. Each generation was slightly or entirely different than the last, and some were born without power altogether.

People like her father.

The magic had skipped over him, which had been one of the major reasons her grandfather had decided it was best to kill him off. He'd been useless as a powerless heir, but Jade...

Fury swept through her and it took everything in her to contain it and keep it from seeping into her expression. She couldn't let anyone in on the fact that she knew. Even that night, before she'd fled, she'd been smart enough to carefully replace the police and medical reports in her grandfather's safe exactly where they'd been.

"Are you mad that your grandfather didn't come for you himself?" Key asked, seeing right through her. Unsurprising, considering how close the two of them had always been.

Used to be.

Jade felt almost nothing for him now, and that was both off-putting and relieving at the same time. She'd thought she'd never get over him, that she'd be stuck in a one-sided love for the rest of her life. And yet, looking at him now, with him less than half a foot away, she remained unaffected.

Was it the drop of blood from the Emperor? Had he done this to her as well?

He'd claimed, just before they'd been interrupted by Koya, that she was wrong about the blood. That it didn't do anything to sway her emotions…Could she believe that? Did she want to?

"Don't be absurd," she told Key. She'd known from the get-go that her grandfather wouldn't bother to waste time going to Bangkok himself.

"Then what is it?" Key knew. He had to know. He wasn't an idiot. When she didn't reply, he sighed. "Jade, this is the best thing for you. He's your family, the Emeralds are your family. This is where you belong."

"Keep telling yourself that," she drawled.

He tensed. "What would you have had me do? Save you and then run off into the sunset with you? Hope your grandfather never finds us? Don't be a child, Jade. You know there's no way out. You were born for this."

Arguing with him would get her nowhere. Like Koya, Key was loyal.

Koya, who'd died at the hands of the man that he'd loved.

Even though he'd been trying to kill her, Jade couldn't help but feel bad for the fallen soldier. He'd been just as obsessed with the Emperor as he claimed the Emperor was with her, to the point he'd even been willing to betray him.

In a way, she understood. That connection the two of them had shared before Jade had arrived and ruined it all must have been important to Koya. Once every month, he gave his body up for the Emperor to possess, a job he'd been specifically chosen for. A job that had given him purpose.

As someone who'd spent most of her life searching for that very thing, Jade could see why losing that purpose had sent Koya over the deep end.

He'd felt threatened by her and he'd acted accordingly.

And the Emperor had killed him with a blade through the throat. Cold. Swift. Unflinching.

Jade shuddered just thinking about it, and Key misconstrued the move, quickly stripping out of his suit jacket to wrap it around her shoulders.

"Are you feeling unwell?" he asked, running his hands up and down her arms as if to help heat them.

"I'm fine." She was hardly going to tell him the truth. That she'd felt like a tangled ball of anxious nerves since the moment they appeared in that alley. That she hadn't felt right since then.

Jade had run from the Emperor out of instinct. Perhaps it'd had more to do with the fact Key had used her grandfather's blood and opened a portal than anything else. There'd been an odd sense in the air, an invisible trail that she'd followed without thinking, and it had led straight to him.

Dust had told her once that power called to power, so it wasn't entirely out of the realm of possibility.

"Come," Key took her hand and pulled her from the bathroom into the hall, "your grandfather is waiting."

Jade allowed him to continue to hold onto her until they stepped out into the main area of the restaurant, then she removed her hand from his and slipped the suit jacket off. Silently, she returned it to him, watching other guests in the packed five-star restaurant as they ate and laughed amongst family and friends.

The French restaurant was built by the water on the fourth level of a tall building. An entire wall of windows to the right looked out over the harbor. A couple of lights flickered here and there from boats that were coming back in, and the sky had already started to grow dark and cast shadows everywhere. The color scheme inside was all reds and golds and mahogany, and Jade paid more attention to the swirly pattern on the thin carpet as she followed Key through to the back than she did the men in black suits peppered about.

They were being discrete, but the Emerald members stood out like sore thumbs to her. If she tried anything, no doubt they'd been ordered to stop her. Tonight, they weren't acting as protection, but as jailers.

She wasn't stupid enough to try running right now, however. No, she'd have to wait it out, bide her time.

She snorted derisively at herself, pretending it'd been a sneeze when Key glanced at her over his shoulder with another one of those slight frowns he loved to wear. She'd literally gone from being locked up in a palace to being locked up in a restaurant. And she hadn't had dinner before she'd gone either. There was some irony in there, she was sure.

The back room had been rented out entirely and the two sentries at the door stepped aside as soon as she and Key made their appearance. She inhaled deeply, bracing herself for what was to come, before following after him into the room.

Her grandfather was seated on the opposite side of the entrance, the large rectangular table big enough for fifteen. There was only him though, him and a vast array of various dishes. The surface of the table was littered with morsels and though she'd been expecting him to take it easy on her because they were in public, this was a bit much.

The private room was meant to fit a business party, and with only the three of them and the half dozen guards stationed at the walls on either side, it looked cavernous. Directly across the entrance, at her grandfather's back, was a massive window that looked out over an accompanying balcony. There was a door that lead out onto it and for a split second Jade considered bolting and tossing herself over the edge.

But she hadn't made it this far just to throw her life away, especially not for someone as disgusting as her grandfather. No, she needed to keep herself composed, wait for the right time.

Dust's words about revenge flickered through her mind. He'd asked her if she wanted it, and she'd told him the truth. That she wasn't strong enough to stand against someone like Owen Blakely and win. Even with the influx of power coursing through her veins, that was still true. Not because he had more magic than she did—there was no way to know that now that she'd consumed the literal power from a god—but because of his position as leader of the Emerald syndicate.

Still, she couldn't keep her brow from furrowing as she and Key approached. When Key pulled out her chair, she accepted without really thinking about it, eyes scanning the full platters and plates. This looked like a celebration when it should have been a punishment.

Maybe he was going to force her to sit there and watch him eat? It wouldn't be the first time he'd starved her for being disobedient, though the last time he'd used that tactic she'd been eleven.

"Jade," her grandfather called her name warmly, but she felt like someone had oozed slim down her spine.

He beamed at her, and it was impossible to tell how much of his happiness was fake. "Welcome home. I trust your travels went well?"

Her...

"I ran away," she blurted, because she wasn't going to let him sweep this under the rug even if that meant making things easier on herself. She wouldn't pretend anymore. Wouldn't live the lie. It was tempting to tell him point blank she knew what he'd done, that he'd killed her parents, but she was stubborn, not suicidal.

"Yes," he cleared his throat, obviously trying to hold on to patience, "well, you're young. You wanted to explore the world and you knew I would oppose it. You're here now, and you've done your trip around the globe, so I trust you're ready to finally take your place at my side."

Key had quietly been filling her plate as her grandfather and she spoke, and she noticed and scowled at him.

"Jade," her grandfather tapped a finger to the table to regain her attention, "there are things we must discuss. For starters, you've been absent a long time, there are things you need to reacquaint yourself with. Business has been steady the past year, but your position in the company has been left vacant far too long. You'll start Monday."

It was Saturday. He couldn't be serious.

But of course he was.

She wanted to tell him he could shove his job where the sun don't shine, but couldn't. How was it that in front of the Emperor, an actual god, she'd been brave, and yet in the presence of her grandfather she was back to that cowering child? She was better than this, stronger, and she knew it, yet...

Owen Blakely was still talking.

"The wedding will be scheduled for next month, it's the earliest we could get everything sorted. You'll have to pick out a dress as soon as possible. I've already told Margret to find all of the best bridal shops on the East Coast and carve out some time in your work schedule to go visit. I'm sure you'll find a dress in no time. And while it goes against my better judgment, Key has convinced me to allow you to invite your friend—" he paused in the middle of cutting his steak and turned to Key, "—what was her name again?"

"Amelia, sir," Key replied smoothly.

"Yes, that's right. Make her a bridesmaid. If it wasn't for her we never would have known where to find you. As for the venue—"

"Hold on," Jade held up a hand, certain she was mishearing things, "what are you talking about?" Wedding? "Whose wedding?"

"Yours, of course." Her grandfather stared at her like they were meeting for the first time and then glanced at Key. "You haven't told her already?"

"I thought perhaps you would like to make the announcement yourself, sir," Key explained.

"Told me what?" And why did she have such a bad feeling about it? At her graduation he'd made a passing joke—that hadn't really been a joke at all—about how she was at a marriageable age and should start looking through the Legends to find her potential husband. There were only two men the right age in that group, and they were both assholes. "I'm not getting married to someone I don't like."

He wanted to force her to work at the company? Fine. She'd do that until she could come up with a viable escape plan. He wanted her to pretend like everything was okay between them and she hadn't run? Whatever. For now, she'd go along with that too. But marriage? To one of those men she hardly knew? A lifetime tied to someone chosen by her grandfather? That's where she drew the line.

"I refuse," she stated sternly. Her gaze shifted to the filled glasses of water set before each of them, and it was tempting to call it out of the glass, turn it to shards of ice, and stab him through the eyes with them.

But she didn't.

Enough Emerald guards were surrounding the place that even if she did successfully murder her grandfather, she'd never make it out of there alive. And Amelia had been mentioned, which meant her friend could be at risk as well. She couldn't act rashly until she knew just how close they'd gotten to her. With any luck, Amelia would have already left the country, but if she hadn't, Jade would urge her to do so. And then she'd cut contact because it was the only way she could guarantee her best friend's safety.

Her grandfather's amused chuckle yanked her from her wandering thoughts and Jade frowned at him.

"You're getting all worked up over nothing, Jade," he told her. "You'll be happy to hear that you're tantrum worked. I understand I was wrong to suggest you marry one of the Legend boys. You're right, neither of them is good enough for you or the Emeralds."

He thought she'd run off because of his insistence she get married? At least it proved he knew nothing about what she'd discovered in his office. It also explained why he'd brought her here first and not straight home. This was an act, meant to coerce her into complacency. They didn't want her to fight this engagement because clearly there still was one.

She tilted her head at him, waiting for the punchline but it never came. "But you just said—"

"You'll be marrying Key!" He pointed the tip of his steak knife proudly across the table at the man in question, smiling from ear to ear.

"What?" Jade felt the ground drop from underneath her.

"Isn't it perfect?" her grandfather continued. "It's what you've always wanted, and it'll benefit us both. You have Key to thank. He helped me realize that this is a battle not worth fighting over. You should be allowed the right to choose your husband."

"If I can choose," she found herself saying, her voice foreign even to her own ears, "does that mean I can refuse?"

The silence was deafening.

Her grandfather's smile fell away, and his gaze hardened. His fists clenched tightly around the handles of his silverware as he glared at her, silently daring her to repeat what she'd just said.

"She's shocked," Key quickly came to her defense, resting one of his hands over hers where it was pressed to the table. "Can you blame her?" He laughed, the sound forced but clearly doing the trick for her grandfather's tensed shoulders eased some. "You've been against our relationship for so long, this must have blindsided her."

"You're right," her grandfather nodded his head, the smile slowly returning. "That's more than understandable, Jade. I'm sure you're elated. The engagement period will begin immediately."

"I'm sure you'll love having Amelia be part of the bridal party," Key said, nodding his head at Jade to get her to agree while her grandfather's attention was back on the food.

She followed suit dumbly even though Owen Blakely obviously wasn't even watching.

"It was kind of your grandfather to suggest it," Key added.

"I need my phone," Jade blurted. If she tried to do or say much more in this room with them she feared she would scream. When both her grandfather and Key tensed she reiterated, "So I can call, Amelia. To tell her."

"Of course." Her grandfather laughed and lifted a hand, waving at one of the guards standing against the wall.

The guard rushed over, pulling her cell phone from his pocket and presenting it to her like it was a damn crown. She almost rolled her eyes but was too caught up in the wave of emotions.

She was most definitely going to be sick. She needed to get out of here.

Jade pointed toward the glass door that led to the balcony. "I'll be right out there."

Her grandfather waved her off. "That's perfectly fine. Have a nice chat with your friend."

This was surreal. Not only had he not mentioned she'd left, but he also hadn't asked a single question about where she'd been or what she'd been doing all of this time. Hell, she'd thought for certain he'd at least have questions about the entire other realm she'd fallen into. But nothing.

He'd only spoken about her engagement to Key which was…

Also a big mind fuck.

Her crush on the older guy had never been a secret, but it also had never been reciprocated. Her grandfather wouldn't have allowed them to be together, true, but Key had also shown absolutely no interest other than brotherly affection. Was she supposed to believe that had suddenly changed? Or was he being forced into this just as much as she was?

She made sure the door was sealed tightly shut behind her and she was alone on the balcony before she turned on her phone and quickly dialed Amelia.

They couldn't actually think she wanted to marry Key, could they? Was this her grandfather's poor attempt to placate her after she'd run?

She'd have to figure that out later. Right now her main concern had to be Amelia and making sure that she was okay.

If only she'd pick up the damn phone.

Chapter 2:

Jade was just starting to panic when the other line finally connected. Bracing herself against the metal railing of the balcony, she exhaled and closed her eyes. She hadn't realized just how badly she'd needed to hear a friendly voice.

"Jade," Amelia sounded tired, "thank god you're all right. I was so worried that they wouldn't be able to find you. Or that they'd be too late."

"I'm fine," she said. "What about you? You met with Key. Did the Emeralds—"

"I'm at a friend's house right now," Amelia interrupted. "I came back to the states a couple of days ago. Your grandfather's men told me not to wait."

She sighed in relief. "That's good. That's safer."

There was so much she wanted to say and ask, but now that she finally had her best friend on the phone, Jade found herself unable to find the right words. How was she supposed to tell Amelia that she might have fallen slightly for the Emperor? Did it even matter now, since she was here and she was never going back?

Since she'd never see him again...

Jade's heart ached at that and she scowled at herself. She couldn't afford to pine over something right now, and certainly not someone like Dust. No doubt he'd already moved on. He'd gotten what he'd really wanted from her, his curse broken, and everything else had merely been a bonus.

Although, he'd sounded gutted when he'd called her name before she'd vanished through the portal...

No.

"Jade?" Amelia asked tentatively, clearly sensing something was wrong even though she wasn't there to see Jade's expression. "What's wrong?"

"What isn't?" she said before she could help it. "My grandfather is acting strange. He's being...nice. Something's wrong. I just don't know what yet." It couldn't just be the public restaurant setting or the fact he wanted her to marry Key. It wasn't lost on her that he thought for certain she'd be grateful about this engagement. There was no reason he'd need to bribe her into it by being kind. "There's something I'm missing."

"You've always been good at following your gut," Amelia told her cryptically and Jade frowned.

"Are you really okay?" Suddenly, Jade had a bad feeling. She'd been so excited hearing Amelia's voice, she'd accepted the idea that her grandfather had simply let Amelia walk away after being an accomplice to Jade's running all this time. That wasn't like the Owen Blakely she knew. "What's the name of the friend you're staying with?"

"You remember Ian from Chemistry?" there was no hesitation in Amelia's reply. "I ran into him at the store earlier and he invited me over for drinks. It's been so long since we last saw one another, and you know how much of a crush I used to have on him."

Amelia had absolutely loathed Ian from Chemistry. He'd cheated on one of her close friend's

Freshman year and had gone around campus bragging about it. The two of them had been paired in a group project as well, and he'd done nothing to contribute so Amelia had reported him to the professor. He'd gotten an F on the assignment, so it was safe to assume that the hatred was mutual by this point.

She would never willingly go anywhere to hang out with him, let alone to his house. This was a tip-off. Amelia was trying to tell her something.

Jade felt her blood go cold. "Yeah," she forced herself to say, keeping her voice light and conversational, "wow I can't believe you're finally getting time with him and I'm not even there to see it."

"It would be better if you were," Amelia agreed. "But you weren't here. It's not your fault."

Her heart sank. This was bad, like worse than she'd initially suspected even. With how secretive Amelia was being, it had to mean that she also wasn't alone and she was being listened in on.

This conversation was being monitored.

"Hey, speaking of long-time crushes," Jade had wanted to avoid bringing this up, but now it seemed like she'd have to or risk it getting back to her grandfather that she hadn't, "guess who's getting married?"

"No way," Amelia sounded horrified for a split second before she cleared her throat and added in a more chipper tone, "To Key? Seriously? Wow, dreams do come true huh."

"You have to come," Jade said, trying not to think too much about that last sentence. "You have to be my maid of honor. You know I'm shit at planning things. Though, I doubt there will be much I actually get to plan. My grandfather probably already has it all mapped out."

"But you've been dreaming of this wedding forever," Amelia reminded. "Why don't you just tell him your ideas? Maybe he'll listen. I'm sure he'll sense how excited you are and how happy you are about all of this."

"Right," she kept her back to the windows looking in on the dinner, worried she'd crack if she looked at either her grandfather or Key, "that's true. Maybe I'll try. Either way, I need you here."

"But you said it was dangerous…"

"My grandfather won't hurt you now," Jade lied, trusting that Amelia was aware of that fact as well. "Not this close to a wedding. He wants it to happen next month, so there's a lot to do in a short period of time. How could he expect me to celebrate anything and behave if something bad happens to my best friend beforehand?"

Amelia hummed her agreement, and it was clear that her friend was scared.

Jade couldn't ask her any more details about where she was without tipping off whoever was listening, which meant her options were limited. She needed to find out where they were keeping Amelia, but Amelia couldn't help and the only place Jade could think of searching for information was her grandfather's office. That was risky, but she'd snuck in before and hadn't been caught.

"You said you ran into Key first when you came back through the portal, right?" She needed to confirm that Key was in on this. If he was, maybe she could ask him for help. She'd have to be very careful, get a read on him first and see if he'd crack, but it was worth a shot if it meant rescuing Amelia. There was no telling what kind of place she was currently being kept in.

"Yeah, he was nice," Amelia told her. "I can see why you've liked him all this time. He treated me better than the Grazer, in any case. Kind of reminded me of Koya. You remember him? From that one party we went to Sophomore year?"

The only Koya either of them knew was from Orremos.

"I heard he died," Jade said, even though she shouldn't. But the image of that knife point slipping through the front of his throat and the way his eyes had bulged...She swallowed the bile back down and exhaled slowly.

"What?" Amelia was shocked by that notion. "How?"

"He was stupid." Now that she'd had some time to think about it, to separate herself from the whole situation, Jade could at least acknowledge that what Dust had done had been for her.

She'd known that before, of course, but it'd still been frightening, seeing him murder someone who'd been so loyal all this time, someone he'd been close with prior to her sudden arrival. Part of her still felt a little badly for Koya even, but when she broke it down, it'd been him or her, and she was glad she was the one who was alive.

Besides, as much as she'd loved Key up until a year ago, she never would have even considered harming someone he liked. If he chose someone else, which she'd always imagined he would, she would accept that and mourn for the relationship that never was alone.

"Jade, I have to go," Amelia said. "Ian is getting bored without me. We're going to watch a movie."

"Call me as soon as you can," Jade told her.

Amelia paused and then, "I'm going to be pretty busy. It'll be easier if you just call me."

"Sure," she clenched her fist, hating that her best friend was going through all of this because of her, "I promise. And I'm sorry."

"Don't be," Amelia said, "none of this was ever your fault. I don't regret a thing."

The call ended before Jade could respond to that and she came close to chucking her phone over the railing. That explained why her grandfather was pretending to let bygones be bygones where her running away was concerned. He knew he had something over her and was just waiting to spring it should she misbehave. The fact that he was keeping closed lip about it just so he could blindside her made it feel even worse.

Why couldn't she have been born into a family that actually cared about her?

No, that wasn't fair. Her parents had cared for her. That's why they'd moved away from her grandfather and had refused to allow him to meet with her. When she'd developed her powers at the age of two, her grandfather had tried to take custody even. The whole reason he'd had them killed was so he could get his hands on Jade and have an heir.

Power and control, that's all it came down to, all it ever came down to.

But Jade had power now, and she wasn't going to sit back and allow the past to repeat itself.

Slowly, she turned to glance back inside, watching as her grandfather and Key laughed with one another.

She doubted she was powerful enough to take down someone like Owen Blakely, but she was strong enough to take away his heir.

Jade needed to find Amelia and then she needed to escape.

Even if the only place she could run to was back to Orremos and the Emperor.

Chapter 3:

They'd finished dinner and had gone back to the estate. Jade's room had been left exactly as it'd been the night she'd run away, but it'd felt like walking into a stranger's bedroom. The designer backpack she'd used all four years of college, hanging on the wall hook next to her mahogany desk might as well have been from a different lifetime. She recognized the various stuffed animals decorating the window seat, some of which had been gifted by Key, but there was no attachment to them like there'd once been.

There was no attachment to anything in the entire manor, in fact, just indifference.

Jade had spent less than an hour inside before it'd become too much and she'd fled outside for some air. Without much thought, she'd traveled to the west grounds where the largest water fountain on the property was located. She had no idea how long she'd been out there, but the sun had long since set and the lights lining the walkways had been turned on, so that lights trailed throughout the dark.

It would have been a magical feeling if she hadn't been so aware of what Blakely estate really was.

A cage.

A cage she'd spent the better part of her life in. One where she was harmed every bit as much as she'd been back in Orremos. The only difference was her grandfather pretended it was training and called it sparring when he allowed grown men three times her size to wield weapons against her.

Jade trailed her fingers across the surface, watching the tiny ripples and the way they caused the lights at the bottom to dance.

The fountain looked nothing like the one she'd practiced with in Orremos, aside from being made from white marble. This one was ovular with one long statue in the center of a panther. The panther had emeralds for eyes, the stones the size of golf balls, and a path outstretched as if he was swiping at the water. When she'd been a child, Jade had loved this fountain. She'd even jumped in once when she'd been fifteen.

Her grandfather had punished her severely for it and she hadn't taken the risk again, but...

She shook her head, mouth tipping up in a partial smile. She was no longer a child and it wouldn't be worth drawing yer grandfather's attention. So far, she'd been lucky. Lucky that he was so distracted trying to plan this wedding that she didn't want. Lucky that he wrongly assumed she'd be obedient and behave because he was "finally giving her what she'd always wanted".

It was true she'd wanted Key in the past. But that was then, and this was now.

Jade tried to pinpoint exactly when her feelings had changed and couldn't. The only thing she could be certain of was there was only one man in her heart, and it wasn't the one she'd grown up with.

Guilt that she was emotionally betraying Amelia filled her and she twisted her hand palm up, calling on the water as her mind raced through a range of emotions. If she could, she'd strip herself of these feelings, of the attachment she felt toward the Emperor.

Of how badly she missed him.

It was absurd—hadn't she spent her entire time in Orremos praying for escape?—but toward the end there things between them had been…honest. Now that she'd been separated from the situation, she could see it. Dust had been trying to get her to open up to him, and she might never know if that was a ploy or not, but Jade wanted to believe he'd been sincere.

She'd thought he was winning her over with the phenomenal sex, getting her addicted to it the same way one became addicted to sugar or caffeine. Making her crave it and him. But as good as it was, that's not what had crept through her defenses.

He'd wiggled his way in through all those times at night he'd held her close. He'd wrapped her in the safety of his arms in the dark and had whispered all kinds of sweet things to her. Things about how she was powerful and strong. About how he'd help her become even more so. How beautiful he thought she was. How sexy he'd found her when she'd been fighting his guards the day she'd first arrived.

She recalled the ring he'd tossed her and Amelia into and the anger was still there, but it burned low, the flames never rising high enough to ignite the rest of her. It wasn't an excuse, but they hadn't t known one another then, and what he'd said had been right.

When a stranger appeared in your territory you treated them as a threat first. She'd learned that at a young age as well, probably would have done the same thing if their roles had been reversed. She'd only felt different because the shoe had been on the other foot.

Would Amelia forgive him though? Jade didn't even have the right to ask her friend that question. She wanted to talk to someone about the Emperor, but she couldn't trust that Amelia wasn't being closely monitored wherever she was being kept, and even if she wasn't, it wouldn't be fair to bring up Dust. No, it would be better to take these feelings of hers, her secret longing for the Emperor, to her grave.

She made a sound of frustration, hating herself a little for even wasting time thinking about this instead of trying to find a way to get to Amelia. Her eyes focused on the water she'd been playing with, and she sneered when she realized she'd made a replica of Pearl in her bird form.

"I knew it," Key's whispered words startled her and she lost control, the water splashing back down into the fountain. He was standing roughly ten feet away, watching her with a look of awe on his face.

A year ago, she would have done anything to see him look at her like that.

She focused on his words and turned on the fountain to better face him. He'd seen her freeze that soldier in Orremos before they'd escaped. She'd completely forgotten. "Did you tell him?"

"Your grandfather?" He shook his head and came closer. "No. And I won't. Not if you don't want me to."

She narrowed her eyes as he came to a stop, close enough she could reach out and touch him if she wanted.

She did not.

"Why?" He'd kept things for her in the past, little things, like one of the maids bringing her an apple when her grandfather had ordered her punished by starving her. Or when he'd caught her messing around with the weapons in the restricted area of the armory. But nothing big.

She wished she could trust him. Wished she was still that naive. It would make things easier in any case. Maybe then she could accept her fate and protect Amelia in the most obvious way. By obeying. Her grandfather hadn't yet mentioned he had her friend, which meant he was waiting to see if he needed to use that card. If she gave him no reason to, he would release her. Jade knew that. And yet...

She was selfish. She didn't want to throw her life away, become a shell of herself, I'd there were any other options.

"We're betrothed now," Key said softly. "My loyalty is to you, Jade. As it should be."

She grunted. "Sure it is. Tell me the truth, how did my grandfather convince you to go along with this plan?"

He frowned. "What plan?"

"This," she flicked a wrist between them. "Us."

"I think there's been a misunderstanding," he told her. "I'm the one who suggested the marriage."

She couldn't hide her confusion, eyes widening when he dropped down next to her and took one of her hands in his.

"When Jeff called us and said you'd vanished…Jade, I've never felt fear like that before. I was terrified you were gone forever. It made me realize that I've been lying to myself this whole time where you're concerned."

"What are you saying?" And why did she suddenly not want to hear it?

"Your feelings weren't one-sided, Jade," he confessed. "I'm sorry for making you believe they were all this time, but I'm aware of it now, and I won't make you wait any longer."

Key was telling her that he liked her, something she'd literally dreamed of happening since she was like ten, and….Jade felt nothing but sadness.

"Key." she placed her other hand over his, trying to decide the best way to be honest with him without bringing Dust into things. She didn't want to hurt him. But she couldn't let him go on believing the feeling was mutual when it wasn't. She has firsthand experience with one-sided love and it sucked. She didn't want that for him. Especially not when he intended to marry her. "If it was your suggestion that means there's still time for you to take it back."

"What?"

"Go to my grandfather and tell him you've changed your mind. Say that you were so worried about me you mistook your feelings, and now that I'm back—"

"But that isn't what happened."

"It could be." She wanted him to catch on so she didn't have to continue. It was cowardly, but Key had always been the epitome of strength in her mind and even the thought of letting him down made her almost willing to take the whole thing back. Almost. Because even if she had no intention of actually going through with this marriage, and letting him believe it would make her plan to run easier, she couldn't do that to him.

"Jade?" He was going to make her say it.

She dropped her gaze, unable to meet his eyes. "I'm sorry, Key."

To say he was surprised would be an understatement. "But you're in love with me."

"I was," she nodded, "yes."

"That's past tense."

"Key—"

"We're getting married." He stood abruptly, pulling his hands free but not moving away. "We're getting married next month, Jade."

"Key, I'm telling you I don't want that."

"You did."

"That was then."

He paused. "Is there someone else?"

She hesitated, an image of pale pink eyes flashing in her mind. "No."

It wouldn't do him any good to tell him the truth. And it wasn't like anything could come of her feelings anyway. She loved here and Dust lived in Orremos.

Key stared at her a moment, searching her expression. "Then there's no reason to call off the wedding."

Her mouth dropped open, but he wasn't finished.

"I don't see why we'd bother. You've liked me for over a decade, Jade. You've only been gone a year. I'm confident I can win you back."

"That's not..." Was he serious? "Key, I'm telling you no. This is me, rejecting your proposal."

"And I'm telling you I won't accept no for an answer," he replied. She was so shocked she didn't even think to move away when he bent down and placed a chaste kiss on her forehead. "You'll fall back in love with me in no time, Jade. I promise. How could you not? I'm about to give you everything you've always wanted."

"What do you mean?"

"Think about it," he said. "Once we're married, I'll lead the Emeralds. Because I don't have power like you, I can't do that on my own, but together we can. I know you want nothing to do with the syndicate. I'll leave you out of it as much as possible. I'll let you live a normal life as you've always wished."

"If this is about taking control of the Emeralds—" She would give it to him. Had made that suggestion several times in fact. The other Legends were weak compared to her grandfather, and the Emeralds were a massive organization. If Key chose to be the next head and had the support of her grandfather's people, no one could stop him.

"This is about you," he stated. "And me. It's about us and the life we can share."

"Even if that's not the life I want?"

"It is," he said firmly, and he sounded so sure of himself that if she'd been the version of herself from a year ago he would have convinced her. "Trust me, Jade. I'll make you happy. That's all I want."

That wasn't all he wanted, but it was clear arguing with him would go in one ear and out the other.

He continued to talk about their future, completely unaware that Jade was now mourning their destroyed past.

She'd never be able to look at him the same after this conversation.

Chapter 4:

"Jade," the Emperor's voice sounded far away. "Jade, come back. Come back to me, little cat."

She struggled to rouse herself from the deep sleep she'd been in, shifting onto her side in her bed, turning toward the sound.

"I'm sorry," he said. "Just come back."

"Dust?" She managed to shake the lingering sensations of sleep and pried her eyes open, only to find she was alone.

"Come home, Jade," the Emperor pleased, his voice distinct despite the room being empty.

Jade bolted upright, scanning the darkness, searching in the shadows for any signs of him, but there were none. "Dust?"

Silence.

"Dust?" She got off the bed and stood there, waiting, hopeful even though that was ridiculous. The silence continued and with a defeated sigh she dropped back down, fingers curling into the comforter.

A dream. It must have been. Now even her subconscious was messing with her.

"Fine," she stated into the dark, still exhausted and stressed and now reminded of just how lonely she was to boot, "I miss him. Happy?" She groaned. "And I'm talking to myself. Pathetic."

She reached for the glass of water and downed its contents, slamming it back down onto the dresser with more force than necessary. After a moment of sitting there in quiet contemplation, Jade stood and went to her closet.

Since she was awake anyway, she might as well make use of the time. The clock read that it was past two in the morning, meaning her grandfather should be fast asleep by now. It was the perfect opportunity to search his office. In the few days it'd been since she'd spoken to Amelia, he'd refused to give her cell phone back, claiming that even though he'd forgiven her, the trust still needed to be earned.

She scoffed as she pulled on a pair of black jeans and a dark sweater. She was a grown-ass woman. He was treating her like a child. It was stupid that it'd taken her discovering his deceit about her parents for her to finally see her life for what it'd been.

Jade snuck out of her room and headed down the dark corridor, careful to avoid the sections of the manor that she knew would still be guarded even this late at night. While her grandfather had people stationed at all the exits to ensure she didn't leave, he preferred his privacy just as much as the next person and kept guards indoors to a minimum.

His study was never under watch since there was a keypad that required a fingerprint scan in order to enter. Jade had spent a week before her graduation plotting how she was going to get in there. It'd taken time and a carefully orchestrated plan, but she'd managed to keep the door from locking by using a piece of tape. Her grandfather amazingly hadn't noticed and had left, and she'd quickly typed in the key code—which she'd also had to plan to find out—and had secretly added her thumbprint to the system.

She could only hope that he hadn't changed it in her absence, otherwise, there was no chance of her getting in there. Now that she was back she was under even more observation than before. He didn't trust her—for good reason.

She didn't trust him either.

The lights were all off and she made her way by memory and with the outside lighting pooling in through the windows. It wasn't the first time she'd slunk around in the dark; she'd been doing it since she was a child, for one reason or another. Even this though, something that should have felt familiar, meant nothing to her.

It was clear that Jade couldn't stay here, couldn't return to the girl she'd once been, the naïve one who'd pinned over Key and desperately tried to please her grandfather. She didn't need the approval of a man who would murder his own son in cold blood.

If only she were strong enough to get revenge for them, she would.

A chill swept through her at that harsh realization, but she didn't fight against it. She hated him. Hated him for what he'd made her. Hated him for what he'd stolen. Hated him for being the cause of so much pain and suffering, hers and now Amelia's.

Jade also blamed herself for ever involving her best friend in her life, knew that if she hadn't been selfish, she would have continued through life alone. But at the time, when she'd gone away to college, even knowing that her grandfather was a monster and ran a syndicate, she'd still been foolish in the belief he wouldn't harm her or the people she cared about.

It was a fifteen-minute walk from her side of the manor to her grandfather's, and she paused when she entered the hallway where his study was located, peering around the corner just to be certain that things hadn't changed and it still went unguarded. A bit of the tension in her shoulders eased when she saw it was empty, and she slipped around and proceeded toward the door.

Her grandfather's bedroom was down another two corridors, so there was little fear of being discovered by him, but that didn't mean she could risk taking her time. She needed to be quick about this, get in and out before anyone else could wander by and catch her.

If there was information on where Amelia was being kept, it would be in one of two places, either his desk or the safe. She'd taken her passport from the safe before, so he had to know about that at least. It'd been stored on a different shelf from the papers on her parent's deaths, and since he'd stated he thought her reason for leaving was because of talk of marriage to someone she didn't like, she assumed her grandfather had no idea she'd seen those.

Still, he would have changed the code on the safe for sure. The door...that was debatable since he couldn't know how she'd gotten in and hopefully assumed he'd forgotten to shut it all the way behind him.

Jade stopped at the keypad and hesitated. If this didn't work she had no other options. There was no Plan B.

She pressed the ENTER button on the keypad and then placed her thumb over the scanner, holding her breath as she waited. The light flickered red once but then turned green. The lock clicking out of place had her silently praying to whoever was listening as she quickly yanked open the door and went to step inside.

Her foot froze just over the threshold.

Key stared back at her from where he was seated in the leather armchair across from the large desk. He had a file open in his hands—possibly a police report or maybe something from one of the companies her grandfather owned—and his ankles crossed. It was obvious he'd been in there a while already, and he was just as taken aback to find her there as she was to find him inside.

Why hadn't she even considered that Key might have access to the study? As her grandfather's right-hand man, and now her fiancé, Key was the prime candidate to help take over the Emeralds. Her grandfather would have spent time training him, preparing him, even though he had another ten-fifteen years left if he was lucky.

"What are you doing here?" Key stood abruptly and rushed over, pulling her the rest of the way inside. He glanced down both ends of the hall and shut the door, turning to frown at her. "What the hell were you thinking, Jade? What if your grandfather had caught you just now? He's been treating you so well—"

A bark of laughter slipped past her lips and she slammed a hand over her mouth to stop any more of it. The damage was already done though.

His angry looked turned to one of confusion. But he didn't ask her about her reaction. Instead, he cocked his head and came to a conclusion about her presence on his own. "You're here because of Amelia."

It sucked, hearing straight from the source that he was in fact in on it, but it wasn't surprising. Which also kind of sucked, in its own way.

What had Jade ever seen in him?

"Tell me where she's being kept," Jade demanded, "and I won't have to go searching myself."

"You think I'm just going to stand here and let you riffle through your grandfather's things?"

"No," she knew better than that, "but do you really think you can stop me?"

"We both know of the two of us I'm the better fighter," he told her, with the same tone he'd used after one of their sparring matches when he beat her.

"It'll make a lot of noise," she pointed out. "My grandfather will definitely hear."

His eyes narrowed. "I'm allowed to be here, Jade."

"Sure, but I'm not. Yet here we are, together."

"He'll never believe you," he stated. "If you plan to tell him I allowed you to come—"

"You're the favorite, I'm aware. I don't have to make anything up. I'll just tell him the truth. I came here to find my friend and you tried to stop me. I'll be punished, sure, but," she took a deliberate step closer to him, "you told me you liked me. Are you really going to stand back and watch me get beaten?"

He'd done it a million times before, and they both knew it, but this was different. There hadn't been a confession then, and when he hesitated, Jade knew she had him.

"Was that a lie, Key?" she asked. "I already told you, you can have the Emeralds. I'll give it to you. You don't need to pretend—"

"I love you," he insisted, and he sounded so earnest she almost believed him. "That's why I'm begging you to please, let this go."

"Let my best friend go?" She quirked a brow, a thread of anger slipping into her tone.

"She won't be harmed," he said, "you have my word."

"The word of someone who would stand by and watch me get hit? At least you claim to love me. You have no connection to Amelia whatsoever. You'd let her rot if it came down to it, don't think I'm not aware of that fact. I'm not a child anymore, Key, and I'm not that idiot girl who followed you around either. You should have stopped them from taking Amelia in the first place. How could you let them use my best friend as leverage? She's innocent in all of this."

"Hardly," he snorted, shocking her into momentary silence. "Without her help, you never would have been able to hide for so long. It's true, she's also the reason we knew where to find you and how to get there, but that's the reason she was allowed to live. She should be grateful for that much."

"Please don't tell me..." Despite what she'd claimed about no longer having feelings for him, her mind wanted to rebel against the thought that had just entered it. "You didn't..."

He sighed. "Yes. I'm the one who suggested we hold on to her. There was no telling how you would react once we got you back. This was the smartest play."

"You kidnapped my best friend?" The downpour outside happened quickly, and a bolt of lightning cracked against the night sky, sending a burst of light through the room. "You planned on using her against me?"

"Jade," he glanced between her and the window, reaching for her arm, "you have to understand. It's for your own good. You've always been stubborn, that's why your grandfather always has to discipline you. But whether you like it or not, you're the Emerald heir. You're the only one who can take on the role of leader once your grandfather passes. You have a responsibility—"

Jade slapped him. Hard.

He stumbled a step even, a mixture of shock on his face as he grabbed at his bright red cheek and stared.

She should do worse. Should toss one of the windows open and call in the rain to drown him. But she couldn't because she still needed him.

She couldn't because all her life he'd been the only safe place for her, and even though she was now discovering what an absolute asshole he actually was, those old feelings were hard to shake entirely.

"Tell me where Amelia is being kept," she ordered, making sure all of the fury could be heard in her tone.

"I can't."

"No," she shook her head. "You won't. That isn't the same."

"She'll be at the wedding," he promised. "She'll be there and after it's done, I'll let her go."

"You'll? Not my grandfather. You."

He flinched. "He's left me in charge of it."

"That means you can let her go right now," she said. "Key, if even for a moment you ever really did care about me, please. Amelia has nothing to do with this and she's already been through enough because of me. If you knew the things she went through in Orremos—"

"I do," he interrupted. "She told me. I know everything the two of you went through right up until the point where she was sent through the portal without you. I've been waiting to ask you about your side of things and what happened after. I was trying to give up space to readjust before bringing it up."

Amelia would have told him willingly in the hopes that he would find a way to get Jade back. There was comfort in that at least, because it meant that she hadn't been tortured for information the same way she had been by the Emperor.

The guilt she felt at that recollection was swift and heady, and Key mistook her expression.

"I understand why you haven't wanted to talk about it yet," he reached for her again, taking her hand gently, "but that's just another reason why I needed to keep Amelia close. What if someone from that world comes for you? You and Amelia are the only two people who know anything about it or who you came into contact with while there."

"No one is coming for me," she said, and it sucked because at that moment she wished that someone would. She wished for it so badly that it ached. If only Dust were here… "There was a monster, in that other world. I thought he was awful."

"He tortured your best friend and held you prisoner." Key's grip tightened comfortingly. "I'm sorry you had to experience that alone, Jade. I came as soon as I could."

"The thing is," she pulled her hand from his and looked up to meet his gaze, "there are monsters in this world too, and you're one of them."

"Jade."

"Tell me where you're keeping Amelia."

"No."

If Key was the one in charge of her best friend missing, that meant there was nothing in this office for Jade to find. Her grandfather wouldn't keep a copy of the information, he would have merely insisted that Key keep him updated and tell him by word of mouth where she was located.

She was in the wrong place.

"I'll never forgive you," she told him.

"She's going to be fine."

"Never." Jade walked around him and headed for the door.

Key didn't bother trying to stop her.

Chapter 5:

"Jade," Dust's voice called out to her, and Jade frowned.

She'd gone back out to the fountain and the sky was high in the sky, heating her skin as she lounged on the stone rim. She'd been in the process of considering her next move, the fight with Key last night replaying over and over again in her mind, when her thoughts had inadvertently turned toward the Emperor.

And now she was hearing him?

She blinked and winced at the bright light above, holding up a hand to block it out as she turned her head to glance around. Like before in her room, there was nothing. The closest person was a guard who was stationed more than thirty feet away, pretending not to be there with the sole purpose of monitoring her.

"Jade."

She heard it again and sat.

"Jade, come back."

"Dust?"

"Come back, little cat. I'm sorry. I'm sorry, just come back. I'll make it right."

"Dust, where are you?" She had to keep it down to avoid being overheard by the guard, but she desperately searched the area, feeling a slight panic when she couldn't find him anywhere.

Was she going insane?

"Jade," he continued to call out to her, "I love you. Come home."

"Home," she whispered. Where was home? She looked around at the estate. This wasn't it. She wanted a home. Wanted somewhere she belonged. She slumped and closed her eyes. "I'm so tired of fighting to be free."

"Come home, Jade," Dust urged. "I'll make it right. I love you."

He sounded so close…Was this a delusion or—

Jade's eyes popped open and she swiveled so she could stare down into the water of the fountain. It was crystal clear, and all she saw looking back at her was her own hopeful expression.

She must have been wrong. For a moment, she'd thought perhaps he was speaking to her through water, using her power. Wishful thinking on her part. She really must be going crazy. And to imagine him confessing his love for her too…Yikes. She was so pathetic, even she couldn't stand it.

"How ironic," she told herself out loud, "that I had to come all the way back to this hellhole to realize I'd rather be there." She almost added with you, but since she wasn't actually talking to him refrained. She was alone, sure, but there was a limit to how ridiculous she would allow herself to become, even without witnesses.

The truth was however, she missed him. She missed him and she wished she'd known sooner that her feelings for him had been real. Because now that they were apart, she also had time to think over what he'd said to her last right before Koya had interrupted.

That drop of his blood did nothing to her emotionally. Was there still a good chance that she was experiencing Stockholm syndrome? Yes. Did that matter? Not really. Those last few days she'd been happy. He'd taught her how to use her power, had praised her when she'd done a good job, and had meant it.

He'd listened to her stories about her life here, had agreed her grandfather's treatment had been awful.

It was true that he'd held Amelia captive and had used her as an incentive the same as Key was now doing, but the second Jade had ordered her injuries treated he'd complied. When she'd returned from her quest to find the vial, Amelia hadn't been in bad shape. And he'd sent her home as promised.

That'd also all been before the two of them had gotten close. They'd been strangers and she'd been nothing more than a tool for breaking his curse. All those nights he'd taken control of Koya's body he'd gotten to know her better.

The Dust Emperor liked her, she believed that wholeheartedly.

"I don't care what he did in the beginning," she admitted, needing to hear the words herself. Needing to stop running from that truth at the very least. "I don't care if it's wrong, or that it makes me feel guilty toward Amelia. I just wish he was here."

She wished—

"Sir!" Key's frantic tone had her straightening, turning to see what the commotion was all about. He was racing across the lawn, a few feet behind her grandfather. A group of men followed closely behind, all of their expressions stern.

They were headed right toward her and recognizing the wild look in her grandfather's eyes had her instinctively standing and backing up a step.

"Sir," Key glanced between the two of them as they approached, "please! This isn't necessary!"

"You!" He pointed a finger at Jade and shook his hand, his fury palpable. "You little bitch! How long did you think you could lie to me, huh?!"

Jade froze in fear, suddenly that twelve-year-old girl again struggling to make her grandfather proud and failing. Afraid. Alone. She turned to Key, silently begging for him to explain what was going on, but he didn't get the chance.

Her grandfather reached her first, slapping his hand across her face so hard she fell over.

She landed on the edge of the fountain, catching herself just before she splashed into the water.

That only pissed him off more.

He grabbed the back of her neck with one meaty palm and shoved her head under, pinning her down when she fought against him.

Just before she could really panic and consider whether or not he intended to drown her, he yanked her back out, shoving her away so that her side dug painfully against the stone rim.

"You think you're so clever, is that it?!" He kicked her and she cried out, curling up against the fountain in an attempt to protect herself. "Sneaking into my office, reprogramming the system! What else have you touched?!"

She glanced at Key but he vehemently shook his head, knowing exactly where her thoughts were going.

"A guard saw you leave last night," he told her, and he sounded just as afraid as she felt, "there's no use denying it. Just confess and apologize."

"Apologize?!" Her grandfather kicked her again, harder this time. "As if that'll be good enough!"

Jade pulled herself up onto the edge of the fountain in an attempt to get away, but she should have known that was futile. The next time he kicked her it was straight into the water.

She hit the base with a heavy splash that had her bones aching and her wrist stinging horribly. Despite the pain, she sat up and shuffled back until she hit the panther statue in the center of the fountain.

"Get out here!" He waved at her, pacing in front furiously. "Get out this second, Jade!"

"Sir," Key tried to step between them, "please! It isn't what you think—"

Her grandfather hit him, his fist connecting with his jaw. Though he was in his seventies, he was still strong enough for the blow to leave a mark, and Key's bottom lip split open. He wagged his finger in his face. "Don't you dare make excuses for her. She hasn't been home a week and already she's sneaking around trying to defy me!"

Jade tried to ignore the tears that stung at the corners of her eyes, wanting to convince herself she wasn't that weak. She could take a few kicks. It wasn't like this was the first time he'd personally beat her. He wouldn't climb into the fountain after her, so there was a slight safety there, and even though she was a grown woman now, she curled in on herself instead of attempting to fight back.

Why bother? This was Owen Blakely.

He was stronger than she ever could be.

If only she'd stayed in Orremos a little longer...perhaps it would be different. Perhaps she'd stand a chance, even with the few dozen Emerald soldiers he had on the grounds right now.

If only Dust were here...

She would have laughed if not for the situation. How funny though, that she was wishing for the same man who she'd despised all this time. How funny that now when she thought of him it was with longing instead of with hatred.

Whether it was because of his magic dick or because she was a foolish idiot who'd fall for the first person who was even remotely kind to her, Jade didn't care. She wanted the Emperor. She was in love with the Emperor.

"You aren't coming out?!" her grandfather screamed then, and she flinched. "Fine!" He pulled his phone from his pocket and dialed a number, waiting for the receiver to pick up. "Jason, beat the girl."

"Stop!" Jade struggled to stand but the pain in her side had her immediately falling back into the water.

"Too late," her grandfather stated, ending the call. As if delivering that single order was as simple as getting a pizza. "You don't want to obey? Your friend will pay the price! That girl Amelia will be a bloody mess before the day is through and it's because of you!"

"Wait," she tried to rise again when he turned and stormed off, "stop!"

He didn't even turn his head back in her direction. The rest of the men fell into step behind him.

Jade twisted her hand up in the water so that it rushed over her palm and she summoned her magic without thinking, forming tiny balls of water in seconds. Before she could do anything with them, however, Key jumped into the fountain and grabbed her, causing her to lose control. The water dropped back in and she let out a frustrated sound, glaring at her grandfather's retreating form as she was pulled from the fountain.

Even now, she was powerless to do anything against Owen Blakely. There were too many people standing in her way. Even Key.

She wished Dust were here.

She wished he was here so badly.

Key dragged her from the fountain and back out onto the patio. "Are you okay?!"

Jade shoved him off of her, hissing at the stabbing pain in her side doing so caused. When he took a step forward as if to help her she held up a hand, stopping him. "Don't touch me."

"Jade, it wasn't me. I didn't tell him!"

"Amelia," she demanded, "where is she?"

He paused. "I—"

"Tell me where she is!" she screamed. Jade grabbed the collar of his suit and shook him, ignoring the way her wrist protested. She might have sprained it when she fell into the fountain. It didn't matter. "Jason is there! You know how he is! You know how much he hates me!"

If they weren't quick, if they didn't help Amelia soon...

A sob escaped her. "I can't lose her. I can't let him take her like he did my parents."

Key froze. "What?"

"He murdered my parents," she said.

"No, he—"

"I'm not debating this with you," her fists tightened on the material of his shirt, "I don't care what you believe. I know he did it. And if we aren't quick, he'll let Jason kill Amelia. He doesn't care, Key, he never has. That's who he is. Life means nothing to him."

"Jade."

"I swear to any god that's listening," she growled, "if something happens to her I'll hold you responsible. I'll spend the rest of my life making sure you suffer."

"Jade."

"Unless you help me," she added. "Help me, Key." Just once, she wanted him to be the man her younger self had fallen in love with. The man she'd deluded herself into thinking he was all this time.

Key searched her expression for a moment, clearly torn. When he finally nodded his head, she thought she might have imagined it even, until he spoke.

"I'll take you to her," he said, "let's go."

Chapter 6:

They were both silent the whole drive over to the small house where Key had left Amelia, except for one comment where Key informed Jade that along with Jason, two others had been left behind to help monitor.

True to his word, he'd kept her close, the street located only ten minutes away from the estate. Even with afternoon traffic, they made good time, though it may as well have been a year for how slowly time moved for Jade.

The thought of what she'd find when they finally got there made her sick to her stomach. She'd seen the damage Jason could do when he was let loose, and her grandfather's order had been purposefully vague. He'd wanted her to panic, to fear for her friend, not knowing what was happening or how bad it was.

He couldn't have known that Key would help her. Honestly, even she was surprised.

"He'll punish you for this," she said when they pulled onto the right street.

"I know." Key sped up.

"Then why—"

"We're here." He took the turn onto the driveway sharply, and she almost hit her head on the window.

But that didn't matter. Jade had her belt undone and the door open before he'd even turned off the engine. Then she was racing up the tiny stone path that led to the front door and forcing her way inside without knocking.

The house was tiny, with the door opening up to a small living area only big enough to fit a single love seat and a TV stand. To the right was a dining room with a wooden table that sat three, and across from that was an open kitchen. This was clearly a place meant for a single person to live comfortably, and yet with three grown men crammed in, there was garbage littered everywhere in the form of old fast food wrappers and dirty dishes.

Laughter spilled from down the straight and narrow hall, the only one in the place, followed by the sounds of thumping.

Jade raced down the hall, not caring if they heard her coming or not, and burst into the room at the very end where the sounds were coming from. She came to a sudden stop, needing a moment for her brain to catch up with what she was seeing.

The bathroom was only slightly larger than expected, most of the size there to help fit the massive bathtub. Amelia was in it, her shirt partially torn off and her pants and underwear missing. Her head rested on the edge, and her eyes stared up at the ceiling unblinkingly.

She didn't make a single sound as the man between her spread legs assaulted her, his reedy moans and the sound of the two other guards' laughter the only thing that could be heard in the small space.

Jason, who was seated on the closed toilet lid noticed her first, and he was startled. His reaction had the other two taking notice as well, and the one who was in the tub sneered at her, not bothering to stop the movements of his hips.

"Get that bitch out of here," he snarled.

"That's the heir," the other guard who was standing by the sink informed him.

"Jade, what the hell are you doing here?" Jason remained seated, a smug look twisting his features. "Your grandfather wanted me to send you photos afterward, but I guess you were so eager you came to see things firsthand."

The sound of Key running up behind her snapped Jade out of her daze.

Without a word, her hand shot out and flicked the tap on, spilling water into the sink.

The guard standing next to it frowned but didn't move away, unable to sense the danger they were now in.

Jade didn't allow herself to think about what she was doing, she simply acted. With a flick of her sprained wrist, she sent water sailing through the air straight toward the man in the tub. Just before they made contact, she turned them to ice.

The sharps penetrated through his skin, straight through his neck. Blood splattered against the pale pink tiles.

Jason gasped and went to stand, but Jade was already sending another burst of ice his way. She made them sharper this time, longer, so that icicles stabbed through his chest with enough force his body hit the wall and rattled the light fixtures.

The last guard, the one closest to the sink, she gutted. Another flick of her wrist and a small wave rose from the basin, sharp as a knife. It sliced through the man's stomach, deep and quick.

He was dead before he even knew it, falling to the ground to bleed out with no way to stop it from happening.

Key rushed past her, stepping over them and reaching into the tub to yank the dead guard off of Amelia. He swore as he pulled her out, cradling her in his arms. He brushed past Jade again, moving down the hall back to the tiny living room.

Jade followed, more slowly, stumbling now and again into the wall and needing to use it for support on her way. By the time she made it to the living room, Key had placed Amelia on the sofa and was kneeling at her side.

His face was pale.

But not as pale as Amelia's.

Even knowing what she was about to see, Jade couldn't stop her eyes from looking. She stared at her friend's immobile body, noted the blood and the bruises. Key had pulled the ends of her shirt closed, but that did nothing to hide the fact she was mostly naked.

It was the angry mark across Amelia's neck that finally broke her. Jade crumbled to the ground right where she stood, hitting hard and not caring. The sobs heaved out of her, tears blinding her as she screamed in anger and grief and guilt.

They'd strangled her.

Amelia was dead.

Key wrapped his arms around her tightly and held Jade close, and she was so lost to the pain that she didn't even consider pushing him away. She just let him cling to her as she cried. He let her for a long while before he broke the silence.

"It's not your fault," he told her softly. "It's not your fault, Jade."

Not her fault?

Her hands fisted, nails digging into her palms until she bled.

She could have let her grandfather beat her by the fountain. Then none of this would have happened. Amelia wouldn't have—

Jade stopped that thought.

Why should she have been beaten either? What had they done to deserve that kind of treatment? To be tossed around and treated worse than dogs? Locked up? Restricted? Used?

"No," she said, her voice hoarse. "It's your fault."

Key stilled around her, his arms going lax when she sat up.

"It's your fault," she repeated darkly, "and it's there's," she motioned over her shoulder back toward the three dead men. "And it's my grandfather's."

She'd been angry about her situation before, but now she was seething. Hatred? She hadn't understood what that felt like until this moment. Hadn't realized how all-consuming it could be. Her parent's deaths had happened so long ago and she'd been so young; there were hardly any memories of them when they'd been alive.

But Amelia…

"I should have told you where she was last night when you asked," Key said, and there were unshed tears in his eyes now. "I'm so sorry, Jade. I'm so sorry. You're right. This is my fault."

He wasn't wrong. But he wasn't entirely right either. He'd believed he could control things, could make the decisions and protect Amelia. He'd believed it because her grandfather had most likely told him it was true. He'd no doubt given Key charge of the situation, knowing that he'd take it back the second it became beneficial for him to do so.

That's how her grandfather was. He never gave up the power. He just tricked others into believing they had choices when in fact they did not. Owen Blakely called the shots.

Or, at least, he had.

"Make it up to me," Jade ordered, and Key nodded before she could even continue.

"Let's leave," he suggested, "together. Right now. Let's go, Jade. I have enough money in a separate account. I can clear it before he even realizes what's going on. We can run, start fresh somewhere new. I should have seen it sooner. Should have known the only happy outcome for us was leaving."

"No," she stopped him. There was no happy outcome for them. "The only place I'm going with you is back to Blakely manor."

"You can't."

"He needs to pay for what he's done."

"Jade, you aren't strong enough," he told her. "Even with my help, we aren't strong enough to go up against the Emeralds and your grandfather."

"I don't care about the rest of them," she said. They were merely soldiers doing his bidding. "I just want him. I'm going to kill him, tonight. Or I'm going to die trying." Most likely the latter, but when she glanced at the couch where Amelia's dead body lay…She didn't care. "I have nothing to live for here anyway."

"That's not true!" He grabbed her arms roughly. "You have me!"

"I don't want you," she stated, not caring how hurt those words seemed to leave him. She pried his hands off and stood, staring down her nose at him. "Make a choice, Key. Are you coming with me or not?"

He stared up at her, defeated looking, so unlike the man she'd grown up with. Still kneeling before her, he reached out a second time, touching her fingers lightly. "I'm coming with you, Jade. I meant it before. I love you. I'm sorry I'm too late."

It was such a weight thing to say, but she could easily read between the lines. He was sorry he hadn't realized it sooner. He was sorry he hadn't trusted her enough. He was sorry for choosing her grandfather over her over and over again.

He was sorry for Amelia.

But sorry wasn't enough. Not anymore.

"Prove it," she ordered.

When he rose to his feet before her, it was clear in his eyes he was ready to.

Chapter 7:

"If we die tonight—"

"Oh, we're definitely dying." There was no other way Jade saw this ending. There were over three dozen Emerald soldiers stationed on the estate, some of which were her grandfather's personal bodyguards. The second her purpose for being there was discovered, they'd sound the alarm and a ton of men with guns would rush in. When they saw that their boss's life was in danger, it wouldn't matter that she was the heir. They'd shoot her to stop her.

Jade only hoped that she could do some damage before then.

Key had been reloading his gun and paused at her words. They were parked just outside the entrance. It was suspiciously quiet with the men who usually guarded the front doors missing. The ones who were stationed at the gate had been there however and had let them in.

"He knows you took me to see Amelia," Jade pointed out. "He'll expect me to be upset, but with any luck, he'll still think I'm weak. So long as you didn't tell him about my enhanced powers."

"No," he promised. "I said I wouldn't and I didn't."

"I'll go in first," she repeated the plan they'd come up with on the drive back. "You come in close behind and tell everyone you see that I want to be alone to beg forgiveness. If it comes from you, they'll believe it. Even knowing that you went against him and took me off the property, my grandfather won't expect actual betrayal from you, and he certainly won't consider me a threat. He'll meet with me alone for sure."

"What if there's no water in the room?"

"I'll make it rain and break a damn window." There were heavy enough objects in literally every room for that to be easily done. Her grandfather had collected old statues and pieces of art to fill a museum.

"He'll fight back."

"Of course he will."

"The second I hear it, I'll come running," he assured her.

"Don't." she shook her head and reached for the door handle. "No matter what happens, act loyal. There's no reason for both of us to get shot. If I successfully kill him, you can take over the Emeralds, and if I don't you're the only one grandfather likes enough to give the job to anyway."

"Your grandfather took me in and raised me," Key said quietly. "I've spent my whole life thinking that I owe him for that kindness, for seeing an orphan and giving him a home. But," he caught her eye, "we grew up together, Jade. Whether I love you as a man or I love you the way a big brother would, I love you. I know now you were the only one who was ever truly honest with me about your feelings. Your grandfather doesn't care about his own flesh and blood. I'm not so arrogant as to believe his affections for me were real. Not anymore. And if he really did kill your parents—"

"He did."

He glanced away. "That means he made you an orphan, just like me. I can't ever forgive him for that. No," he corrected, "I won't."

"I would thank you but…"

"It's too late." He smiled sadly then pulled open his door. "I know."

He stepped out onto the driveway first and Jade followed, the two of them moving toward the entrance to the manor confidently. The gun he'd loaded was slipped into his belt to keep anyone from being suspicious. He'd offered her one as well, but she'd refused, knowing that if she was seen with it they'd stop her from getting close enough to have a hope of using it.

"Wait." She pulled him to a stop just as they were about to enter. "When they kill me—" he opened his mouth to interrupt but she shook her head curtly, "—when it happens, I want you to remember that this was my choice."

She could never forgive him for his hand in the way her life had played out or for what had just happened to Amelia. But she didn't want him living the rest of his life suffering the way she was currently. Eaten by guilt.

Her grandfather had been right all these years. She was too soft to be the leader of a criminal organization.

She smiled up at Key one final time and then before he could say anything else, walked into Blakely manor.

They made it through the foyer and were halfway down the next hall before she started to grow uneasy. A glance over at Key showed that he was feeling the same way.

"Where is everyone?" she asked. It was around dinner time, which typically mean a slew of servants were busy setting the table and getting everything ready for her grandfather.

He took dinner seriously; it was a meal that both she and Key had to attend nightly without fail, the three of them sat around the table pretending to be a real family for an hour or two before they returned to reality. No matter how angry at her he was, there was no way he'd call dinner off. He wasn't the type to lose his appetite over an argument.

"Something's not right." Key shifted to take the lead. "Stay behind me, Jade."

They kept going, aiming for the dining room at the back of the house where they'd already agreed it was most likely for her grandfather to be. The doors were closed, and as soon as they saw that they both hesitated.

The dining room was never closed off. Ever.

"What's going on?" Jade asked, keeping her voice down. Logically she knew that Key was just as in the dark as she was, but old habits die hard. Whenever there'd been a problem in the past, she'd turned to him for answers.

"We should go," Key suggested. "This isn't right."

"No." She refused to run. Not again. Jade searched around, spotting one of the vases filled with fresh flowers cut from the garden. Her grandfather liked to keep them around to spruce up the place, as if anyone who visited would be fooled into thinking he was a kind old man simply because there were fresh tulips on the mantel.

Jade tossed the flowers to the ground and carried the vase back over to where Key was waiting. She held it up and shook it, silently answering his unasked question. The vase was about a foot long, with a round bottom and a narrow neck. It was more than half filled with water. "Change of plan."

He nodded and then inhaled before leading them the rest of the way to the closed doors. He stopped with his hand on the doorknob, turning to her to confirm she was ready. The second she nodded, he twisted it and pulled it open, stepping into the room as if everything was all right.

A gun went off and Jade rushed in after him, processing that he'd avoided the bullet and it'd hit the wall just a few inches from him.

A guard stood off to the side of the room, someone she recognized as belonging to her grandfather's personal staff, and he was aiming a gun at them.

Jade smashed the vase on the ground and lifted the water, turning it into a shield of ice in front of Key a second before another shot rang through the room. The bullet hit the wall, shattering it, but she reformed it in less time than it took to blink.

"Stop," a strong voice vibrated throughout the room, rich with command.

Everyone froze, including Jade. It couldn't be…

"Little cat," the Emperor purred, "look at me."

He hadn't used his power, but that didn't matter. She dropped the ice shield to the ground, turning to find him seated at the head of the long dining room table. He was dressed in a black silk shirt and matching pants, somehow fitting in amongst the many guards that lined the room.

And there were many.

Jade counted at least twenty before she stopped bothering and turned back to him with a frown. "How…?"

"You summoned me," he grinned at her, that familiar arrogant look causing her stomach to leap into her chest.

"I didn't…" The fountain. Her eyes widened. "That was really you. I was hearing you."

"I called to you many times," he confirmed, "this last time, you called back."

"Jade," Key moved up to her side and rested a hand on her elbow protectively, "what's going on?"

The Emperor's eyes flashed with anger. "Step away from her and pull that gun from your belt," he ordered, his power ringing through the room. "Put it to your head."

Key did as he was told, pressing the side of the barrel to his temple.

"Wait!" Jade yelled. "Don't! Don't hurt him!"

Dust cocked his head at her, silent for a moment before, "Ah. So this is the famous Key I've heard so much about."

"Don't," she repeated.

"Tell me, little cat, why shouldn't I? Getting rid of the competition seems like it'd be in my best favor. Not to mention the fact that he stood by while your grandfather kicked you earlier has me enraged. Killing him quickly like this would be a mercy."

"I don't want you to," she said. "I don't want you to hurt him. That should be reason enough."

"Should it?"

"Yes." She was glad to see him and relieved, but she couldn't trust those feelings. Not because she believed in his blood controlling her, she didn't anymore, but because she'd thought she was in love with someone before and look how that had turned out. Key was on her side now, but now it was too late and the damage had already been done.

Jade needed proof from the Emperor. Proof that her love wasn't misplaced. Proof that it wasn't one-sided again.

Even though she wanted to yank the gun out of Key's hand, she forced herself to remain still, to hold the Emperor's gaze. To wait.

"Tell me how you feel, Jade," he surprised her by asking then. "Don't be afraid to tell the truth. If you love him, I won't harm him."

"I don't," she said.

He didn't appear to believe her. "I give you my word that I won't hurt him. It's true that I'm jealous, but you're right. You asking me not to is reason enough for me to listen."

"I don't love him," she insisted.

His brow furrowed. "When you first arrived—"

"That was then," she cut him off. "How could I still be in love with him after meeting you?"

"Jade," Key sounded wounded but she didn't turn to spare him so much as a glance, keeping her focus on the Emperor instead.

"I can always order you to tell me the truth, little cat," Dust warned, but she simply took a step closer.

"Do it," she said. "I mean it. I won't hold it against you, I hardly believe it myself, of course you want proof." She wanted proof of his love as well. "Do it, Dust. Order me. It's okay."

His frown deepened but he shifted in his seat, leaning forward. "Jade, tell me how you feel about me."

His power skittered down her spine making her shiver, but not in a bad way.

"I love you," she confessed. "Do you love me?"

"I do." He seemed caught off guard by her words, as if he really hadn't believed her.

"Then tell Key to drop his gun."

"Put the gun on the table and step away," the Emperor commanded.

Key moved to the side of the table and placed his weapon down, then he took several steps away. The second he had completed the task, he shot forward once more, reaching for Jade.

"Don't," she told him sharply, and he froze.

"You can't be serious." He searched her expression.

"I am." She turned back to Dust then, dismissing Key at the same time with the move. "Where's my grandfather?"

It was obvious that the guards in the room were under Dust's control. He must have used his power to command them to obey him. It was also clear that she'd somehow called him through a portal in the fountain that she hadn't been aware was there. But that didn't explain how he'd come to be seated in her grandfather's spot at the table.

A table that was fully set for a large meal.

She took in the many dishes spread out, pausing when she saw that there was only one other place setting made up and it was at Dust's right.

"Do you really want to know, little cat?" he asked. "You might change your mind about loving me."

"I won't." She didn't know why she was so certain of that, but she was.

The Emperor motioned to one of the nearby guards and pointed to the largest platter that was on the table. It was at the center and had a lid.

The guard moved forward and lifted the metal cover off.

Jade and Key both gasped at the same time.

Her grandfather's severed head stared back at her. Someone had even taken the effort to place it on carefully arranged lettuce leaves, and there was an apple stuffed in his mouth.

"I gathered it was meant to be a pig," Dust said calmly, "but I decided I liked this better, and it's important to cater to guests. Your grandfather didn't initially agree, of course, but," he grinned when she looked back at him, "he came around to the idea."

"You made him do it himself, didn't you." Something about the wicked glint in his pale pink eyes gave that fact away.

He lifted a single shoulder. "For as long as he was able, at least. He passed out long before the deed was done, but the goal was met."

Dust had commanded her grandfather to take his own life.

She searched him now for any signs of injury, but there was nothing.

He chuckled at her. "I'm unharmed, little cat. He may have been considered powerful in this world, but in mine he'd be nothing. He turned one of the statues outside into liquid gold and attempted to smother me, that was interesting. But only mildly so."

"You played with him." Because if her grandfather had even been able to do that much it'd been because Dust had been curious enough to let him.

His grin widened and he leaned forward, resting his elbows on the edge of the table. "Jade," he used his power again, "tell me how you feel about me."

Did he think something like this would change her mind? On the contrary. She'd come here tonight willing to die just to injure her grandfather, that's how much she hated the man. Yet, thanks to Dust, she was alive and her grandfather was worse than injured.

And he'd gone slow and painful.

Did it make her a monster to be pleased by that?

Probably.

But that was no longer something she cared about.

At least now she was choosing to be monstrous.

That made all the difference.

"I love you," she said, grinning herself when his expression slipped again into one of surprise. "I love you even more than I did three minutes ago. If you take me home, I'll love you even more than I do now."

"Home?"

"Yes," she nodded and held out her hand to him, "Let's go home."

Chapter 8:

They left Key at the fountain with orders to give Amelia a proper burial and take control of the Emeralds. To help avoid an uprising, Dust commanded the Emeralds who were there to accept Key as the new leader. What happened from there was up to him and how he handled things.

He tried to stop Jade from going, but he was no match against the Emperor's power either, and the last they saw of each other, she was opening a portal to Orremos.

There were no great goodbyes or final words. There was nothing left to say, really, nothing that could be said that would change her mind. She wasn't able to forgive Key, and he wasn't able to convince her to stay.

And there was nothing to stay for anyway.

Amelia had been the one thing keeping her and now...

Jade didn't take anything when she went either. Didn't pack a bag or grab anything from her room. She simply led Dust out to the fountain, opened a portal, and went. The thing about her power was, she didn't need to take anything that second.

She could come and go as she pleased.

"No more cages, little cat," Dust promised, pressing his warm lips to the back of her neck as if reading her thoughts. They were in their room in their palace, with him snuggled up behind her.

It'd been over a week so it was no wonder that the blood and any signs of Koya had been cleaned already, but Jade had hesitated at the entrance a moment before Dust had swept her off her feet and carried her to the bed. He'd helped her forget all about bloodshed and the horrors of the past month—begging for forgiveness all the while for the ones he had a hand in.

Jade had grieved the loss of Amelia again, and he'd held her close, silently waiting for her to let it all out. Comforting her with silence and his presence in a way no one had bothered to before.

She did not mourn her grandfather.

It'd all happened so suddenly, and there was little doubt she needed more time to adjust and process everything, but he got what he deserved. She may not have been the one to deliver the killing blow, but at the end of the day, that didn't really matter to her. The only thing she cared about was being free.

Amelia would have wanted that for her as well.

A tear slipped past her defenses and Jade quickly brushed it aside, not wanting to cry again. Her eyes were already red and puffy and her throat was sore from all the sobbing she'd done. Tomorrow, she'd succumb to the guilt again, but for now, she wanted to set everything aside and just be.

"I'm so grateful you called me to you," Dust told her then, the words whispered against her ear as he settled even closer against her back. "I was so afraid I'd never see you again. That you would never forgive me."

"You have a lot of making up to do," she replied, smiling some to keep the sting from her words.

"I do," he agreed. "I will."

"I didn't even know I was calling you." She'd thought she was hearing things, but she didn't repeat as much now.

"You summoned me," he confirmed. "Whenever you thought of me in your world, a small portal would open up nearby. The first time, you were in a puddle outside. The second time in my bathing water."

She quirked a brow and turned her head to glance at him over her shoulder. "Are you saying I appeared in your bathtub while you were naked?"

He chuckled. "You like me naked."

She rolled her eyes.

"I couldn't see you," he told her. "I only knew you were there. I could sense you."

"I couldn't see you either."

"But you could hear me."

"Yes." She twisted around so she could bury her face against the curve of his neck. "I hated how badly I missed you."

"I'll prove to you I'm worthy of your love."

She snorted but didn't argue. "Where did the portal open up?"

"In the fountain," he said. "The one we trained with. It's interesting, I get the sense that it wasn't here before you created it."

"Is that something I can do?"

"We'll have to find out." He brushed a strand of hair off her face and smiled at her. "You've only just begun learning about yourself and your power. I'll be with you every step of the way."

"No more cages," she reminded.

He kissed her, deeply, lovingly, and though it was nothing like their past kisses, there was enough passion in it to set her soul on fire and have her rubbing against him all over again.

"I'll give you everything you've ever wanted and more. You want to control what you do and where you go? Done. No one will ever order you again, not even me. You want to learn who you are and what you're capable of? I'll help you. You want to belong?" He cupped her cheek. "You belong, Jade. Here, with me, in Orremos."

"Those are pretty words, Dust." She sighed. "But that's all they are."

"For now," he agreed. "I'll prove it."

"And your power? What about when we argue— because we will. Will you use your power against me, or will you remember this promise?"

He rested his forehead against hers and closed his eyes. "I'll only ever use my power on you if you ask it of me. I only hope you agree to offer the same courtesy. If we fight, we do so without magic. In the past I was vicious, but I don't intend to ever physically hurt you again."

It was a truce of sorts, and one her grandfather never offered to her. There was always the chance that the Emperor would slip up, would go against his word…But…

"I'm good at running," she reminded him. "I don't want to run anymore, but that doesn't mean I won't. If you betray me, all the power in the world won't be able to keep me by your side."

"Understood, little cat." He stroked a path down her spine with the tips of his fingers, the touch light and gentle. Familiar and comfortable.

"I want to be your equal, Dust," she said. "And I want everyone to know it."

"I was going to wait to propose marriage," he grinned. "If that's something you want, we can make you Empress immediately."

She lifted a shoulder. "I was going to get married next month anyway—"

His smile turned into a scowl. "You have no idea how badly I wanted to break that man's neck for even suggesting you marry someone else."

"Well, you did cut his head off so, close."

He paused, but before he could say anything she shook her head to stop him.

"I'm not mad. You did me a favor. We both know I'm not strong enough, and even if I was…" Could she have really murdered her own grandfather in cold blood? Acting on the rage she'd felt for Amelia, she'd believed as much at the time, but there was no way of knowing for certain what might have actually happened if the Emperor hadn't arrived to the deed in her stead.

"You will be strong enough," he told her. "With more training, you'll be strong enough to take on anyone in this world or yours. Master Mist was powerful, and not only are you Valued by him, you drank the vial."

"Will I become more powerful than you?" she teased, only partially serious.

"You already are," he surprised her by saying. "I am the God of Command, and yet you rule over me, Jade. Anything you want from me is yours. All I ask is you stay with me. If you want to go somewhere, go, just don't run. I won't hold you back but I also don't want to lose you."

"Keep your promise," she said, "and you won't."

The corner of his lips tipped up at that, and then he was kissing her again, his tongue sweeping into her mouth. His cock hardened against her stomach and his arm banded around her waist to keep her close.

"Command me, little cat," he pulled away to whisper. "I'm yours to do with as you please."

Control over the God of Command? She could get used to that. Her gaze wandered over his shoulder toward the top corner of the bed and she smirked, an idea entering her mind.

She cupped his jaw and stroked her thumb over the rise of his cheekbone, a thrill racing through her when he nuzzled into her touch. She'd never had anything like this before. Never had anyone look at her that way, like he couldn't live without her, like he really would do anything she asked.

She'd never been touched like this either, like she was precious and important.

Like she mattered as more than a thing.

He'd said he'd help her discover who she was, and Jade was eager to begin. Eager to put her past behind her and look ahead, to the future and all of the possibilities it held.

"Dust," she eased him onto his back and straddled him before reaching forward to grab the handcuff hanging from the bedpost, "give me your wrist."

He grinned wickedly and without hesitation held up his hand for her. "As you wish, Empress."

Oh yes. She could get very, very used to this.

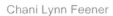

Acknowledgments:

This was my first official attempt at a rapid release with novellas, and while I'm not sure how successful it will be, it was definitely a learning experience. My goal for 2022 was to challenge myself and my writing by trying out different things, and I think between this and my MM Sci-Fi Romance, I've done that.

That being said, I hope you all enjoy the glimpse into this world I created and the dark characters that dwell there. As of this moment, it's unclear if I'll ever return to it, but I've set it up so the option is there should I ever decide to.

Big thanks to Brie whose enthusiasm for the first two novellas helped keep this project alive, despite how often I almost gave up on it. And thank you to my street team for BETA reading and giving me feedback and notes.

As always, thanks to my family, friends, and Matt and Lisa.

Chani Lynn Feener has wanted to be a writer since the age of ten during fifth grade story time. She majored in Creative Writing at Johnson State College in Vermont. To pay her bills, she has worked many odd jobs, including, but not limited to, telemarketing, order picking in a warehouse, and filling ink cartridges. When she isn't writing, she's binging TV shows, drawing, or frequenting zoos/aquariums. Chani is also the author of teen paranormal series, *The Underworld Saga*, originally written under the penname Tempest C. Avery. She currently resides in Connecticut, but lives on Goodreads.com.

Gods of Mist and Mayhem is Chani's first novella project.

Chani Lynn Feener can be found on Goodreads.com, as well as on Twitter and Instagram @TempestChani.

For more information on upcoming and past works, please visit her website: HOME | ChaniLynnFeener (wixsite.com).

Made in United States
Orlando, FL
02 August 2022

20484031R00246